THE SEVEN SYMPHONIES

A Finnish Murder Mystery

by
Simon Boswell

Finnish Evolutionary Enterprises

in

Bookloc

International Edition
Copyright © Simon Boswell, 2005
ISBN 1-59113-652-0

Updated from the original Finnish edition
Copyright © Simon Boswell, 2004
ISBN 952-91-6878-0

The ideas expressed in the seven Sibelius lectures by the novel's fictional character Dr Nick Lewis are to be understood as the genuine thoughts of the author, Simon Boswell. As such, the lectures should be taken as a serious (non-fictional) attempt by the author to express an original commentary on the life and works of the great Finnish composer, Jean Sibelius. Quotations from Sibelius and his contemporaries, as they appear in the lectures, mostly derive from the Robert Layton translation of Erik Tawaststjerna's Sibelius biography which, in the author's opinion, is a primary source for any researcher of the subject.

Claims are made by fictitious characters in this novel that the texts of the letters sent to (or intended to be sent to) 'The Ainola Residence' are direct quotations from Sibelius's diaries and letters. These claims are themselves fictitious. In reality, the texts are not direct translations into English of anything that Sibelius wrote himself, but merely loose paraphrases.

With the obvious exception of the historical people referred to in the seven Sibelius lectures (and occasionally elsewhere), all characters in this publication are fictitious and their resemblance to any real persons, living or dead, is coincidental.

The following trademarks appear in this novel: BMW, Coke, Esso, Fiat, Formica, Guinness, Honda Civic, Hotmail, Identikit, Kalashnikov, (Apple) Macintosh / Mac, McDonald's (restaurants), Mars (confectionery), Michelin, MiniDisc, Monopoly, Nokia, Opel Corsa, Pizza Hut, Polaroid, Renault, Semtex, Volvo, VW (Volkswagen). [However, the drug Comatin is an invention of the author.]

The front cover is a composite of photographs depicting Sibelius Park, Helsinki. In the background may be seen a glimpse of the Sibelius Monument, sculptured by Eila Hiltunen.

Finnish Evolutionary Enterprises
in association with Booklocker.com Inc.

http://www.SevenSymphonies.com

This book is dedicated with all my love

to Leena

(who will never read it)

& with very special thanks

to Carolyn Brimley Norris

(without whose help and encouragement
I would never have written it)

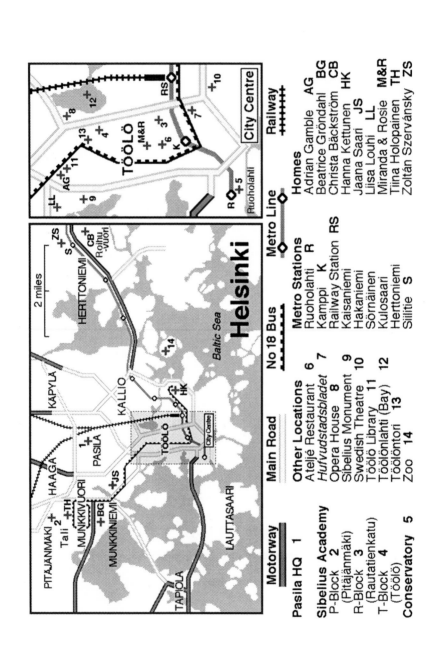

Helsinki

Motorway ▬▬▬

Pasila HQ 1

Sibelius Academy
P-Block 2
(Pitäjänmäki)
R-Block 3
(Rautatienkatu)
T-Block 4
(Töölö)
Conservatory 5

Main Road ▬▬▬

Other Locations
Ateljé Restaurant 6
Hufvudstadsbladet 7
Opera House 8
Sibelius Monument 9
Swedish Theatre 10
Töölö Library 11
Töölönlahti (Bay) 12
Töölöntori 13
Zoo 14

No 18 Bus ▬ ▬ ▬

Metro Stations
Ruoholahti R
Kamppi K
Railway Station RS
Kaisaniemi
Hakaniemi
Sörnäinen
Kulosaari
Herttoniemi
Siilitie S

Metro Line ◇

Railway ┼┼┼┼

City Centre

Homes
Adrian Gamble AG
Beatrice Gröndahl BG
Christa Bäckström CB
Hanna Kettunen HK
Jaana Saari JS
Liisa Louhi LL
Miranda & Rosie M&R
Tiina Holopainen TH
Zoltán Szervánsky ZS

NOTES TO THE READER

When setting one's story in **a bilingual** (or, as here, **trilingual**) **environment**, there's always the problem of how to represent the changing languages within a monolingual narrative.

I ask the reader to follow these guidelines:

(1) Discussion between native English speakers may be taken as is.

(2) When Finns converse together, they are, in reality, using Finnish.

(3) If a character employs a language other than his or her own, this will be clarified in the text.

(4) The occasional use of Swedish (Finland's official minority language) will be specifically indicated.

Street names in Finland generally end with the suffixes -tie or -katu, as in *Mannerheimintie* & *Mariankatu*. These are roughly equivalent to the English-language 'Road' & 'Street'.

The **Finnish police ranks** of *ylikonstaapeli*, *komisario* and *ylikomisario* have been converted to their nearest British equivalents: Sergeant, Inspector and Chief Inspector.

Since the novel's conception more than five years ago, new buildings have sprung up in Helsinki where my narrative sees none. Mobile phones have grown in sophistication and ubiquity. As a result, *The Seven Symphonies* is already taking on characteristics of **a historical novel!**

The Sibelius Lectures

The concept of presenting fiction and non-fiction within the same volume is by no means new, but many would question the wisdom of incorporating a series of lectures on Jean Sibelius's life and music into an otherwise mainstream crime thriller. Of the dozen and a half people who generously read my draught manuscript, some complained that the lectures were an irrelevance and interfered with the plot line; others insisted that the lectures were an important and integral part of the reading experience and must on no account be omitted.

My original inspiration for writing this book was to combine two things that I love: Sibelius's music and the jigsaw-puzzle intricacies of the detective story. After reviewing the contradictory but valuable feedback from my reader guinea pigs, I've decided to attempt a compromise. The lectures remain, but **certain sections have been bracketed off as optional**. The reader must be the ultimate judge of whether this approach is a success or failure.

Simon Boswell: Helsinki, January 2005.

Symphony No 1
in E minor

I

Andante, ma non troppo—Allegro energico

*　　*　　*

[8.54 pm; Friday, 24th March]

*M*en are so weak. It doesn't mean a thing. Most of the time they
can't help themselves. But how could I have been so stupid — to try
and change your mind like that? It's only left me more humiliated.
Damn you! Damn all men! Why do I keep getting myself in situations
like this? And why did I have to threaten you? It was so cheap! I'd
never follow through anyway. Oh, I know I did something of the sort
once... but that time was completely different.

 The big question's 'What next?' I can't give you up! You have to
give me another chance. What if I come back and apologize for being
such a bitch? No, you've probably already left. And why do I always
end up losing my temper? It hardly does me any favours. If I'd kept
my head, you might've taken me with you... though I doubt it!
Ashamed of what your precious friends would think.

 And how ridiculous to play the diva — refusing to let you walk me
home. Perhaps I could've persuaded you to come in for a while...
made it hard for you to leave again. Then I wouldn't be wandering
round here alone in the dark — alone in this freezing, miserable park.
But I can't face an empty flat feeling like this... Though I suppose the
cats are some kind of company. At least they'd pretend to listen. And
the poor things need feeding. I should never've taken them on. I'm so
damn irresponsible. I can't even look after myself.

Preoccupied with her own thoughts, she was unaware of the one

3

who'd been watching and had now followed her here. Only at the last moment did she experience a subliminal warning, a primordial flash of insight that someone or something was close behind. But, as so often in her less than twenty years of life — and now at the point of death — she had her timing wrong. The wire was slipping over her head and there could be no escape.

Such a level of fear was unknown to her. She was immobilized, outstretched toes grasping at the ground, back arched and frozen; in terror of making any movement that would pull the noose tighter. Only her fingers were active, tearing at her throat, trying to prise beneath the wire, to release the deadly pressure. With an enormous act of will she overcame the panic and pain, wriggling her body round in an attempt to reach the gloved hands that were making such a brutal assault on her future.

Thus it was, in the cool impersonal floodlighting which illuminated this small hallowed space beneath the trees, that she came face to face with her attacker. The shock of recognition was fleeting. Certainly the outward features were familiar. But that familiarity was contradicted by eyes unlike any she'd earlier seen or imagined: devoid of compassion, reptilian in their self-containment and single-mindedness — holes into a dark and empty place that surely no human soul could inhabit. With the last conscious moments allowed her, she recognized in those unblinking, unflinching eyes her imminent death... and abandoned all hope.

*   *   *

Hours passed. The natural silence was complete. There were no leaves on the trees to answer the chill, almost windless air. The only sound, muffled by the cold and distance, was man-made and came from the occasional passing car on one or other of the two roads which, west and east, flanked this modest area of unfenced urban parkland. Often crowded by day, especially in the summer months, it now stood empty... shunned by any living, breathing human presence. But this place, created to celebrate human excellence, must sooner or later draw to itself some other aspiring or despairing human spirit and, with one of time's gentle little ironies, the next to pass this

4

way would be another in preoccupied self-torment.

He'd told himself so often over the last weeks that it couldn't go on. He had to put a stop to it. Of course, it would take a certain courage... though he persuaded himself that, looking back on his earlier life, he hadn't often been lacking in nerve, or even daring. He could surely summon up what was necessary. It was a problem that had to be faced and the sooner the better.

He nearly missed her. She was out of his immediate line of sight as he walked towards the shoreline. But, once his eyes locked onto that solitary and lifeless figure, set in an almost staged tableau before him, he was unable to turn away. He drew closer, responding with a tumult of emotions and thoughts: some irrelevant, others of an intensity that threatened to overwhelm him and seemed to be drawing him in surprising directions.

His normally reliable sense of time abandoned him. He would afterwards have no concept of how long he stood transfixed by this unexpected and cruelly compelling sight... But then he shook himself — physically and mentally. He couldn't stand here staring. He had to act.

"You're late, Miranda," said Tero as she passed his desk en route to her own.

She didn't need telling, thank you very much! Some forty minutes earlier, stepping onto the pavement outside the flat she shared with her younger sister, Rosie, Miranda had found her treasured, two-year-old Opel Corsa boxed in by a battered old van and a flashy red BMW. They'd left her no more than a few inches either end. And neither vehicle was even displaying a resident's parking permit! At first she'd tried to manoeuvre her way out by tacking back and forth. It was hopeless. Digging out her mobile, she phoned Leena in Registry. The van was from out of town — somewhere up north — and its owner didn't appear to have a cellphone. Fortunately, the BMW's owner did, and Miranda dialled the number. It rang for over a minute. She was wondering whether to give up and call a taxi, when an irritable male voice grunted something unintelligible. She didn't know what she was interrupting and didn't care. She threatened him with tow trucks, with swarms of traffic wardens crawling over him and his pretentious penis-substitute, with an eternity of police harassment. He'd better get down here pretty damn quick and let her out! Grudgingly he agreed, but kept her waiting another ten minutes... with full malevolent intent, Miranda was sure. Having sat in her car and ignored him — to avoid any risk of getting physical — she pulled out into the traffic stream and focused on reining in her emotions. No way would a creep like that affect the quality of her driving.

But now she'd arrived at Pasila HQ almost half an hour late.

"The boss already left," Tero went on, prompting Miranda to halt by his desk. "Wants you at the crime scene, soon as poss'. Tasty one this morning. A murder."

Much as Miranda sympathized with Tero's enthusiasm for a professional challenge, she wished he'd show more sensitivity towards what was probably another tragic and unnecessary death.

"Only been gone ten minutes," Tero added. "It's over at the Sibelius Monument."

Miranda's eyes widened. "Won't be hard to find then. How come *you're* still here?"

"Paperwork. Going to court first thing Monday. Might be along later."

Not bothering to visit her own desk, Detective Inspector Miranda Lewis hitched her bag more securely over her shoulder and walked back the way she'd come.

The Sibelius Monument, in Sibelius Park, is less than two miles from Pasila Police Headquarters. Miranda took her own car and parked in a quiet residential street along the park's northern edge.

With the benefit of her bi-cultural background, she realized how hard it might be for a non-Finn to grasp the full national significance of the composer Jean Sibelius. In the Finnish psyche he occupies a place which, for most countries, would be reserved for kings, military heroes or saints. It's true that modern times have seen other popular figures rise to prominence in the Finnish iconography: extraordinary Olympic athletes like Paavo Nurmi and Lasse Viren; more recently, in motor racing, Keke Rosberg and Mika Häkkinen. But Sibelius towers over them all as the grand old grandfather-figure of the nation. He was there at its birth, nurturing the struggle for independence with his *Kullervo Symphony*, his *Karelia Suite* and *Finlandia*. Later his art would transcend geographical and political boundaries and reach out to all humanity, placing Finland, with its small isolated population, on the world's cultural map for all time.

The sculptress Eila Hiltunen's memorial was unveiled in 1967, ten years after the composer's death, and it followed the fashion for later-twentieth-century civic sculptures by puzzling many who saw it. A large stainless-steel relief of the composer's head, reassuringly comprehensible, now greets the onlooker from the face of a natural granite outcropping. But that was an afterthought — a bowing to public pressure. The main structure, which still dominates the scene, is more esoteric. Steel pipes of varying lengths and diameters are bundled together in a broad vertical array, at its tallest reaching to fivetimes human height. Many of the pipe ends are frayed, with deep irregular gashes reaching far up into their coarsely textured bodies. Despite the creator's claims that the design represented music in the abstract, for most people a visual association with organ pipes was hard to avoid. Some critics pointed out that, as Sibelius had written very little organ music, a reference to the symphony orchestra would have been more appropriate. Miranda didn't subscribe to such nitpicking. Her fondness for the monument was based on childhood visits with her Welsh father. They'd indulged in much less sanctimonious pursuits, chasing each other around the pipes and sticking their heads up inside to hoot, scream and laugh at the resonant echoes.

Approaching the monument on this bitingly subzero, late-March morning, Miranda saw that the Scenes Of Crimes Officers (the SOCOs) had already established themselves and were hard at work. The focus of the crime was screened off from public view, and just outside the screen she spotted the imposing figure and head of close-cropped white hair that identified her superior officer, A police photographer standing beside him, though not a small man, seemed almost dwarfed in comparison.

Apart from his exceptional height, Ylenius was powerfully built with little excess fat for someone of his fifty-four years. And, unlike many men of exceptional height, conditioned by years of banging heads on structures designed by those of lesser stature, Ylenius had no tendency to stoop. Amiable and avuncular features moderated the effect of this potentially intimidating size. Children warmed to him. Miranda had several times witnessed his ability to win their trust with a few soft-spoken and uncondescending words. As a boss he couldn't be faulted: fair-minded, supportive in times of crisis, never failing to give credit where it was due. Not much concerned with formality, he encouraged his subordinates to work together on a first-name basis. He would have been totally at ease with younger colleagues calling him Aleksi, but for the most part, they preferred 'Chief Inspector', 'Chief' or simply 'boss'. Miranda held him in considerable respect, both as a person and as an experienced police officer. She was grateful for the last eighteen months under his command.

"Sorry I'm late, Chief."

"A rare event, Miranda. I'll tell you what we've got so far..."

The police photographer nodded to Miranda and disappeared behind the screen.

"...The call came in at 6.48 this morning. The victim was found by a man walking his dog. The duty officer alerted me at home, so I sent the SOCOs in first to do some of the preliminary work. The pathologist's been and gone. He estimates death occurred between eight and eleven yesterday evening. You'd better have a look."

Miranda wasn't squeamish, but such moments in her chosen career were always unpleasant. In a way, she hoped they would never become routine — preferring to keep her humanity unjaded and intact.

She followed Ylenius into the screened area and adjusted to the scene, letting professional training and experience take over. The victim was seated with her back propped against the rock face, little more than a yard to the left of the fourtimes-natural-size relief of Sibelius's head. Her legs were straight and splayed out at an angle of about thirty degrees. It was difficult to guess her age. Death had disfigured her youth, but she was clearly very young — somewhere between seventeen and twenty-five, Miranda supposed.

The girl's hair was thick and Nordic fair, gathered luxuriantly around her shoulders: beautiful, healthy hair which only accentuated the frightful distortion of the face it now framed. The eyes bulged; the tongue protruded slightly between pale, bluish lips. Cause of death was obvious. The girl's neck was tightly encircled by some kind of noose that bit viciously into the flesh of her throat and had entrapped large amounts of hair.

The victim's clothes had been interfered with. Her red and yellow quilted winter jacket was open and pushed back over her shoulders. A dark-red ribbed top and the bra beneath were pulled up to her armpits, exposing her breasts and stomach. Her jeans had been unzipped and tugged only part-way down her hips, as if the spread of her legs had prevented further removal. The fact that her pants were still more or less in place seemed to preclude outright rape, but the sexual implications were unavoidable.

"And there's this extra grisly little feature," said Ylenius, drawing Miranda's attention to the arm lying inert at the girl's right side. "Her fourth finger's been removed — severed from the right hand. Some kind of trophy, I suppose. The pathologist pointed out there's been very little bleeding, so she must've been dead when it was cut off. Let's be thankful for small mercies, shall we?"

"Any indication how it was amputated?"

"Nothing found yet that's suitable for the job. We'll be widening our search, of course."

"And the violin? Was it found like that?" She pointed to a violin case leaning against the rock just below Jean Sibelius's austere and impassive face.

"Yes, the SOCOs had a quick look inside, but I asked them to put it back in situ — so you could get an overall impression of the scene."

Both detectives now allowed themselves some greater distance from the victim, backing away to stand beside the monument's towering metal pipes.

"Any ID?" Miranda asked.

"Nothing useful on her. A solitary door key in her jeans pocket and a few coins in the jacket. No sign of a handbag."

"What about inside the violin case?"

"Address label, you mean? No, just the instrument and some printed music."

"A violin dealer might give us a lead on the instrument — suggest it's provenance, help us locate its owner. But how about the music? Can I have a look?"

9

"Forensics already bagged it. What've you got in mind, Miranda?"

"I'm not sure."

But the music was located and Miranda studied it through the clear plastic evidence sleeve.

"Debussy's Violin Sonata," she said.

"So?"

"On the whole it's a lyrical piece — not exactly virtuoso stuff. But it needs some technical skill to attempt. And she does seem to have been working on it. The music's covered in pencilled bowing marks. She could be a professional — though, judging by her age, I'd guess a music student. Perhaps at the Sibelius Academy."

"Worth looking into."

"But we've got a problem now it's Saturday. The Academy admin's closed for the weekend. A bit ghoulish to hawk a PM photo of her round random students in the corridors — the way she's looking now."

" You could at least try the porter on the door. Get the photographer to do a Polaroid of her face. Perhaps he can flatter her appearance a bit — keep the noose out of the picture. But, before you follow up on that, let's go and interview the man who found the body."

Martti Hakala lived close to where Miranda had left her car, in a block of flats overlooking Sibelius Park from its northern perimeter. More or less contemporary with the 1952 Helsinki Olympic Games, the building looked in need of a major renovation. So did Martti Hakala. Although, according to his identity card, he was in his early forties, he could easily have passed for fifty. His face was colourless, drawn, conveying an impression of worry and fatigue. In his bearing there was a curious mixture of military preciseness and slouching indecision which gave Miranda the impression of an ex-soldier fallen on hard times. As he edged past her in the narrow hallway, she caught a whiff of stale vodka.

Hakala showed them into a living room cluttered with ugly furniture. An overweight golden Labrador was sprawled inside the door. Its only reaction to their arrival was a brief raising of one eyelid.

"Wife's at the shops," Hakala said vaguely. "Like some coffee?

Only take a moment."

"Not necessary, thank you," replied Ylenius.

They sat down and the Chief Inspector made a start: "Can you tell us, Mr Hakala, exactly how you found the body?"

"Okay, so I got up before dawn. Already been awake a couple of hours. Not sleeping too well lately. You know how it is… a lot on my mind. Anyway, I made some coffee and tried reading the paper. Couldn't concentrate. Looking at the words and nothing going in. So I went out for some fresh air. Took Saara with me, of course. She can't wait too long in the mornings. Her bladder isn't what it used to be."

Miranda assumed he was referring to the dog rather than his wife. Ylenius gave an encouraging nod.

"Usually we go for a slow stroll round Sibelius Park — seeing as it's so close — along the edge of the kiddies' playground, past the monument and down to the seashore. I almost didn't see her — the girl, I mean. Lost in my own thoughts probably."

"Was it the dog spotted her first?" Miranda asked.

"You must be joking," he said mildly. "Poor old Saara wouldn't spot a hare if it hopped up and bit her. Practically blind. Don't think her sense of smell's up to much either. Suppose I should have the vet put her to sleep. But she's still game for a walk, as long as I don't rush her. Difficult when you've been together so long. You get so attached. Just like a marriage. Better than a marriage, to be honest. The wife tells me I should just get on with it and have the poor thing put down. But there's not much me and her agree on nowadays."

Ylenius brought him back to the real issue. "Could you estimate the time when you found the body?"

"Must've been a bit after six-thirty. Can't be more precise than that, I'm afraid. Six-thirty-five or six-forty shouldn't be far from the truth."

"And did you go up to the girl when you saw her?"

"Not closer than a couple of yards. Obviously stone dead. No sense checking her pulse or anything. Not the first time I've seen a corpse, but it took me back a bit. Sort of rooted me to the spot. Her tongue sticking out and her eyes staring like that. There'd obviously been some funny business… With that thing round her neck and her clothes all pulled about. I came straight home and called the police."

"You didn't touch her?"

"No, I just said that." Hakala was showing signs of irritation.

"Or anything else in the vicinity?"

"What kind of anything else?"

"You didn't pick anything up nearby? Or notice anything lying on the ground?"

"I came home, I made the call, and that's it... Well, there was a violin leaning against the rock. Is that what you're getting at?"

"No, I wondered if anything else caught your eye."

Hakala shook his head.

"And the dog didn't go anywhere near her?"

"Don't think she'd even noticed."

"Well, that seems clear enough," Ylenius said.

But Miranda had another question.

"You said you regularly walk the dog on the same route. Did you go that way yesterday evening?"

"Yes, I wanted to watch the ice-hockey on telly, so I took Saara out just before it started."

"And did you walk past the Sibelius Monument?"

"We came back that way — at about twenty to nine, I suppose."

"Did you see anybody in the park?"

"No, it was deserted for a Friday evening. Probably the cold. Not used to temperatures like this so close to April, are we?"

"And you're sure the girl wasn't already there by then?"

"No, we walked straight past the place. I'd've seen her, wouldn't I?"

Miranda and Ylenius exchanged glances. That narrowed down the time of the murder to later than eight forty.

Ylenius pushed himself up from the sagging sofa.

"Thanks for your cooperation, Mr Hakala. We'll send a constable round in a day or two to take a formal statement."

Hakala nodded... but then seemed to hesitate, as if he had something to add. Ylenius paused expectantly.

"There's one thing, Chief Inspector. I might not be here much longer. The wife and me, you see — we haven't been getting on too well recently... and I've found this little one-room-and-a-kitchen round the corner. It's up for rent. I thought I'd give it a try... and take

Saara with me. Don't know if it'll work out. But things have got to such a head, I don't see as I can go on like this — not under the same roof."

When he appeared to have finished, Ylenius shifted position in the direction of the door.

"If you do decide to change address, Mr Hakala, you *will* inform us, won't you?"

"Yes, yes, of course. At once." He seemed relieved, and Miranda wondered if they were the first to hear of his impending escape.

Outside on the pavement, Ylenius stopped beside Miranda's car.

"What about the Sibelius Academy?" he asked.

"It'll be time-consuming. They've got three main buildings scattered round the city. Two in the centre and one out in Pitäjänmäki. And there are so many departments nowadays:" — she counted them off on her fingers — "Theory and Composition, Church Music, Performing Arts, Opera, Music Education, Folk Music, Jazz, Music Technology... Nearly two thousand students, and no way of knowing which department she might've been in. My guess is she'll turn out to be a Performing Arts student. They're the ones aiming at a solo career or hoping to join a professional orchestra — just like my sister Rosie, in fact. Officially they're based in R-block — the one on Rautatienkatu. But the dead girl could've visited any of the buildings on a regular basis — going to different classes or looking for an empty practice room."

Twenty yards behind Ylenius, Miranda noticed a tight-faced woman with two plastic bags of shopping turn into the apartment block entrance they'd just themselves exited. *Mrs Hakala?* she wondered.

"Okay, Miranda, this lead's going to keep you busy for a while," Ylenius said. "But identifying the girl's a priority. Could your sister give us some help?"

"To be honest, boss, I wouldn't want to put her through it. She's so sensitive. A PM photo like this could give her nightmares for months. Anyway, she's in London right now — on a Royal Academy cello scholarship. She won't be back for another fortnight."

— * —

13

The rest of Miranda's day proved to be a series of cul-de-sacs. Showing the victim's photo to the porters at the three Academy buildings drew a blank; although she did get a list of personal phone numbers for the various department secretaries and student affairs officers. Miranda visited some of them at their homes. But no one could identify the dead girl.

At one point during these meanderings across the city, Miranda passed through Pasila to check her in-tray and email. She found Sergeant Tero Toivonen in their open-plan office peering at a selection of Sibelius Monument crime-scene photos that he'd laid panoramically across his desk. At the same time he was chewing on an outsize burger needing both of his hands for successful control. The amount of junk food he ingested, Miranda often wondered how he could retain the same lean and wiry build — 'rat-like' she privately described it to herself, corresponding to his pointed, somewhat sneering features.

"A lot of people'll be screaming sacrilege when this gets in the papers," Tero said, through a mouthful of burger. "Committing such a dastardly deed under the eyes of our beloved Jean."

Miranda stared back coolly. "The sacrilege, Tero, was on that poor young girl — whoever she might be. Her whole life ahead. You probably find the idea trite, but I think it's an appalling waste. And Sibelius would've agreed. He had six daughters of his own and loved them dearly."

"So you haven't managed to ID her?" he asked, ignoring the lecture.

"Not yet. Any luck with missing persons?"

"No one matches the description."

"Well, I've still got a few Academy personnel to visit."

"How's about taking me along? Get me out of the office for a while?"

"No, you'd better stay and hold the fort."

"Ah, the trials of a subordinate officer," he said, though without any sign of rancour.

This gave Miranda pause for thought. At twenty-nine, Tero was exactly her own age, but Miranda's university degree and resultant accelerated promotion had left him one clear rank behind. Many men would have resented taking orders from a woman under such circumstances. For all his faults — and he had plenty — Miranda considered herself fortunate that Tero was in some ways so unambitious. He seemed content to just drift through life doing his job commendably enough from day to day; then, in his free time, playing endless computer games over the internet while listening to *Nirvana* on one of the largest, most expensive hi-fi systems Miranda had ever seen outside an arena rock concert.

"How did the press conference go?" she asked.

"Caused a bit of a stir. Of course, we suppressed most of the details: the missing finger, the tampering with the clothes, the ligature, the placing of the violin. They know she was strangled, but not how."

This was standard procedure. Knowledge of such facts by a later suspect could indicate guilt. Conversely, the police needed some way to eliminate false confessions that always attended a crime of this nature.

"When's the PM?" asked Miranda.

"Tomorrow morning. The boss wants us here by ten for a conference of war."

"So much for a quiet Sunday at home."

Tero nodded. "Yeah, I was looking forward to a relaxing one hundred decibels of Kurt Cobain."

Miranda went trekking off again in search of someone who could identify the dead girl. But, throughout this fruitless and frustrating day, her thoughts turned repeatedly to an altogether more private matter — to events in her own life over the last three days, and especially to the Wednesday evening Sibelius lecture where she and the Englishman had first met. . .

II

Andante (ma non troppo lento)

" **J**ohan Julius Christian Sibelius was born on the 8th of December 1865, in Hämeenlinna. Johan, or Janne as his family and friends would always call him, was only two years old when his father, a regimental doctor, was struck down by typhus — presumably contracted from one of his patients. Although Janne never knew his father, he appears to have inherited from him a kind-hearted, engaging character and a love of social gatherings. Janne could be lively and amusing, but there was a complementary dark side to his personality: an unpredictable moodiness or moroseness; a tendency to withdraw into a world of his own which others found disconcerting."

Miranda had made it into the Sibelius Academy Wegelius Hall only moments before the lecture began. It was her boss's considerate dismissal from a late-afternoon-stretching-tediously-into-early-evening brainstorming session with the Community Relations Committee that had made it possible for her to get here at all for the seven-thirty start. In his empathetic way, Ylenius had remembered the upcoming English language lecture series on the seven symphonies of Sibelius and the reason why Miranda was especially keen to attend. As she dropped into the last remaining aisle seat in the fifth row, she received a welcoming smile from a tall, darkly moustached man in his early- to mid-thirties on the adjacent chair. Miranda then managed to embarrass herself by upsetting her shoulder bag and scattering personal items around and about his feet. With reassuring humour he helped her gather them up. He spoke in English, so she thanked him in the same language. His response was a melodramatic tip of the head...

"Do I detect a lilt of the hills and valleys in your delightful, velvety voice?" he enquired. "A resonance from the great Land of Song? A reminder of the bardic realm of..."

Before he could finish, or Miranda could adjust to this extraordinary manner of speech and frame an answer, the evening's speaker had climbed onto the lecture platform, and the audience was sprinkling the hall with polite and expectant applause.

Dr Nicholas Lewis was something of a celebrity in the world of music literature. He'd written several well-researched and critically acclaimed books that had explored the symphonic cycles of, among others, Brahms, Bruckner and Mahler. His ability to combine erudite scholarship, a strongly personal musical sense, and an appealingly readable and approachable style had won him a small but enthusiastic following. On his return to Finland, a country in which he'd spent nearly three earlier decades of his life, he was at last focusing his attention on Sibelius. This Wednesday lecture series would embody developing plans for a new volume he hoped to have ready for publication by the end of the year. He had begun this first lecture by introducing himself to the audience, and now he was giving a brief account of Sibelius's early years.

"Apart from the untimely loss of his father, Janne was fortunate in his childhood. He grew up in a small and attractive provincial town, in the warm and loving embrace of a cultured middle-class household. The whole family was musical, especially on his mother's side, and they actively played chamber music together. Although clearly talented, Janne didn't exhibit the gifts of a child prodigy. His musical development would be slower than that of a Mozart or a Mendelssohn but nonetheless inexorable. At twenty years old, Janne dutifully followed his family-elders' wishes by entering the Faculty of Law at the University of Helsinki. After only two terms, he abandoned an academic career in favour of the Helsinki School of Music. His mother bowed to the inevitable with an apprehensive heart. How could she have known that, as a consequence, this very school would one day change its name to hers and become the Sibelius Academy.

"Janne's ambition of becoming a professional violinist was painfully thwarted — probably because of his late start... not taking formal lessons until the age of fourteen. But his talent for composition was spotted by Martin Wegelius, the director of the Conservatory, and Janne's career was set on its proper course."

Miranda watched the speaker with affection. He was a man of short but stocky build who had, she knew, achieved success in his younger years as a prop forward for one of the better South Wales rugby teams. His hair bore traces of its original dark colour, though now almost overtaken by grey. He also sported a thick grizzly beard which, in combination with his body shape, reinforced the impression of an ageing teddy bear.

"At this point," he went on, "I should mention the composer's Uncle Johan, who was a sea captain by profession. In those days it was customary for such international travellers to adopt a French form of their name when abroad and, one day, Janne stumbled on a stack of old visiting cards bearing the name Jean Sibelius. The ring of this combination so impressed the younger Johan that he decided to follow his uncle's example."

* [Having completed this short biographical introduction, Dr Lewis chose to explore more provocative ground...

"I'll now ask you to follow me on a small detour — one that I personally find of great interest. Let us consider the concept of Sibelius, the Finnish composer...

"His music is so Finnish. This is a statement one often hears, especially in the land of his birth... so often that it seems to be a truism. But what exactly do people mean by this claim? *Sibelius's music is so Finnish.* It's very easy to feel sympathy for a Finn wishing to express an affinity with his or her own cultural heritage. I, myself, am deeply proud of the fact that I was born on the same island as William Shakespeare, and that the language he moulded into such extraordinary dramatic and evocative forms is also my own. No matter that Shakespeare's genius is separated from my mediocrity by a geographical distance in birthplace of one hundred miles and a temporal separation of about four hundred years. I feel a proprietary sense of oneness, of somehow being myself a part of his genius. Why then should I be surprised if, for example, a thirty-five-year-old systems engineer, working for Nokia in a present-day Helsinki that Sibelius would scarcely have recognized, takes comfort in associating

---

* As suggested in the introductory **Notes to the Reader**, these bracketed sections of the Sibelius lectures may be treated as optional.

himself with his own national giant of creative genius? Sibelius was indeed one of the great geniuses of Western musical civilization, and he was most certainly born a Finn. This doesn't however, in itself, help us to answer the question of what is really meant by the statement: *Sibelius's music is so Finnish.*
"In what ways is his music Finnish? Wherein does this Finnishness lie? Is it a product of the musical culture into which he was born? Hardly... In 1865, the concert music tradition in Finland was mainstream European. Janne grew up in an environment of Bach, Haydn, Mozart and Beethoven; of Schubert, Mendelssohn, Schumann and Brahms. There was no Finnish composer, past or present, who hadn't trained in and modelled himself on this predominantly Teutonic tradition. The same musical influences were paramount in Janne's formative years. He played many works of these masters with the family trio: consisting of himself, his brother and his sister. Should we then be calling Sibelius's music Austro-Germanic? No, let's withhold judgment for the time being and look elsewhere. Let's turn our attention to Finnish ethnic music.
"Finland has a long tradition of folk music covering a wide range — from the genial dances of the 'pelimanni' violinists to the grief-laden cries of the professional lamenters. So perhaps this is where Sibelius's Finishness derives: from Finnish folk music. Unfortunately not! Sibelius isn't a nationalist composer in the way that could be claimed for such figures as Grieg, Smetana or Bartók. Incidentally, Bartók was a composer that Sibelius would, in later years, come to admire, so I'll take the Hungarian as an example... Bartók's music, although not relying directly on quotations from ethnic sources, is imbued with Hungarianness in its rhythms and scale structures. There is ample justification for calling his music Hungarian. In Sibelius's case, however, although the composer had a fair knowledge of the Karelian folk-music tradition, relatively little seems to have found its way into his own work."
Miranda looked surreptitiously around the lecture hall. The majority of the audience would undoubtedly be Finns, and what the speaker appeared to be implying was tantamount to treason. She detected puzzlement on some of the faces but nothing more.
"Sibelius himself denied any direct influence from Finnish folk melodies and wrote a rebuttal to anyone he discovered making such claims for his music. But can't we anyway reassure ourselves by considering the composer's fascination for the *Kalevala*: Finland's national epic poem? The titles of many of his pieces testify to it: *The*

Symphony No 1

Kullervo Symphony, Lemminkäinen's Return, The Swan of Tuonela, Pohjola's Daughter, Luonnotar, Tapiola. Surely these literary sources of inspiration demonstrate the Finnishness of Sibelius's music? Well, if they do, by the same logic we are forced to declare that the incidental music he wrote for Maeterlinck's *Pelleas et Melisande* demonstrates Belgianness and the incidental music for Shakespeare's *The Tempest* demonstrates Englishness! We have clearly gone astray.

"Of course, we might still resort to Sibelius's patriotism. Everyone knows that he composed *Finlandia* as a stirring thumb-on-the-nose at nearly a century of Czarist rule. Yes, that's true, as far as it goes. However, politics is politics and, although music can sometimes be drawn into the service of political creeds, music of itself does not, indeed *cannot* express political thoughts. Its language is of a totally different nature."] *

But now Dr Lewis announced that it was time to embark on a detailed study of the composer's First Symphony, opus 39, in E minor...

Glancing to her left, Miranda caught her neighbour's eye. He grinned broadly, and whispered: "Intriguing stuff!" His face was curiously irregular, with one eye noticeably higher than the other and a nose that looked as if it had at some stage been broken. Although his style of dress was conventional, the impression he made on Miranda had something piratical about it. His voice had been a sonorous baritone — an actor's voice — its accent plainly English. She wondered about his connection to Finland and if he'd been in the country long.

"It's something of a tired joke," Dr Lewis continued, "that Sibelius's First Symphony should really be called Tchaikovsky's Seventh... and, yes, there *are* clear traits inherited from the Russian composer. In his autumnal years, Sibelius acknowledged a 'youthful' fascination for the cosmopolitan Tchaikovsky. He was, however, less ready to admit any debt to the more nationalistic Russian composers like Borodin or Rimsky-Korsakov. Perhaps he felt it would be 'politically incorrect' for a Finn whose patriotism had come to be considered a cornerstone of his country's recently won independence."

The remainder of the lecture provided an analysis of each of the four movements, effectively illustrated with short examples — some played enthusiastically at the piano by the speaker himself, and others on CD in a full orchestral version. Dr Lewis held his listeners spellbound. And, on drawing his presentation to a close, invited everyone to join him the following Wednesday evening for an exploration of the *Second* Symphony. The audience showed its appreciation with vigorous applause.

As they were all standing to leave, the Englishman leant over and asked Miranda: "Have you heard Dr Lewis lecture before?"

"You could say that," she laughed. "At breakfast and dinner for most of my childhood."

The Englishman's brown eyes twinkled. "Am I encouraged to suppose that finding two persons of the druidic persuasion sheltering under the same far-flung roof is no mere coincidence?"

Miranda gave herself a few moments to interpret this idiosyncratic verbal style, and nodded: "He's my father."

"Tempting to be wise after the event," said the Englishman, "but I believe I *do* detect a plausible resemblance to the illustrious doctor — especially around the mouth. Not the colouring, of course... not your flaming Titian red hair and striking green eyes, Ms Lewis." He hesitated. "Or perhaps I err in assuming your name conforms to that of your paternal lineage?"

Again she made the necessary mental translation, and smiled. "I did try another name for a while, but Lewis turned out better after all. I'm Miranda... Miranda Lewis."

"Wonderful to make your acquaintance. And if I may introduce *myself*?" He offered his hand... "Phillip Burton — though I'd be grateful if you limited your usage to the Phillip bit. And while we're participating in the social graces, allow me to introduce a fellow countryman." He turned to the man now hovering beside him: "Vagabond and composer extraordinaire, Adrian Gamble."

And that was it. Not love, of course. Miranda wasn't naive. But powerful attraction at first sight — admittedly a rare occurrence for her in recent years — was entirely possible; though nothing to do with Hollywood screen-star looks. This man wasn't tall — not as tall as Phillip, for example; nor as dark. His eyes were strikingly blue.

And his hair was a halo of tight curls. When he spoke — "Yes, I'm Adrian Gamble. Nice to meet you, Miranda" — he had a soft, reticent, tenor voice. His boyish smile came in appealing contrast to his otherwise manly features, and she suddenly realized how much he reminded her of a whirlwind teenage romance ten summers ago on the island of Crete.

Miranda offered to introduce the two Englishmen to her father. They eagerly took up the offer, and were soon praising Dr Lewis on his lecture — Phillip hyperbolically, Adrian more directly. Both were obvious Sibelius enthusiasts, and Nick Lewis suggested they all four visit the nearest pub for a quick "post-proscenium pint"; adding that, although he and Miranda had a prior dinner engagement *à deux* — having not seen each other for several months — all his prattling on about Sibelius had left him with a raging thirst which he'd enjoy quenching right now *à quatre*.

Phillip and Adrian protested they didn't want to impose on a family reunion; but Nick, with Miranda's unspoken endorsement, overrode their objections.

"Blissfully resident in this 'Pearl of the Baltic' for a couple of years now," Phillip Burton explained. "No plans to leave. Suits me admirably."

"And you, Adrian?" asked Miranda.

"I only got here last autumn. Spent last year in Stockholm."

"Why change to Helsinki?"

"*Cherchez la femme,*" said Phillip archly. "Or, in this case, *la femme cherchée.*"

Adrian looked disconcerted: "Don't be absurd, Phillip. You know I only came to keep a parental eye on you — that and the lure of the Sibelius Academy." He turned back to the other two. "I won an Arts Council scholarship in Sweden for composition and decided to bring it over here. Now I've got a couple of part-time teaching jobs to supplement the grant, so things are working out fine. Meanwhile Phillip's pursuing his career as an English teacher," he added, shifting the focus from himself.

"Yes, spreading our winsome tongue to the natives," Phillip agreed. "Immense good fortune, don't you think? A worldwide market demand for something we acquired effortlessly in the cradle. Potential for travel and personal enrichment! Been exploiting it most of my adult life."

"You and adult life strike me as incompatible concepts," quipped Adrian.

"I admit I've been a slow developer," Phillip responded. "But subtle depths of maturity await discovery for the trained observer."

"Why do I get the impression you two've known each other more than just a few months?" asked Miranda.

"You've penetrated our guilty secret!" exclaimed Phillip. "We do go back a long way — as far, one might say, as the redbrick halls of Edgbaston — the confluence point of our fateful first meeting so many life-enhancing years ago."

"What Phillip's trying to say is we met at Birmingham University. I was doing Civil Engineering, and he was doing English Literature and Modern Languages. We seem to have been recrossing paths ever since."

Nick turned to Phillip. "You're a linguist, eh? So how's your Finnish?"

"Ah... well, I can manage in French, German and Italian," Phillip replied, "and pass muster in five other world languages. But Finnish, I humbly admit, still defeats me!"

Miranda picked up on *Adrian's* degree subject: "Civil engineering to composition? That's quite a leap!"

"Maybe not," said Nick. "Bach might've made a stunning mathematician if he'd been born in another time and place."

Adrian nodded. "Yes, I've always felt a close affinity between compositional and mathematical processes. But, Phillip, shouldn't we be making a move?"

"Quite so," Phillip agreed. "We'll leave you to your family tête-à-tête and wend our separate way. Although might I suggest another occasion to further this agreeable acquaintance? Adrian and I shall imbibe two days hence at the Ateljé Restaurant. Any chance of joining us?"

"Personally, I'm off to the country for the weekend," Nick said, "to our lakeside cottage. It's been locked up the whole winter. But I'd like to set myself up there for the summer months and work on my

Sibelius book. Though I'll be back in Helsinki for my Wednesday lectures. I'm sure we can find another chance. But, Miranda, nothing to stop *you* this Friday, is there?"

"I've got an eight o'clock start Saturday morning. But, I suppose if we don't make too long an evening of it..."

"Hope you didn't mind me putting your name forward, my dear, for meeting our new English friends again."

Father and daughter had by now settled themselves at a corner table in a restaurant nearby: one specializing in traditional Finnish farmhouse cuisine.

"No problem, Dad. Could be fun. Phillip's quite a character, isn't he?"

"Gay, do you suppose?"

"I doubt it. I know he talks like a frenzied Shakespearean actor, but it doesn't come across especially 'camp'. More Lord Byron than Oscar Wilde."

"Just asking. Women are better judges of these things. But I got the impression Adrian interested you more."

"Was it *that* obvious?"

"I've known you a long time, darling."

"And was there a hidden motive for setting me up on Friday evening? Trying some match-making, are you?"

"And why not? You've been alone too long. Time to put the past behind you, Miranda. I've had to do it. Any news from Johannes by the way?"

"Someone told me he's in Brussels."

"I never thought you were a good match. You'll find someone better. But only if you put yourself in the path of opportunity. I know your job's important to you. Just try getting out a bit more."

"It's not that bad, Dad!" Miranda objected. "I've still got the string quartet." This was an amateur ensemble she'd played in since university. "Though we only manage once a month nowadays. Haven't done a recital for ages."

"Did you get your viola sorted?"

"It only needed an adjustment to the sound post... Hey, we're running through Opus 76, No 2 tomorrow — just for fun, of course."

"One of Haydn's best. Can I tag along and listen?"

"Of course! And why don't you join us more actively sometimes? We could do a Piano Quintet together."

"Tempting thought. How about the Brahms F Minor? Are we up to it?"

"There'll be nobody else to hear us. We can make as big a mess of it as we like."

The waitress came for their order. Both chose the braised liver with cowberry sauce.

"See how it compares with your mother's culinary skills, shall we? Always was one of my favourites."

Miranda leant forward, resting her chin on interlocked fingers.

"Are you coping, Dad?"

"Ups and downs. Sometimes I think I'll be fine. Then everything comes flooding back. Work's excellent therapy. I'm keeping myself busy with this new book."

"It's wonderful to have you back in Finland. I'm glad we'll see more of each other, but I wish things could've gone better for you in Edinburgh."

Nick reached out to touch Miranda's cheek. Tears had formed in the corners of his eyes and she felt her own burning in sympathy.

"You and Rosie have been wonderful daughters," he said, summoning up an affectionate smile. "I've often wondered if I should've left you so soon after your mother passed away."

"Dad, we both understood. You had to take that second chance. And we weren't babies anymore. I only wish you and Eleanor could've had more time together."

She studied her father intently. The pain of nursing two successive wives through terminal cancer in less than five years had left its mark. She realized how hard it would be for him to risk a third commitment.

"Tell me, Dad, did you see Rosie while you were in London?"

Nick rallied at once. "Yes, she was radiant, and making excellent progress. She proved it to me with a private recital in my hotel room: Bach's C Minor Cello Suite."

Miranda laughed. "I wish I'd been there. She said in her last letter she'll be back in a fortnight."

"So how about us meeting her at the airport?"

Symphony No 1

"Dad, that's a great idea."

Over the following two days, Miranda's work was largely routine: domestic violence, a couple of bar brawls. Nothing out of the ordinary. But, at last, on Friday evening Miranda arrived at the Ateljé Restaurant — no more than a few minutes past the agreed time of 8 o'clock — for her triangular date with the two Englishmen. Phillip spotted her at the door and rushed gallantly over.

"Miranda, you look stunning. I'm bowled over." He escorted her to the table, pulled out a chair and tucked it under her with practised skill. Miranda found the attention mildly amusing. Somehow he managed to be neither obsequious nor overfamiliar.

"May I order you a drink?" he suggested. "Something to eat? Or shall we wait for Adrian? He's invariably late. It's the artistic temperament, so we must endeavour to excuse him. In the company of his creative muse he's oblivious to the passing hours."

Miranda accepted a glass of red wine and gazed at the surroundings. The Ateljé, a restaurant much frequented by professional musicians and music students, was more popular for drinking than for eating. Apart from the nearby television, whose volume was turned mercifully low, the place retained much of its original 1940s atmosphere.

"A long time since I was here," Miranda said. "I'd forgotten the sensation of stepping through a time warp."

"A little gloomy — even a little seedy. But, yes, it has a certain aura of old-fashioned Bohemianism, does it not? Talking of which, I was treated to an extravagant dinner at the Kämp last week."

Miranda was impressed: the Kämp being the only 5-star hotel in Finland with 5-star prices to match.

"Courtesy of a company that employs my English teaching services," Phillip went on. "Some top management wining and dining me as they practised their English skills — all on the company expense account, naturally."

"The perks of a language teacher?"

"Exactly! Of course, the Kämp was a regular haunt of Sibelius and his cronies back in the 1890s," Phillip said. "The new owners have striven to recreate that *fin de siècle* image — with excellent results, I must say. Easy to picture Jean at a corner table: the painter Gallen-Kallela to his left, the conductor Robert Kajanus to his right — discussing the human condition, peeling back the layers of illusion to reveal the innermost secrets of life, death, hope and despair. Well, that's the Romantic version. All probably just pissed as wombats most of the time."

In spite of herself, Miranda grinned at the change of register.

But still there was no sign of Adrian Gamble. Several times Miranda drew the conversation round to Phillip's missing friend, quizzing him about Adrian's previous and present life. If Phillip felt disappointment or envy at not being the focus of Miranda's interest, he concealed it very well, fielding her questions with attentive good humour.

Miranda learned that the *femme cherchée* Adrian had followed from Sweden to Helsinki was a young and rising opera star: an exceptionally gifted Finnish soprano who'd been studying in Stockholm. Unfortunately, back in the singer's home country their relationship became tempestuous and survived little more than a month. She ran off to Milan with an Italian tenor and, according to Phillip, it was two or three months before Adrian was able to compose again.

"Never seen him so affected by a member of the very much fairer sex," Phillip admitted.

Miranda might've preferred being spared some of the more delicate details of the romance, but Phillip's manner of recounting them was highly entertaining.

At exactly nine o'clock, Adrian phoned Phillip's mobile to say he was on his way. He finally appeared twenty minutes later.

"Good heavens, Adrian," Phillip chided, "this is extremely tardy, even by *your* long-practised standards."

"I'm really sorry. Something came up I had to deal with right away. I'm glad you're still here, Miranda. I was afraid I'd missed you."

Miranda now found *herself* the focus of both men's curiosity. They were predictably intrigued to learn about her job at the Homicide Unit, and pressed her to give an outline of her daily duties as a detective inspector. She found the chore less irksome than with most new acquaintances, but was still relieved when the discussion turned to Wednesday's Sibelius lecture.

"Have you noticed," said Phillip, at one point, "a family resemblance between the First Symphony's opening clarinet melody and the main theme for Coppola's *The Godfather*?"

Adrian considered this proposition. "Yes, if you give it to the trumpet. Though I doubt Sibelius ever saw the film. Something that interested me, Miranda, was your father's reference to Bruckner in the third movement. He's right, of course, about the opening scherzo passage — though Sibelius's touch is lighter, much less megalithic. That insistent pulse, those ambiguous cross-rhythms — they could almost be lifted from a previously unknown Bruckner symphony. The trio section's another matter. Nothing could be more idiosyncratically Sibelius, could it?"

Speaking on a subject that truly interested him, Adrian took fire. Miranda found herself drawn by his enthusiasm and more than anything by his eyes — such vividly blue eyes, of a hue seldom seen in Finland where a much greyer blue was commonplace. Some would find the intensity of those eyes unsettling. Miranda thought them extraordinarily attractive.

By half past eleven, she knew she'd have to leave if she wanted to function successfully the next day.

"You've been fantastic company," Miranda told them, "but I promised myself I'd be home by midnight."

"In that case, fair Cinderella," Phillip declared, "I trust you'll allow these two ugly sisters to escort you to your home portals. Didn't you say earlier your flat overlooks the Church in the Rock? 'Tis but a stone's throw from here, and 'twould be an enormous privilege. I'm convinced Adrian feels the same. Speak up, Adrian!"

"Yes, of course," Adrian nodded.

Some fifteen minutes later, as they were saying their goodbyes outside Miranda's apartment block, Phillip proposed they met again the following Monday at Mamma Rosa's Italian restaurant. Miranda had been wondering how to ensure her association with Adrian — such as it was — wouldn't end right here and now. Fortunately Phillip had taken the initiative.

And as she climbed the stairs to her flat, she experienced a sensation unfamiliar in recent years: a glow of anticipation — a feeling that her life was moving in a promising new direction.

Of course, she had no way of knowing how tomorrow morning would bring discovery of that young woman's body at the Sibelius Monument, and how this event would begin an unfolding sequence of horror overshadowing her life and numerous others for many weeks to come. . .

III

Scherzo: Allegro—Lento (ma non troppo)—Tempo I

At ten-thirty on Sunday morning, Miranda and Tero sat down in Chief Inspector Aleksi Ylenius's cosy, though unspacious office. Miranda often wondered how this colossal man could be content with such a tiny place of work, or how he managed to keep everything in order without the limited surfaces becoming permanently littered by papers and files.

"The preliminary post-mortem and forensic reports on the Sibelius Monument murder," Ylenius said, handing each a folder. Miranda and Tero studied the contents in silence...

The pathologist estimated the girl's age at around twenty. She was healthy, well-nourished, and had never given birth. She was 5' 5" tall and lightly built — a mere 7 stone (98 pounds). The cause of death was no surprise to anyone: strangulation performed with a length of lightweight electrical cable fashioned into a simple noose. The knot, situated at the back of the neck, had been designed to make the tightening process difficult to reverse. The remaining free end of the cable had then been tied into a fixed loop, presumably for hooking over the killer's wrist. The cable itself was of little help, consisting of two parallel grey strands fused along the middle — typical for connecting loudspeakers to domestic stereos, and *as common as spaghetti* the report wryly commented in a hand-written footnote.

Apart from the neck area, there were no obvious signs of bruising on the body. The position of the ligature knot at the back of the neck suggested the victim had been taken by surprise from behind with little chance of defending herself. The skin and blood found beneath her fingernails were her own — the result of a fruitless attempt to tear the noose away.

Despite no obvious signs of rape, sexual intercourse had recently taken place. A semen sample was being processed to generate a DNA profile.

And there was evidence to indicate the kind of tool used for amputating the little finger. Under a magnifying lens, the bone and cartilage remaining at the severed joint showed clear marks of a blade with extremely fine concave serrations (approximately three to a millimetre) suggesting either kitchen scissors or garden secateurs. But a detailed search of the crime scene area had turned up no such item — nor, in fact, anything else relevant to the investigation.

A study of the body's hypostasis indicated that the sitting position the victim was found in had been adopted soon after — if not immediately after — death. The time of death itself was now given more accurately: between 8.15 and 10.00 pm.

And then there was the door key found in the girl's jeans pocket. It was attached to a clear plastic tag advertising a popular brand of Finnish beer — so common as to offer no viable leads in itself. But the surface of the plastic bore two clear fingerprints: an index finger on one side, a thumb on the other. Neither belonged to the victim, nor disappointingly to any known felon on record.

"Not much to go on, is there?" complained Tero.

Ylenius sighed. "And we still don't know who she is. Missing Persons can't offer us a match. If she lives alone, it's possible nobody's even noticed her absence. Any luck with the door-to-door enquiries?"

"Not yet," said Tero. "Seems the cold snap and the ice hockey on telly kept everyone tucked up at home with the curtains drawn."

Miranda flicked back through her folder. "According to the report, there's no evidence the victim was forced to have intercourse. But, once he'd got the noose in place, she could've been frightened enough to comply. The most likely sequence would've been the rape first, the murder by strangulation second, and the removal of the finger last. So something doesn't add up."

"The clothes," said Ylenius.

"Exactly, boss. Her jeans and pants were more or less pulled back up. Why would he bother with that after he'd raped her? Seems curiously prudish under the circumstances."

31

"Perhaps the girl did it herself," suggested Ylenius. "A reflex action to hide her nakedness afterwards."

"But she didn't get them all the way up," Tero added, "because he started tightening the noose and she had other things to worry about."

Miranda grimaced at the image.

The meeting broke up a few minutes later. Being a Sunday, and with so few leads available, Miranda and Tero settled for completing the paperwork on their outstanding cases so they'd be free to concentrate on the Sibelius Monument murder tomorrow.

In fact, when Monday came, Miranda had no greater success at the Sibelius Academy than on Saturday. She could find no one able to identify the dead girl, and felt her next best bet would be the Helsinki Conservatory: a rather less prestigious music school recently drawn under the umbrella category of 'polytechnic college'. Most of its students were training to become instrumental or music-playschool teachers. After decades confined to cramped and unsuitable premises in the centre of the city, the Conservatory had, the previous autumn, moved into a brand-new building located a convenient twenty yards from Ruoholahti metro station.

It was already 3 pm when Miranda pushed her way through the clear-glass entrance doors. The porter's cubicle and the concert hall cloakroom lay to the left beyond a stairwell and a branching corridor. A large cafeteria opened up to the right, reaching as far as the building's glass-fronted facade. Few people were in sight. The lunch-time rush was over, and only a handful of the cafeteria tables were occupied. Behind the cloakroom desk a tall, heavily-built man was pulling on his jacket. Miranda approached him, her eyes drawn involuntarily to the long strands of fair hair combed from one side across the pink dome of his otherwise bald head.

"Are you the porter?" she asked.

"That's the one you want," he said, and nodded towards a much older man nearing the porter's cubicle from the direction of the stairwell. Miranda followed him as far as the threshold and introduced herself. He smiled back crookedly, and apologized for the fact that talking intelligibly might be a problem.

"Just came from the dentist," he explained, gingerly massaging his jaw. "Anaesthetic hasn't worn off yet. Gave me hell last week when it flared up. Didn't sleep a wink. Rushed straight to the dentist next morning. But she's been digging around again today. Says she can't do a root filling till the antibiotics've got the infection under control. Mind you, I always think the most painful bit's the bill at the end, don't you? Oh, sorry, Inspector. Rambling on as usual. How can I help?" He was about sixty, with friendly eyes and a wispy salt-and-pepper beard. Miranda warmed to him instantly.

"We're trying to identify a dead girl we think might've been a student here."

His cheery expression clouded. "Dead, you say?"

"I've got a postmortem photo. Not pleasant, I'm afraid. But, if you wouldn't mind taking a look... perhaps you'll recognize her."

"True, I know all the students here. Deal with them on a daily basis — passing on messages, booking practice and rehearsal rooms."

He took out a pair of reading-glasses and perched them on his nose. His response to the photo was immediate.

"This is Liisa Louhi. She's a first-year violin student."

"Are you sure?"

"No doubt about it. What happened to the poor girl?" He made a sudden connection. "Was she that one found at Sibelius Park?"

Miranda nodded.

"Oh, my goodness! I read about it in the newspaper. Never occurred to me she might be one of ours."

"I'm trying to trace her movements over the days leading up to her death. Can you help in any way?"

"I don't remember her being here much last week. Maybe she was in on Friday... Yes, I saw her in the afternoon. She was just leaving the building."

"What time would that've been?"

"We were just changing shifts — me and the other porter. We overlap shifts mid-afternoon, and we'd just made the changeover when I saw her going out. So it must've been three o'clock, or very soon after."

"Did she have her violin with her?"

"Yes, I think so."

"How about a handbag?"

He considered for a while. "Sorry, I can't remember."

Miranda scanned the ceiling of the hallway and located a video camera trained on the main entrance. "Could we check the security tapes for Friday afternoon?"

"There aren't any! The cameras are up, but the recording room's not fitted out yet. They didn't plan a security system for this building at first. But there've been so many problems since it was opened last autumn — kids wandering in off the streets stealing the students' instruments. So now one's being installed, but it won't be ready till next week."

"Pity," said Miranda. "But you've been an enormous help, Mr..."

"Koskinen. Olli Koskinen."

"If you think of anything else, please get in touch." She handed him a card, and asked for directions to the student affairs office where she hoped to get more details about the murdered girl.

Passing the cafeteria, Miranda noticed a group of female students chatting at one of the tables. On impulse she joined them.

There was initial shock at the news of Liisa Louhi's death. But they were all willing to talk. Unfortunately, getting background on the dead girl proved difficult. It seemed that Liisa Louhi hadn't confided much in her fellow students.

"No close girl friends here as far as I know," said one of the group. "Kept to herself. And that's unusual. We're a tightknit bunch in this place."

"How about boyfriends?"

"The boys took an interest in *her* all right. But she stayed sort of aloof — like she thought they were too young for her or something."

"That didn't stop her taking advantage when it suited her," said a second girl. "She could turn on the helpless-little-woman act at a moment's notice. Had them running round fetching and carrying, helping her with her music theory homework, stuff like that. But I'm pretty sure she wasn't dating any of the students here. We'd've heard about it."

A third girl, very blonde, with a face — so it struck Miranda — like a picture-postcard angel suddenly spoke up: "I was in here last week sitting at the next table to her, and I overheard a phone conversation she was having. Sounded like a boyfriend. She was talking to him in English."

"How do you know it was a man?"

"Well... the tone of voice, a bit flirtatious, sort of bantering. Sounded like trying to talk him into letting her visit him. But without much success. She was getting a bit annoyed. And then she gave up. Said she'd phone again later."

"When was this?"

"Could've been last Monday. Yes, that's right. I'd just had my horn lesson."

"Did she ever refer to this person by name?"

"Not that I remember. I only picked up the general feel of it all."

"Thanks, anyway. I'm trying to build up an overall picture of her life, so everything helps."

"There was some kind of scandal last autumn," said a girl with short henna-ed hair and a stud in her lower lip. "Some trouble between Liisa and her violin teacher. Rumour was she'd been having an affair with him. Frowned on, of course: teachers consorting with their students."

"I heard something different," said Angel-Face. "That he came on too strong and made a pass at her during a lesson."

"That could've been it. Anyway the teacher left. Don't know if he resigned or was kicked out."

Sounds promising, thought Miranda. "So who was this teacher?"

"Not a Finn. From Eastern Europe."

"Hungarian," someone else chipped in. "Don't remember his name."

"No, it was something unpronounceable," said Studded-lip. "He was only here a few weeks. Dishy to look at, I can tell you that much," she grinned. "I expect the office'll give you his name."

The secretary-of-studies was a prim, conservatively dressed woman of about sixty who allowed Miranda into her office with a minimum of fuss but no more than sufficient politeness to maintain professionalism. Miranda assumed she was annoyed at having her Monday afternoon routine disturbed. With a moue of distaste, the secretary confirmed Liisa Louhi's identity from the photograph, and then provided the dead girl's full name, birth-date, address, next of kin, etc. To Miranda's surprise, there was also a photograph — taken for an upcoming concert programme. She studied the lovely face that posed smiling for the studio camera. It was hard to recognize the distorted parody that death had left at the Sibelius Monument. The girl looked so young: a child's face, though with more than a hint of womanly sensuality. The secretary allowed Miranda to fax the photo and other details straight to Pasila.

Nineteen-year-old Liisa Louhi was originally from Turku: Finland's third-largest city, a hundred miles to the west of Helsinki. Her mother still lived there, and somebody from the local Turku station would have the unenviable task of telling the woman about her daughter's death. Liisa's address in Helsinki was a flat close to Sibelius Park in the same network of streets as lived Martti Hakala — the dog owner who'd found her body.

Full student attendance records weren't submitted to the Conservatory office until the end of term, but the secretary prepared a hand-written list of Liisa's teachers and their telephone numbers. Miranda immediately spotted Adrian Gamble's name near the top. She also noted that the replacement violin teacher was a woman. A calculated move to avoid further problems?

In fact, the secretary refused to be drawn into any discussion about Liisa's previous violin teacher, Zoltán Szervánszky, or his sudden departure from the Conservatory, saying simply that one of the Helsinki orchestras had offered him employment, so he'd decided to give up teaching for the time being. The secretary also declined to comment on the rumours of impropriety in the Hungarian's behaviour, although she did agree to look up his address.

Miranda managed to interview three of Liisa's teachers presently in the building. The solfège teacher had a look at his attendance lists and confirmed his recollection that Liisa had been absent from both the Tuesday and the Thursday sessions. The harmony and figured bass teacher hadn't seen her either at his Wednesday lesson. On the other hand, Liisa had managed to turn up for her personal violin tuition at a quarter past one on Friday — albeit more distracted and unprepared than usual, having left most of her music at home. They'd been able to work extensively on only one of her pieces — the Debussy sonata — and the lesson had ended at two o'clock.

Miranda would have welcomed the excuse to speak to Adrian Gamble as well, but apparently he didn't come in on Mondays. Never mind, she'd be seeing him this evening at *Mamma Rosa's*. Before leaving the building, Miranda visited the Conservatory library and learned that Liisa had dropped in at about twenty to three on Friday afternoon to enquire about a symphonic score for a future form-analysis project. No copies remained on the shelf, so the librarian had checked on the internet and located one at the public library in Töölö. This was only four or five hundred yards from Liisa's flat and would have been directly on her route home, so Miranda decided to drive straight there and ask if anybody remembered the dead girl.

Miranda's luck held. The young librarian in the music department looked up Liisa Louhi on his computer.

"Yes, she borrowed a miniature score of Mozart's 'Jupiter' Symphony on Friday at 3.41 pm. I remember her," he added. "I helped her find it on the shelves."

The wistful look in his eye suggested he'd been another male victim to the aura that Miranda was beginning to suspect had accompanied Liisa wherever she went.

"Was she carrying a violin?"

"Yes."

"And a bag?"

"Perhaps... Yes, she took her library ticket out of it. Dug around for ages. Made some joke about old ladies and their handbags. And she put the score in there afterwards."

"Could you describe this handbag?"

"I'm not exactly an expert on ladies' handbags. But she did have it up on the counter." He frowned, trying to summon up an image. "A shoulder bag, about this big..." He indicated something the size of an encyclopaedia... "in a sort of light-brown suedey material. Soft-looking. Lots of tassels on it. Sort of like Indian moccasins."

Miranda nodded. He'd managed quite well for a non-expert.

"Do you remember what she was wearing?"

This he found easier, describing the same clothes Liisa had been wearing at the murder scene.

But the young librarian had even more to offer: "Don't know if it helps, but I saw her later on — after she'd left the library. I went out on the balcony for a smoke. Spotted her down on the street. She was over on the other side, walking back down Humalistonkatu. Then she went into the corner café."

"How long was this after she left you?"

"Less than ten minutes."

"Was she still carrying the bag and violin?"

"Not sure about the bag... but I can picture the violin in her hand."

Miranda considered the implications. The library had no side entrance, so Liisa must have left by the front door and doubled back along the side of the building — up Humalistonkatu towards her own flat. Why then was she coming back *down* the street so soon? Her own flat was a good third of a mile away. If the librarian's estimate of less than ten minutes was correct, she wouldn't have had time to get home and back — even if she'd run the whole way. So where had she been in the meantime? Perhaps she'd started walking home but changed her mind and decided to go to the café instead.

Before Miranda left the library, she made a formal request that Friday afternoon's security videos be retained, promising to send an officer round for them later with the necessary paperwork. Her own next move would be the corner café. But the staff there proved unhelpful: Yes, they'd both been working on Friday afternoon. No, they couldn't remember anyone fitting that description. The place was always full on Fridays. No way could they be expected to remember one particular girl. But, as Miranda noted, the café staff were both girls themselves.

By now Ylenius and Tero would probably be at Liisa's flat with a forensic team. Miranda wondered whether to join them. She was already close by. But it was getting late, and her meeting with Adrian and Phillip was scheduled for 8 o'clock. The most productive way to spend the remaining time might be following up on the Hungarian violinist.

She called Chief Inspector Ylenius on his mobile and brought him up to date. She also asked about Liisa's flat...

"Have you come across her handbag, boss?"

"No, but we found two desperate cats. Obviously hadn't been fed since Friday. The smell of ammonia from the litter tray practically knocked us out. But there was *something* interesting. One of the speaker cables on the stereo's been chewed up — presumably by the cats. The other one's missing altogether. Seems to be the same kind of cable Liisa was strangled with."

"Doesn't that suggest the killer had access to her flat?"

"Maybe, but I don't think we should read too much into it. As Forensics already pointed out, this kind of cable's very common. Anyway, after you've interviewed this Hungarian fellow, call it a day." — *Thanks, boss, but I already intended to!* — "No need to rush in early tomorrow. We've all been putting in a lot of overtime. Get yourself a good night's sleep."

Miranda dropped in at Pasila HQ. The interview with Zoltán Szervánszky might turn out more than just a fact-finding mission. She'd better take another officer with her. While in the building, she checked her email. Nothing of significance. But as she was leaving her desk to find a suitable backup, the phone rang...

"Inspector Lewis? I'm Jaana Saari from the Conservatory. You came over to our table this afternoon... gave us all your card. I was the one who overheard that phone call of Liisa's."

"Yes, Jaana. I remember you." It was Angel-Face.

"You see, something sort of popped into my head on the way home. You asked me if Liisa called the guy on the phone by his name."

"You've remembered it?"

"No, no! Not exactly. But I did remember something peculiar," she said, and hesitated... "I'm not sure if this'll make any sense."

"Try me."

"While she was talking to him, a few times she said stuff like *'Come on, eh!'* or *'What about it, eh!'* and then once *'Hey, eh!'* It sounded really odd. I remember wondering if she was saying "eh" to make a question — you know, like you stick on the end to get a reaction. But most of the time it didn't sound like a question. And then I wondered if she was throwing in the Finnish word *"ei"* — instead of using the English *"no"* — sort of mixing the two languages together. But that didn't seem to work either. Now I've thought of another explanation... and this is the really silly bit. Try not to laugh. What if *"eh"* was his name? I don't mean his whole name. Just a nickname. Or the first letter 'A' of his name — like calling somebody by their initial." She paused again. "Sounds far-fetched, doesn't it? I expect you think I'm crazy. Wasn't sure whether to tell you or not."

"I'm glad you did, Jaana. Everything's worth considering."

Miranda took the girl's phone number, and ended the call. In truth, she didn't see how Jaana's information would help much. But as Miranda stood up to leave, and before she could even grab her bag, the phone rang again.

The caller introduced herself as Hanna Kettunen...

"I heard you've been asking about Liisa Louhi, so I thought I'd better let you know she came to visit me on Friday afternoon. We rehearsed a violin sonata at my place. I've got my own Steinway, so I prefer to play at home rather than on a Conservatory instrument."

A rich mummy and daddy somewhere, Miranda supposed.

"How long was she at your place?"

"From half past four. We played for an hour and a half. So she must've left at ten or quarter past six."

"Where do you live, Hanna?"

"In Mariankatu."

An expensive area! *And doubtless an expensive flat*, Miranda speculated, *to provide a suitable setting for the Steinway.*

Mariankatu would have been a twenty or thirty-minute ride from Töölö library on a number 18 bus. If the librarian saw Liisa going into the corner café at about ten to four, and she stayed long enough to drink a cup of coffee, then she must have travelled directly to Hanna's flat to arrive by four-thirty.

"Did Liisa seem in any way different from usual?"

"Not that I noticed. She was always a bit distant — sort of scatty. But she liked the piece we were playing. We were going to perform it in a couple of weeks. Anyway, we started practising, and she really got in to it. She played the second movement beautifully."

"You mean the *Intermède*?"

Hanna paused. "Yes, that's right." She seemed bemused by Miranda's clairvoyance. But Miranda didn't bother to explain how she'd guessed the piece was the Debussy sonata.

"Did Liisa tell you where she was going next?"

"No, she wasn't very forthcoming about her private life. With people like that, you give up asking after a while. I offered her some coffee, but she was in a hurry to get away."

Hanna confirmed that Liisa owned a suede shoulder bag, but she hadn't noticed it on that final Friday visit...

"She would've left it by the door with her coat. Anyway somebody phoned me just after our practice session, so Liisa ended up letting herself out."

Miranda had now managed to construct a picture of Liisa's movements between one o'clock and quarter past six on the afternoon of her death. But what had happened in those last few critical hours?

Zoltán Szervánszky lived in Herttoniemi, five miles east of the city centre. Since the element of surprise could be a useful tool for gauging a suspect's veracity, Miranda took a chance and didn't phone him beforehand. As backup she took along a chatty, twenty-year-old constable from the uniformed branch. Only six months on the force, Riitta was full of enthusiasm, and reminded Miranda of herself at the same stage in her own career. That was probably why she'd chosen Riitta.

The Hungarian's apartment block, although convenient to the metro line — only 150 yards north of Siilitie station — was an ugly box-shape, painted in a drab olive-green. As they climbed the stairs to his second-floor flat, Miranda heard strains of the Sibelius Violin Concerto permeating onto the landing. Not a recording: the real thing — though, of course, lacking an orchestral accompaniment. Miranda waited for a breathing space in the musical line before ringing the doorbell. She knew how irritating an interruption could be when you were concentrating on a fine piece of music. No need to aggravate the violinist before the interview even began.

When Szervánszky answered the door, he'd decided to be annoyed anyway, making it plain that he wished to rid himself of these unexpected callers — whoever they might be — as soon as possible. He was forced to amend this attitude when their identity and purpose were explained, and begrudgingly invited them in. His sitting room furniture looked shabby: most likely acquired from second-hand shops and the Salvation Army. Apart from the kitchen and the bathroom, this seemed to be the only room. There was no sign of a bed. Probably the sofa performed a dual function. But despite the meanness of his domestic surroundings, Szervánszky took obvious pains with his personal appearance. His clothes were immaculate — almost dandified — and his dark wavy hair was expensively cut to create an impression of casual bohemianism. One heavy lock fell across his forehead and he frequently brushed it aside with his left hand in a graceful but, Miranda felt, overly self-conscious gesture. She suspected him of having perfected it in front of a mirror. Difficult to guess his age. Mid-thirties, perhaps? Undeniably good-looking, with a swarthy complexion and dark, fiery eyes. His features were sharply drawn: an 'artistic face' one would have to say. But Miranda also detected arrogance, even insolence, and the near-perfection suggested more than a hint of effeminacy. Although she realized how some women would be reduced to whimpering jelly at the mere sight of this man — Riitta was already showing dangerous symptoms — he only made Miranda squirm inwardly.

"We're trying to learn as much as possible about the dead girl," Miranda began brusquely once they were all seated. "I understand you were Liisa Louhi's violin teacher last autumn."

"That is correct. I taught her for two months, perhaps for three months. She was not a satisfactory pupil." Szervánszky spoke Finnish well enough, though with a clear Hungarian accent.

"Why do you say that, Mr Szervánszky?" Miranda felt her back stiffen in Liisa's defence.

"She had much talent, but she did not like to work. She was lazy. I gave her good teaching, and she wasted it. I set her many excellent études to make her technique better, but she did not practise them. She made little progress. It was not my fault."

"Did you have any other problems with her? Personal problems, I mean?"

Szervánszky sighed theatrically with pinched lips, and cast his eyes back and forth across the room before answering.

"So this is why you have come. Can I never be free of ugly gossip? She was not a nice person. She was difficult. It is true that I allowed temptation to control me once. But only once. It was to be excused. I drank some wine that evening. It was a celebration. I had been taken into the Tapiola Sinfonietta to be leader of the second violins. That was a good thing for me."

Miranda noticed his fingers. Long and tapering, with scrupulously manicured nails.

"Are you telling us you had a relationship with Liisa?"

"It was not a relationship," he said irritably. "I slept with her once. That does not make a relationship. But afterwards she thought she could own me. She would not leave me alone. At the end I lost my temper. I told my true opinion of her. That was a mistake. She went to the principal with a story that I had tried to make sex advances. It was the opposite. But the principal — I think she did not believe me. And you will not believe me, either. You are also a woman." He stared a challenge at Miranda, but she held his gaze until he broke eye contact first.

"So you left the Conservatory because of this 'problem' with Liisa," Miranda suggested.

"No, I did not leave the Conservatory because of Liisa," he replied with emphasis. "I left because I had a job in the Sinfonietta. I did not want to teach so much. And now I want time to practise my instrument. I will enter the Sibelius Violin Competition this year. It is my last chance. I will perhaps win it."

At least he didn't lack self-confidence! But Miranda now had to correct her estimate of his age. Candidates for this famous international violin competition weren't accepted beyond their thirty-first birthday.

"Did you stay in contact with Liisa?"

"Of course not. I did not wish to see her again. That is obvious."

"And she didn't try to phone you?"

"Once she did. Two weeks after I left the Conservatory. Very late. She awoke me. I think she had too much to drink. She told me she was happy I had lost my job. I did not lose my job. I left because I did not want to stay. I took the telephone plug out of the wall. She never called me again."

"And you haven't met her since?"

"Never."

"And can you tell us, Mr Szervánszky, what you were doing last Friday evening, between eight and ten o'clock?"

The Hungarian stood up abruptly and threw his arms in the air with affected exasperation. "So now you think that it is certainly I who killed her." He walked round to the back of the sofa and leaned across it. "You are quite mad. I have not seen Liisa for a half year. I have no wish to see her. You say she is dead. Such a pity! But I did not kill her."

"Please answer my question, Mr Szervánszky." Miranda's voice sharpened. "Can you account for your movements on Friday evening?"

"Yes, I can tell you what I did." He turned momentarily to Riitta, and gave her a conspiratorial smile. She blushed like a schoolgirl. "On Friday evening I sat in the orchestra of the Finnish National Opera House. Sometimes a player is sick and they ask me to take the place. It is not a permanent work, but I have done it often. It brings extra money. I did it last Friday. I hope I do not make you very unhappy, Inspector."

Miranda had to admit some disappointment that this odious person might have an alibi for the evening of the murder. They'd, of course, check it, but there was now no point in pursuing the interview. Miranda made her escape, with a reluctant Riitta trailing behind.

Back at HQ, Miranda paid her desk a final visit. Tero was still in the office, typing up a report with one hand and grasping a Mars bar in the other. Miranda told him about the interview in Herttoniemi.

"What d'you reckon?" he said. "Are all Hungarians like him?"

"I've met plenty of others and had no trouble liking any of them. Obnoxious people can be born in any country, Tero. Even in Finland," she added pointedly.

But Tero seemed oblivious to the irony.

"Will you check out his alibi tomorrow?" Miranda went on brusquely.

"And tear it down in shreds for you?"

"That's just wishful thinking. But since you've probably never set foot in the Opera House, it'll be an educational experience for you — a broadening of your cultural horizons. Something might even rub off while you're there."

"That's just wishful thinking," Tero echoed, and then brought Miranda up to date on the search of Liisa Louhi's flat...

Little had been found that might generate any new lines of enquiry, although the forensic team had lifted two unknown sets of fingerprints: one of them from the cats' food bowl.

"There's something else that might interest you," Tero went on. "Guess who we bumped into on the stairs outside Liisa's flat? Martti Hakala with his moth-eaten Labrador! The Chief introduced us. He's moved into a bedsit on the floor above. Bit of a coincidence, eh? That's probably all it is, though. Hard to see what connection there could be. He didn't move in there till yesterday — three days *after* the murder."

When Miranda arrived at *Mamma Rosa's* that evening, she found Adrian sitting alone. He explained that Phillip was standing in for a sick colleague, and would be ten or fifteen minutes late. Miranda was glad to have Adrian to herself for a while.

"Thanks for taking me home on Friday," she began. "Did you go on somewhere afterwards?"

"No, we just walked to my place. Phillip came up for a nightcap."

Miranda steered the conversation round to Adrian's composition: "Phillip told me you use synthesizers a lot."

"Yes, there's been this desperate struggle over the last decades to discover new timbres, to somehow squeeze out the last drops of novelty from the traditional concert instruments. Some composers seem worried nobody'll take them seriously if they don't experiment with more and more extreme uses of the violin or the flute or whatever. Personally I don't find many of these so-called 'novel' sounds attractive. They're hardly ever as expressive as the more traditional uses of the instruments. No, the whole approach seems a cul-de-sac to me. Rather pointless too, because there's a wide range of beautiful new timbres available from electronic instruments — synthesizers, and so on. It's true that synthesizers have earlier tended to sound — well, synthetic — at worst, mechanical. But let's face it, nothing could be more mechanical than the piano. The piano's basically just a complicated piece of machinery. But that hasn't stopped great music being written for it. It's all a question of adapting to each new medium. Synthesized sounds are getting more malleable every day — more under the spontaneous control of the player. What can't be done on the spot can be added to or adjusted later with computer software, so your imagination's the only real limit. Anyway, I like to combine electronic sounds with real players on *traditional* instruments — especially the ones with a wide range of emotional nuance like violins, saxophones, and electric guitars. That way you get the best of both worlds: exciting new timbres forming a backdrop to the immediacy of live musicians."

Miranda was acutely aware of a warm ache somewhere low in her stomach. It was intensifying with every moment she sat near this man. There seemed no reasonable excuse for doing so, but she wanted to reach out and touch him — to place her hand against his face or his neck.

Later perhaps...

"And how's the world of detecting?" Adrian asked suddenly.

Miranda was unwilling to change the subject, but answered his question: "We're investigating a murder. A girl's body was found at the Sibelius Monument on Saturday morning. She'd been strangled."

"I heard something about that. In fact, I live quite near there — just beside the library."

"We only found out today who the girl was. A student at the Helsinki Conservatory. Her name's Liisa Louhi."

If Miranda had been looking in Adrian's direction, she might have seen the blood drain from his face. But she was distracted by Phillip's flamboyant entrance at the far end of the restaurant. Phillip threw them a wave and was immediately sidetracked by an acquaintance sitting near the door. By the time Miranda turned back to Adrian, he'd recovered his composure.

"I think you must've known her, " Miranda went on. "You teach at the Conservatory, don't you?"

"Only a couple of counterpoint classes."

"Don't you recognize her name? Liisa Louhi," she repeated. "Perhaps you can tell me something about her. She seems to have been a rather secretive person."

"Well, I have a lot of trouble remembering all these Finnish names. And the classes are quite big."

Phillip arrived noisily at their table.

"News from the fatherland, or should I say from motherland?" He waved a page of computer print-out at Adrian. "An email from your darling sister. She informs me the long-awaited addition to the Gamble clan has issued forth mewling and puking into this desolate world we unconvincingly call home. And she bids me convey the glad tidings to her errant brother. Shall I read it to you?"

Miranda frowned. "How come it's *you* that gets the momentous news, Phillip? Why not Adrian?"

"Because, Miranda, Adrian prefers to cold-shoulder the twenty-first century, to forego mobiles and modems, to turn his back on micro and radio waves and exist purely on the artistic plane of his own inspirational brain waves."

Miranda turned to Adrian. "A moment ago you were telling me how deeply you're into music tech. Is Phillip saying you don't even own a mobile phone?"

Adrian shrugged. "I like my privacy. There are too many ways for the world to break in on one's personal thoughts these days. On the other hand, music tech lets my thoughts break out on the world — which is another matter altogether. Anyway, Phillip's exaggerating. I've got an email address at the Sibelius Academy. Trouble is I usually forget to check my inbox."

"Come on, you two! Do you want to hear this email or not?" Phillip asked, in mock impatience.

"Yes, of course. Go ahead."

Phillip began reading:

"Little Lily was born on Saturday morning at 4.09 local time. By that I mean the clock on the delivery room wall. James insists the real time was 4.06 — according to his tediously reliable personal chronometer. The last couple of hours were heavy-going, but everything turned out okay. 8 pounds and 4 ounces okay! Such a darling little girl. Just like her Mummy. She makes warning noises when her next meal's due, but in general she's a cheerful, alert, artistic, mathematical genius — just like her Mummy. She practises her t'ai chi exercises daily,

wriggling her arms and fingers around in graceful, meaningful movements. And, at regular intervals, she tests out her rear-end jet-propulsion capabilities — just like her Daddy. Before long she'll be reaching supersonic speeds round the corridors of the maternity hospital.

Can't get to a computer right now, so James has promised to type this lot in for me when he gets home.

Love and kisses
from mother Theresa.

P.S. Please pass on the news to A., at your earliest. I've tried calling him, but he's never home. He'd better be delighted, or else!"

Phillip handed the paper across the table.

"So, what *do* you think, A.? Sufficiently delighted?"

"Of course," said Adrian, studying the email for himself. "Fantastic news!"

"Personally," Phillip went on, "I'm inclined to go for *James's* estimate of the magical moment. Allowing for the time difference between the UK and Finland, it would, from our point of view, place the minutes and seconds of birth exactly synchronous with my own. Quite a coincidence, wouldn't you say? If it had been a boy, do you think they might've named him accordingly — after myself, I mean?"

Miranda wasn't listening to Phillip's garbled rigmarole. She felt suddenly and shockingly distanced from the celebratory proceedings. "What did you call Adrian just now?" she interrupted.

He looked puzzled for a moment... "Oh, you mean 'A.'?"

Miranda nodded.

"Dear Theresa's nickname for him," Phillip explained. "Short for Adrian, of course. She's called him that since they were nippers."

"And Phillip gets the urge too, sometimes," added Adrian. "When he's feeling especially sisterly."

Miranda's face still carried an amused smile, but now it felt like a rictus. This had to be coincidence. It didn't make sense... But that was the trouble — it made altogether too much sense. Too many connections: the Helsinki Conservatory, the phone call in English, the

48

nickname, the location of the body near Adrian's flat, his turning up unexpectedly late at the *Ateljé* on Friday evening.

The anticipatory glow Miranda had been basking in earlier drained away, leaving a hard knot in her solar plexus.

Phillip was meanwhile expounding on his feelings for Adrian's sister...

"Yes, Theresa and I have enjoyed a wonderful and rewarding relationship for many, many years. Purely platonic, you understand. A rare occurrence in my colourful and multifaceted life, it's true, but when you meet a kindred spirit... Are you all right, Miranda? You're looking rather tense."

"I think I've got a migraine coming on," she lied. "Flashing lights and stuff. Only get them a couple of times a year, but they can be absolute blinders."

Adrian looked concerned. "Would you like to leave? I can take you home if you like."

"No, no, I'll hang on for a bit, thanks. Perhaps it'll come to nothing. By the way, Adrian, did you say you live somewhere near Töölö library? "

"In Humalistonkatu — the street running alongside the library building. You know it, I suppose?"

She certainly did.

A few minutes later, while Adrian was visiting the toilet, and Phillip was engaged in conversation with someone at the next table, Miranda picked up Adrian's empty beer glass. Gripping the lip carefully between forefinger and thumb, she dropped it into her handbag — registering the inappropriateness of her behaviour in view of her station in life as an upholder of the sanctity of private property.

When Adrian returned, she made her excuses and left in a taxi. But she didn't go home. She went straight to Pasila HQ where she transferred the glass to a plastic evidence bag. This would have to be done discreetly as a personal favour from one of the fingerprint team. The whole thing was too unlikely — too tenuous to go official.

Unfortunately, her instincts were telling her otherwise.

IV

Finale (Quasi una Fantasia): Andante—
Allegro molto

Miranda put the phone down and returned to the kitchen table. She stared out of the window, her coffee getting steadily colder.

So, there it was. The fingerprints matched. Adrian had definitely handled the key found in Liisa's pocket. The identification was decisive and, if necessary, she'd been assured, would stand up in court. It was already past nine o'clock and, although Aleksi Ylenius had suggested she made a later start this morning, she should go in at once to inform her boss of this new development. They'd have to bring Adrian in — possibly even charge him.

Twenty minutes later Miranda was still sitting there, her coffee now completely cold. She was at last raising it to her lips when the front doorbell rang jarringly. Who the hell was that? At this time of the morning?

Miranda went to the door and peered through the spy-hole. She could only see the closed door of the flat opposite. Whoever had rung the bell had either left or was standing somewhere out of sight. She released the latch and pushed the door open.

"Ah, Miranda. I thought you must've left for work already." He was halfway down the first flight of stairs, but now climbed back up to the landing. "You left your credit card on the table last night — when you paid for your drink. Thought I should drop it in on my way to the Academy."

Miranda stared at Adrian with a sense of unreality. He was the last person she'd expected to find on her doorstep.

"Your flat number was on the list of residents downstairs," he explained superfluously.

Miranda still said nothing, and Adrian began to look uncertain.

"Are you in a hurry? I've got some time before my composition seminar. I could stay for a while. But if it's inconvenient..."

Against all better judgment, Miranda turned and walked back into the kitchen, leaving Adrian to follow her and close the apartment door himself.

"Nice," he said, looking round. "These older buildings have a special solidity, don't they? Thick, strong walls. And the high ceilings are marvellous. Gives a sense of space and airiness."

Miranda didn't sit down. She stared at him, leaning back against the kitchen worktop, shoulders hunched forward, arms folded tightly and protectively across her chest.

Adrian clearly found her silence disconcerting, but he tried again.

"How's your migraine? Did it pass off all right?"

"You knew her, didn't you?'"

"Knew who?"

"The dead girl found in the park... Liisa Louhi. You knew her." *What in heaven's name are you doing, Miranda? Confronting a possible murderer alone in your kitchen! This should be happening in an interrogation room.*

Adrian gazed back, alert but outwardly calm. He said nothing.

"Did you know her, Adrian?"

He seemed to reach a decision: "Yes, as you pointed out yesterday, she was in one of my counterpoint classes."

"Were you having an affair with her?"

Another hesitation... But then he nodded. "...Yes."

"Did you murder her?"

"Good God no, Miranda! What on earth are you saying?" His calm had evaporated.

"Your index finger and thumb prints were found on her door key."

"I can explain that," he said, showing no curiosity as to how Miranda had made the match.

"Did you have sex with her on the evening of her death?"

No answer.

"Somebody did."

She waited again for a response.

51

"Look, Adrian, they can do a DNA analysis with the semen. They can find out, you know."

"She seduced me."

Miranda's mouth opened; then closed again.

"I beg your pardon," she said, at last. "Would you care to rephrase that?"

"Okay, so it sounds pathetic, but you've got to realize she was a sexual terrorist. She took no prisoners. She knew all the tricks — exactly how to draw a man on. For goodness sake, Miranda, try to understand. She was only nineteen, and she was sexy. I'm not a saint. There aren't many men could've resisted her."

"Are you saying you were a rape victim?" Miranda was startled by the wave of jealousy that swept over her.

Adrian had turned away. But not for long. Pulling a chair from under the kitchen table, he sat down, speaking with quieter intensity: "All right, I won't try to justify myself. I'll tell you, as objectively as I can, everything that happened. Okay?"

Miranda gave a cursory half-nod, and slipped behind a fragile veneer of professionalism. She didn't join him at the table.

"It started three or four weeks ago. We met a couple of times on the bus — on the way home from the counterpoint class. I usually catch the metro to Kamppi and change to a number 18. She was on the same bus. Her flat's not that far from mine, so we got off at the same stop. The first time was probably an accident, but I suspect she engineered the next meeting. When we got off the bus that second time, at Töölö library, she asked me to walk her home. Claimed some bloke had been following her around and she was afraid he might be lurking somewhere. Probably made the whole thing up. She never mentioned him again. Anyway, when we got to her place she offered to make us an omelette. I hadn't eaten anything all day, so I said yes."

"What about your other appetites?"

"All right, so we ended up in bed."

"And she engineered that too, did she?"

Adrian ignored the question. "But, you see, I didn't want it to become a habit. Fact is I regretted the whole thing. Not clever getting involved with your students. I tried to keep a healthy distance after that — without hurting her feelings, of course. But she was very clinging. Immature, I suppose. Not that she ever made any scenes at the Conservatory... Thank God! But anyway she kept phoning me and turning up at my flat unannounced. It was starting to interfere with my composition work. Then, last week, she went off to Turku for a few days. Her mother was coming out of hospital — after an operation or something — so Liisa went to give her a hand."

Miranda realized how that could explain Liisa's absence from the Conservatory those three or four days just before her death.

"But she needed someone to feed her cats," Adrian went on. "Quite frankly I was pleased to get rid of her for a while, so I agreed to do it. That's why she gave me the key."

"Incidentally," said Miranda, "did she phone you that Monday morning?"

Adrian considered for a moment. "Yes, sometime between nine and ten. That was when she asked me about the cats. She wanted to come round straight away with the key, but I knew it would break my concentration. I told her no. But, hey! Why the hell is this important, Miranda?"

"I'm tying up loose ends. And while we're at it... Did she call you A., like your sister does?"

This question seemed to puzzle him even more. "Well, yes, she found a letter on my desk one day — a letter from Theresa. Just picked it up and started reading it. No permission asked, of course. That's what she was like. As usual the letter was sprinkled with what Theresa calls my 'fratronymic'. It was A. this and A. that. Theresa's got this chatty style when she writes. I ended up having to explain the whole thing to Liisa. So then she decided she'd use it too. Probably thought that would bring us closer together. Truth is it irritated me to hell."

"But let's get back to Monday. She phoned you that morning, and you put her off."

"Yes, but she came round later anyway. That must've been about six. I think the key business was more of a pretext than anything."

"An excuse to seduce you again?"

"Something like that," Adrian admitted. "The next morning she left for Turku."

"So when did you see her again?"

"At the end of the week, on Friday. I'd been at the Academy working on some tubular bell samples. They've got fantastic software at R-block. So I lost track of the time and suddenly realized I'd have to rush home to shower and change. I was supposed to meet you and Phillip at eight o'clock. Well, I'd just got out of the shower when Liisa turned up. She was in a right old state. Claimed somebody had stolen her handbag. Said she'd got back from Turku around midday and taken her luggage home. Then she'd tried to locate me. But I wasn't at home yet, so she went to the Conservatory for her violin lesson, and afterwards to Forum shopping centre. She put her violin and handbag down to try on a coat, and that was when the bag disappeared. God, she was in a total panic when she got to my place! Carried on and on about losing her credit cards, and that the thief might try to use them. Said she ought to phone and report the theft."

"Did she?"

"Not to my knowledge. She was all over the place — mentally, I mean. Couldn't focus on anything for more than a few seconds."

"Did she tell you which clothes shop it was?"

"No."

"And did she report the theft to the shop?"

"No idea. It would've been the logical thing to do, but she was unpredictable when she got herself worked up over something."

"So when did she arrive at your place?"

"Half past seven. It could've been twenty-five or twenty to eight. Like I said, I was about to leave."

"Did she mention anything about a rehearsal at another student's flat?"

"For God's sake, Miranda! Are all these questions necessary? Can't I tell everything in the proper sequence without you continually interrupting me?"

"Sorry," she said curtly.

"The main thing's what happened *after* she arrived at my place, isn't it?"

"Perhaps, but I need a proper picture of everything she did that last day. By the way, it seems she tried visiting your flat at around quarter to four on Friday afternoon."

"How the hell do you know that?"

"Because I'm a detective! She'd just been to the library. Of course, you weren't home at the time. But let's carry on with your story."

Adrian stared back for several seconds before complying: "Okay, so I tried to calm Liisa down. But she wasn't having any of it. Not to start with. Stormed round my flat ranting and raving. Then suddenly she sort of collapsed into my arms. I held her for a while. But she started wanting more. I told her we should be trying to slow the relationship down, but it wasn't a very opportune moment to bring that up, was it? Anyway, she didn't take any notice. Told me I didn't really mean it, did I? And then... well, she sort of..." He fell silent.

"No need to act so bashful, Adrian! I get the picture." Miranda recalled his first words on arriving late at the *Ateljé* last Friday: *Something came up I had to deal with right away...*

"The next bit was really unpleasant," Adrian went on. "I told her I had to go — that I was already late meeting you and Phillip. You'd said you wouldn't be able to stay long, Miranda, and I didn't want to miss seeing you." He paused, perhaps hoping for some positive response. Miranda remained stony-faced.

With an audible sigh, Adrian continued his story: "After that she completely lost her rag. Leapt out of bed. Started throwing her clothes back on. Screaming what a bastard I was. How I'd just been using her."

And hadn't you? screamed Miranda, in silent sympathy.

"I offered to walk her home, but she just grabbed her violin and ran out of the flat. She slammed the door right in my face. A few moments later she was back again, ringing the doorbell. When I opened the door she just pushed past me and grabbed her spare key off the hall table. Of course, she needed it. Her other keys were lost with the handbag. But I've been thinking... perhaps, if I'd walked her home — insisted on it — she'd still be alive today."

He looked up, suddenly boyish and vulnerable, searching Miranda's eyes for a hint of clemency or détente. In spite of her suppressed anger, she felt a surge of desire for him.

"So what time did Liisa finally leave?" she asked, letting a fraction more warmth into her voice, though still resisting the urge to sit opposite him.

"About quarter to nine."

55

"Did she threaten you with exposure?"

"What does that mean?"

"Did she threaten to tell the Conservatory admin about your affair? Or accuse you publicly of sexual harassment?"

"Of course, she didn't."

But there'd been a slight delay. Miranda was inclined to believe everything Adrian had told her so far. Why did she suddenly feel he was lying?

"Look, Adrian, you'll have to go to the police station. Right now!"

"Turn myself in, you mean?"

"Go and make a statement."

"Go and make a confession is what you'd prefer, I suppose."

Miranda's pent up anger burst out: "Hey, I want to believe you — and your version of what happened. As far as it goes, it fits in with what I already know. But you shouldn't have lied to me yesterday evening. And you can't go on trying to withhold evidence. It makes you look guilty as hell. I'm not absolutely sure I believe you, but you can be damn certain no one else will if you don't get your shrinking-violet arse down to Pasila police station posthaste and tell them everything you know. You can say you only found out who the girl was this morning — from the newspaper or something. That'll throw a better light on the delay. But, for heaven's sake, don't let on we've had this conversation at my place. They'll crucify me for not doing things by the book and with another officer present. So this is what happens next. We leave straightaway in my car and I drop you off near the police station. But we go in separately, okay? And then you tell them everything you've just told me. Everything!"

On the journey, they spoke only once. Miranda asked: "Have you never heard of protected sex, Adrian?"

He turned his head, but Miranda wasn't looking at him. She was concentrating on the road.

"With Liisa," he said, "there wasn't always time for such niceties."

Tero Toivonen was just stepping into the little kiosk across the square from Pasila Police HQ to purchase his daily three packets of chocolate-coated raisins, when he spotted Miranda dropping somebody off twenty yards down the road. He paused and watched as the man walked up to the police station entrance and went in. Miranda meanwhile drove round to the other side of the square and down into the underground car park. Tero was naturally curious about the identity of this stranger, but he was anyway about to find that out. . .

The interrogation was carried out by Detective Chief Inspector Aleksi Ylenius and Detective Sergeant Tero Toivonen. Miranda was present as a passive witness. The whole interview was recorded on tape, and Adrian presented his reasons for coming in exactly as Miranda had suggested: that he'd only just heard about Liisa Louhi's death. It reassured Miranda that the story he told deviated in no way from the version she'd already heard.

Ylenius asked Adrian if he'd visited Sibelius Park on Friday evening.

"No," came the reply, "but I do go there quite often. The last time was probably Wednesday afternoon. I like to walk through the park and along the seashore. It helps if I get a creative block. Always useful to put some physical distance between yourself and your work when things aren't going well."

They kept Adrian at the police station for a full twenty-four hours. During the day he gave a blood sample to allow a DNA check. Although he admitted to having sex with Liisa on the evening of the murder, confirmation was needed that the semen was really his. His fingerprints were also taken, this official procedure overriding the informal (and highly irregular) test on the beer glass from *Mama Rosa's*. With much relief, Miranda realized that her ally in Forensics intended keeping last night's print comparison to himself.

Apart from being on the door key, Adrian's prints also matched samples taken from Liisa's flat. No surprise there. He'd been in her flat on several occasions — most recently to feed the cats.

When Ylenius requested permission to search Adrian's Humalistonkatu flat, the Englishman agreed. He wasn't so foolish as to think the police couldn't get a search warrant. He did however insist they were careful with his music tech equipment.

It must have struck Tero as odd that, during the interview, Adrian Gamble failed to mention how Miranda had brought him to Pasila in her own car. The fact that Miranda and Adrian knew each other had come out clearly enough. Their meeting with Phillip Burton at the *Ateljé* was discussed at length. Why, then, had Adrian given the impression his arrival at the police station was entirely under his own steam? If Tero harboured any thoughts on this matter, he kept them to himself.

That same afternoon, while her colleagues were at Adrian's flat, Miranda faced the grim task of taking Liisa Louhi's mother through the formal identification of her daughter's body.

Mrs Louhi was driven the hundred-mile journey from Turku in a police car. Ylenius had deemed it appropriate to give her every support at this distressing moment in her life — especially so soon after a major operation. But Miranda's apprehensions about the ordeal didn't fully materialize. Liisa's mother was quietly composed and, although she appeared frail, was perfectly capable of holding her emotions in check. Her back and neck were poised and straight. Her face was impassive. She looked Miranda unflinchingly in the eye, but maintained a tranquil detachment that gave away nothing of her emotional state. Miranda had met this personal bearing before, and associated it with the Finnish rural population, especially with the smallholding farmer or farmer's wife. She'd theorized that such stoicism was a necessary protection against the unpredictable elements that could buffet the worker of these northern lands through more lean times than fair.

Miranda placed the woman's age at sixty. Her hair was white with no sign of its original colouring. And she wore inexpensive but well-cared-for garments, favouring muted colours and sober traditional lines.

After they'd exchanged a few quiet words about the journey, Miranda escorted Mrs Louhi to the small mortuary in the basement where Liisa's body had been laid in readiness for viewing. The stark simplicity of the room was alleviated by vases of fresh flowers at the head and foot of the bier, and by several candles burning with motionless flames on a small table in one corner. Mrs Louhi drew close and stood for a long time staring down at the dead girl's face.

Miranda waited for a full minute before asking, in the gentlest tones she could muster: "Is this your daughter, Mrs Louhi?"

There was a further delay before the woman answered in the same carefully modulated voice. "No. This is not my daughter."

Miranda was taken aback. She'd been so sure.

But Mrs Louhi hadn't raised her head and, after a while, she spoke again, hesitating between each sentence.

"My daughter was full of life... She was restless... She tired herself out searching for novelties — for something to believe in."

There was an even longer silence, but Miranda understood not to interrupt.

"It's Liisa's body, of course... But only the empty shell... My daughter is gone."

Mrs Louhi turned to Miranda and asked: "May I sit here for a while? Is it permitted?"

Miranda nodded and withdrew to the furthest corner of the room where she stood perfectly still, hands clasped formally in front of her. She wasn't at liberty to leave the dead alone with the living, but she endeavoured to make her presence as unobtrusive as possible.

After ten or fifteen minutes, Mrs Louhi rose placidly and still dry-eyed, indicating that she was ready to leave. Miranda took her to a small conference room on the third floor with an east-facing window that overlooked the multiple tracks and platforms of Pasila railway station. A constable provided them with a Thermos of hot water, two cups and saucers, and tea bags of various blends. Miranda poured some water and they each selected a tea bag to tear open and methodically immerse in their cups. It was a comfort to follow this commonplace ceremony.

Mrs Louhi was clearly a woman of few words who would speak only when she had something of importance to say. That she now began, with no further prompting, to talk at length about her daughter was, Miranda realized, a truer indicator of the woman's feelings than her tightly reined-in appearance. It was almost as if she were holding a conversation with herself — carefully working through this necessary process to retrace the route that had brought her and her daughter to such a bleak, final confrontation. The task seemed unfamiliar but, once begun, the unfolding of her story became a steady, unrestrainable flow...

Symphony No 1

"Liisa was a beautiful child, but perhaps I never really knew her. She came to me late in life. I was already more than forty. Her father was a dance-restaurant musician. I suppose that's how she came by her musical gifts. He was ten years younger than myself, and I was foolishly flattered. I'd lived a sheltered life. I wasn't used to the attentions of such a man. But when he learned I was pregnant, he disappeared. We neither saw nor heard from him again. Liisa never met him. Well, if he was so ready to leave us, I was just as ready to be rid of him. But life wasn't easy alone with a child. My own parents had recently died. I was left with a small farm to manage on my own. But that became too much for me, so I sold up and moved into the town to find other work."

She went on to speak of an affectionate but temperamental child who grew up into an intelligent and wayward teenager. Liisa was considered bright by her teachers, but consistently failed to fulfil their expectations. Her innate musicality was spotted by a primary-school teacher, and Mrs Louhi economized and denied herself all luxuries to finance years of violin lessons, and to invest in better and better instruments. Liisa practised minimally, but she made surprising progress. Violin-playing was, in fact, the only unbroken thread through her fretful adolescence — the one thing that reliably held her interest and provided the emotional outlet she seemed unable to find elsewhere. Leaving school with indifferent grades was probably one reason why, despite her musical talent, she failed to gain admission to the Sibelius Academy. Instead, she enrolled at the Helsinki Conservatory to train as a violin teacher.

Although Liisa was capricious, she could occasionally be a dutiful daughter — as when she'd spent several days the previous week tending her convalescent mother. But there was little personal communication between parent and child. Liisa's life in Helsinki had remained a closed book to Mrs Louhi, who confessed knowing nothing of her daughter's men friends. Liisa hadn't brought a boy home since the age of fourteen.

Miranda's overall conclusion was that Liisa had become a precarious composite of her mother's reserve and her father's impetuosity. Her interest in men significantly older than herself complied with the fashionable psycho-theories — whose insights

Miranda didn't necessarily buy into — that Liisa had been seeking a father figure: although the idea of Zoltán Szervánszky being *anybody's* father, either now or in the future, struck Miranda as appalling!

Saying goodbye at the police station entrance, Mrs Louhi expressed gratitude for the consideration that had been shown her; and she climbed into the car that would take her back to Turku, displaying the same controlled dignity with which she had arrived. Miranda wondered if, in the privacy of her own home, she would finally give way to grief.

Ten minutes later, Ylenius and Tero returned from their search of Adrian's flat. The forensic team were still there, but nothing incriminating had turned up: "No extraneous fingers in the fridge", Tero said, with obvious disappointment. And Ylenius was doubtful that anything useful now would.

"We've taken various items of clothing for analysis," he explained, "and samples from the furniture and rugs. But our problem is Gamble doesn't deny Liisa was in his flat — or even in his bed. And he's told us how he regularly takes innocent walks down to the Sibelius Monument. It could hardly make things more difficult. Any defence lawyer worth his salt can explain away our trace evidence as transferred between Gamble and the victim or between Gamble and the murder scene on some other occasion than the crime itself."

Adrian was released the following morning with instructions to keep himself available for further questioning. Meanwhile, attempts were made to locate the shop where Liisa might have lost her bag, and to find out if she'd informed the relevant authorities about losing her credit cards. Neither line of enquiry was successful, so there was no corroboration for Adrian's version of how the handbag had disappeared. The only certainty was that it was still missing.

There were, however, two significant contributions to the investigation later that Wednesday, and Miranda was witness to both.

At half past three, a teenage couple approached the front desk of Pasila police station and explained that they'd like to speak to someone about the Sibelius Park murder, because they thought they might've seen something important. Miranda and Tero sat the youngsters down in a comfortable conference room — a less intimidating environment than a poky interrogation room in the basement.

Tommi was a friendly open-faced boy of sixteen who seemed immediately at ease with the situation. But fourteen-year-old Laura, despite Miranda's efforts, remained nervous.

"Please promise you won't tell my dad," she begged. "I didn't want to come, but Tommi said we had to. If my dad finds out I was in the park with Tommi, he'll murder me." She stopped, and flushed bright pink. One hand moved involuntarily to her mouth. "I didn't mean it like *that*. I'm not trying to be funny or anything. It's just I was late home on Friday and I told Dad I stopped off at a girlfriend's place. If he knows where I really was, he'll go ballistic. You won't tell him, will you?"

Without making any false promises, Miranda tried to reassure her: "We wouldn't want to get you in trouble with your father, Laura, but this is a murder investigation. It's a very serious matter. So if you can tell us something that might help... " she tailed off, and Laura dropped her head in resignation.

It was Tommi who decided to take up the story: "You see, last Friday evening we were at the Töölö sports hall. I was training with my floor-ball team, and Laura was doing aerobics. We finished about quarter to eight, and met up for a burger. Then we went for a walk in Sibelius Park. That's how we ended up going past the monument."

"So this would've been about half past eight by now, would it?" asked Tero.

"No, well... we weren't going that fast. We kind of stopped from time to time."

Laura blushed crimson this time, and Miranda moved on quickly: "Did you see something special in the park?"

"Two people over at the monument," said Tommi, "kind of squatted down on the ground up against the rock — just next to the big metal head. I thought they were a couple of drunks, so I didn't pay much attention."

"Can you describe them?"

"We weren't close enough — we weren't on the path going nearest to the monument. But one of them was sort of sitting back against the rock. I think it was a woman because she had a lot of hair — very blonde hair."

"Can you describe her clothes?"

"She had a coat with bright colours — red perhaps, or blue."

"Red and yellow," said Laura. "But we couldn't see her properly because the other one — a man, I suppose — he was kneeling down in front of her."

"Was he tall? Was he short?"

"He was all hunched up, so you couldn't tell."

"Was he blond, too?"

The youngsters looked doubtful.

"I think he was wearing a hat," Tommi said. "A woollen hat. All his clothes were dark."

"And he didn't turn round," said Laura. "So we didn't see his face."

"But a bit later on," Tommi added, "I looked back, and he wasn't there any more. He'd disappeared. I thought he might've gone for a leak in the bushes."

"Could you see the girl more clearly this time?"

"No, we'd walked down the hill by then. There were some bushes in the way."

"What about her clothes? Were they pulled open? Was she fully dressed?""

The teenagers seemed puzzled by Miranda's question, so she didn't pursue it. "And now there's something very important I have to ask you both," she said. "Do you think the girl was still alive when you saw her? Did she cry out? Did you see her move at all?"

They shook their heads. No, she hadn't done either of those things.

Miranda watched the implications sink in. On Friday night, they'd witnessed the immediate aftermath of a murder, and they'd been only a few dozen yards from a dangerous killer! Laura looked especially unnerved. But Tero — certainly without realizing it — came to the rescue: "Can you estimate what time it was when you saw them?" he asked.

"We can do better than that," said Tommi, brightening at once. "We can tell you the *exact* time. Just before we spotted them, I asked Laura, shouldn't I be getting her home? I checked my watch and it was dead on nine o'clock. Then Laura said the ice-hockey was just starting, and her father'd be so fixated on the telly, he wouldn't notice whether she was there or not. And my watch is really accurate." He showed it to them across the table. "I check it every morning with the radio. It hasn't lost or gained a second since Dad gave it to me."

Tero eyed Miranda curiously. She was smirking like a Cheshire cat. Of course, this was valuable information, but her reaction seemed a little over the top. Some kind of private joke perhaps? Anyway, prompted by his own enthusiasm for ice-hockey, Tero then turned to Tommi and asked: "Didn't you want to watch the match yourself?"

The boy shrugged. "I wasn't that bothered."

Miranda could guess why. Laura was a pretty little thing, and for a sixteen-year-old boy with romance on his mind, even a match between arch-rivals Finland and Sweden might have to take second place.

"Did you walk straight past the monument?" Miranda asked. "Or did you stop at all... between when you first saw them and when you looked back and the man had gone?"

Laura stared at her lap, but Tommi gave a sheepish grin: "I suppose we did hang around there for a minute or two."

The sequence of events was becoming clearer in Miranda's mind.

"What's got into *you*?" Tero asked, as soon as they'd seen the young couple off. "Won the National Lottery?"

Miranda at once toned down her buoyant mood...

"Useful stuff, though, wasn't it, Tero? Narrows the murder down to just before nine o'clock. We already knew it had to be after eight-forty because that's when Hakala walked his dog past the monument. But now we can pinpoint the murderer at the crime scene at exactly 9 pm. Let's tell the boss."

Ylenius was also pleased with the information, but regretted they still had no useful description of the killer.

"The way I see it," said Miranda, "the murderer was interrupted when the kids came past. They stopped for a while in sight of the killer — presumably for a snog — so he probably thought they were watching him and ran off."

"Which might explain why he'd only just started removing her jeans," Ylenius considered.

Miranda pulled a face.

"So you reckon he was planning a bit of 'necro'?" asked Tero, with no compunction about voicing what Miranda had merely been thinking.

"No, something *still* doesn't fit," Miranda objected. "It's the order of events. If he ran away before he got her clothes off, he must already have amputated the finger, because he took it with him. But you'd expect him to do the rape first and take the finger as a trophy afterwards. It's the wrong way round."

"Unless," said Ylenius, "removing the finger had some special sexual significance for him."

Tero nodded approval: "Yes, to get himself in the mood. It's obvious we're dealing with a total 'loony' here."

Miranda picked up smoothly on this last comment: "Some kind of psychopath," she said. "A random killer. The setup doesn't suggest a definite motive or even a *crime passionel* in the traditional sense — by someone who knew the victim. So I don't see how Adrian Gamble fits the profile anymore."

"You reckon?" Tero stared at her long and hard.

"Especially," Miranda went on, "as he's now got an alibi."

Both of her colleagues looked baffled. Ylenius tilted his head in enquiry. "Could you explain that for us please, Miranda?"

"Okay, now we can place the murderer at the crime scene at exactly 9 pm. At that same time, I was sitting in the *Ateljé* with Phillip Burton. In fact, we noticed the ice-hockey match starting on the TV, and Phillip suggested that was the reason Adrian hadn't turned up — that he'd stayed home to watch the ice-hockey. Phillip found the idea amusing, because apparently Adrian has no interest in sport at all. Anyway, just seconds later, Phillip's mobile rang, and it was Adrian calling to say he'd been held up but was now leaving home. He got to the restaurant less than twenty minutes later. So, if he was phoning from his flat at exactly nine o'clock, he couldn't have been the one Tommi and Laura saw at the Sibelius Monument, could he?"

Ylenius massaged his temples, considering. But Tero wasn't anywhere near convinced; perhaps because he'd remembered

Miranda's strange high of half an hour ago and was growing suspicious about her motives for wanting Adrian out of the frame.

"What about Gamble's mobile phone?" he challenged.

"He hasn't got one. He can't stand the things. Go ahead and check if you don't believe me," she said, a touch too defiantly; but catching herself out in this revealing 'you versus me' faux pas, added: "As a matter of routine, of course... But I think you'll find I'm right. And there's no public telephone anywhere near the murder scene. If Adrian called Phillip that close to 9 o'clock, he couldn't have been at the Sibelius Monument, and he can't be the killer."

Tero left immediately for his computer terminal, and soon confirmed that Adrian Gamble held no account with any mobile phone operator in Finland. He even checked Swedish and UK operators but came up with the same result.

At the first opportunity, Miranda slipped off to an empty conference room and telephoned Adrian. It seemed only fair to set his mind at rest — to let him know at once he was no longer a suspect.

"Does that mean I'm off the hook, so to speak?" Adrian asked.

"Looks that way. At least, for now." Miranda's voice was playful. "Though perhaps we can conjure up something else incriminating... if you give us time."

This weak attempt at humour met a stony silence; so she tried a different tack: "Are you coming to Dad's lecture this evening?"

"Yes, and Phillip too. We've talked a lot about last Wednesday's session. No way we'll miss any of the series from now on."

"Look, Adrian..." Miranda hesitated... "I'm feeling uncomfortable about all this business with Liisa..." Then the rest came out in a rush: "Would you let me take you for a meal sometime? A kind of peace offering? Do you like Indian? My treat, of course. What do you think? Is it a good idea?"

She expected him to punish her with a series of prior engagements, but he agreed at once — although he insisted on paying his own way. He even suggested they follow up the plan that same evening after the lecture. Miranda had been visualizing just the two of them sitting there across the restaurant table... But never mind. If it had to be another *ménage à trois* with Phillip, so be it.

66

"I'm afraid Phillip won't be able to join us," Adrian added. "He's got something else on straight after the lecture — some kind of company cocktail do. How about your father? Do you think he'd like to come?"

"I think he's made other plans too."

"So I hope that doesn't matter? If it's just the two of us?"

"No, that'll be okay," she said.

Miranda was returning to the office, when Tero rushed up in the corridor.

"There's been another development," he said, steering her towards Ylenius's room.

The Chief Inspector stood up as they entered, passing Miranda two transparent plastic sleeves across the desk.

"The Järvenpää police just couriered us these," he said.

Inside one sleeve was a plain white envelope — addressed, stamped and postmarked. It was already torn open, and Miranda supposed its contents was the short letter displayed in the second sleeve. Both the envelope address and the text of the letter were in Swedish — Finland's official minority language spoken by six percent of the population. The address was curious:

Helsinki City Police Force / Homicide Unit
c/o The Ainola Residence
Järvenpää, FINLAND

Ainola was the name of the Sibelius home where Jean and his wife, Aino, had lived together for most of their married life. Situated twenty miles north of Helsinki, it was now a museum and much visited by the public.

The letter itself appeared to be a computer print-out; not only curious but disturbing:

Symphony No 1

Sibelius Park
Friday, 24th March

Symphony No 1 in E minor

Dear A.
Let the voice of my inner being and the spectres of dream and fantasy direct me. There are things to be done that cannot be delayed. Life is so very fleeting!

At the bottom was an initialed signature: *JS*. And beside that was the most striking detail of all: a single, darkly-inked fingerprint with all of its lines and whorls perfectly defined.

Miranda glanced up at her colleagues. "Are you thinking what I'm thinking?"

Both nodded.

Taking the lift to the fourth-floor lab, they soon had their suspicions verified. The inked impression matched a sample lifted from the heel of Liisa Louhi's violin bow. There could be no doubt that the letter bore a print from the murdered girl's missing fourth finger.

Symphony No 2
in D major

I

Allegretto

Dressing for the evening took unusually long. After several false starts, Miranda settled for a demure, creamy-coloured silk blouse and a dark skirt that just covered her knees. She applied her make-up with care but kept it discreet and simple: a quiet, almost natural shade of lipstick; a subtle hint of emphasis to the eyes. Standing in front of the full-length bathroom mirror, she appraised the results.

Miranda was a genetically genuine redhead and had the pale complexion and freckles to prove it. She'd often considered cutting her hair shorter. It would have been easier to handle than the present wavy tangle reaching almost to her shoulders. It would certainly have looked more business-like. But she was aware of how it flattered her face and body shape. Somewhat less than average height, Miranda was compactly built — rather like her father, but with a considerably more female result. Her waist and hips were on the boyish side, but her breasts were relatively fuller. Soon after puberty she'd noticed how men of all ages had difficulty holding their gaze at the level of her face. Not that her face wasn't worthy of attention: the large cat-like green eyes had been inherited from her mother but, as Phillip noticed at their first meeting, her mouth was completely her father's — Pan-like, too wide to be classically beautiful, and prone to a transforming impish smile.

Adding a last hint of green eye shadow, she decided that would have to do, and turned from the mirror. Still a quarter of an hour too early. She paced round the flat, glancing at her watch every couple of minutes and staring at intervals out of the window. The latest events in the Liisa Louhi case were tugging at her thoughts. That strange message, apparently from the murderer himself, had arrived at the

Ainola Museum on Tuesday. But the part-time secretary who dealt with Ainola's correspondence had Tuesdays off. Her first reaction on opening the letter the next day was to take it as a meaningless prank. She'd tossed it to one side. Not until later in the afternoon, as she was tidying her desk ready to leave, did she reconsider and make a connection between the place and date heading and the Sibelius Park murder reported in her Sunday newspaper. Feeling somewhat foolish, she phoned the local police. To her surprise, the officer on duty took the matter seriously enough to send someone over for a look. This act of professional caution had led to the letter reaching its intended destination: the Pasila Homicide Unit, where it was now being forensically processed. Miranda didn't expect any revelations. Unlikely that the sender would be stupid enough to get his fingerprints or saliva on the stamped envelope or its contents.

But what should they think about the letter's contents? The message was cryptic, although Miranda already had suspicions about its origin, and wondered if her father might be able to help. She intended showing him a transcript after this evening's lecture.

Leaving the flat — in fact, half-way through the door — Miranda turned back. Rushing into the bedroom, she changed into a scoop-necked, figure-hugging, knitted dress in a rich dark green that threw her hair into relief and highlighted her eyes. It was considerably shorter than the skirt now discarded on the bed. Slamming the apartment door behind her, she ran downstairs.

"As a young man with suitable school-leaving qualifications to gain a place at Turku University, Baron Axel Carpelan expressed a desire to dedicate his life to the violin. His parents opposed the notion. So Axel flew into a rage, smashing his instrument into small pieces and scattering the remnants in the river. He followed up this melodramatic act by rejecting a university career to do little more than indulge his personal passion for books and music. It soon became apparent that Axel lacked the staying power to develop his own artistic gifts — such as they were — and he remained, for the rest of his life, little more than a well-informed dilettante.

"I regret to say that the young baron's love-life was no greater a success. Like a devoted dog, he hovered outside the home of a certain high-born, tempestuously intellectual and, for him, quite unattainable lady — on the off-chance that he might catch a glimpse of her. When she lost patience and drove him away, he banished himself from Turku altogether to take up a lonely bachelorhood in Tampere, eking out a frugal existence on an allowance that barely exceeded subsistence level.

"Now why should this rather pathetic, foppish, pince-nezed little man concern us in the context of our present lecture series? The answer, astonishingly enough, is that he acted as a long-term muse to our main protagonist: the composer Jean Sibelius. Yes, Axel and Jean shared a lively correspondence for nearly two decades — right up until Carpelan's death in 1919. Admittedly, it was Axel who, wanting to feel somehow at the centre of contemporary artistic life, had initiated the relationship. But Sibelius came to depend on his friend's loyalty and devotion to a surprising degree. In their exchange of letters, Carpelan adopted a wide gamut of roles from flattering sycophant to nagging mother. He offered opinions on all matters musical, literary and political.

* ["For example, it was Carpelan who proposed the name *Finlandia* for the popular work which had already borne several other less stirring titles. We also know he was the first person to suggest that Sibelius compose a second symphony, a violin concerto, a string quartet and music for Shakespeare's *The Tempest* — all of which ultimately came to fruition. Sibelius responded respectfully to Carpelan's comments and proposals, sometimes sending back detailed analyses of ongoing musical projects.] *

"But the baron was also very free with his advice on more personal matters, never hesitating to inform Jean on what course his life should take next — even lecturing him on the evils of intoxicating liquors. Carpelan later advised the despairing Aino Sibelius to remove her husband to the country — away from the temptations of the city — thereby rescuing him from his slide into chronic alcoholism and creative torpor. But that belongs later in Jean's life-story, at the time of the Violin Concerto. Let's instead turn our attention to the major work preceding that concerto — our focus for this evening's lecture... Symphony No 2 in D major, Opus 43."

Miranda was now comfortably sandwiched between Phillip and

Adrian. All three had managed to arrive in good time at the Wegelius Hall; and, despite an even better turn-out than last week, had secured seats in the front row. In the narrow confines of these tightly-packed chairs, Miranda was very conscious of the warmth of Adrian's upper arm and thigh against her own. *Like being a teenager again*, she thought ruefully.

* ["The Second Symphony has, for a long time," continued Dr Lewis, "been the most popular and most performed of Sibelius's seven symphonies in the Anglo-Saxon countries; and not without good cause. It possesses a special radiance — a softly incandescent aura, highlighted by the composer's shifting, unpredictable turns of imaginative fancy. The orchestra has been streamlined. The bass drum, triangle and Tchaikovskian cymbals are gone, and Sibelius will never use them again in a symphonic context. The swirling Romantic harp has also been omitted. The underlying mentality is still nineteenth-century but, with the possible exception of the fourth movement, we are no longer distracted by suggestions of other composers. Sibelius appears here as a fully formed and unique musical personality.

"The first sketches for the D major symphony were made while Jean was in Italy with Aino and his daughters. Axel Carpelan had been the one to propose this trip, pointing out the importance of similar Italian excursions in the musical development of Tchaikovsky and Richard Strauss. But Axel went much further than idle suggestion. He persuaded two wealthy patrons to finance the whole trip anonymously, turning his proposal into a reality. That Carpelan's own straitened circumstances made it impossible ever himself to engage in such an adventure beyond the borders of Finland is, I find, rather touching."] *

Dr Lewis now approached the grand piano and, leaning with one elbow on the edge of the instrument, smiled at his audience.

Adrian and Phillip — in perfect synchronization — turned their heads to Miranda. Unaware of the reason for this sudden attention from either side, she rewarded each of them with an exact replica of her father's endearing and infectious grin.

Over the next forty minutes, the audience was carried, step by step, through all four movements of the symphony...

* ["The claim occasionally heard that Sibelius begins the first

movement with mere motivic fragments which he only later welds into coherent themes is misleading. The melodic material is certainly motivic. And yes, it does consist of relatively short phrases. But mere fragments they are not. Each melodic idea is an interesting and perfectly formed entity — although, when considered as a group, we notice how they share a strong family resemblance, as if grown from a common ancestor. Allow me to attempt, in my own way, a demonstration of this melodic affinity..."

Dr Lewis now did something that surprised even his daughter. He sat down at the piano and started to play in an improvisatorial, almost jazz-like fashion. For several minutes he worked with the main themes of the movement, weaving and bouncing them around, allowing them to mutate and transform back and forth from one to the other. By so doing, he graphically laid bare many of their similarities and, for those in the audience who knew the symphony well, the experience was a revelation. When Dr Lewis stopped playing and stood up, the audience burst into spontaneous applause.

"What I've here tried to do, ladies and gentlemen, is akin to the processes that Sibelius himself has applied — although perhaps only subconsciously."

The speaker went on to explain how the motives were brought into closer contact in the development section of the movement and, in the recapitulation, actually superimposed upon each other as counterpoint.

"The second movement begins in triple metre with mysterious low pizzicato strings, and we shall here witness an early example of a special Sibelian trick. A series of lugubrious bassoon phrases appear as an overlay to the pizzicato, conflicting with the strings in a rhythmic ratio of 'two against three'. The contradictory effect is heightened by the fact that every duplet phrase is syncopated off the beat. This juxtaposition looks so simple on the score but generates in the listener the impression that each layer is travelling at a different speed — the bassoons are floating in slow motion over the underlying stream of pizzicato triplets. We shall see this kind of kinetic illusion used to extraordinary and shattering effect at later key moments in the symphonic cycle. It's also instructive to notice what happens next. When the oboes and clarinets take over the bassoon melody, they stabilize it by placing it squarely on the first beat of the bar. Hey, presto! The two-layered effect vanishes! The woodwinds and strings lock into each other to produce a single and unified sense of ongoing motion that carries us smoothly away. This, ladies and gentlemen," he added, with another broad grin, "is nothing less than magic!"

The speaker later presented the third movement *scherzo* with its "classical sense of energetic yet controlled fleetness"; and the contrasting trio section, whose repeated-note oboe theme "has sometimes been compared to the gentle, poised inflections of Gregorian chant".

In the fourth movement, Dr Lewis experienced "a vivid premonition of the Seventh Symphony" in the rippling viola and cello quavers that underlie the short and "lamenting woodwind phrases" — phrases which, according to Aino Sibelius, were inspired by the tragic suicide of her sister Elli Järnefelt. But the speaker went on to express some reservations about the appropriateness of the finale's "big theme", finding it excessively "grandiose and operatic" for the restrained and intimate atmosphere found elsewhere in the work.

"Nevertheless," he admitted, "whenever a performance arrives at the splendid coda, and that same theme is transformed into ceremonial and imposing majesty, I have no choice but to bow my head in humble recognition of the genius that is Jean Sibelius."] *

Dr Lewis then played a recording of the symphony's closing passage; and, having allowed the final chord to die away, brought his lecture to an end...

"Thank you for your kind attention, ladies and gentlemen. I hope to see you next Wednesday, when we'll join Sibelius in an interesting new experiment: his Symphony No 3 in C major."

Half an hour later, Miranda found herself sitting with Adrian in the Maharajah restaurant. They had walked the quarter mile from the Sibelius Academy to stretch their legs and sharpen their appetites. The weather was changing and the temperature had risen several degrees above zero. As they removed their coats in the restaurant's cloakroom alcove, Miranda was once again keenly aware of Adrian's physical presence. He had a firmly packed, athletic body which, in combination with his facial features and curly hair, reminded her of Michaelangelo's David. *Though a more mature David*, she thought. *One come to full manhood.* Amused by this comparison, she followed Adrian to a corner table on the non-smoking side of the restaurant. A short distance across the room, two musicians sat cross-legged on a low platform playing the sitar and the tabla drums. Their music was unobtrusive and atmospheric.

Miranda and Adrian settled themselves at the table and, once they'd ordered their food and a bottle of wine, Adrian talked at some length about ragas and talas and the exacting demands made on musicians who wished to train in traditional Indian musical skills. However, he changed topic when the wine and starters arrived, beginning instead to quiz Miranda on the other Lewis-family members. Perhaps it was the lubrication of Beaujolais on an empty stomach, but Miranda soon found herself describing her sister Rosie's personality and history, and revealing the tragedy of her father's double confrontation with cancer — first with her own Finnish mother and then with a second, Scottish wife.

The narrative was interrupted as they investigated the various main dishes that suddenly appeared before them, and enthused together over the delicious aromas. But, while they were serving themselves, Adrian returned to his interrogation...

"So your father's a celebrated commentator on the compositional gurus of western music, and your sister's pursuing a cello career at the Royal Academy. That's quite a musical background! How come you ended up in the police force?"

"Not as weird as you'd think," said Miranda, ladling chicken pasanda over a generous helping of basmati rice. "For one thing, my mother was a lawyer. She loved music too, but she never had any formal training, and she never learned to play an instrument. A shame really. She'd probably've been a natural. Anyway, I somehow followed in her footsteps by starting a law degree. The trouble was I'd always been so wide-ranging at school, and that didn't change at university. I enrolled in loads of extra courses — especially psychology ones. And then later I discovered criminology, which seemed like a synthesis of the two — law and psychology, I mean. The academic stuff was interesting in a way, but I've always had a strong physical component in my life — I've needed it really — and the thought of a sedentary desk job surrounded by case files and law books... that wasn't what I wanted for myself. I needed to be more at the sharp end of life, doing something with a potential for physical excitement — danger even. Then I heard about this graduate training scheme with the police force and decided to go for it."

"They must've snapped you up. Bit of a change in salary prospects though," he added wryly.

"It'll never be 'big bucks', but I don't have extravagant tastes. And the work makes up for it. It has its routines like any other job, but you never really know what to expect from one day to the next. That unpredictability's the biggest bonus. I've never regretted my choice."

Miranda now decided it was time her dinner date said something about his own background.

"So tell me about *your* parents, Adrian?"

The answer was a long time coming... "They're both dead," he said at last.

This stalled Miranda long enough for Adrian to ease in another question of his own: "Did you never learn an instrument, Miranda?"

She knew she was being side-tracked, but gave in gracefully: "The violin — from the age of five. But I never had Rosie's dedication. There were always too many other things going on in my life. When I left school I changed to the viola."

Adrian's eyebrows rose. "Surely you didn't think that would be easier?"

"No, no! The viola's a tough instrument to master. But I've always enjoyed ensemble playing — orchestras and chamber music. In those contexts the viola tends to get easier stuff. I was a member of the Helsinki university orchestra for years. It was great fun. And I usually managed to live up to the demands of the viola part, even with my limited practising. Four of us still meet up about once a month to bash out a quartet or two — just for fun, of course."

Adrian scooped up some sauce with a piece of naan bread. "Viola players say it's great being in the middle of the texture."

Miranda agreed: "Yes, in a string section or string quartet you're listening to the surface melodies of the violins above and following the bass line underneath — like being the glue that holds everything together."

Adrian smiled his boyish smile across the fast diminishing debris of a very enjoyable meal... But how could she get him to open up and talk a bit more about himself?

"I've never heard what *your* instrument is," she ventured.

"I haven't got one — unless it's the Macintosh computer..." He explained how he'd been a late starter, not getting actively involved in music or composition until he was an engineering student at university. Since then he'd picked up some rudimentary keyboard skills, but claimed he was incapable of performing in public: "I envy your training with a stringed instrument, Miranda. I'd love to play in a quartet — even as an amateur. Phillip was luckier that way. His parents weren't musical, but his mother considered it *de rigueur* for her child to have piano lessons. He's let the whole thing lapse, but he can still hammer out a mean blues — especially after a few drinks."

"Phillip's a genuine one-off," said Miranda. "Does he always talk like that?"

"You mean like an out-of-work Thespian in search of an audition? No, it's mainly with people he doesn't know very well — a sort of nervous reaction, I suppose. He gets less florid as you get better acquainted. And when he's in a serious mood — which does happen from time to time — he can do a fair impersonation of a normal human being."

Miranda smiled down at her plate as she scooped up her last forkful. "Perhaps I shouldn't say this — well, it was meant harmlessly enough — but my father asked me if I thought Phillip might be a touch in the gay direction."

Adrian nodded. "That's a common reaction. All I can say is, if he *is* gay, he's made a damn good job of hiding it from *me*. Truth is he's a bit of a womanizer. I sometimes wonder if he generates the gay impression on purpose — to give women a false sense of security. Then, as soon as they're overwhelmed by his fascinating personality, he dons the wolf's clothing."

Miranda laughed. "Well, he didn't fool me."

"That's because you're a professional observer of human nature trained to see beneath the superficialities."

"If that's the case, how come I'm having no success with *you*?" she risked. "I can't seem to get a handle on who you really are. You're ready to talk about music — even about your own composition — but you don't give much else away. You get me talking about my family and my personal life and, at the end, I realize I know nothing more about yours."

"I told you about Liisa," he countered.

"You didn't have much choice there, did you?"

Adrian shrugged and focused his attention on pouring the last of the wine. He wasn't going to pursue this direction without further prompting.

"Phillip told me you had a stormy relationship with an opera singer last autumn. He said it shook you up badly."

"Phillip's got a big mouth. He also told me he thinks you've been married, and for some reason it didn't work out."

"Phillip *has* got a big mouth," agreed Miranda.

They eyed each other circumspectly, but with genuine warmth.

"I'll show you mine if you'll show me yours," she said, affecting a coy smile.

"An intriguing proposition. But who goes first? My grammar-school upbringing taught ladies always get that privilege."

"How can I be sure you'll keep your side of the bargain?"

"Oh, I assure you, I'm a paragon of integrity."

"Now you're sounding like Phillip."

"Hang around him long enough, and it starts to rub off."

The waiter came to clear away the plates and dishes. But once they were alone again, Miranda gave an account of her failed marriage to a postgraduate law student who, unlike herself, had followed up his vocation to become a successful corporate lawyer.

"He was elegant. He was dashing. At the time, he impressed me, but I should've known better. We were heading in different directions. He never understood my decision to go into policing and he resented the hours I had to keep. He worked hard too, but expected me to be there the moment *he* came off duty. Surprising we lasted as long as we did! Four years and he'd moved out. In all fairness he treated me well over the divorce. He left me his share of the flat. Probably thought he could recoup the loss quickly enough on the salary he was making. Since then, I've fought shy of getting involved. I've kept my head down and concentrated on the job. When Dad went to Scotland, Rosie moved in with me. It's been nice having her around, though some days we hardly see each other. She does her stuff and I do mine."

Over a dessert of *pista kulfi* ice-cream, Miranda's patience was rewarded. Adrian took his turn and spoke about his own ill-starred romance. Less forthcoming than herself in the details, he seemed to be making an effort to meet her part of the way. One revealing moment was when he said: "I've lost my taste for high levels of drama in a relationship. It was very painful. I don't want to expose myself to anything like that again."

Miranda felt she was making progress.

Outside, the wind had picked up, and a growing dampness in the air added a raw edge. Miranda was grateful for the ankle-length coat that enveloped her skimpy dress. She'd expected Adrian to take her arm, perhaps her hand — at the very least to place his arm across her shoulders. He'd done none of these, and Miranda's need for physical contact was throwing her off balance.

When they reached the outer door of her building and were standing together on the pavement, Miranda heard herself invite him up for a cup of hot chocolate...

"It'll thaw you out for the journey home," she explained, assuring herself things would go no further. They'd share a cosy beverage at the kitchen table, and then she'd remind him of her eight o'clock start the next morning, and then he'd leave.

Closing the apartment door, she removed her coat and took Adrian's to hang them up in the hallway. Suddenly he was there behind her, placing his hands lightly on her shoulders and stroking the nape of her neck with his thumbs. Miranda found this simple gesture electrifying. Somehow she succeeded in draping the coats across two empty coat-hangers, but then remained motionless. If she turned to face him now, all vestiges of self-control would be lost.

Slowly his fingers travelled the length of her neck and probed the lowest margins of her thick red hair. They stood this way for a long half minute. But then his hands slid back to her shoulders and, meeting no further resistance, he gently swung her around. She expected him to kiss her, but he only gazed into her face, mapping every detail with those intense blue eyes — totally absorbed in the task. With unhurried deliberation he raised his fingertips to her face to lightly trace the lines of her forehead, her cheekbones, her mouth and chin. When his hands glided softly down again to her neck they hesitated, speculatively encircling her throat. Miranda felt a momentary *frisson* of fear... but the hands were moving lower, as if counting the delicate bony ridges of her chest beneath the creamy freckled skin, venturing downwards to explore the deep tapering valley exposed by the scooped neck-line of her clinging knitted dress; drawn still further to circumscribe and savour the soft pliable curves that lay immediately beneath the dark-green material.

Miranda had scarcely moved, her arms hanging forgotten at her sides. She was hypnotized by his eyes, by his concentration. Only now did she hesitantly raise both hands to frame his face and lay them caressingly along his cheeks. This seemed to awaken Adrian from his trance. Slowly at first, but with steadily increasing passion, he passed his hands down her waist and across her hips to reach for the hem of her dress — sliding it, working the close-knit wool upwards around her buttocks and beyond, to expose her belly... then even higher, prising his fingers beneath her bra to push it and the now bunched material over her breasts and into the haven of her armpits.

With a slight gasp, he backed her urgently against the wall, tugging his own upper clothing free to uncover his chest, pressing his body against hers.

And, at last, he kissed her. Miranda was overwhelmed by the explosive combination of sensations: the hard insistent textures of his body, his skin against her skin, his lips against her lips. Her rational mind fought to reach the surface...

"Adrian," she managed, struggling for breath, "with me, you're going to have to observe the niceties."

"Yes, Miranda. I realize that."

Later... And then again much later, Miranda was lying with her legs curled around Adrian's, and her head buried in the crook of his shoulder. Her fingers toyed with the curly down that covered his chest. Such furriness was unfamiliar to her. Finnish men generally carried less body hair, and her excursions into the manhood of other nations had been few and far between. *A furry Michaelangelo's David*, she thought.

The Englishman sighed and shifted position beside her.

"What's your middle name?" Miranda asked tentatively.

"You mean between 'Adrian' and 'Gamble'?"

"Yes."

"Matthew."

After a pause — more as a statement of fact than a question — she said: "So, you're Mr Adrian M. Gamble."

"That's right."

Miranda allowed a lengthier silence before making her main point. "Have you noticed, Adrian M., that our names are anagrams?"

He did the mental arithmetic. "Curious," he said. "Curious but fitting. We're obviously made for each other."

"Or made to scramble up each other's lives."

Adrian smiled into her hair. "Let's try being a bit more optimistic, shall we?"

II

Tempo Andante, ma rubato

Miranda arrived at work one minute before eight o'clock, short of sleep but elated. She told herself she'd have to get down off this cloud by a few thousand feet if she intended doing anything productive today. As it happened, she was brought to earth with a jolt.

Passing Ylenius' open office door, she paused at the sight of her boss standing behind his desk — as if he'd just arrived himself, but hadn't yet managed to sit down. Facing him across the desk, also standing, was Tero. They turned their heads in her direction. For several moments, all three were motionless — the two men staring out, Miranda staring in. No word of greeting was uttered, and Miranda felt her face flushing. To hide this unaccountable confusion, she said: "What's up?"

Tero turned back to Ylenius and, after a further pause, the Chief Inspector spoke: "Tero thought of something on his way here this morning. The same thing occurred to me during the night."

Oh, oh! This was sounding ominous.

Tero took it upon himself to drop the bombshell: "Gamble could've phoned from the Sibelius Monument using Liisa Louhi's own mobile. He could've taken it from her bag. We've only got his word for it her bag was stolen. He might've removed it from the crime scene himself. Perhaps he thought he could make the whole thing look like a mugging that went wrong, until he realized the theft story would give him a better alibi."

"Do we know Liisa even had a mobile phone?" Miranda countered. She sounded overdefensive — even to her own ears.

"It was one of the first things we checked on Monday," said Tero, "when we got your fax from the Conservatory. I even tried phoning her number, but I only got a pre-recorded 'number unavailable' message. Either the phone's switched off or the battery's run down."

"Surely the operator can verify if that nine-o'clock call was made from Liisa's mobile," Miranda argued.

"There was an oversight," said Ylenius. "The constable scheduled to apply for the information came down with a stomach bug and never made it back to work on Tuesday. Nobody else noticed the job hadn't been done. Of course, a lot's happened over the last thirty-six hours. Gamble turning up on our doorstep threw everything off keel. And then that business with the letter and the fingerprint... It's all distracted us from the obvious routines. But excuses won't help." He straightened to his full height. "Let's get on and initiate the paperwork for a complete run down of Liisa's calls over the last three months. Hopefully it'll reveal something useful. And it's vital to know if someone switches her phone back on. Get the operator to monitor that too."

"I'm on it!" said Tero, and left the room.

Miranda was following, when Ylenius called her back.

"Adrian Gamble isn't off the suspect list," he said. "You'd be wise to maintain a professional distance."

Thanks for the advice, boss, but I expect he's still asleep in my bed!

Miranda nodded, and stepped into the corridor, recalling yesterday's telephone conversation with Adrian. *Just give us time,* she'd teased him. *Perhaps we can conjure up something else incriminating.* Sixteen hours had proved enough! And the nightmare was back. The uncertainty and suspicion. With it came the unpalatable truth that Ylenius was right. She'd allowed her attraction towards Adrian to interfere with her judgment. Now she was deep in the mire. If the others got an inkling how deep, she'd be dropped from the investigation. But that mustn't happen! Her sense of obligation to the victim was now a personal matter. Liisa Louhi had acquired a solid reality for her, and Miranda believed she could contribute a lot to the investigation. The woman's angle was needed. But first she'd have to recover some objectivity.

An hour later, Miranda's father phoned from the country cottage.

85

"How'd it go last night, darling?"

"The jury's still out," she said evasively. "Any luck with that text I gave you yesterday?"

"So I'm being fobbed off, am I? All right, it *was* Sibelius — just as we suspected. I found the passage in Tawaststjerna's biography: from a diary for the year 1914. But what's it's all about, Miranda? Why did you want me to check it?"

She hinted at a possible link to the murder enquiry. "Sorry, Dad, I can't tell you more at present."

"Fair enough. I'll put my curiosity on hold. And that goes for what happened last night as well!"

Miranda reported the Sibelius connection to her colleagues, but it did little more than suggest the murderer was educated, and with a deep interest in music. As Miranda pointed out, that could apply to any number of people.

Tero didn't miss his opportunity: "People like Adrian Gamble," he said.

Meanwhile the forensic check on the letter had drawn a blank. The post mark was as good as useless. Letters collected from post boxes around the capital were all franked at the same central sorting office with the broad, unhelpful designation HELSINKI: so it was impossible to know exactly where the letter had been posted. The envelope was nondescript and freely available from any stationers. With rapid and efficient cooperation from the Järvenpää police, the few fingerprints found on the envelope were eliminated as those of the Ainola Museum secretary and a sorter at the Järvenpää post office. Hopes that human saliva had been used to seal the envelope or attach the stamp were likewise thwarted. And the paper of the letter itself was standard Rank Xerox material, used by thousands of photocopying machines and computer printers across the city. One marginally useful piece of information was that a careful examination of the computer font used for the letter's text indicated a Macintosh computer rather than a PC.

Tero then reported that he'd been checking the Töölö library security videos for the afternoon of Liisa Louhi's death: "I tracked her movements through the building," he explained, "but all she did was go up to the music department on the third floor, borrow the book and leave again. The place was more or less empty at the time. She didn't pass any males of a suitable age on the stairs. Apart from the librarian who served her and the girl who processed the book on the way out, nobody seems to have paid her any attention... And no suspicious-looking psychopaths hovering behind the bookshelves."

"How about the Conservatory?" Ylenius asked. "Any luck with the students and staff?"

Tero shrugged. "Most of the male students and teachers can account for their movements on Friday evening. And on the admin side they're all women. But there *are* two porters. The younger one's Jorma Mannila. He's about thirty — a big bloke, heavily built — ponderous is how I'd describe him. He's got a reputation round the Conservatory for being a religious crank, and he *looks* weird. Practically all the hair on top of his head has gone, but he combs a bunch of long strands over the bald bit. Looks ridiculous!"

Miranda remembered seeing the same man when she'd visited the Conservatory on Monday.

"The porters work two shifts," Tero went on. "The early one's from eight till three, the other from two forty-five till nine fifteen in the evening. So they overlap by fifteen minutes in the middle of the afternoon. That's when they make the changeover. On Sundays the building's closed, but each porter keeps the same shift for a six-working-day stretch from Wednesday to the following Tuesday. Then they swap over so neither has to work evenings the whole of any given week. The office provided me with a copy of the computerized work sheets. Last Friday Mannila had the later shift. He clocked off with his personal code at 9.15 pm, so he's in the clear. Louhi was already dead by then."

"You haven't mentioned the other porter," Ylenius pointed out.

"Oh, he's too old — about sixty. This is an able-bodied, *young* man's crime. Not a geriatric's."

"Olli Koskinen's hardly a geriatric," Miranda said, though without emphasis. She'd personally warmed to the older porter. But, true enough, he was a small, lightly built man — almost frail. She remembered his movements as carefully measured, like those of a person acutely aware of his physical limitations. It was impossible to

imagine him overpowering a young, healthy, energetic woman —
even one as insubstantial as Liisa Louhi.

Later that morning, the forensic lab came up with a small update.
Their investigation of Liisa Louhi's flat hadn't been exhaustive —
after all, it wasn't the actual murder scene — but something curious
had caught their attention. In addition to the large number of cat hairs
found on every surface a cat could reach, there had been a few dog
hairs adhering to the cushions and seat back of the sofa. *Pale
brownish-yellow*, said the addendum to the report. *Possibly golden
Labrador.* This raised the team's collective eyebrows, but the implied
connection to Martti Hakala — the man who'd found Liisa's body —
was too tenuous to take seriously.

Miranda felt the investigation had ground to a halt with everyone
waiting for Liisa's telephone log. A lot seemed to hinge on it.
However, as they would eventually discover, the telephone log could
not provide the specific information they sought...

On the evening of Friday 24th March — the evening of Liisa
Louhi's murder — a telephone engineer named Jyrki Penttinen was
scheduled to do one of his infrequent night shifts. He was functioning
well below par. His baby daughter (upon whom he doted beyond
reason) had cried almost nonstop for three days and nights. The
doctor's diagnosis was teething troubles. Since Jyrki's wife seemed
capable of sleeping through anything short of the Apocalypse, it fell
to Jyrki to walk the child up and down for an hour or two at a time
until she cried herself into unconsciousness.

Jyrki's task that particular Friday night was to update the computer
software which recorded data on every call passing through the
exchange. Such updates with improvements, refinements, and
corrections of 'bugs' were made at least once a year. During the
changeover, the recording system was inoperative for several
minutes, and no calls made during that period could be logged and
subsequently billed; which is why updates were performed in the
early hours of the morning when telephone traffic was at a minimum.
During the preliminary routines, and at exactly twelve seconds to 9
pm, Jyrki made a tiny error. Taking into account his problematic
domestic situation, this would, by another human being, have been

perfectly understandable. Computers, however, are notoriously unforgiving, and this one promptly ceased recording. A full minute and fifty seconds passed before Jyrki noticed his mistake and brought the computer back on line. He wondered whether to keep quiet. Perhaps nobody would notice. In the end he chose not to put his job on the line, and confessed to his immediate superior. The older man shrugged. The company could bear the loss of a couple of minutes' revenue, but he duly documented the event. After all, he had to cover his own back.

At one o'clock, Miranda received a call from the young librarian at Töölö Library's music department: "Thought you'd like to know," he said. "That pocket score of Mozart's 'Jupiter' Symphony — the one that Liisa Louhi borrowed... It's turned up in a strange way. Some shabby old bloke wandered in with it about ten minutes ago — you know, the type that sleeps in hostels and sits all day in our journals room to stay out of the cold. Says he found the book in the park. He seemed to expect a reward, so I gave him a couple of ciggies, and promised him more if he'd hang about till you got here for a chat. I didn't tell him you were police. Thought it might scare him off."

Twenty minutes later, the white-haired, stubble-chinned vagrant was showing Miranda where he'd found the book on the grass near a rubbish bin that he'd been rummaging through for empty bottles. The spot was only a few yards from the side wall of the library building, and almost exactly opposite Adrian Gamble's flat. She called in the SOCOs, but they found nothing else of interest in the area. The vagrant admitted he'd tried to clean the book up before returning it, and given it a thorough wiping on his sleeve. Any earlier fingerprints were irretrievably smudged.

Back at headquarters, Miranda reminded Tero that Liisa had put the Mozart score in her handbag: "The librarian saw her do it. So now it's turned up at Sibelius Park suggests the person who stole her bag at Forum shopping centre also trailed her to Töölö, and was waiting beside the library for her to come back out of Adrian's flat. Maybe the book fell out of the bag by accident. Or maybe he dumped it. But whoever he was, he could've been the one that afterwards followed Liisa to the monument and strangled her."

Tero tilted his head vaguely from side to side. "That's assuming the bag really was stolen from the shopping centre," he said.

Miranda turned away to hide her annoyance.

Towards the end of the afternoon, Adrian called to suggest a follow-up date for that evening. Miranda was obliged to put him off, trying unsatisfactorily to explain the awkwardness of her position.

"Are you saying it was just a one-night stand!"

"Don't be absurd, Adrian. It probably meant more to me than it did to you."

"Don't count on that! So does this mean you still suspect me? Whatever happened to my alibi?"

"As far as the investigation's concerned, of course, you're still a suspect. How could it be otherwise? You were the last person to see her alive — by no more than ten or fifteen minutes. The telephone alibi isn't necessarily conclusive. And you've admitted you were having an affair with her. Which doesn't mean I personally think you killed her. I find that very hard to believe."

"Methinks the lady protests too much."

"Please don't start misquoting Shakespeare at me!"

"Can you honestly say you don't harbour any doubts?"

She wasn't ready to answer the question that baldly stated.

"All I can 'honestly say' is I have to keep a professional distance — until the real culprit is found. Surely you can understand that?"

"I think I've got the picture." And he hung up.

"Oh, shit!" she said aloud. *So I've hurt his feelings. I've told him he's still in the frame. What the hell does he expect me to do? Resign? Look for another career?*

Miranda was grateful nobody else had been around to overhear even the one half of that conversation. Especially Tero! Thank God *he'd* been elsewhere.

The workday ended with no sign of the court order for Liisa's telephone log. Miranda went straight home where she fell into bed hungry but not caring, and slept for nine hours without once breaking the surface.

Almost a week had elapsed since the Sibelius Monument killing. But, shortly before ten on Friday morning, Tero lifted Liisa Louhi's much awaited telephone log from the print tray of the fax machine. He studied it for a minute or two before taking it to Ylenius's office. Miranda was already sitting there, but she stood up to circle the desk and peer over Ylenius's shoulder at the list of data.

At first glance, the most significant fact was that no calls had been made from Liisa's mobile phone later than 6.24 pm on the evening of her death.

"So there's nothing for 9 pm," said Ylenius. "That puts Gamble's alibi on firmer ground."

"In fact, boss, it doesn't," Tero stated flatly.

"How do you mean?" demanded Miranda. "It shows he couldn't have been using Liisa's mobile when he phoned Phillip and me at the *Ateljé*."

"But if you look at the footnote here," Tero pointed obligingly to the place, "it says there were two data-recording blackouts on Friday-stroke-Saturday night. The second one from 3.29 to 3.41 am doesn't concern us. But there was a shorter one straddling that critical time of 9 pm — about a minute either side of it — which means we still can't be sure where Gamble made the call from."

"Let's request a log for Gamble's home telephone?" suggested Ylenius.

"That won't help," said Tero. "It comes through the same exchange. Liisa Louhi's operator runs the national grid."

Although Adrian's alibi remained inconclusive, that final listed call at 6.24 pm — less than three hours before Liisa's death — was startling in itself: because further checking revealed that Liisa had made it to the mobile owned by Phillip Burton. What was *his* connection to the murder victim? He wasn't himself a suspect. He'd been sitting in the restaurant with Miranda for most of that evening — in fact, from at least an hour before the time of the murder. But this tantalizing question needed following up, and Tero volunteered.

"I remember Phillip telling me," Miranda offered (on her best behaviour since yesterday's veiled reprimand from the boss), "that he teaches at the School of Economics on Fridays.

"Right," said Tero. "I'll go and look for him."

— * —

91

Forty-five minutes later, having caught Phillip Burton in the staff room between lessons, Tero approached the matter tangentially and explained to the Englishman how there was reason to believe that Liisa Louhi might have tried to phone him during the evening of the murder — perhaps between six and seven. Had Mr Burton received any such call last Friday?

Tero made no mention of the hard evidence provided by Liisa's telephone log. He wanted to try a 'truth test' — to see if Burton was inclined to peddle him any lies.

In fact, Phillip began by pointing out that he didn't know the girl and had never even met her. But then an idea seemed suddenly to strike him...

"There *was* a mysterious call while I was on my way home. It must've been about half past six. A girl's voice... But she didn't introduce herself. She just asked for Adrian. I told her he wasn't with me, but I could take a message if she so desired. She said, 'No, thanks!' and rang off. It could've been Liisa Louhi, I suppose. Perhaps Adrian had given her my number."

Tero went on to discuss Adrian's nine-o'clock call to the *Ateljé*, and Phillip was very cooperative. He even offered to show Tero his mobile's internal register of calls. "Help yourself," he said, and handed the phone over. Phillip anyway knew there was no item in the memory that could incriminate Adrian, because he'd already taken the precaution of removing it...

Earlier that same morning Phillip had dropped into a café for breakfast. Sipping his coffee, he'd suddenly remembered the brief Friday evening call from that anonymous 'mystery girl'. Taking out his phone, he ran back through its record of the previous twenty received calls: twenty being all his mobile's memory could retain. Every number listed was from a known caller until he came to the twentieth and oldest entry. For this the telephone had found no crosscheck in its directory of Phillip's friends and colleagues, and only showed the number. Phillip memorized it long enough to dial directory enquiries. The owner of the number turned out to be Liisa Louhi!

Phillip had then stared thoughtfully out of the café window. A pretty Asian girl came up to the glass and peered in, presumably looking for an acquaintance. She soon gave a charming pout and strutted away, her bottom swinging in an intriguing manner. "Vietnamese," thought Phillip, with uncharacteristic vagueness considering the attractiveness of the girl. But his thoughts were elsewhere. Picking up the mobile again, he weighed it in his hand, at a loss to explain how Ms Louhi had got hold of his number. Not that her name was unknown to him. The newspapers had been full of the Sibelius Monument murder. He'd also belatedly learned about Adrian's involvement with the victim. Well, it wasn't the first time Adrian had been cagey about his girlfriends. He could be absurdly secretive sometimes.

But sitting there in the café, Phillip felt particularly uneasy. He suddenly wanted Liisa Louhi's number removed from his mobile phone's memory. Of course, as soon as the next call came in, Liisa's number would be pushed off the end of the list and be erased automatically. But could he wait for that to happen? One alternative would be to erase the entire list. Instead, he stepped across to the café's public telephone, inserted a coin and dialled his own number.

While Tero was at the Helsinki School of Economics, Aleksi Ylenius made some informal enquiries of his own. Those dog hairs on the sofa had been ringing alarm bells. He wanted more information about Martti Hakala. Like Miranda, he'd detected something military about the man and, on impulse, logged on to the police database. It was an easy job to verify that Hakala had once been a career soldier — which suggested Ylenius's next move.

The Chief Inspector was himself ex-army. On finishing his compulsory military service he'd signed on for a further five years and been detailed to the military police. When the contract ran out, he'd taken up a career in the civilian police, but he still had some useful army contacts — and that was fortunate, because army personnel were quick to close ranks against outsiders. Ylenius selected someone in the military records department who owed him a favour and, within an hour, had received a fax revealing plenty of valuable background...

Hakala was trained in special ops, for which he'd shown a natural physical aptitude. During the Bosnian crisis, he was sent in as a member of a Finnish battalion assigned to the UN peacekeeping force. All had gone well until he was arrested, along with a number of other UN soldiers, and held for six days under suspicion of raping and murdering a fourteen-year-old Bosnian girl. He was ultimately vindicated when the real perpetrators were identified, but this experience soured him against his superiors and against the army in general. He became noticeably less cooperative, and he displayed an increasing apathy towards his duties. Everything came to a head when, on a routine delivery of medical supplies to a village in the foothills, his small detail came under attack from unidentified snipers. It was Hakala's first time under genuine fire and (in the words of his commanding officer) he "lost it completely". Ignoring all orders, he cowered in a ditch until a couple of his mates risked their own lives to drag him to safety. Hakala never recovered from the crushing humiliation, and three months later was retired from service on psychiatric grounds.

Ylenius had only just put the fax down, when Tero stepped into the office to report on his meeting with Phillip Burton. Almost immediately, Miranda appeared in the doorway behind Tero, obviously anxious to say something herself — and, as soon as Tero had finished, she broke in: "Boss, I've been checking through Liisa's phone log. Guess who she called at 5.32 pm on the Monday before she died? Martti Hakala!" she announced in triumph. "Still at his old address, of course."

"Most interesting," nodded Ylenius, and then told them about his own afternoon's research.

"All right, Tero," he said, rising from his desk. "Bring Hakala in, please."

III

Vivacissimo—Lento e suave—Tempo primo—Lento e suave

"This won't take long, will it?" asked Martti Hakala.

Ylenius faced him across the table, flanked by Tero and Miranda. Hakala looked edgy, as if he were about to leap back up from his chair.

"We won't detain you any longer than necessary," said the Chief Inspector. "Just a few questions — more or less informally. You don't mind if we record the conversation, do you? An aid to memory, you understand?"

"Suit yourself," said Hakala. "As long as we get this over a.s.a.p. It's my dog Saara. She's been poorly the last couple of days — not herself at all. I hate leaving her like this. I was just about to take her to the vet when your Gestapo arrived. Can't understand why you've dragged me in here. I've already told you everything I know."

"Ah, but I'm afraid that's the problem, Mr Hakala," said Ylenius blandly. "We're not sure that you have."

Hakala eyed him warily.

"For example, you led us to believe you'd never met the murder victim, Liisa Louhi, before finding her body at the Sibelius Monument."

"That's right, I hadn't. What are you on about?"

"And that you'd never been inside her flat. You do know where it is, don't you?"

"Of course, I do. Now! But I didn't move to that block till after she was dead."

"In that case, I'm sure you won't mind us taking your fingerprints to check them against prints we found in her home. That way we'll be able to eliminate you from our enquiries."

95

"What is this? Are you suggesting I killed her? Hey, I'm not answering any more questions without a lawyer here."

"I think you're overreacting, Mr Hakala. We're only checking a few facts. But it is your legal right, of course. Do you have a lawyer of your own, or would you like us to provide one?"

Hakala looked bewildered by the practicalities. "Well, *I* don't know. Suppose you'd better get me one."

"Certainly we can do that. There's no lawyer on the premises, but it shouldn't take more than three or four hours to arrange things."

"Three or four hours?" Hakala was horrified. "I can't leave Saara that long. This is ridiculous!"

Ylenius smiled attentively across the table and waited for Hakala to make his next move. The man wasn't stupid. They could obviously drag this out for the rest of the day if he didn't cooperate.

"And what makes you so bloody sure I was in her flat?" he said at last — although much of the fight had left his voice.

Ylenius told him about the Labrador hairs. Hakala tried to laugh that one off. But next came the phone call from Liisa to his old address, and he seemed to realize the weak hand he was playing.

"All right, so I *had* met her before, but it was only the once."

"Why didn't you tell us straight away?" Miranda chipped in.

"Because I didn't recognize her. Not in the park. I doubt her own mother would've recognized her that morning. It wasn't till I saw the police crawling in and out of her flat that I made the connection. But then I thought I'd better keep quiet. I was afraid you lot'd start jumping to conclusions. I know how it works."

"Do you?" asked Tero. "Why's that?"

Hakala ignored him. "I didn't have anything new to tell you — not about the murder. Like I said, I only met her the once."

"So can you now please tell us all about that once, Mr Hakala," suggested Ylenius, settling back in his chair as if about to enjoy a favourite TV programme.

"Well, it was the weekend before she got killed," Hakala began... "On the Sunday afternoon. I'd heard about this place coming up for rent, so I went to have a look. The previous tenant showed me round, and afterwards I was going down the stairs when this girl comes rushing out of her flat in a right old tiz-woz. *My cat, my cat*, she keeps shouting. *He's going to fall. You've got to help me.* She practically dragged me in through the door. Took me some time to figure out what was going on, but there's this sort of narrow metal sill outside her kitchen window. It runs along the wall past the end of the window till it meets up with the side of her balcony. Go and have a look. You'll see what I mean. Anyway, one of her cats had jumped up on the balcony rail and walked along this ledge, and there it was, sitting calm as you like, right outside the largest pane of her kitchen window staring across the road at the kiddies' hospital. Obviously hadn't occurred to the stupid animal there wasn't enough room to turn round. It was stuck there with a drop of three floors as the only way off again. So Liisa wanted me to reach out of the opening window at the side to try and get it — said she was afraid of heights. Well, they've never bothered me, so I sort of half hung out and grabbed the damn thing by the scruff of its neck. Scratched the hell out of me for my trouble. But then the girl — this Liisa — she insisted on me stopping for coffee. That's when I sat down on her sofa. Saara's hairs must've come off my coat, 'cause I didn't have Saara with me that day."

"Flattering, was it?" asked Tero. "This little adventure with the girl next-door?"

"What do you mean?"

"Pretty young thing like that — damsel in distress, so to speak — crying gratefully on your shoulder."

"Don't know what you're getting at," said Hakala, bridling.

"Give you any ideas, did it? Nice and cosy over the coffee cups... Thought she might fancy some maturity and experience? Make a move, did you?"

Hakala's face reddened, and Miranda was relieved when the Chief Inspector intervened: "Can you explain, Mr Hakala, why she phoned you the next day? We've been rather puzzled about that. But I'm sure you can clear the matter up for us."

"She said she was going away." Martti said, relaxing slightly, "to look after her mother or something. And could I take care of her cats? Go and feed them once a day? So I told her I was more of a dog person myself. But she talked me round..." *That doesn't surprise me!* thought Miranda. "...and she said she'd have an extra key cut and drop it round at my flat on Monday evening."

97

"So did she?" asked Ylenius.

"No, she phoned instead. Said she'd found someone else to do the cats — someone living in the same building, I suppose. And that's the last I saw or heard of her — alive at any rate."

"You didn't run into her next Friday evening in the park?" needled Tero. "About nine o'clock? Stop for a friendly chat? Try picking up on your little tête-à-tête?"

"No, I did not!" Hakala burst out, and leant belligerently across the table at Tero. "Stop dropping your insulting little hints or I'll *make* you stop, you rat-faced little prick. Don't think I couldn't. I haven't forgotten my army training."

"That's *exactly* what I was thinking," said Tero, apparently enjoying the reaction he'd provoked.

"Calm yourself, Mr Hakala," said Ylenius, reaching out a restraining hand. "I think, Tero, it's better if you leave the rest to us. Go and write up that report, will you? The School of Economics...? By the end of the day, if you please."

Tero nodded and left the room with a lingering smirk. Not for the first time, Miranda wondered why the boss took such a conciliatory line with him after behaviour of this kind.

"Please believe me, Mr Hakala," Ylenius carried on placatingly, "I find your explanation of the facts convincing — really I do. But we'd be grateful if you could let us take a quick look round your flat — in your presence, of course — just to reassure ourselves there's no further connection between yourself and the unfortunate victim. Only take an hour, I expect."

"You mean right now?"

"For example."

"And I'd be coming along too?"

"Certainly."

Hakala brightened at once. "Let's do it! The sooner the better." He seemed more concerned about getting back to his ailing Labrador than anything the police might find.

But there was a distressing postscript...

On arrival at Hakala's bedsit, they found the dog lying inert on the door mat. She appeared to have been waiting for her master's return, but was evidently dead. Hakala tried vainly to revive the poor animal before standing up to harangue Ylenius and Miranda.

"You bastards! Dragging me away for no good reason. I should've been here. She shouldn't've had to die on her own!"

For a moment it looked as if he might physically attack the Chief Inspector. Instead he collapsed on the floor beside the dog and burst into tears.

What a thankless task policing can be sometimes, Miranda thought.

They did a superficial search for items that might connect directly to the murder: secateurs, nooses, biographies of Sibelius, etc — but found nothing obvious, and left the SOCOs to finish off the job.

On the way out, Ylenius expressed his regrets at how things had turned out. Hakala was still huddled on the floor, stroking the dead animal's ears.

"My advice, Mr Hakala — and I speak from experience — as soon as you feel able, get yourself another dog. She won't replace the one you've lost, but it will help."

Friday evening, and Miranda was at home resisting the temptation to phone Adrian. Uncertainty remained about that nine o'clock call to the *Ateljé*, but Miranda felt reassured by how the search of Adrian's flat had come up negative. Since she'd taken him directly from her flat to Pasila HQ, he'd had no chance to go home first and remove any incriminating evidence. Tero would, of course, point out there'd already been three days for that little operation. But she was no longer inclined to discuss the matter with Tero.

At nine-thirty she tried phoning her father at the lakeside cottage. He was almost the only person she could talk to about her personal (and sometimes professional) problems. He always listened sympathetically and was never judgmental. Miranda loved Rosie dearly, but had always tried to protect her sister from the uglier aspects of life. She never told Rosie details of her work at the Homicide Unit. In many ways Rosie was an innocent, and Miranda preferred to keep it that way.

Her father's number gave nothing but a recorded message. His mobile must be switched off. Probably deep in his writing.

Miranda put her restlessness down to the fact that she'd missed both her Thursday evening aikido session and her Friday early-morning swim. For some women, training in aikido and keeping physically fit was important because you never knew who you might find chasing you one dark and lonely night. In Miranda's line of work, it was more a case of never knowing who, one dark and lonely night, you might find yourself chasing. Actually, she'd just been trying to burn off some excess energy with an hour's jog around Töölönlahti bay. That and a stingingly hot shower to follow had helped... but not nearly enough.

She toyed again with the idea of calling Adrian.

Better not! Give it a few more days. After all, the boss had warned her off, and she owed him that much deference. Choosing a Mozart string quintet from the CD shelf, she curled up on the sofa with a book.

As it happened, Adrian might have been hard to reach. He and Phillip had arranged to meet for a late-night movie at the Tennis Palace Arts Centre. Apart from a couple of brief phone calls and the Sibelius lecture — the whole of which they'd spent in Miranda's company — there'd been little chance to discuss the events of the last few days. Their plan was to sit down over a pizza before the film began. . .

A little earlier than Adrian and Phillip's scheduled rendezvous, and five miles east of the city centre, a young photojournalist was walking from Siilitie metro station towards her flat in Roihuvuori. She'd just been talking on the hoof to an old schoolfriend, and now returned her mobile phone to a handbag hooked over one shoulder.

It was a surprisingly mild evening. The woman unzipped her black leather jacket, enjoying the sense of freedom the warmer spring weather always brought. A smile played briefly across her lips. . .

*   *   *

[9.43 pm; Friday, 31st March]

I can't believe I did that. Not my first in a public place, of course — but with a bloke like that! Not exactly a thing of beauty, was he? Face like a forest troll... not to mention overweight! But, my God, he was strong as an ox. Bit of a caveman stunt really. Have to admit, there was an overwhelming 'maleness' about him. And such a hilarious sense of humour. That's always a killer turn-on. Now I can't even remember his name, for Christ's sake! Definitely one Guinness too many! And the queue waiting outside... the look on their faces! Sorry, wrong door, he says! Didn't know whether to laugh or cry. No choice but to brazen it out, was there? But definitely time to split after that... And the early-morning 'shoot' tomorrow's important.

Wonder if I'll run into troll-face again. Doubt whether I want a repeat performance...

By now, she was climbing up through the trees on her usual short cut home, a battered violin case clasped under one arm. At the top of the steep incline loomed several blocks of flats, their outlines just discernible against the even darker sky. Illuminated windows, some curtained, some revealing interiors with pastel-coloured walls and flickering reflections of TV screens, cast a broken light through the branches, allowing her to pick her way on the rough path. Startled by a noise behind and slightly to her right, she turned with a rush of adrenaline to see a human shape emerging from the undergrowth. A patch of light caught the person's face and she knew him instantly.

"What the fuck are *you* doing here? Christ! You scared the living shit out of me creeping round in the dark like that!"

As the figure advanced towards her, his purposeful, calculated strides transmitted a sudden and absolute certainty that he wished her serious harm. She turned and broke into a run, the windows ahead seeming to offer some hope of refuge. But the irregularity of the path caused her to stumble, and that gave him the chance he needed. He was upon her at once, slipping the noose over her head from behind. She struggled onto her feet, but he forced her face-first against a tree, pinning her there with the weight of his body as he continued to pull the noose tighter.

Through the terror and pain of the constriction to her throat, she was aware of his erection pressing against the small of her back and his left hand groping under her jumper. She tried to shout, but could only produce an incoherent croak. The words, unable to escape, screamed and rebounded back and forth inside her own head: "You fucking madman, you'll never get away with it! No way you'll get away with it!" — until finally she blacked out.

His excitement took several minutes to subside. The shattering force of the orgasm had taken him by surprise. He felt no remorse: just a sense that he'd been an instrument of justice. The bitch had deserved it. His only regret was the realization that he'd missed an opportunity — that, had he been sufficiently prepared, he could have achieved an even higher level of fulfilment. A different approach would be necessary next time. Not that there would be any next time, of course! It must end here. He already carried responsibility for two deaths. But despite this assertion — made here in the presence of his victim — the notion, once permitted access, would feed his fantasies for days and nights to come.

*   *   *

Phillip was sitting at a window table in Pizza Hut when he spotted Adrian crossing the road from the direction of Kamppi metro station. Presumably he'd just got off a number 18 bus.

Half an hour late to the minute, Phillip noted to himself. *Nothing unusual about that.*

For all of Phillip's own self-confessed "colourful and endearing" faults, lack of punctuality was not one of them. It could even be said that he was punctual to a fault. He detested turning up late for anything. If at risk of missing an appointment through force majeure, he'd generally try to find some way of informing the offended party. Nevertheless, Phillip was surprisingly tolerant of other people's failings in these matters. He rarely showed annoyance at being kept hanging around and seemed capable of shrugging off the longest waits with a good-natured quip.

"Not late, am I?" asked Adrian. "Half-past ten, wasn't it?"

"My recollection, dear friend, is we agreed on ten sharp. But no matter. I've been pleasantly distracted. The girls in here are of the highest quality. Look at that beauty over there. Not a day past eighteen and a picture of pulchritude."

"When does the film start?"

"Another forty-five minutes. Still time for a pizza. I haven't ordered. I've been waiting for you."

Over their food they discussed Adrian's "incarceration" (as Phillip chose to characterize it) and the police suspicions about his involvement in Liisa's murder. Adrian had explained on Wednesday about the nine-o'clock alibi. But, after a couple of days to consider, Phillip had doubts of his own.

"Why didn't you tell me earlier you knew this Liisa Louhi?"

"She was a student of mine. I wasn't exactly proud of the fact I'd been giving her extra counterpoint lessons in my bed."

"Your sense of discretion is impressive, Adrian — or should I say your sense of misdirection. Never caught a whiff of it. But you always were a dark horse."

"True, I've never felt the need to broadcast my private life to all and sundry."

Phillip was too familiar with Adrian's ways to feel hurt by being categorized as 'all and sundry'... "But there is a dark side to you, isn't there, Adrian? Is to all of us, naturally. But I wonder if yours might be darker than any of us realize."

Adrian made no response to this melodramatic suggestion, so Phillip carried on: "I didn't tell you, did I? Liisa Louhi phoned me on the evening of the murder. Called my mobile around six-thirty and wanted to speak to you. Any idea how she got my number?"

Adrian looked baffled at first, but then shrugged. "She was always nosing round my things. Suppose she could've found my address book. She certainly knew you existed. I'd spoken about you. Probably she thought your number would come in useful for reaching me some day. Well, that's what she was trying to do, wasn't it?"

"There's something else. I tried calling your flat last Friday from the *Ateljé* to find out what the hell had happened to you. Miranda doesn't know. She was in the toilet. But surely you were alone by then? Liisa must've left by five to nine. How come you didn't answer?"

Adrian considered for a moment. "I do remember the phone ringing. But when Liisa stormed out I just collapsed on a chair in the hall. It was such a mess — that business between me and her. I was trying to figure out the best way of handling it. When the phone rang, I ignored it — often do, in fact. But then a couple of minutes later it struck me it might've been you trying to get through, so that's when I made the call back... at nine o'clock, as you know."

They ate in silence for a while.

Then Phillip decided to approach the subject from a different angle: "I had a policeman sniffing round today. A Detective Sergeant Tero Toivonen. Know him?"

Adrian grimaced.

"He was asking me about that nine-o'clock call. I reckon he's got the idea you called me from the Sibelius Monument with someone else's mobile. Didn't say so, but I think he meant Liisa's."

"That's ridiculous! It was stolen with her handbag."

"Yes, yes, quite so. Which is why I lied to him."

"You did what?"

"I told him I saw your name come up on the display when I answered your call... which would prove you were calling from home. It's the only number my phone recognizes as yours. But I was lying. I don't remember even looking at the display."

Phillip's greatest source of uncertainty was that, although he knew at least *one* call had come in to his phone from Liisa's mobile, he had no way of knowing if there had been a *second* one. Recent models showed the dates and exact times of every incoming call listed in the memory. But his two-year-old 'dinosaur' showed only the names and numbers. It was possible that the call he'd seen recorded as the *oldest* of the twenty listed in his phone's memory wasn't the six-thirty call at all, but a later one made at nine o'clock from the Sibelius Monument!

Phillip finished his food, and laid down his knife and fork, ready to take the plunge: "So where did you *really* make that nine-o'clock call from, Adrian?"

The ensuing silence stretched almost to breaking point.

"Was that a serious question?" Adrian asked, at last.

Phillip stared back, trying to penetrate the thoughts of this long-term but sometimes infuriatingly inscrutable friend... "Oh, I suppose not," he said, and stood up. "Better get going. The film starts in five minutes."

* *

~ *I'm trying hard to understand.*

~ Aren't we all. Part of the human condition.

~ *Be serious! You've got to help me through this... to see the larger picture. But we need a starting point, and there's something comes to mind from way back. Remember the Biology Tower? We were on the eleventh-floor landing waiting for Val to come out of the physiology lab.*

~ I think I recall the occasion.

~ *We'd been talking about suicide — not right then, but over the previous weeks — about whether life was worth all the hassle... about how death's inevitability negated everything — negated ambition, negated love, negated hope. Everything was futile in the context of the infinite universe — swallowed up by the enormity of Time and Space. And we agreed God was a self-delusion. So, if we couldn't come up with a logical, reasoned argument for going on, the only intellectually honest alternative was to accept the inevitable, and bow out straightaway.*

~ We were young and stupid. Correction: younger and even more stupid.

~ *At the time it seemed crucial... an unavoidable decision to be taken one way or the other.*

~ So I climbed into the stairwell.

~ *Exactly! You climbed over the banister rail and hung at full stretch by your fingers in the stairwell — a sheer drop of eleven floors! I'd had my back to you, staring out of the window across the campus. Suddenly you called my name. I turned and there you were. It was terrifying.*

~ I recollect feeling rather nervous myself.

~ *But you were stuck. To pull yourself back up out of danger you needed to flex your arms. But that would've moved your centre of gravity away from the rail, towards greater peril. You didn't trust your fingers to take the strain on their own, so I had to help you. I had to reach over the abyss and grab you under the armpits — lift your whole weight up by myself until you could reach over the rail and scramble to safety. You placed the burden of responsibility for*

preserving your life in my hands and I was terrified of failing.
~ I did say thank you afterwards.
~ *People claim moments as intense as that are written indelibly and with perfect detail on the memory. But I can remember almost nothing of it. I suppose my mind rebelled — refused to accept what was happening. All I can remember is the pair of us lying there afterwards on the floor of the landing, shaking uncontrollably with muscle fatigue and a backlash of fear.*
~ Do you know why I did it?
~ *Presumably you wanted to prove you had the strength and determination to go on. Placing yourself in the jaws of death would test whether you had the genuine will to choose life — the courage to face anything fate might later try and throw in your path.*
~ Something like that.
~ *What a fucking crazy trick, you irresponsible moron!*
~ A fine turn of phrase you have when paying a compliment.

* *

Saturday morning at Pasila police station began with deceptive calm. Miranda was planning some routine phone enquiries — hoping to reach the last few people listed on Liisa's log of calls. One of them might know something important to the investigation. But, if possible, she'd get away at lunchtime and spend the rest of the weekend at home. She wanted to invest some time readying the flat for her sister's return. Rosie would be flying in from London on Monday evening.

Miranda was coming back from the canteen with a breakfast tuna fish sandwich, when Tero intercepted her. He was in an obvious state of excitement.

"We've got another one! Another murder with the same MO. Out at Roihuvuori. They want us over there right now. The SOCOs and the pathologist are on the way. I've phoned the boss at home. He'll meet us at the scene. That's another weekend lost, I suppose!"

"Another *life* lost, Tero!" Miranda said sharply, and stalked off to fetch her coat.

IV

Finale: Allegro moderato

The similarities to the Sibelius Monument murder were striking. The victim — now attended by the pathologist and police photographer — sat with her back against the trunk of a tall pine tree, legs extended and widely spread. Her leather jacket was pushed back over her shoulders, and the clothes beneath lifted to expose her breasts. Her skirt was bunched up around her hips. Both tights and pants had been completely removed from one leg, and remained trailing from the ankle of the other. The cause of death was clearly strangulation — the noose design similar to the earlier one with a looped hand-hold at the back. But the wire itself wasn't identical, consisting of a rather thicker single strand of white electrical cable. Despite the slight variations in the modus operandi, two other features made a convincing case that this was the work of the same killer: all three joints of the woman's right little finger had been removed; and, leaning against an adjacent tree to the left of the body, was a violin case.

"She seems a bit older than Liisa," said Miranda. "Something close to thirty." *My own age*, she remembered, with a shudder.

Ylenius turned to one of the local officers who'd secured the site. "Know anything definite about her?"

"No, sir. It was obvious she'd been dead for hours, so we radioed in and kept our distance. Didn't want to risk contaminating the scene. But a lot of trace evidence will've gone. It started raining at 3 am. Absolutely tipping down! Didn't let up till well after seven. Did you notice, sir? Her handbag's lying over there by the bushes. Well, I

107

suppose it's hers. We haven't touched it. There could be some ID inside."

The presence of a handbag was a further divergence from the previous murder.

"Who found the body?" asked Tero.

"A woman jogger, at around twenty past eight. Heard the victim's phone ringing in the trees and got curious. Probably regrets it now. She was in quite a state when we got here. We took her details and sent her home. Hope that's all right, sir," he added, a shade uncertainly.

Ylenius nodded his approval.

"I doubt if she'll fancy jogging solo round *here* again," said Tero, apparently amused by the thought, and earned himself a withering look from Miranda.

After the handbag had been photographed and its position properly mapped, Ylenius asked Miranda to take a look inside. She pulled on a pair of latex gloves, and gingerly poked around amongst the contents. There was the usual bric-a-brac of toiletries and cosmetics, a mobile phone, and a wallet which Miranda carefully opened. According to the driving licence, the woman's name was Christa Bäckström and her age was twenty-nine. Miranda lifted out and unfolded a picture postcard from Antananarivo, Madagascar, bearing a message in Swedish: *The adventure begins!* It was signed with the initials B-M — not relevant in itself, presumably — but the card did provide Christa Bäckström's address: Lumikintie, a street no more than 300 yards away.

"She's got a press card," said Miranda, still digging in the wallet. "It says she worked for *Hufvudstadsbladet*."

At that moment the victim's telephone rang inside the handbag with a reedy and unmusical rendering of a traditional Irish tune: *"It's not the leaving of Liverpool that grie-ieves me, but my darling when I think of you!"*

Miranda winced.

"That's the fifth time since we got here," said a passing SOCO man.

The three detectives exchanged glances.

"Shall I?" asked Miranda, and Ylenius nodded.

Easing the phone out of the bag, she blessedly pressed the ANSWER button before the tune could start up again.

"Hi," she said, and was answered, not in Finnish, but in Swedish.

"What the hell are you playing at Christa?" The man's bellowing voice forced Miranda to move the handset half an inch from her ear. "You're over an hour late! Left us hanging round here like a bunch of dicks. And why'd you take so long to answer your bloody phone?" He dropped his voice to an angry whisper: "I know we've had our little differences recently, but that shouldn't affect one's professionalism. There's a job to be done!" He paused... but, when he got no response, returned to his earlier decibel level: "Are you still there, Christa? Are you bloody listening to me?"

Miranda glanced at the mobile's display to see if the caller's name had been recognized.

"I am listening to you, Mr Sirén," she said, replying in Swedish. "The problem is I'm not Christa."

"What do you mean, you're not Christa? Is this a wrong number?"

"No, you've reached Christa's phone, all right."

"So who the hell are *you*?"

"Detective Inspector Miranda Lewis," she answered, ignoring the man's rudeness. "With the Helsinki Police. I'm sorry, but I have some bad news for you. Christa has met with an accident. I'm afraid she's dead."

"Dead? What do you mean? How *can* she be? What kind of an accident?" He sounded more bewildered than shocked.

"I'm not at liberty to tell you right now, except we're treating the circumstances as suspicious." *Something of an understatement, Miranda!* "Look, I'm sorry, Mr Sirén, I have to ring off now. I'll get back to you later in the day."

So we've had our little differences, have we? Miranda mused, and then she related Sirén's half of the conversation to her colleagues.

"Right, you'd better follow up on that," said Ylenius. "If nothing else, he can give us some background on the victim."

"And while I've got Ms Bäckström's phone in my hand," Miranda ventured, "shall we raid its memory?"

Miranda dictated to Tero who wrote down the names, numbers and times of the latest calls made and received. Three text messages had also arrived within the last half-hour — both from Sirén, and both asking "where the bloody hell" Christa was. Miranda then checked the list of 'missed' calls: incoming calls that had been left unanswered. Cross-referencing all of this information led to an important conclusion. Apart from Miranda talking to Sirén a few minutes earlier, the last 'answered' call had been received at 9.41 the previous evening. Soon after that there were two missed calls: at 9.58 and 10.11. The implication was that Christa Bäckström had died between answering one call and failing to answer the next — between 9.41 and 9.58 pm. The pathologist's preliminary estimate for the time of death confirmed this as a possibility. And all three of those last calls had come from the same number, so they'd need to speak to the person who'd made them.

Meanwhile, the murdered woman had acquired a name. Their next job was to build a life around that name — to reconstruct Christa Bäckström's personality, her daily habits, her social contacts, and most importantly the sequence of events which had led her to this sordid, violent end.

The victim's appearance gave some preliminary insights: Christa was a woman of smallish build — like Liisa Louhi, but with a tighter, less fleshy body. Her hair was solid black — obviously dyed — and it was cut short and spiky. Every item of clothing, even her underwear, was a corresponding black. The large earrings, the stud in her nose, and the rather aggressively applied make-up all contributed to a hard-edged sexiness. As far as one could tell under present circumstances, her face hadn't been beautiful or pretty — not in any traditional sense — but Miranda was in no doubt that many men would have been attracted to her.

One of the SOCO team approached Ylenius: "Something over here you should see, Chief."

He led them some twenty yards to where a rough, muddy path climbed steeply through the trees.

"Better not get too near," he said, pointing to a tall spruce that stood beside the path. "We'll need a closer look round here. Do you see those black threads caught on the twigs sticking out of the trunk? I think we'll find they're from the victim's clothes. My guess is she was attacked right here as she was walking along this track. He held her against the tree while he strangled her, and then dragged her body over to where it is now. It'll be hellish difficult to figure out anything for sure after all this rain."

"Any cutting tool this time?" asked Ylenius. "Something to sever the finger?"

The SOCO man shook his head.

Ylenius then suggested that Tero stayed to monitor the SOCOs progress while he and Miranda visited the victim's home. At that point they noticed the absence of any keys: none in the handbag, or in the victim's pockets, or lying anywhere about the site.

"This is a reversal," said Miranda. "A key was almost the *only* thing we found at Liisa's murder scene. Anyway, boss, before we go, shall I have a look at the violin?"

Miranda's verdict was unflattering: "Just a cheap fiddle," she said. "Even then, it's seen better days. The body's cracked just here below the bridge. And the bow hairs are tatty. Hasn't had a service for years. If ever! We can definitely rule out Christa Bäckström being any kind of serious musician."

Forearmed with the knowledge from HQ's database that the murder victim was unmarried and lived alone in her Lumikintie flat, Ylenius and Miranda climbed to the third floor and rang the door bell. They weren't surprised to get no response, and spent the next twenty minutes locating the caretaker — an enormous bear of a man — in the basement of the neighbouring block where he was doing some repairs on the plumbing. Although he agreed to let them into Christa's flat, he was reluctant to stay: "Better get back and finish the job," he said. "Nobody's got any hot water."

So the two detectives stepped alone into Christa Bäckström's tiny hallway.

"One problem solved," said Miranda, pointing to a bunch of keys on a small table inside the door. "Must've forgotten to take them with her."

They moved down the short corridor and peered into the kitchen. There were fitted cupboards around the walls, all painted in a sunflower yellow that was beginning to peel. A couple of dirty dishes lay in the sink, and a half-drunk mug of coffee stood abandoned on the table. Otherwise, the place was clean and tidy. Further exploration revealed a cramped bathroom, and a combined bedroom-cum-sitting room furnished with a sofa, a portable TV, and a platform bed raised on stilts. An impressive-looking computer dominated the far corner like an altar.

"Start going through her stuff, shall we?" said Miranda.

Ylenius didn't answer. He was standing motionless in the middle of the room, facing the window.

Miranda waited, matching his stillness, and became acutely aware of the silence. She had the strangest impression that the flat itself was waiting... for its owner to return and resume her everyday existence: to unload the shopping into the fridge, to switch on the coffee machine, to sit down at the computer.

Ylenius turned and spoke with quiet urgency: "Call it a sixth sense, if you like, Miranda, but I'm almost certain he's been in here, and it was the murderer who put those keys on the hall table. We'll leave this place to the SOCOs."

By half-past one, they'd picked up Tero, and were all three back at Pasila, jammed into the Chief's tiny office.

"So what's the scenario of this second murder?" Ylenius asked.

Miranda spoke first: "I think we can assume that Christa was using the track through those trees as a short cut between her flat and, most probably, Siilitie metro station — on her way home or on her way out remains to be seen. The station surveillance videos might tell us. But I wonder how the killer selected her. Was it a random choice? Had he been stalking her? Did he follow her into the trees, or was he lying in wait? If she used the track as a habitual route, he could've planned the attack in advance."

"And what's the significance of the violins?" mused Ylenius. "Each of the victims was carrying one. That's surely more than a coincidence."

"Perhaps the killer hates the sound of the violin as much as I do," said Tero.

Miranda huffed audibly.

"We can't discount the possibility," said Ylenius, "that the murderer knew both victims personally. Our best course is to search for connections between Liisa Louhi and Christa Bäckström. Who did they know in common? Which places did they frequent? What routes did they travel regularly? Did their lives intersect in any way at all?"

"What about our Hungarian friend, Zoltán Szervánszky?" Miranda speculated. "The violin motif's an obvious connection. And we know he had a reason for bearing Liisa a grudge. Is it pure chance that the second victim's turned up dead less than half a mile from where he lives? Could he have known Christa as well?"

"Perhaps he was giving her violin lessons?" Ylenius suggested.

But Miranda shook her head in grim amusement. "I think Szervánszky would consider it an indignity to occupy the same room as an instrument like Christa's. But there might be some other connection we don't know about. By the way, Tero, did you check Szervánszky's alibi for the evening of Liisa's death? Was he playing at the opera house?"

Tero looked uncomfortable. "In the end, I didn't. The investigation seemed to be moving in a different direction."

Yes, much too busy concentrating on your pet Adrian Gamble theory, Miranda thought, and surrendered to the pleasure of seeing Tero put on the spot in front of the boss. Good heavens, he actually looked embarrassed!

"I'll visit the opera house this evening," he said, quietly emphatic.

"You'd better," agreed Ylenius. "And I want you to mobilize door-to-door enquiries. Did anyone know Christa — if only by sight? Did anyone see her that evening? Was anybody using the same path or travelling on the metro at the critical time? Have there been any suspicious characters hanging round her apartment block recently? All the usual stuff! We'll need more personnel. I'll put in an application. The Louhi death was bad enough, but now it looks like we're up against a serial killer. Miranda, can you request a court order for Christa Bäckström's telephone log? Let's not make *that* mistake again. In the meantime you can check out the calls we already know about. This Sirén fellow... I think you should go and interview him face to face — preferably this afternoon."

"What do you make of that *difference of opinion* Sirén mentioned over the phone?" asked Tero.

"Well, on second thoughts, I doubt it has any bearing on the murder," said Miranda. "If Sirén killed her, he'd know exactly why she didn't turn up for work this morning. His repeated calls to her mobile would have to be a conscious attempt to feign ignorance. But if that's the case, I can hardly see him giving away a possible motive within seconds of some stranger answering Christa's phone."

"Unless it was a double-bluff," suggested Tero.

"Easier to judge when I've spoken to him."

Kaj Sirén turned out to be a journalist with *Hufvudstadsbladet*: the same Swedish-language newspaper that Christa Bäckström had worked for. Miranda tracked him down at their headquarters in Mannerheimintie.

Sirén was an energetic-looking man in his mid-forties; slim-bodied and with large amounts of striking silver-grey hair. He led Miranda into a large open-plan office on the fifth floor where they sat down either side of his desk. Sirén seemed willing enough to speak about Christa Bäckström and his professional association with her — especially when told this was now a murder enquiry. He explained that Christa had only recently joined *Hufvudstadsbladet* as a photographic journalist — last autumn, in fact. Prior to that she'd been with a small provincial newspaper in a predominantly Swedish-speaking area on the northwest coast. Having reached the 'big city', she had ambitious dreams of working for one of the large international syndicates. Sirén had tried introducing her to the right people, but nothing came of it.

"And now nothing ever will," he added. "Hard to believe she's gone — just like that!"

"Did you work a lot together?" Miranda asked.

"This job's very dynamic. We're always on the move. I do stuff with a lot of different people. I wouldn't say I worked with her more than anyone else."

Sirén seemed strangely jumpy — unable to keep himself still for any length of time. His hands and feet were as restless as a five-year-old's, and he was continually swivelling to left and right in his office chair. Miranda didn't put this down to any special nervousness on his part but guessed it to be habitual.

"Was Christa talented?" she asked.

Sirén pursed his lips, rocking his upper body from side to side as he considered Miranda's question. "Competent... but I doubt she'd ever've made it big time. Of course, a lot of it's luck in the end." He paused again. "Didn't turn out so lucky, did she?"

"I understand Christa played the violin," Miranda went on.

"Irish folk music. Never heard her myself."

"She was carrying her violin yesterday evening. Any idea where she could've been going to or coming from?"

"Sorry, can't help."

Miranda broached the subject of the *little differences* Sirén had complained about over the phone that morning, but he brushed the whole thing off.

"Always like that in our line of work," he explained. "You have one idea how to go about the job, and your colleague has a completely different one. Gets heated sometimes. That's normal."

"There's a routine question we'll be asking everyone who knew Christa. Can you account for your movements yesterday? Between 9 and 10.30 pm?"

"Good God, do I need an alibi? Well, I probably don't have one. I went home about half-past seven. And that was it. Listened to a couple of CDs, read a book, went to bed around eleven. Nothing else I can tell you."

"Do you live alone?"

He shrugged a yes.

"Did you make or receive any phone calls?"

"Not that I remember."

"And did you know a music student by the name of Liisa Louhi?"

"Never heard of her. Look, I'm sorry to rush you, Inspector, but I'm supposed to be at a Metalworkers Union press conference in twenty minutes. Hopefully I've told you everything you need."

Miranda had little choice but to let him go. Then, hoping to gain a little more from the visit, she sought out the personnel office and — from the Saturday skeleton staff of one — obtained details of Christa's employment and a recent photograph. She tried chatting to a few people in the open-plan office area, but they were all too busy for her — apart from one individual who cheekily tried to pump *Miranda* for information.

Symphony No 2

She'd just entered the lift to return to the ground floor, when a woman slipped in beside her and eyed her with a mocking smile. The lift began to move and the woman spoke in a rough-edged, mannish voice: "Don't believe all the crap Kaj Sirén tells you. I heard him spinning that line about professional differences. A damn sight more than that, I can tell you. He was screwing the bitch. But then she gave him the cold shoulder. Royally pissed him off, I imagine!"

Bemused by this gratuitous tirade, Miranda could only stare back. The woman was pushing forty and, despite an attempt to hide the fact with an overgenerous layer of make-up, the skin of her face looked tight and lined. Too many cigarettes over too many years, Miranda supposed. A stale smoky odour was already detectable in the confined space they shared.

"Of course, she was only using him." The woman gave a contemptuous sneer that accentuated the creases descending from the corners of her mouth. "Christa bloody Bäckström was ready to screw anyone she thought could further her career. A scheming, self-serving cow and I, for one, won't be sorry to see the last of her!"

The lift stopped at the second floor and the woman stepped out, vanishing as abruptly as she'd appeared. Miranda watched the doors slide shut again, and pursed her lips in displeasure. She could almost taste the sour grapes.

Meanwhile Tero's expedition to the Finnish National Opera confirmed that Zoltán Szervánszky had indeed been employed for a ballet performance on the Friday of Liisa's murder. The programme that evening, entitled *String Serenade*, was danced to a collection of five different pieces. Tero recognized only two of the composers: Bach and Tchaikovsky — although the name *Brandenburg Concerto* sounded familiar. Perhaps he was thinking of the Brandenburg Gate in Berlin. The curtain went up at 7.30 pm and the performance had ended at about twenty past ten. There was one interval of twenty minutes between the third and fourth pieces, starting at almost exactly nine o'clock. This meant that the Hungarian was in the clear. The Sibelius Monument lay almost a mile from the opera house. No way could he have been there with the victim by nine.

Just to make sure, Tero spoke to some of the musicians arriving for a last-moment rehearsal of that evening's *Madame Butterfly* premiere. Most of them had no idea who Zoltán Szervánszky was, but Tero found three who did — all female — and they were ready to verify that Szervánszky had definitely been sitting at the second desk of the first violins on the critical evening of the 24th.

So much for *that* suspect! But what about Adrian Gamble? Tero would dearly love to know what the Englishman had been doing at ten o'clock *yesterday* evening. Had he by any chance been somewhere in the vicinity of Roihuvuori or Siilitie metro station? Tero found himself only a short distance from Adrian's flat. Rather than go straight back to Pasila and write up his reports, why not confront the man straightaway? Perhaps he could catch him wrong-footed...

But Tero's initiative was wasted. Gamble wasn't at home... though maybe Phillip Burton would know where to locate him. Tero patted his pockets, and drew out a little black notebook. Surely he had Burton's number scribbled down somewhere.

Several minutes later, just as Phillip was returning his mobile phone to his jacket pocket, the doorbell rang. That would be Adrian.

"Fancy a glass of red stuff?" Phillip offered, taking his visitor's coat. But Adrian was more in the mood for a cup of tea — *preferably strong* — and they filed into Phillip's small but lovingly maintained kitchen.

"That Tero Toivonen fellow just called me," said Phillip, filling the electric kettle. "Regular bloodhound! Said he'd been trying to track you down, and did I know where you were?"

"So you told him I was coming here?"

"In fact, I didn't." Phillip placed two bone china teacups and saucers on the table followed by a small matching milk jug and a bowl of sugar. "He's still got it in for you, I'm afraid. Seems there was another murder last night, and he was trying to worm out of me what your movements were yesterday evening. So I told him about our ten-o'clock arrangements for a pre-cinematic pizza at the Tennis Palace. One could almost smell the man's disappointment seeping down the telephone line. He seemed desperately anxious to learn if you'd arrived punctually for our little rendezvous. I deemed it appropriate to

117

bend the truth a fraction — by thirty minutes, to be precise. I told him you'd arrived on the stroke of ten. Hope you don't mind me taking mendacious liberties with the biographical details of your life."

Adrian stared thoughtfully across the kitchen table. "Perhaps it'll keep him off my back for a while," he said.

"Exactly. And by the way," Phillip went on, pulling a chair up to the table, "you never actually explained why you turned up late yesterday evening."

Adrian frowned. "Yes, I did. I got the time wrong. I thought we'd agreed on half past ten."

"Ah, you did say that, didn't you? Silly me. Chocolate biscuit with your tea?"

Symphony No 3
in C major

I

Allegro moderato

"**S**o Phillip Burton's provided Gamble with an alibi again," said Tero.

It was Sunday morning, and they were catching up on each other's news.

"Very convenient, I call it! Claims they met at the Tennis Palace Pizza Hut at exactly 10 pm on Friday night."

"Perhaps it's true," said Miranda.

"Sure! But those two've obviously been hanging around each other for a very long time. Wouldn't put it past Burton to cover for his little buddy. *And* I suspect it's more than just chumminess — if you get my drift?"

Miranda felt Tero's surreptitious scrutiny, but was too much on her guard to take such easy bait. Her face and body language remained flawlessly impassive.

"Did you check at Pizza Hut?" she asked, studying the notes on her lap.

"Short-staffed that evening. One waiter vaguely remembers serving a couple of Englishmen over by the window, but he couldn't put a time to when they arrived or left."

"So, for now," said Ylenius, "we'll have to take Burton's word for it. And, assuming Christa Bäckström was still alive having a telephone conversation at nineteen minutes to ten, there's no way the killer could've committed the murder, dragged the body further into the trees, cut off the finger, and still have made it to the Tennis Palace pizzeria by ten o'clock. It's a good three minutes to the metro station, even at a run, and another ten or fifteen on the train to Kamppi station. A taxi or car would've taken at least as long crossing the city centre. If Burton's telling the truth, Gamble's out of it. By the way, Miranda, any luck with those last three calls to Christa's mobile?"

"They came from Anita Söderblom, living in Haaga. So far we haven't been able to raise her. She's not at home, and her mobile's not answering."

Miranda then reported on her interview with Kaj Sirén and her vitriolic encounter in the lift. "Suppose I should've found out who it was. Caught me off balance. But she struck me as a nasty piece of work."

"They're my favourites," said Tero. "They can never keep their mouths shut."

"I should be able to locate her again, to see if she's got any more sulphurous secrets."

They went on to assess the preliminary postmortem and forensic reports. No big surprises. The time and cause of death were as expected. The black fibres caught on the tree trunk beside the track were verified as coming from Christa's own jumper. Several small scratches on the victim's nose, cheeks, forehead and lower abdomen were embedded with tiny fragments of bark and lichen, supporting the earlier suggestion that she'd been pushed face-first against the tree by her attacker. She appeared to have had sexual intercourse within hours of her death, but it was impossible to say more because the only indications were traces of latex lubricants, prophylactics and artificial food additives: a condom had been used — one synthetically impregnated with a strawberry flavour.

"So could our 'freako' be a believer in safe sex?" asked Tero facetiously.

The forensic report went on to describe a study of the bone and cartilage at the site of the fourth finger amputation. There were scratch patterns suggestive of the tiny serrations found on the blades of many garden secateurs. The microscope also revealed the track of a small nick at a point along one of the blades. A similar track had been found at the site of Liisa Louhi's amputation. So it seemed probable that the same secateurs had been used on both victims.

Unfortunately, no other useful trace evidence had turned up at the Christa Bäckström murder scene. As feared, the heavy rain had washed the area clean. Fingerprints and fibres had been lifted from the victim's flat, but the data was still being processed.

There was one additional fact that looked helpful. The victim's stomach contents included more than a litre of beer, and the pathologist thought it was probably Guinness — a rather uncommon choice amongst beer drinkers in Finland.

"So it looks like she'd already been somewhere and was returning home," said Miranda. "Guinness and Irish folk music... A suggestive combination. Perhaps she'd been to one of the Irish pubs. There are three in the city to my knowledge. We'd better check them out later. Fancy a pub crawl, Tero?"

He grinned immoderately, fluttering his eyelashes.

Miranda turned hurriedly away and spoke to Ylenius: "Are we getting more staff backup, Boss?"

"I was coming to that," he replied. "They're placing a further ten officers at our disposal. I'll give them their initial briefing at eleven o'clock, so I need you both there. In the meantime, follow up what leads you can."

Copies of all the metro station videos for Friday evening reached the Pasila team by midday. Tero spent a couple of hours viewing the most relevant ones, and he established that Christa Bäckström had boarded the Vuosaari-bound train at Central Station at 9.25 pm, apparently alone; and had then got off, still unaccompanied, at Siilitie station twelve minutes later. Timing tests for the walk homewards had been carried out by a female officer (with a range of paces from leisurely to strenuous) and the intersection of Christa and her killer at the murder scene was now estimated at a quarter to ten.

Miranda later scanned through the Siilitie videos herself.

"*There's* a familiar face!" she exclaimed, and rewound the tape for Tero's benefit. "Strutting down the platform in all his glory — Mr Zoltán Szervánszky."

Having never seen the Hungarian in the flesh, Tero leaned forward to peer at the screen: "But, Miranda, the train he just got off... it's not the same one Christa was on."

"No, it's the one before. A pity Szervánszky's got an alibi for the first murder. I'd love to pin them both on this puffed-up little peacock."

123

"Well, he lives near the metro station, doesn't he? Probably just going home in this shot."

Miranda had to agree. And reviewing the tapes from earlier stations showed that Szervánszky hadn't even joined his train at the same place as Christa. He'd got on one stop earlier at Kamppi. Catching the previous train from the previous station seemed rather an impractical approach to following one's intended victim.

"Anyway, Tero, can you do some backward tracking of any males of a suitable age that got off the train with Christa? Also find out where they got on, and have some blow-ups done for ID purposes. We'd better put someone at Siilitie station over the next few days and try to trawl them in. That way we can check their eligibility as suspects."

"Sounds complicated," said Tero. "I think I'll delegate the video bit. Watching any more of this metro stuff'll make me cross-eyed."

Towards 6 pm, Miranda and Tero set off on their pub crawl. First stop was O'Malley's: a self-styled 'Irish pub' in the centre of the city. The clientele was small at this time of the day, but business would soon be picking up. The place was popular, even on a Sunday evening.

They let the barman finish pulling someone a pint of draught Guinness before introducing themselves. Miranda showed him the photograph she'd been given at the *Hufvudstadsbladet* office: "Do you know this woman?"

"Sure! That's Christa. She plays the violin here. One of the regulars at our Irish 'ceilidh' on Friday evenings."

"Do you know if she was here last Friday evening?"

"Yep! I usually work Fridays. And she came in... oh, about six o'clock. Brought her violin with her. Played a few numbers with some of the other guys."

"Did you notice if she was with anyone in particular?"

"Well, she was chatting to Sammu for about an hour."

"And where can we find this Sammu?" asked Miranda.

"Try that corner over there. He's the one with the beard."

This was an unexpected windfall. The person in question was sitting alone, nursing a half-empty beer glass, and studying the national broadsheet.

"Are you Sammu?" asked Tero.

"That's certainly what everyone calls me," came the reply. He was in his mid-thirties, not tall and rather squat; clearly of a cheerful disposition but overall rather seedy-looking.

"And what were you called at your christening?" Tero said, displaying his police warrant card.

"That would've been Samuli Junttila — or so they tell me. What's the problem?" He had a clear regional accent betraying his origins in Ostrobothnia, an area of Finland a few hundred miles to the north.

"Do you know a Christa Bäckström?"

Sammu stuck out his lower lip and shrugged. "Don't think so. Should I?"

"The barman claims you were talking to her in here last Friday evening. For an hour, he said."

"You mean the photographer? The violinist? Hey! She hasn't been making silly accusations, has she? Now, come *on*!" He spoke more in genial disbelief than in outrage. "She was well up for it. Surely you don't believe bullshit like that!"

Neither detective had a clue what Sammu was talking about.

"If you don't like *her* version," said Tero, fishing blindly, "you'd better tell us yours."

Sammu didn't hesitate: "Look, we got nattering at the bar. I'd seen her playing in here before, but it was the first time I'd ever spoken to her. A real tasty-looking lady. And she seemed to be coming on to me. Happens sometimes. Anyway, she went off to the toilets — they're down in the basement, away from the general hubbub. A few minutes later, I notice the call of nature myself — nature and three pints of Guinness — so I head off in the same direction... Just as I'm passing the door to the ladies, out she comes and gives me a really dirty smile. Well, I sort of backed her into the cubicle — on the spur of the moment — locked the door, and there we were. Just a bit of spontaneous fun. No question of me forcing the issue. She was giggling her head off the whole time."

"Make a habit of this kind of thing do you?" asked Tero, a touch wistfully.

"It has become a bit of a hobby of mine in recent years," Sammu admitted, in mock expansiveness. "Some blokes collect stamps. I collect venues."

"And this particular venue last Friday?" Tero was grinning now. "I presume you took prophylactic measures?"

"I may be a randy old goat, but I'm sure as hell not stupid."

"What brand do you use?"

For no apparent reason, Sammu suddenly slipped from Finnish into trans-Atlantic English:

"Why? D'you wanna borrow one, pal?"

"You can cut the wisecracks!" mimicked Tero.

"Hey, lighten up, man! You'll get a heart attack and miss your old age."

"Answer the question, smartass!"

Miranda's jaw dropped at Tero's complicity in this absurd charade. *My God!* she thought. *They've been watching the same American cop operas.*

Just as abruptly — and much to Miranda's relief — Sammu dropped back into the vernacular: "You'd better take a look, officer," he said, pulling a colourful packet from the back pocket of his jeans — *A regular boy scout*, Miranda concluded — which he then unfolded like a wallet. "Still a couple left," he said. "Help yourself, if you need one? If you're in a bit of a rush, so to speak?"

"Don't mind if I do," said Miranda, and reached forward to pluck out one of the bright red plastic wrappers. She slipped it into her handbag, noting — as often before — how it more resembled a piece of confectionery than an item off a pharmaceuticals shelf.

Sammu's eyes twinkled. "Would you like some help opening that?" he said, and his face creased into an engaging smile. Miranda had to admit there was something strangely charming about this man — in spite of his pudding nose, watery eyes, and wiry hair. A small part of her understood Christa's intemperate behaviour... *A very, very small part*, she hurriedly assured herself.

"So what about *after* your loo escapade?" Miranda asked. "Did you leave the pub together?"

"No, she vanished. Had my back turned for a couple of minutes and she'd gone."

"Didn't you follow her out? Try to catch her up?"

"Wouldn't've been much point. If she wanted to slide off, that was her business. No, I was here till closing time solving the barman's marital problems. They don't call me Auntie Sammu for nothing. Isn't that right, Jukka?"

Jukka turned out to be the barman Miranda and Tero had spoken to earlier. He was emptying a nearby ashtray into a bin, and confirmed that: yes, Sammu had remained in the pub until well after midnight.

Which seemed to put Sammu in the clear. But Jukka could also give an estimate of when Christa left the pub...

"Just after nine," he said. "I was storing her violin behind the bar, and she asked for it back. I said: *A bit early to leave, isn't it, Christa love?* But she just grinned and walked out."

When the barman moved off again, Sammu turned to the detectives: "Are you going to tell me what she's been saying? About our little 'loo escapade' as you so charmingly put it?"

"I don't think you need worry," said Tero. "She won't be pressing charges. She got herself murdered last Friday on the way home from this very pub."

Sammu suddenly appeared to have lost his talent for a quick retort.

Miranda spent much of Monday sifting through the mountain of reports accumulated by the rest of the team. She also checked the numerous messages phoned in by the general public. These included the usual garbage from loony time-wasters, and from psychics promising to divine the name of the murderer by means of 'auras emitted' from an article of the victim's clothing. But everything had to be given consideration. There was always a risk of missing some tiny detail hidden away in that daunting stack which could crack the case wide open.

One piece of information uncovered by the door-to-door enquiries seemed interesting. An elderly neighbour had seen a man leaving Christa's flat during the early hours of Saturday morning. Miranda took what she felt was a well-earned break from all this paperwork, and drove to Roihuvuori to reinterview the woman herself.

Mrs Perkiö turned out to be well into her eighties with a tendency to dither, and Miranda wondered about the reliability of this witness's testimony — especially if she were later subjected to cross-examination in a court of law.

Over a cup of coffee, accepted mostly out of politeness, Miranda asked Mrs Perkiö about the man she'd seen leaving Christa Bäckström's flat two nights earlier.

"No, not exactly *leaving* Miss Bäckström's flat. I tried to explain to that young policeman yesterday. He was very nice, but he did rush me a bit, and sometimes he put words in my mouth I didn't mean to say. You see, I was up in the middle of the night. It's often like that. My back doesn't like lying down too long at a time. Sometimes I go into the kitchen for a cup of tea and play patience at the table."

"What about on Saturday night?"

"It must've been four o'clock in the morning. I wanted to play cards, and I was looking for my reading-glasses. Couldn't find them in any of the usual places, so I went to look in my coat. It was hanging up in the hallway. And then I heard a door bang shut on the landing."

"Whose door was it, Mrs Perkiö?"

"That's the thing, isn't it? I can't be sure. Four of us on every floor. So it could've been any of the neighbours' doors. I went and peeked through the spyhole. Naughty of me, I know, but us foolish old ladies... not enough excitement in our lives. We get curious about the silliest things."

"So what did you see through the spyhole?"

"Not much. But a man came past my door and went on down the stairs. He didn't take the lift. And what seemed a bit strange was he didn't put the lights on either. That's why I couldn't see him clearly."

"Were you wearing your glasses by now?" Miranda asked suspiciously.

"No, I wasn't. But it wouldn't have made much difference. It was so dark — only the street lamps outside shining through the landing window."

"Can you be sure it wasn't a woman?" Miranda said, playing devil's advocate.

"Well, no..." said the old lady hesitantly. "But I *think* it was a man. Then I went into the living room to watch from the front window. But he didn't come out that way. He must've left by the back door, and there's nothing out there — only trees." After a pause, she added: "I suppose it might've been the silver-haired gentleman again."

Miranda was alerted. "Which silver-haired gentleman, Mrs Perkiö?"

"I've seen him twice before. Once from the window when he went off with Miss Bäckström in a car. Then another day I came up in the lift with him. Got a good look at him that time. Tall, quite nice-looking really. What you noticed most was his hair. I don't think he was very old — forty perhaps. It's hard to tell people's ages as you get older yourself. But his hair was completely turned. It was all silvery-white. When we got out of the lift, he went to Miss Bäckström's flat and she let him in."

"Did you hear her say his name?"

Mrs Perkiö looked flustered. "I don't think so. At least, I don't remember it any more if she did."

"Can you tell me when were these two earlier occasions that you saw the silver-haired man?"

"Oh, dear! You ask such difficult questions. I suppose it was two weeks ago. Or three perhaps. Every day's much the same when you're retired and live alone like I do."

Miranda learned nothing more of importance. Mrs Perkiö was unable to give a description of the dark figure on the landing, and her suggestion that it *might've been the silver-haired gentleman* — a perfect descriptive match for Christa's journalist colleague, Kaj Sirén — was obviously only surmise.

But this sighting of someone on the stairs in the early hours so soon after the murder seemed to support the boss's conviction that the murderer had visited the victim's flat. That the mystery man seemed to have left by the back door was also suspicious... unless he hadn't left the building at all. Every male resident of the block — especially those on the floors below Christa's — would need to be scrutinized.

Miranda next decided to pay another visit to the *Hufvudstadsbladet* newspaper office. Relocating the venomous person she'd encountered in the lift was easy, but learning anything else useful from her was another matter. Contrary to Tero's prediction of further indiscretions, she clammed up under direct questioning. Miranda came to the conclusion that it wasn't to avoid giving away how *much* she knew but how *little*. Her earlier attack on Kaj Sirén seemed to have been little more than speculation and personal spleen. However, it drew attention to the possibility that Sirén was holding back on some of the truth. Asking around amongst other members of the office staff, Miranda concluded there probably had been some other-than-professional relationship between Sirén and Christa Bäckström; that it had ended in acrimony — apparently over a job they'd both hoped to get with *Time* magazine — and that Christa had afterwards been leaking ugly stories about her ex-lover to people in high places.

Clearly Sirén warranted a follow-up interview. But, for the time being, that proved impossible. He'd taken several days leave of absence to embark on a freelance project in Lapland and wasn't expected back till Thursday. The rumours Miranda had heard so far didn't justify dragging him back to Helsinki under police escort. She'd have to be patient and let Sirén return in his own good time.

That evening, Nick picked Miranda up in his old Mercedes and drove her to the airport. Rosie arrived on a Finnair flight from Heathrow and emerged from baggage reclaim all smiles and exuberance. Nick had to be satisfied with a quick peck on the cheek before he was left in charge of the luggage trolley and his daughter's precious cello. Then Rosie threw her arms impetuously around her sister's neck. She'd seen her father a mere fortnight ago. The separation from Miranda had been almost three months. Miranda herself realized how much she'd missed her baby-sister. It would be wonderful to have her around the flat again.

The Töölö flat was where they headed next, making a brief 'pit stop' — as Nick referred to it — so that Rosie could drop off her belongings, change out of her travel-weary clothes and freshen up. Their ultimate destination was a pre-booked table at a popular Lebanese restaurant in the city centre where they'd hold a fitting celebration of their family reunion.

Next morning, the person who had made those last three calls to Christa's mobile on the evening of her death got in touch with Pasila HQ. Miranda drove straight to the woman's flat in Haaga.

Anita Söderblom led Miranda into a tidy, conventionally furnished living room where they sat down facing each other across the polished pine coffee table. Miranda categorized her as a prematurely middle-aged thirty-something — frumpishly dressed, with short, straight, mousy hair, and no apparent interest in attempting to enliven her rather plain features with make-up or any other adornment. She was obviously suffering from a heavy cold. Her nose was red and chafed, and she clutched a well-used paper handkerchief. But, even taking into account the poor state of her health, one got the impression this was a woman who'd already adopted the role of a confirmed spinster — whether through choice or necessity was impossible to judge. She seemed shy, even a little nervous, but Miranda detected a spark of higher-than-average intelligence in the eyes that, from time to time, made an effort to engage her own. The extensive library stretching the full height and length of one wall further testified to Anita Söderblom's being a woman of some intellectual substance.

"I'm sorry I didn't call earlier, Inspector," she began. "I started a bout of flu up at my weekend cottage, and decided to stay on an extra day. I only found your message when I got back an hour ago."

"You've heard about Christa Bäckström?"

"Your officer told me when I called this morning, but it was a terrible shock. I spoke to her myself just a few days ago... on Friday evening."

"That's why we were so anxious to get in touch. You called her three times, didn't you — in the space of half an hour?"

"The first time I just phoned to say hello. We hadn't been in touch for months. But Christa was walking home from the metro station. She asked me to call her again in fifteen minutes — so she could settle down on her sofa for a long gossip, she said. But I tried twice later on and there was no answer. In the end I gave up and went to bed."

"How well did you know Christa?"

"We were at school together up in Vaasa. But I was never that close to her. We've met a couple of times for a chat since she came to Helsinki... Not that she was interested in *my* boring little life — well, I can understand that — but she enjoyed telling me all the wonderful things *she'd* been doing. I suppose I'm an attentive listener."

"And did she discuss her problems at work — or problems with colleagues?"

"No, she didn't." Anita seemed a little surprised by the question. "But our conversations were very superficial. It was Christa and Britt-Marie who were the real friends — at least, they spent a lot of time together when we were still at school in Vaasa. Britt-Marie's my twin sister."

Miranda's eyes widened with interest. "Identical?" she asked.

"No, no! Like chalk and cheese: looks, temperament, interests... everything different. But that made it easier growing up together. We never had to compete for the same things."

"So Christa and your sister, Britt-Marie, were close, were they?"

"In a way... but it was rather unbalanced. Britt-Marie's so independent. She always knows where she's going and why. I think that impressed Christa. She wanted to be the same. She seemed to measure her own achievements or lack of them with Britt-Marie's life as a yardstick. But I'm afraid Christa wasn't cut out to be another Britt-Marie. She lacked the originality. She was always going to end up a poor second."

"Maybe your sister knows something about Christa that could help us," Miranda said. "Can you tell me where to reach her?"

"No, I can't! I haven't seen her for over a month, and I don't exactly know where she is."

Miranda frowned in surprise. "Do you mean she's disappeared?"

"In a sense. She's off on another of her adventures. She does these big articles for magazines, colour supplements and the like — travels rough in outlandish places, meeting the people, pitting herself against the elements. The best I can offer you is that she's somewhere in Madagascar."

Miranda was even more astonished: "And is there no way to get in touch with her?"

"Sorry... she just takes her backpack and sets off into the unknown. It's all part of her philosophy. The old-time adventurer turning her back on the modern world."

"Sounds extraordinary," said Miranda, genuinely impressed.

"Eccentric, that's for sure."

"When she *does* turn up, please ask her to contact us."

On the drive back to Pasila, Miranda was in whimsical mood: *Wonder if the department would finance a trip to Madagascar? I could follow up on this lead with my own backpack... and go looking for the missing Ms Söderblom.*

Earlier that morning, a second suspicious-looking letter addressed to 'The Ainola Residence' was spotted by the Järvenpää post-office sorter who'd handled the original one. After all the rigmarole last week of having her fingerprints taken, she'd alerted the local police. By the time Miranda returned to the Pasila office, the letter had arrived and was being studied by Tero and Ylenius.

In outward appearance the envelope was the same, except that the reference to the Homicide Unit had been dropped from the addresses. And the letter inside — again written in Swedish — followed the earlier format:

Roihuvuori
Friday, 31st March

Symphony No 2 in D major

Dear A.
Such a vision of wonder: the slow movement of a symphony —
malaise, mould and maggots — fortissimo strings muted and
fading to silence. Oh, but the godlike power of it all! To be
carried away in joy by the surging rush of strings.

At the bottom, beside the initials *JS*, was another boldly inked fingerprint.

This time, nobody bothered to rush up to the fourth-floor lab. They were sure whose print it would be.

"How many symphonies did Sibelius write?" asked Tero.

"Seven," Miranda said, barely above a whisper.

II

Andantino con moto, quasi allegretto

"**B**eatrice! Haven't you forgotten something?"

Beatrice Gröndahl was on her way out through the main doors, laughing uproariously with two girls of about the same age. Turning round, she shrieked in embarrassment and ran back to retrieve her violin case from the outstretched arm of her teacher.

"Thanks, Miss Hållman. See you next Tuesday!"

"Please try to be on time for a change, Beatrice. Six o'clock — not five or ten past!"

"Yes, Miss Hållman. Sorry!" And, with that, Beatrice dashed off after her friends. Mikaela grabbed her arm and pulled her into step.

"Bea, I was just telling Lotta about last Sunday. Hairy Henrik came round to my place. A surprise visit. Thought I'd die. Suddenly there he was walking up our drive, and I'd been vegging out all day in front of the telly. Looked a total wreck. Wearing the scuzziest clothes possible. No make-up. Hadn't even brushed my hair since I got up. Total disaster. So darling bro' kept Hairy talking about ice-hockey or something — so I'd have time to hide in my room and salvage the mess."

"Personally, I wouldn't've bothered," said Beatrice. "A boy should love me as much when I'm slobbing. Still the same me underneath, isn't it?"

"You liar, Bea! Not even *you've* got that much self-confidence."

"Maybe you've just been hanging with the wrong boys," teased Beatrice.

Lotta, the third girl, cut in: "Hey, I never told you, did I? 'Bout this awesome fella I met last summer on the ferry back from the zoo. He ended up walking me all the way home. That was the fab bit. But the next day he turns up on our doorstep completely unannounced."

"Doesn't sound like a problem," said Mikaela.

"The problem was I didn't hear the door bell. Mum goes and let's him in, brings him into the hall, and just bangs on my door. No explanation. No word of warning. I come bursting out of my room, and there he is... And there *I* am, in a filthy old shirt of my Dad's, wearing this face pack with just my eyes and mouth showing through and looking like a total zombie!"

The other two exploded with laughter.

"He must've thought I'd stepped off an alien spaceship."

"So what happened?"

"He did an instant flit. Never saw him again."

"Poor you! Hey, there's the bus. Let's run for it!"

The number 18 braked to a halt at the last moment, and the three girls piled on, hugging their instruments close to their bodies. The driver gave a friendly grin and waved them through without checking their bus passes. Mikaela collapsed into a single seat near the front, while the other two huddled round her, clinging on as the bus accelerated away.

"What about Saturday? You going?" asked Lotta.

"Haven't decided," said Beatrice.

"Luscious Lars will be there."

"More your department than mine."

"What do you mean? You couldn't keep your eyes off him last week!"

"Hey, Bea!" said Mikaela, prodding her arm. "Have you heard about Lotta phoning his mum?"

Beatrice looked blank.

"Thought not. You see, Lotta posed as a radio programme researcher and spent twenty minutes asking Lars's mum all these weird questions: like what are your son's interests, and what are his favourite bands, and where does he hang out, and all kinds of other stuff."

"Are you totally gaga?" laughed Beatrice, delighted. "That's got to be illegal!"

"Who cares?" said Lotta. "She didn't suspect a thing. And now I've got all the gen. He doesn't stand a chance. I can pull all the right levers. Press all the right buttons. He's in the bag."

"But you haven't even spoken to him yet, you total wimp!"

The girls went on giggling and taunting each other noisily. They were all speaking Swedish: presumably the language they also used at home and at school. And they were drawing a lot of attention from other people on the bus — especially from the male passengers. Not surprising, because they made a pretty trio. Beatrice in particular was striking, with her sultry Latin-American looks and thick raven hair.

Soon Lotta pressed the bell and jumped off the bus with a breezy wave. A couple of stops later, Mikaela did the same, leaving Beatrice the empty seat.

Towards the back of the vehicle was someone else who would normally have left by now. He'd missed his stop. But that didn't concern him. He was ready to sit here until the dark-haired girl with the violin reached her destination. It was suddenly very important to know where she was going.

Several minutes before next morning's briefing session with the rest of the team, a more detailed forensic report arrived on Ylenius's desk concerning both the second murder scene in Roihuvuori and Christa Bäckström's flat. He invited Miranda and Tero into his office for a preview.

The report offered no new leads. The condom they'd brought back from O'Malley's pub was the same brand and 'flavour' as inferred from the vaginal swabs taken at Christa's autopsy. This, however, gave no evidence as to whether the murderer himself had performed penetration. The report dryly pointed out that the killer could simply have the same 'taste' in condoms as Christa's trysting partner an hour or so earlier in the pub.

A few unidentified partial handprints and fingerprints had been found in the bathroom and the bedroom. But, as none of them looked fresh, it was impossible to prove or disprove that someone had visited Christa's flat on the night of the murder.

"The elderly neighbour claims she saw a man leaving at around 4 am," said Miranda. "Christa died around 10 pm. So, if it *was* the murderer, what the hell had he been doing in there all that time?"

"More trophy hunting?" suggested Tero.

"For six hours or more?"

"Perhaps he had a lie-down on her bed," said Tero, "and did a Goldilocks."

"No, we didn't find any bowls of porridge in the kitchen," countered Miranda.

Tero's eyebrows rose. Miranda rarely picked up on his little wisecracks.

"A likely explanation," said Ylenius, "is he waited till the early hours before going in — so there'd be less chance of the neighbours spotting him."

"In that case," Miranda probed, "did he go away and come back again, or did he just stay in the neighbourhood? Better check if any of the locals noticed someone hanging about from ten o'clock onwards."

"I was talking to one of our technical people," said Tero. "They've been checking Bäckström's computer. Found masses of text files and pictures — which you'd expect of a photo journalist — and they're categorizing and cataloguing them for us. A mammoth job. But so far nothing significant's turned up. Except when they looked at her email programme the whole contents of the 'sent mail' folder had been erased."

"Could Christa have done that herself?" asked Ylenius.

"It's possible," Tero considered. "I go through my email every week or so and chuck out all the junk. But to get rid of everything — one hundred percent — strikes me as odd."

"I erased *my* 'in-box' by mistake a couple of months ago," admitted Ylenius. "Perhaps the same happened to Christa."

"Can the techs recover the lost data?" Miranda asked.

Tero gave a qualified nod. "If it's been erased recently it's probably still intact somewhere on the hard disk. We've been promised a hard copy if they can rescue it."

Miranda and Rosie were working their way through the crush of people in the corridor outside the Wegelius Hall when Phillip bounced up from nowhere — a more subdued Adrian in tow. Of course, Miranda had known this would happen. The Englishmen had said how keen they were to attend all of her father's lectures. But she was still disconcerted by this rather public encounter with Adrian.

Fortunately Phillip took over the situation with characteristic panache: "Miranda! Wonderful to see you again. Looking in the peak of health..." *Shameless liar!* thought Miranda, feeling thoroughly worn down by recent events. "...But who's this? Could it be the long lost sister returned from the shores of beloved Blighty? Allow me to introduce myself. I'm Phillip Burton," he informed Rosie, bowing slightly. "Regrettably, I don't recall if anyone's apprised me yet of *your* name..."

"Well, everyone calls me Rosie," came the smiling, if somewhat bewildered response. "My real name's Rosalind."

"Ah, yes!" Phillip beamed. "Further evidence of the Williephile in your family."

"Sorry? The *what* in my family?"

"The Shakespeare enthusiast — the believer in the Bard. I'm talking about your pater, my dear!"

"I see!" laughed Rosie. "Yes, I suppose you're right. I've heard Mummy wasn't too keen on the name Miranda at first..." She nodded towards where her sister and Adrian had removed themselves by several feet, and were talking earnestly... "You see," Rosie went on, "Mummy was afraid the average Finn would just think of a cabaret belly-dancer or something. But Daddy persuaded her in the end, of course. He absolutely adores *The Tempest.* As far as I know, Mummy liked *my* name from the start."

"And who wouldn't?" enthused Phillip. "*What's in a name?* I believe someone once asked, but I'm *enraptured* with Rosalind. 'Tis a *delightful* appellation. I shall carve it on every tree!"

Rosie laughed out loud at this silliness.

"Sorry to interrupt the fun," said Miranda, returning, "but the lecture's about to start. Let's grab some seats."

"In October 1907, the famous Austrian conductor and composer Gustav Mahler visited Helsinki; and, during his brief stay, spent some time in the company of the local national hero, Jean Sibelius. Writing home to his wife, Gustav remarked: *Like all Finns, Sibelius seems to be a particularly sympathetic person.* Mahler's comments on his host's music, however, were far from flattering: *These national geniuses are the same everywhere*, he complained. *They turn up in*

Russia and Sweden — and Italy is overrun with such whores and their ponces. Strong stuff! And he went on to describe a Sibelius work he'd heard at a concert the previous evening as mere 'kitsch' spiced up with 'a kind of national sauce'. The concert in question had, in fact, only featured orchestral 'pops' and bagatelles — none of which offered a genuine picture of the composer's originality and artistic reach. But had Mahler never heard *En Saga,* or the Second Symphony, or the Violin Concerto? Or even *The Swan of Tuonela*? Apparently not! And this disparaging indifference towards Sibelius's talent — whether or not inspired by Mahler, I cannot say — seems to have taken permanent root in the German-speaking world, where popular respect for the Finn has never matched that found in the Nordic or Anglo-Saxon countries.

* ["Well, such were Mahler's impressions of this historic meeting between the two musical titans," continued Dr Lewis. "But what of Sibelius's own? At the time of their encounter, Jean was forty-two years of age. But it wasn't until reaching his late sixties that he recorded in writing his recollections of a conversation the two composers had shared on the subject of 'The Symphony'. Sibelius tells us how he himself expressed a personal admiration for the symphonic style — for its severity of form and the profound logic that could create an interrelationship between all of the motives. Mahler declared that, on the contrary, the symphony could not be so confined. It must be 'like the world' and should 'encompass everything'. The reliability of this anecdote, told at a distance of a quarter of a century, must carry an element of doubt. Sibelius seems to have had a tendency to dress up or modify his memories (albeit unconsciously) if the events in question conflicted with what might or should've been. Nevertheless, these two opposing views of the symphonic ideal — Mahler's and Sibelius's — have entered classical music lore, and are much quoted. If we look at the exact timing of this supposed conversation, we realize that both composers were expressing their current preoccupations...] *

"Mahler had recently completed his mammoth, all-singing, all-dancing, bells-and-whistles Eighth Symphony. And Sibelius had, the previous month, conducted the first performance of his own, decidedly unpretentious, C major symphony: the Third, opus 52." Dr Lewis sat down at the piano and casually — almost as if thinking aloud — picked out the latter work's opening four or five bars with his left hand.

* ["*Severity of form and a profound logic that creates an interrelationship between each and every motif,*" he quoted again. "This manifesto of Jean Sibelius does indeed apply to his Third Symphony. But what does Sibelius really mean by the term 'severity' — in reference, that is, to symphonic form? The first movement of the Third employs 'sonata form' of a clarity which had scarcely been heard since the time of Beethoven's Eighth, nearly a hundred years earlier. In such a context, severity appears to mean self-disciplined structural control. It means conciseness. It indicates a dissatisfaction with the loose, subjective, programmatic and pseudo-programmatic symphonies of many of the nineteenth-century Romantic composers, with their story-telling and scene painting. 'My symphonies are music,' wrote Sibelius. 'They have no literary basis. I am not a literary composer and, for me, music begins where words cease.' "] *

Miranda shifted position on her hard wooden seat. As the four of them had taken their places, she'd pointedly allowed Phillip and Rosie to file into the row between herself and Adrian. She regretted it now. How petty it must have looked! *Oh, for heaven's sake, Miranda, forget all this nonsense and listen to the lecture!*

"Classical sonata form," her father was explaining, "as practised by Joseph Haydn, for example, is an architectural shaping of the musical materials which can most often be found in the *first* movement of a symphony, sonata or string quartet...

* [It achieves its effect by generating a tension between passages of tonal stability and passages of tonal instability. By tonal stability, I mean a situation where the listener is aware of a clear and fixed tonal centre which everything in the musical action seems to revolve around. If the music is predominantly in C major or C minor, that tonal centre is the note C. There may be occasions when the music sidesteps or slips into other key areas — but these are no more than fleeting, temporary modulations — they pull elastically away from the real key centre only to be tugged back again. The listener is not allowed to 'lose sight' of the *true* centre of gravity."

Swiveling round to face the piano keyboard, Nick Lewis played the opening section of Haydn's C major Piano Sonata, No 60. Every so often, he paused abruptly and, in the ensuing silence, sang the tonic note C.

"This is the acid test," he explained. "If you can stop the music and every time locate the same note as the centre of gravity, the musical passage is in a state of tonal stability. But how does this fit into the larger sonata form process?

"A typical sonata-form movement passes through three clear stages: the 'exposition', the 'development' and the 'recapitulation'." To emphasize their importance, Dr Lewis repeated the three terms, allowing a pregnant pause after each one.

" The first of these, the 'exposition', can *itself* be subdivided. It begins by presenting one or more thematic ideas — generally referred to as the 'first subject group' — all of which lie in a more or less stable tonal environment. They establish the main key centre of the movement. Then comes the so-called 'transition' where the integrity of the initial key centre is undermined and a *new* centre of gravity is suggested. A further theme or collection of themes is usually introduced at this point — referred to technically as the 'second subject group' — and these themes revolve around that new tonal centre, aiming to convince the listener of its validity: something which may not be fully achieved until the very end of the exposition process."

Dr Lewis returned to the Haydn piano sonata and played the whole of its two-minute exposition, simultaneously calling out the various events as they happened.

"In Haydn's time, the convention was to repeat the whole exposition; but, later on, in the nineteenth century , composers usually preferred to move straight on to the next stage: the 'development' section. The development is the *central* portion of the movement and is characterized by a state of tonal *instability*. The key centre is continually changing and no one centre of gravity is allowed to fully establish itself before being swept away by the next. There may be small islands of repose on the way, but the predominant feeling is one of restlessness, of travelling ever onwards, of exploring a succession of new and contrasting musical territories." Nick Lewis began to play the Haydn sonata's development section, naming and singing the tonal centres as they changed. Then suddenly he stopped...

"Now comes one of the most important moments in the whole sonata-form structure. The restlessness, the rootlessness gives way to a growing feeling of suspense, an awareness that there is some kind of gravitational pull drawing the music towards a specific goal.

And the goal, when it arrives over the temporal horizon, will turn out to be the same tonal centre that began the whole movement. To emphasize this fact, it is nearly always stamped with the very same first-subject-group thematic material as at the beginning of the exposition. This whole process of rediscovering our original centre of gravity is called 'the return' and it initiates the third section: the 'recapitulation'. Here both the first- and second-subject-group material is restated — not necessarily in the same order — but all of it now rotating more or less around the same single centre of gravity. The transition passage which, in the exposition, drew the music toward a different tonal centre will this time only chase its own tail. The recapitulation and indeed the whole sonata-form movement ends with a satisfying and irrefutable confirmation of the 'home key' — which, in our present example, is C major."

To illustrate the return to the recapitulation, Dr Lewis picked up the Haydn movement again, and played the piece through to its conclusion.

Having outlined the principles, the speaker went on to show how the first movement of Sibelius's Third Symphony followed the same procedures — with an exposition, a development and a recapitulation. He was particularly enthusiastic about the *economical but resounding return to the home key* at the end of the development section, which he felt was *comparable to any achieved by Haydn or Beethoven*.

"But what about the rest of the symphonic creed that Sibelius expressed to Mahler: the profound logic that creates an interrelationship between each and every motif? In fact, we've already seen it in the first movement of his *Second* Symphony. And we'll find it again here."

Dr Lewis now proposed an experiment. He took the opening theme of the Third Symphony and played it at the piano in a modified form that, although still recognizable, adopted the rhythmic characteristics of the main *second*-subject theme. When he followed that with the second-subject theme *itself*, the audience could hardly fail to recognize the melodic kinship.] *

Miranda suddenly had the sensation she was being watched. Glancing to her left, she locked eyes with Zoltán Szervánszky seated on the far side of the hall. He stared for several seconds longer, and then, with supercilious deliberation turned his face back towards the stage. Miranda, refusing to be intimidated, did likewise.

* ["This kinship between the first and second subject themes is clearly not an unconscious accident," her father continued. "Towards the end of the development section, Sibelius tries a rhythmic experiment similar to mine with fragments of the opening theme — step by step, transforming it back to its *original* rhythmic form just in time for the beginning of the recapitulation."

The lecture proceeded through the remaining two movements of the symphony and, on reaching the majestic second half of the finale, Dr Lewis introduced another important point...

"This passage offers a striking example of Sibelius's tendency towards what I can only describe as 'minimalism'. The 'minimalist' school of composition which appeared in the 1960s and is exemplified by such American figures as Steve Reich, Terry Riley, Phillip Glass and John Adams typically employs the hypnotic mantra-like repetition of a melodic cell which gradually transforms itself over extended periods of time. The concept of maximum exploitation of minimal thematic material is not, however, entirely new to Western music. Earlier examples spring to mind: Guillaume Dufay's *Gloria ad modum tubae*, the first movement of Bach's *6th Brandenburg Concerto*, the first minutes of Beethoven's *Grosse Fuge*, and the *scherzo* of Bruckner's Eighth. Sibelius's persistent use of a single short motif at the end of his Third Symphony fits the same minimalist pattern, and we shall see him carry the idea to its most telling fulfilment in his very last orchestral work: the symphonic poem, *Tapiola*."] *

Shortly before nine o'clock, Dr Lewis was ready to sum up...

"The Third Symphony has never received the public attention it deserves. This is Sibelius indulging himself in a 'neoclassical' work more than a decade before the neoclassical movement — that we generally associate with Stravinsky or Hindemith — had been officially invented! However, it's as if Sibelius needed to get this out of his system... and, having proved to himself and everybody else that he could carry it out successfully, he headed off in a more radical direction. Indeed, nothing could be more radical than his following symphony: the Fourth in A minor — and that, ladies and gentlemen, is the subject of next Wednesday's lecture."

The audience began to disperse, and Miranda was momentarily diverted by a viola-playing friend from the university orchestra.

While they were exchanging news in the aisle, Miranda spotted Zoltán Szervánszky drifting toward the exit. He was obviously engaged — so she noted — in *charming the knickers off* an attractive young blonde he seemed only just to have encountered. That was probably why he paid Miranda no further attention.

Nick and the others had already congregated down at the front of the hall, and when Miranda joined them, Rosie turned to her gleefully.

"It's all settled! Dinner at our place on Friday evening. Daddy's in town, and Phillip and Adrian are coming too. You'll be free, won't you? You absolutely *have* to be! I'll do the cooking, of course."

Miranda hadn't forgotten Ylenius's pronouncement about consorting with suspects. But what could she do? It was her sister's home too. She could hardly dictate who Rosie was allowed to invite to dinner. Actually, Miranda was pleased about the timing. It would be useful to have Adrian under surveillance on Friday evening. The last two Fridays had been unpleasantly eventful and... Well, heaven forbid anything similar should happen again! But sitting round a dinner table with friends would give Adrian an unequivocal alibi.

"I'm not sure yet, Rosie," said Miranda. "I'll make it if I can."

The next few days of the investigation were productive only in the sense of checking alibis and eliminating some potential suspects: men, for example, who lived in Christa's neighbourhood or shared her work place.

Kaj Sirén finally returned from Lapland on the Friday morning flight from Rovaniemi. When he heard the police had been trying to get in touch, he called Miranda, and she immediately invited him to Pasila HQ. Tero joined them for the interview.

"Last time we met," Miranda began, "you told us, Mr Sirén, that you were at home alone last Friday evening."

"That's correct," he replied.

"Can you please cast your mind back, and tell us what you were doing the *previous* Friday evening?"

Sirén seemed disconcerted. "Same thing, I suppose. Went home and went to bed. Why do you...? Hey, is it that Sibelius Monument murder? Am I a suspect for that as well?"

"You also led me to believe your association with Christa Bäckström was purely professional. But there was a good deal more than that going on, wasn't there?"

"Ah, so you've been tuning into the office gossip," he said. The fidgety mannerisms Miranda had noticed at their earlier interview were again much in evidence. Sirén's right foot tapped the floor to some lively music that only he could hear.

"All right! We did have something going on for a while," he said, ruffling one hand through his silvery-grey hair. "But not any of your big romantic stuff. Just a few meals together, a couple of nightclubs, ending up in the same bed from time to time. Neither of us took it seriously."

"Were you ever at her flat in Roihuvuori?" Miranda asked.

"I spent a couple of nights there. And once I took her home in the middle of the day to pick up a camera."

"Did you visit her flat the night she died?"

"Good heavens, no! Why would I do that?"

"Not in the early hours, between 3 and 4 am?"

"I was tucked up at home fast asleep. I had work the next day, didn't I? Look, you're going completely overboard. There was nothing serious between us."

"But weren't you competing for the same job with *Time* magazine?" Tero pressed him. "That must've caused some friction — led to some harsh words."

"No, no! You've been misinformed. There *was* a project up in Lapland, but *Time* had already offered it to *me*. I needed a photographer along, and Christa convinced herself she'd be the one — that at last her photos would get an airing on the pages of a big international magazine. But it didn't work out. *Time* assigned me someone of their own — someone already living up there in the north. Christa decided it was all my fault, of course — that I'd told them she wasn't up to the job. Absolutely untrue. I had no say in the matter."

"Is that when she decided to take revenge?" asked Tero.

"Yes, yes, I can see you've done your homework," said Sirén, "but you're wasting your time. The only thing that happened was she tried easing herself into my boss's good graces — into his boxer shorts too, no doubt. I found out later she'd been saying all kinds of stuff behind my back — like I was taking backhanders from companies to give them publicity in my articles, that I was leaking our best scoops to the competition for a fee. Loads of other bulldroppings."

"Must've got you riled up," prompted Tero.

"Yes, I gave her a ticking-off — the day before she died, it was. I said to her: *Perhaps you're hoping the faeces'll hit the fan. Better watch out it doesn't all fly back in your own face.* Me and the boss've known each other for years. He can tell unwarranted muck-stirring when he hears it. Ask him yourself."

"But surely you resented her behaviour," persisted Miranda, as reluctant as Tero to give up on what had seemed a productive line of enquiry.

"Let's get realistic, shall we?" responded Sirén. "I'm an ordinary sort of bloke. Sure I get annoyed sometimes — like everyone else — but this isn't the kind of thing I go around murdering people for... if that's what you're implying. So she bad-mouthed me! Big deal! It hasn't done me any harm. I sussed out early on she was only hanging round me for what she thought she could get out of it. Why should I care? It was fun while it lasted — especially the bits in bed. All things considered, I've had very little to complain about."

Miranda and Tero stared back. He was making a very convincing case.

"And you asked me about that earlier Friday," Sirén went on, "when that other girl was murdered. Fact is I spent most of it with Christa. We logged in a story at the office at about eight, and then headed off to my place. I ordered a couple of pizzas in and opened a bottle of red wine. It was all going fine till she asked about the *Time* assignment. I had to tell her she wasn't getting it. Didn't expect her to take it quite so badly. Things really went sour after that. Definitely the end of our little affair."

"She walked out on you?" asked Tero.

Sirén nodded.

"Pity you didn't tell us about this earlier!" Miranda complained.

Sirén gave a humourless laugh. "Wouldn't've made any difference. And giving Christa as my alibi's a waste of time. She's hardly in a position to verify it, is she?"

At about seven-thirty that evening, while Rosie was laying the table ready for the arrival of her dinner guests and Miranda was hurriedly changing in an adjoining room, Kaj Sirén — several miles away — was looking forward to a meal of his own. The doorbell to his flat rang vigorously. That would be the pizza delivery boy: Kaj recognized the style. Several times a month, after a busy day at *Hufvudstadsbladet*, he'd phone the local Turkish-owned kebab and pizza place and order one of their excellent *Paradiso* pizzas with ham, blue cheese and pineapple. Grabbing his wallet, Kaj went to answer the door. The dusky-skinned teenager on the doorstep grinned and handed over a large, square cardboard box that felt temptingly warm in Kaj's hands.

"I have the right place this time?" the boy asked cheerfully.

At Kaj's uncomprehending look, the young Turk went on in his pleasantly accented Finnish: "You remember? I try to give you another person's pizza last week. I not look so careful at the address. I think it is for you, like usual."

"Oh, right!" smiled Kaj. On that occasion, he'd staggered from the sofa, awoken from an impromptu but heavy sleep, only to discover the insistent doorbell was a false alarm. The pizza had been ordered by his next-door neighbour.

"Hey, hang on!" exclaimed Kaj. "When *was* that? It wasn't last Friday, was it?"

The delivery boy scratched his head. "Perhaps," he said. "Yes, I am sure now. Friday, just before ten o'clock. I was in a big hurry to end work and meet my girlfriend."

Kaj looked delighted. "I believe," he said, "you've just solved a serious problem for me."

III

Moderato—Allegro (ma non tanto)

"**P**artial to a bit of Gershwin myself," said Phillip. "You know... like *Corgi and Bess* — that charming little opera based on the daily life of the Windsor family."

This elicited a smile from the diners in general, but Rosie ended up spluttering through her food.

"Please, please, Rosie," said Adrian, patting her gently on the back. "Phillip's killing quips aren't worth dying for."

The living-room table had been extended with an extra leaf to accommodate five; and, as promised, Rosie had spent several hours in the kitchen preparing a delicious three-course meal. They were just finishing off the raspberry sorbet in a nest of meringue.

"Heaven forbid I should be the cause of any harm to our fairest Rosalind," said Phillip, "but I do recall reading somewhere that people literally *have* died of laughing."

Miranda remembered her psychology studies: "Yes, they're documented in the medical literature. Like the librarian in Philadelphia who suddenly got a terrible laughing fit. She was shaking all over — just couldn't stop herself. It went on for an hour and a half. Finally she collapsed, went into a coma, and was dead within twenty-four hours."

"Extraordinary," said Nick. "What on earth caused it?"

"She'd had a stroke, and bled into an area of the brain associated with the laughter reflex."

"The case I heard was even more bizarre," said Phillip. "Don't know if it's true, but there was a funeral, and they were just lowering some poor woman into her grave when the husband started laughing

148

his head off. Shocking behaviour! Everybody knew the couple had loathed each other for years... but, to carry on like that — in front of all the mourners! Turned out the same as your librarian: a brain haemorrhage. He ended up dead himself within a few days. So you could say," Phillip added wickedly, "that his wife had the last laugh."

"That's a horrible story, Phillip!" Rosie reprimanded him.

"Forgive me; please do!" said Phillip penitently. "I solemnly pledge to refrain from any more graveyard humour."

"Anyone for coffee?" Rosie asked promptly. So everyone trooped into the kitchen bearing plates, bowls, serving dishes and empty wine bottles. Rosie shooed them out again: "Thanks," she said, "but loading the dish-washer's a one-person job."

Back in the living room with the last remnants of the wine, Miranda and her father settled down on the sofa, while Phillip and Adrian took opposing armchairs.

"The workings of the brain are an intriguing mystery," said Adrian, resuming the earlier topic in Rosie's absence. "How can so much be contained in a lump of jelly no bigger than a grapefruit? Everything we've learned, everything we've done in our lifetime — it's all in there somewhere. Faces, for example. We recognize a person we haven't set eyes on for years. And it needn't be an old friend either. It could just be somebody who used to live in the same street. We've never even spoken to the man, but we pick him out instantly. And we must have a lot more faces like his stored away just waiting for the right trigger. Most of them'll *never* be retriggered. So how many are there? Thousands? Tens of thousands? Even hundreds of thousands? Where do we keep them all? How can there possibly be room?"

"What fascinates me," Nick joined in, "is the concept of 'personality'? We'd prefer to keep the whole thing sacrosanct — our individuality, the way we interact with everyone around us, the choices we make between good and evil. Disconcerting to think it might all just boil down to neuron connections and brain chemistry."

"There was a famous case back in the nineteenth century," said Adrian. "A railway worker had an accident when he was tamping down some explosives for rock-blasting."

"Phineas Gage," said Miranda.

"That's him, and he ended up with the tamping rod shot straight through his head. Went in through his cheek and came out through the top of his skull! The miracle was he survived. But his personality had changed. Before, he'd been friendly, polite, hard-working. But, after the accident, he was impossible — a liar, a cheat, incapable of holding down a job."

"You don't need a serious accident to show personality shifts," said Miranda. "I see a lot of it in my job. You arrest a man for wife-beating, and the next day you see him helping an old lady across the street. Or you meet a wonderful father who pampers his children and reads them bedtime stories, but put him behind the steering wheel of a car and he turns into a selfish, arrogant bully. The list's endless. A different persona for every social occasion. I suppose we all do it to a certain extent, but some cases reach Jekyll and Hyde proportions."

Phillip was gazing absently across the coffee table — whether in Adrian's direction or simply into space was hard to tell.

"Am I boring you, Phillip?" Miranda asked.

"Good heavens, no!" he exclaimed, startled out of his reverie. "Your tale, Madam, would cure deafness."

But Miranda guessed he was only functioning on autopilot.

"Of course, we don't just have social personas," said Nick. "What about our internal ones? The persona that's hidden from everyone else — the one that holds long monologues with itself, or imaginary dialogues with others. You know, constructing a sort of mental future: what we'll say when we see someone next time, what we'd tell the boss if we only had the nerve, putting words into somebody else's mouth — the words we'd like to hear them say back." He tugged, with a habitual gesture, at his wiry, grey beard. "Sometimes, of course, you're rethinking the past — rewriting the script: what you'd say if you got another chance, that cutting retort you weren't quick enough with at the time, things you should've said that might've changed the whole course of your life." His expression darkened slightly. "And the conversations it's too late to hold with those who've passed beyond reach."

Miranda registered his pain, but to distract him, kept the conversation going.

"Imagine," she said, "if there were some kind of magic bugging device that let us listen in on each other's thoughts. My guess is somebody else's mind would turn out a disturbing and mysterious place."

Phillip lifted his long, bony body out of the armchair. "Perhaps now Rosie can use some help in the kitchen," he said, with uncharacteristic brusqueness, and left the room. The others watched as he closed the kitchen door behind him.

"By the way, Miranda," Nick said quietly, "that other quotation you gave me was from the same source. November 1914."

Miranda threw her father a warning glance. She didn't want this subject discussed in present company. But Adrian was already cocking a curious eyebrow.

"Hard to fathom the mentality of someone committing such awful crimes," he went on, oblivious of his daughter's discomfort. "Don't know, darling, how you can deal with it on a daily basis."

Miranda only shrugged, willing him to change the subject. But he placed his empty wine glass on the coffee table without looking her way: "The world's such a violent place, don't you think?"

"Perhaps not," said Adrian. "Most of us come into contact with very little physical violence during our lives. Human interaction's more often peaceful with lots of negotiation, lots of cooperation. Compared to a lot of other species, humans are surprisingly non-violent."

"Doesn't that contradict the traditional wisdom?" said Nick. "Man: the only animal capable of engaging in wars and committing cold-blooded murder."

"But things like that horrify and disgust most of us," said Adrian. "We fixate on them and sensationalize them in the news for the very reason that we're fundamentally pacific. Violence shocks and appals us."

"But isn't it always there beneath the surface?" Nick persisted. "Surely it's only social pressures and fear of the heavy hand of the law — present company excepted," he added, with a paternal smile in Miranda's direction — "it's only external pressures that prevent violence from erupting." Take Bosnia or Kosovo: people who've lived in apparent harmony and tolerance for more than two generations start murdering and raping each other. How's it possible? Could it happen *here*? Could we end up behaving the same way, given the right or, should I say, the wrong circumstances?"

"People do things in a group," Miranda said, "that they'd be incapable of individually. It's the crowd mentality. Two or three's often enough to form a critical mass. They feed off each other's negative emotions — whip themselves up into more and more extreme acts."

Phillip re-entered the room, and started clearing the coffee table — moving the wine glasses to one side.

"And there's what I'd call the 'victim-anonymity principle'," Miranda went on. "If we discount spontaneous attacks of anger or jealousy, it's usually only possible for humans to commit acts of violence on another if the victim's somehow perceived as anonymous. Blanket terms like 'nigger', 'jew', 'whore': they're all designed to dehumanize the target — to distance oneself and provide some kind of self-justification, however spurious."

Rosie was hovering by the door with a tray full of coffee cups: "Do we really have to talk about such horrible stuff? Aren't we supposed to be enjoying ourselves?"

Phillip rushed to take the tray out of her hands, and carry it to the table.

"Quite right, Rosie," he said. "How full of briers is your sister's workaday world! Why don't we talk about *yours* instead."

"Oh, yes," said Miranda contritely, "tell them about your recital next week."

Suddenly all smiles, Rosie said, "Bach's D Minor Cello Suite. On Monday at the Academy. I'm stepping in for someone at the last moment."

"How about giving us a preview?" said Nick, with his trademark grin. "Right now!"

"Yes, yes! Please do!" chorused the other three.

Rosie beamed. "I suppose I should show more modesty and make lots of excuses," she said merrily, "until every one ends up begging me. But I just *love* to play for people — anytime, anywhere!"

"And that," said Phillip, "is our very good fortune."

As soon as they'd finished their coffee, Rosie fetched and tuned her cello, and played them not the D Minor but the D Major suite —

"So you'll all have to come to the concert anyway!" she laughed.

Adrian and Phillip hadn't expected such technical skill and depth of feeling. When Rosie started playing, she seemed to shed her girlish mannerisms and take on *an almost mystical aura*, as Phillip described it to Adrian later. *As if she'd stepped out of a Pre-Raphaelite painting* was Adrian's counter comment. Indeed, her long wavy fair hair, her sensitive narrow face, the delicate, fine-boned shoulders and arms, and her thin, childlike body all contributed to Adrian's allusion.

Rosie performed from memory and with one hundred percent concentration. Her bow arm moved with grace and fluidity. From time to time she leaned forward, as if to catch the whispered intimate secrets of her instrument.

When the last note of the closing *gigue* died away, the others gave her a standing ovation. Rosie gazed around at them each in turn, glowing with delight.

Towards midnight, Adrian cornered Miranda alone in the kitchen. It was obvious what he wanted to suggest, but Miranda pre-empted him.

"Please! Don't ask! I can't! I really can't!"

Adrian turned and stepped back into the living room. "Right, Phillip," he said, "time we were off. Don't want to outstay our welcome, do we?"

* *

~ *It's so hard to understand the motivation. You've got to help me with this.*

~ What's bothering you now?

~ *I just remembered an incident from ages back. You didn't tell me at the time. It came out much later when you were deep in your cups one night... about that poor devil who crossed you in love.*

~ Plenty've done that.

~ *No, this one was special.*

~ Perhaps you're referring to Rapier. Post-graduate structures engineer.

~ Bruce *Rapier, wasn't it? Nothing wrong with the bloke as far as I could tell.*

~ He was a total tosser with the brains of a tree frog.

153

~ *Very popular with the ladies.*

~ Makes you wonder how many female tree frogs there were on the campus.

~ *Your problem was that he fancied the same girl.*

~ You called him as special. He wasn't. But the *girl* was. She went by the intriguing name of Sally Primrose.

~ *As I recall, she was a botanist's wet dream.*

~ A regular country girl. A fresh young bloom from the woody glades of Gloucestershire.

~ *So you decided she was a perfect specimen for picking and pressing between the sheets of your favourite taxonomy manual.*

~ Look, I'd invested a lot of time in getting close to Miss Sally Primrose! Weeks of hard graft! Then this Rapier jerk slips her out from under my nose. Adds her to his *own* collection. And with that obscene smirk on his face all the girls seemed to think was a grade-A Robert Redford smile.

~ *Don't you think you overreacted?*

~ He deserved everything he got. The thought of him engineering her structures was a greater load than I'd been designed to bear.

~ *Giving his name to the police strikes* me *as over the top!*

~ Actually it was his name that suggested the idea in the first place. Seemed so appropriate somehow. And his face had been all over the newspapers.

~ *He didn't do it though, did he?*

~ Of course, he didn't do it! But he was a dead ringer for the Identikit picture. Only took an anonymous call from a public phone box and he was neck-deep in shit.

~ *His own, I shouldn't wonder.*

~ Seems he didn't have a satisfactory alibi. But they only questioned the bastard for forty-eight hours. He got off lightly in my opinion.

~ *Perhaps you'd've preferred to see him banged up for life.*

~ It would never've come to that.

~ *Could you really get so hung up over losing a girlfriend?*

~ Don't tell me you've never felt the same way. I know better than that!

~ *But to carry things to such lengths.*

~ Anybody would've wanted revenge. I just went about it with more imagination…

* *

Throughout Saturday, the team-members working Liisa Louhi's and Christa Bäckström's murders were in a state of suspense. Would this be the third Saturday in a row when a young woman's body was discovered somewhere in the city? Whenever a phone rang in the open-plan office, Miranda found herself straining to hear the first words of the conversation — to reassure herself this wasn't the call they all dreaded. But, apart from Kaj Sirén informing Miranda about his pizza-boy alibi — which checked out — the day was uneventful. Definitely no breakthroughs.

Meanwhile, the technical department had recovered Christa Bäckström's email messages. There were nearly five hundred of them, dating back as far as September of the previous year. Miranda and Tero independently ploughed through the complete sequence, but afterwards agreed they could find nothing that threw any light on Christa's death. Why then had the messages been erased? Was it just an accident — a mistake Christa had made herself?

Long before the day's work ended, Miranda was planning her evening. First she'd go for a run, and then she'd suggest to Rosie they dig out one of their store of board games from the living-room cupboard: something to distract her from the recurrent vision of Adrian's exasperated face in the kitchen yesterday evening.

Beatrice came bursting into the kitchen. "I'm going now, Mum!"

Eva Gröndahl looked up from the evening tabloid and smiled. As so often recently, she was struck by how grown-up her daughter looked: dressed and made-up for the Saturday evening party. Of course, Beatrice wasn't *really* her daughter — not biologically. But Eva had been the girl's surrogate mother for the last twelve years and felt she could never have loved any child more.

Beatrice was from far away — from the other side of the world. Certainly from the other side of Eva's life. So much had changed. Things hadn't worked out as she'd hoped and dreamed. Life had been parsimonious with its gifts and impatient to reclaim too many of them. But she still had Beatrice.

When Erik and Eva applied to the Red Cross as a husband and wife team, they'd volunteered to go anywhere in the world. Had they just been running away? Running from the awful discovery that, after the fifth and most distressing of her miscarriages — just four months before reaching full term — she was now barren? They would now never be able to have a child together.

Erik had done his best to comfort her, but his desolation was as palpable as her own. Perhaps it would offer some solace to redirect their parental yearnings into a more abstract and idealistic arena: to offer their medical and nursing skills to the world at large. That was how they'd found themselves in Nicaragua.

To an extent, their tactic succeeded. Conditions on the edge of the jungle were harsh, especially for a Nordic couple used to a cooler climate and first-world sanitation. The work was arduous and frustrating, but it gave them little time to consider their own misfortunes. They were surrounded by so much genuine suffering: so many people who needed their assistance, and for whom they could make a difference.

Erik and Eva nursed little Beatriz's parents through the last days of an indeterminate tropical illness. They'd done everything in their power to save the couple, but death had claimed its victims within an hour of each other. The beautiful dark-haired child with the enormous brown eyes sat patiently on the floor beside her mother and father, watching the life force drain away — unable to understand the reasons, but with a clear sense of the momentousness of the occasion.

Eva had taken the brand-new orphan to her own tent — to share her own hammock and mosquito net. Over the next days a bond formed. The small girl followed Eva around during the daytime and slept soundlessly beside her at night. She began to perform small unsolicited errands: fetching water for Eva's patients, holding Eva's notebook and pencil.

Some evenings, Erik would sing to little Beatriz in his soft baritone voice. She'd sit and listen politely, showing no obvious emotion, and then climb quietly into Eva's hammock to curl up and fall asleep.

Eva would never forget that first smile. Erik was in one of his sillier moods, entertaining the child with imitations of various animals — performing all of the appropriate noises and actions. Suddenly he placed his palms on the ground and raised himself upside-down into a vertical position, walking precariously around for several seconds before losing his balance and falling in an untidy heap. Beatriz's face began to light up with a transfiguring smile... and, before long, an infectious laugh came gurgling to the surface. Eva knew she was seeing the true person for the first time. The real Beatriz had broken through the tragedy and, as tears of joy formed in her own eyes, she picked up the little girl and hugged her.

The adoption process was complicated and took almost a year. But eventually, having completed their current contract, Erik and Eva returned to Finland with their precious human bundle. Her name was officially changed from Beatriz to the more Swedish-sounding Beatrice; and, because they could only guess at the child's age having been about three when they first took charge of her, an official date of birth had to be fabricated. They chose May 2nd, the estimated delivery date for the last of their own half-children that had failed to survive.

"Okay, darling!" Eva said to the girl bobbing effervescently at the kitchen door. "Will you be back by ten-thirty?"

Beatrice pulled a face. "Mum, do I have to?"

"Well, eleven at the latest. If it gets any later and you have to come home on your own, for heaven's sake call me! I'll pick you up in the car."

Beatrice shrugged and disappeared with a quick wave. Seconds later, Eva heard the apartment door slam.

*   *   *

[10.39 pm; Saturday, 8th April]

Oh, bliss! Oh, heaven! I have to keep telling myself until I believe it. It's really going to happen. Not just another disappointment. Think, Hans! My gorgeous, clever Hans! Now we'll see each other every day. How can I wait till August? Well, we've survived this far. Suppose we can hold on a bit longer. Wish I'd remembered to recharge my mobile. Still, only five minutes to home. Then I can call and tell you the glorious news. Wonder how Mum's going to take it. She'll probably try and stop me. But I won't let her. This is too important, and it's my *life after all! Oh, Hans, I hope you haven't found that email yet. I wish I hadn't sent it. I want you to hear directly from me. I want to hear your reaction with my own ears! Did you go straight home as promised? You knew I was expecting to find out today. Surely your concert's over by now.*

Ours went fantastically — apart from that jerk Zoltán afterwards. Why did I go and accept a lift from him*? He's creepy. Of course, it made the journey quicker. Obvious, though, what he had on his mind. Couldn't keep his hands to himself. Think again, octopus! The last man on earth, etc. Really put his nose out of joint when I told him about you. He had to get all snide about my chances in Amsterdam. Said they'd never take anyone like me. Now he can have his disjointed nose rubbed in it as well.*

But who cares? He probably can't help being a total moron. Impossible to be in a bad mood with anybody *right now. Though I'm wondering if I should've taken the long way round and kept to the roads. It's getting spooky under all these trees — and with all the terrible things happening lately... But Hans, my darling Hans, don't be angry with me! I just* couldn't *wait a moment longer than necessary to share the news with you. And there's no need to worry. Nothing could possibly go wrong this wonderful evening. Tonight I feel invulnerable!*

Was it really about to happen? Was he really going to do this? He'd watched himself, as though from a great height, assembling the additional equipment — carefully, methodically, over a period of several days — convincing himself it was all a theoretical exercise detached from any practical reality. He'd never actually follow through, would he? Yet here he was, heart in mouth, stomach churning with excitement, and the girl walking towards him in the semi-darkness. She was taking exactly the route he'd predicted, and his timing had been perfect. Well, he could always stop before the end. He needn't let the game run its full course. He could take things just so far and then... But, scarcely below the surface — certainly nowhere as deep as any subconscious layer — he knew that, once begun, nothing could stop him from carrying the process through to its conclusion. Her fate would no longer be within his control.

She saw him approaching along the path, obviously a man's figure from the height and bulk. She reassured herself there could be no danger — that he was perfectly harmless — perhaps even one of her own neighbours walking this popular pedestrian route between two residential suburbs. But she gave him a wide berth, taking steady, controlled steps, her gaze fixed on the gravelled path a few yards ahead to avoid any suggestion of eye contact.

He didn't change course. He kept more or less to his side of the path and, as they passed at a distance of several feet, she realized she was holding her breath. *Oh, this was silly!* She forced herself not to glance over her shoulder and make sure he wasn't turning back. If she'd done so, there might still have been some chance of escape. But she didn't. And, in one easy movement, he'd grasped her from behind, applying pressure to her throat with the inside of his elbow. For the moment his arm and the knife were enough to subdue her — to ensure submission. The noose would come later, when he had total control, when he could take his time.

She didn't attempt to scream. The dull glint of sharp metal close to her right eye was threat enough. The quiet, mildly gloating words spoken into her hair as he dragged her into the trees were redundant. Yes, she'd behave compliantly. Yes, she realized she had no choice. He'd do what he had to do and then, please God, he'd let her go.

*   *   *

Symphony No 4
in A minor

I

Tempo molto moderato, quasi adagio

"**W**hat happened to *you* last night, my elusive friend?"

Phillip's question seemed to embarrass Adrian. "We didn't make any definite plans, did we?"

It was Sunday afternoon, and they'd just sat down with their coffees at a pavement café on Hesperiankatu: a dual carriageway whose central reservation, lined with tall horse chestnuts, also served as a park. The weather was gloriously warm... the first real day of spring — perhaps one could say of summer — and the population of Helsinki were out in force to enjoy it.

"I thought we'd left the whole thing open," Adrian said. "I dug myself in at the Academy working on some sound samples. Hope it didn't put you out."

"Oh, don't concern yourself. I'm not in the habit of playing wallflower. No tears shed beside the phone waiting for that special call from that special boy. Went out and cruised a few bars. Hit a couple of discos. No problem!"

"Any success?"

"I'm not complaining," Phillip said, with a fleeting, satyric smile. "Wonderful time of year this! In the winter one can almost forget how many beautiful girls there are filling the Helsinki streets — when they're all wrapped up in their hats and scarves and fleecy jackets. But a sudden warm day and everything comes off. Absolutely breathtaking!" He took a long sip of coffee. "So, Adrian, now you've had a couple of days to reflect, tell me your impressions of the fair Rosalind? A marvellous introduction on Friday, don't you think?"

They'd shared a taxi from the dinner party with Nick. He'd dropped each of them off home separately, on the way to his own place in Munkkiniemi. This was the first real chance they'd had to discuss the occasion.

"Rosie's playing's a knockout," said Adrian. "She's amazingly talented."

"Isn't she just? Somehow she reminds me of your darling sister Theresa."

"Mmm... the same thing occurred to me. But where's the similarity?"

"That sunny smile, perhaps," suggested Phillip, "and the girlish spontaneity."

"Rosie's a ray of sunshine, all right. But Theresa also has a penetrating intelligence. I don't want to undervalue Rosie — she's very charming — but, well... she doesn't exactly come across as a super-intellect."

"Oh, I don't know. She laughs at my jokes," said Phillip.

"That's what I meant."

"Well, of course, you're right. The Rosalind of *As You Like It* is one of Shakespeare's most streetwise female characters — not that they had many streets in the Forest of Arden. She's sharp, witty, quick on her feet, and with more than a dash of feminist daring. Perhaps Nick should've named his daughters in reverse."

"Tricky to know in advance. I suppose any newborn could look like a Miranda or a Rosalind "

"I'm sure *I* never did," said Phillip. "Although, they do say I was a very pretty baby. Oh, *please* refrain from making any contemporary comparisons. My beauty's been transformed, that's all — remodelled into a more spiritual form. And, talking of spiritual forms," he gave a sharp intake of breath, "take a look at the legs on *that* one!"

Adrian followed Phillip's gaze to the street's central reservation where a tall girl with straight blonde hair halfway down her back and a tight skirt halfway up her thighs was walking a well-groomed Afghan hound between the trees. On this summery day, Adrian was ready to indulge his friend's little quirks, and made a few appreciative noises.

"The *girl's* legs aren't bad, *either*!" added Phillip.

But Adrian wanted to change the subject: "I think I might ask Rosie to collaborate with me," he said, "on a solo cello sonata. I made a few sketches for one last summer. Could be a good moment to resurrect them. I'd like to put a contact mike on the cello and use electronic effects to modify its sound. I mean the kind of things you normally associate with electric guitars: chorusing, overdrive, wah-wah — stuff like that. What do you think? Should I ask her?"

"I really cannot see her turning you down," said Phillip.

"Okay, I'll bring it up after the Bach recital tomorrow," Adrian concluded.

"As long as you're still motivated to compose, I suppose things can't be going too badly," said Phillip.

"Meaning?"

"Meaning, Adrian, you've been looking peaky lately."

"You don't look so wonderful yourself," Adrian retaliated.

"That's just a hangover from last night. Any improvement on the Miranda front?"

"Let's not get into that!"

"Hey, I don't relish the prospect of watching you fall apart like you did last autumn."

"It's nowhere near that serious."

"I detect the warning signs."

"She still thinks I did it. I'm still her prime suspect."

"Surely not," said Phillip. "I furnished you with a perfectly good alibi for *both* murders. What more could she want?" He seemed genuinely troubled by Adrian's dilemma. "Life can be a real bastard, can't it? But we don't have to suffer in silence. Don't you ever feel a need to get things off your chest? All the stuff that's keeping you awake at night? You must know what I'm talking about."

"You mean, do I feel a need to confess my sins?"

"I don't know... well, perhaps that *is* what I mean."

"So, now *you* think I did it *too*!"

"I'm only talking theoretically, Adrian. We've all got dark secrets somewhere — skeletons hidden in the depths of our personal cupboards. Don't you sometimes crave the relief of getting your most destructive worries out in the open and confiding in someone you trust?"

"What's your point, Phillip?"

"I'm not actually sure myself. Expect I'm just gibbering." He gave a sheepish grin. "No more coffee for me. Time for something less stimulating. How about if we find a place where they serve a large and very cold draught of beer."

Most of Monday, Miranda was engulfed in paperwork. She'd set herself the task of reading and cross-referencing every statement collected by the investigative team over the last week. These included door-to-door enquiries within a five-hundred-yard radius of Christa Bäckström's home; also the screening of Christa's work-mates and neighbours, and her fellow metro travellers on the evening she died. Miranda could have delegated all this drudgery, but she was anxious that no important lead be overlooked. In fact, there had been numerous sightings of a suspicious-looking character in the vicinity of Christa's flat — both on the night of her murder and during the preceding week. Unfortunately, the witnesses were unable to agree on whether he was tall and dark, or short and fair; on foot, or sitting in a large red (or could it have been a small blue?) car; wearing a dark-green tracksuit, which might've been a light-blue denim jacket; etc, etc.

Miranda stuck it out till 7 pm. Then, too late to go home and change for Rosie's recital, she drove straight to the Sibelius Academy R-block and squeezed through the concert hall doors just as the usher was closing them. Adrian, Phillip and her father were on the far side. They'd obviously saved an extra place, but it was too late to join them. Her sister was already emerging from the wings. Rosie played the D Minor Suite with spontaneous warmth and intensity — especially the slow *Prelude* and *Sarabande* movements — and she brought out the implied contrapuntal lines in the first *Minuet* with astounding clarity. It was clear to Miranda that she'd made important strides in London.

There were two other items on the programme. But, afterwards, Rosie's family and friends whisked her off for a celebratory drink. She was thrilled when Adrian proposed they collaborate on a new solo cello sonata. She bounced up and down like a six-year-old and leaned across the table to give him a thank-you hug. Adrian seemed touched and gratified by her enthusiasm.

"And I have a proposal of my own," Rosie smiled. "This one's for everyone! Let's go to Estonia next weekend — all five of us. We could take the hydrofoil on Saturday afternoon, stay a couple of nights in Tallinn, and come back on Monday morning."

Phillip was instantly in favour. Nick agreed it was a great idea, but he'd already committed himself elsewhere for the coming Sunday.

Adrian and Miranda said nothing.

"Oh, come on, Adrian!" said Phillip. "You've never been to Estonia. This is a golden opportunity to broaden your geographic horizons, and acquaint yourself with Finland's fair sister."

"And the hydrofoil's ever so fast," Rosie added. "We'd be back on Monday morning — ten-thirty at the latest."

"I suppose I could fit it in with my teaching schedule," Adrian agreed, and glanced pointedly at Miranda.

"It's a wonderful idea," she began, looking uncomfortable, "and I'd love to come... But..."

"No buts, Miranda!" pleaded Rosie. "You mustn't give us any buts!"

"I'm sorry..." Miranda stood her ground. "There's one very big 'but', and that's my job."

Adrian dropped his eyes to his beer glass, and Miranda could guess how he'd interpreted that 'very big but' in connection with her job: although keeping her distance from Adrian was only a part of the problem... "I know it'd be a lot of fun, Rosie. The trouble is this current investigation doesn't allow me so much time away from Helsinki. We're more or less on 24-hour call."

"But you'll probably catch that horrible man by next Friday," Rosie persevered. "Then your Chief Inspector will be so pleased he'll give you the weekend off."

Miranda didn't share her sister's optimism. The shortage of leads made their chances of apprehending the killer any time soon almost vanishingly small.

"Look, I know what we'll do," said Rosie. "Tomorrow I'll go and book everything for the four of us, and then you can cancel at the last moment — if it's *absolutely* necessary."

Miranda didn't have the heart to argue any further, and began questioning Adrian about his ideas for the projected cello sonata. Her attention seemed to appease him, and he was soon expounding on his plans for applying rock music electronic effects to the medium of the classical cello. A little later the conversation broadened to encompass Bach's six cello suites and the unusual use he'd made of the lower strings in his 6th Brandenburg Concerto. When the gathering broke up at ten o'clock, Miranda found herself promising Phillip and Adrian that she'd seriously consider the trip to Tallinn and do everything in her power to join them.

Of course, she couldn't know that the murder investigation was about to enter an even more distressing and time-consuming phase.

As soon as Miranda arrived at work the next morning, Ylenius handed her two A4-sized plastic sleeves: "These reached us twenty minutes ago."

Miranda almost recoiled when she saw the now familiar contents: an envelope addressed to 'The Ainola Residence', and another letter in Swedish bearing the trade-mark fingerprint:

Pitäjänmäki
Saturday, 8th April

Symphony No 3 in C major

Dear A.
A symphony is always more than a musical composition in the generally accepted meaning of the word. In a very important sense it is also a personal confession relating to a specific point in the composer's life.

"But there hasn't been another murder," Miranda protested. "Why would he...?" She broke off.

"Exactly, Miranda." Ylenius gave a dispirited sigh. "There hasn't been another body, but we'd better start looking for one... and presumably in Pitäjänmäki. I've asked Tero to mobilize a search party. We'll begin with patches of waste ground — especially ones sheltered by trees. There are plenty of those, so it could take time to sweep the whole area."

In fact, it took until late in the afternoon.

— * —

Pitäjänmäki, a suburb four miles northwest of the city centre, was a blend of light industry and medium-high-rise apartment blocks bisected east to west by a main bus route. The initial search concentrated on the larger northerly portion. When that failed, the team moved south of the principal road to a narrow belt of offices, car showrooms, and other buildings including the so-called P-block of the Sibelius Academy. This again produced no result. So the search was extended even further south into a green swathe consisting of a golf course, sports fields and open parkland. Known on the map as Tali, this area was technically no longer part of Pitäjänmäki, but it did include numerous secluded spots where a body might remain undiscovered for days. Tero, who was overseeing the search, felt they should give Tali a try. By four o'clock, the search party had reached the southernmost edge of the parkland and was almost ready to give up; when the third victim was finally discovered.

The area was sealed off and the SOCOs and police pathologist summoned. Ylenius arrived with Miranda a little later, at a few minutes past five. They parked on the northern perimeter road of Munkkivuori, a suburb bordering Tali to the south.

Tero led the way into a dense belt of trees separating Munkkivuori from the playing fields.

"The pathologist reckons she's been dead about three days. The crows have had a go, so she's not a pretty sight."

Miranda found Tero's warning an understatement. It wasn't just the damage the carrion birds had done to the corpse — hideous as that truly was — but also the utter desolation of the scene: how it conveyed so graphically the victim's lonely death at the hands of a *human* desecrator.

In many ways this crime matched the earlier two. The young woman sat with her legs splayed apart and her back against the vertical face of a large isolated boulder. She was wearing a black, knee-length, formal-looking dress, but the front had been split open from top to bottom — cut rather than torn — and the remnants were still hanging pathetically from her shoulders. Her bra was, as before, pushed up to expose her breasts. A coat, black shoes, pants and tights were scattered around on the ground at various distances from the

169

body. A little to the right of the victim, standing up against the same boulder, was a violin case.

There were, however, some new features. The noose circling her throat, though of a similar design to the earlier two — at least, with regard to the knot — wasn't of wire. This time the killer had favoured a soft, silky-textured rope. In addition, the girl's wrists were bound together with silver duct tape, her conjoined arms raised and hanging loosely hooked over the top of her head. Miranda squatted down to inspect the victim's right hand. No surprise to find all three joints of the little finger missing!

Tero continued his report: "The doctor's impression is she was sexually assaulted, quite possibly raped. Not where she is now though. It looks as if the killer had her standing up against this tree over here..." Tero pointed to a tall pine about fifteen feet away. "You see? Up there? Some duct tape wrapped around the trunk. I reckon he taped her wrists together and then secured them to the tree itself, up above her head. That wouldn't have stopped her kicking out, but she'd still've been pretty helpless. It also explains why he had to cut her dress down the front. Once her wrists were taped, there was no other way to get it off. When he'd finished with her, he took her down and sat her up against the rock for his usual set piece."

The victim looked young again — no more than mid-twenties. In life, she might have been pretty: dark-haired, not tall — about five-foot-six — and full-figured.

"Do we know who she is?" asked Ylenius.

"I think so, boss. A handbag was found about fifteen yards away over there." He pointed off into the trees. "And beyond *that* there's a footpath. It cuts through the trees from Munkkivuori to the Tali playing fields. I reckon she was dragged in from the path and dropped her bag half way. We've had a look at the contents. The photo on the ID seems to match the victim — as far as any match is possible with the current state of her face. But until we can compare her fingerprints with what's on the bag, I'm assuming she's Tiina Holopainen: twenty-four years old, and a student at the Sibelius Academy. A pay slip in her purse shows she's been working for —" he referred to his notebook — "the Tapiola Sinfonietta. And her home's here in Munkkivuori, just a few hundred yards away."

"Did you find any keys?" Ylenius asked.

"There's a fair-sized bunch in the handbag, which suggests our Freako didn't pay her flat a visit this time. Maybe he couldn't find her bag in the dark... though we can't be sure yet the attack happened at night."

"It's a reasonable assumption," said Ylenius. "These footpaths must be used a lot in daylight hours. Risky to carry out a crime like this with other people around."

"Something puzzling me," Miranda said, "is why the killer put Pitäjänmäki at the top of his Ainola letter. We're over a mile from Pitäjänmäki. Wouldn't Munkkivuori have made more sense?"

"My guess," said Tero, "is the killer took the same route we did in our search. He started following her from Pitäjänmäki, trailed her across the Tali playing fields and didn't realize how close he'd ended up to somewhere else."

That same Tuesday evening, Beatrice Gröndahl attended her weekly violin lesson in Töölö. Much to her teacher's surprise, she'd managed to arrive before six o'clock. And the lesson had gone especially well — much to Beatrice's surprise, as she'd practised even less than usual.

Afterwards, she found her friend Mikaela waiting in the corridor. "Lotta not here?" asked Beatrice.

"She's ill. You taking the bus home?"

Ten minutes later, they were installed on the back seat of the number 18, leaning close together and enthusing over the boy pinups in the latest issue of a British teenage-girls' magazine Mikaela had been secreting in her guitar case.

"Oh, my *God* — is this one *gorgeous*?!! Why don't we ever meet boys like that, Bea?"

After an extended ogle, Mikaela turned to the horoscopes. "Essential reading," she said. "Mine first! Sagittarius: *You'll be feeling extra flirty this month! If you're boy-free now, don't expect it to last. The moment you see someone cute, you'll be tempted to go and nab him. Turning on the killer charm will certainly have him head over heels, but it could turn out to be mutual! Do you really want to give up your independence with the summer holidays looming?* Yes, yes! I do! *Wouldn't it be better to keep your options open?* No way, sister!

171

Wheel him in! If he's cute I'll take him now!"

Beatrice laughed. "And what about me?"

"Taurus, aren't you? Hey, it's your birthday soon!"

"In three weeks. Second of May."

"And you'll be *sixteen*!"

"A regular old biddy! Legally able to get married. What an awful thought!"

"Is it?" asked Mikaela, unconvinced. "Anyway, listen to this: *Someone new and astonishing will be entering your life before long. Could it be the proverbial tall, dark stranger? But beware! Perhaps there are too many planets coming into alignment. Things may not turn out as you would wish. You'd better hang on to some good sense and remember to use your natural caution in all things. Any recklessness at this point could land you in dead trouble.*"

"I'm always in dead trouble."

"Rubbish! Nobody cruises through life the way you do. Hot-headed, yes! But that's your South-American bit. Wish I had the same to-hell-with-the-rest-of-em attitude."

"I wonder sometimes if you know me at all," said Beatrice, grinning with pleasure. "You make me sound like a totally self-centred bitch."

"Not what I meant. Hey, here's my stop. Call me!"

Beatrice waved to her friend's shrinking form through the back window of the bus.

In fact, Mikaela wasn't far from the truth. Beatrice could usually keep on top of life's problems or, at least, make it look that way. When things got out of hand or someone got on her nerves, she'd flare up and show her Latin-American temperament — as Mikaela had put it — but it never lasted long.

Getting off the bus near the start of the Helsinki-Turku motorway, Beatrice crossed at the traffic lights and picked her way round the back of the petrol station and the burger restaurant. From here she joined a quiet tree-lined cul-de-sac leading to an underground staff car park for the computer research building that was perched on a ridge to her left. After the cul-de-sac came a short cut through the local secondary school playground to her home apartment block a few hundred yards beyond. The residential area she'd just entered was

Munkkiniemi. It lay directly south of Munkkivuori where Ylenius's team of SOCOs and detectives were, even now, working on the latest murder scene.

Beatrice climbed the gently curving slope with the motorway embankment dropping away to her right. She was vaguely aware of a solitary vehicle parked facing her on the other side of the street. Perhaps she noticed someone sitting behind the steering wheel... but the sun was low in the sky and shone directly into her eyes.

The driver of the vehicle was nevertheless paying considerable attention to *her*. He savoured every detail: The raven hair falling across her shoulders and back; the sensuous, child-like face; the plump shoulders and arms exposed by a sleeveless yellow top that clung to ripely pointed breasts but, in failing to reach the top of her jeans, gave a teasing glimpse of navel buried in the last remnants of puppy fat. She was so young, and so strikingly like that other girl — that earlier one who had haunted his dreams, and who now seemed to be reincarnated before him — as if conjured up by some malevolent spirit. Was he being offered a second chance — a chance to relive his profane and treacherous fantasies?

As he watched her, his mind was working on other levels, calculating the risks. A row of tall birch trees concealed this twenty-yard stretch from even the highest windows of the research building behind him, and not one vehicle had passed in either direction since his arrival ten minutes ago. True, the place was in view of the motorway below, but who would notice anything from there? They'd be too concerned with the road ahead to crane their necks in this direction. Perhaps it could be done. Perhaps even in daylight. But there was still much to consider; arrangements and preparations to be made elsewhere.

"The connections! We've got to focus on the connections!" Ylenius brought the flat of his hand down several times on the surface of his desk for synchronous emphasis.

Miranda and Tero looked as weary as their boss. None of them had snatched more than a few hours' sleep since the previous afternoon's discovery.

The murderer had again been either extremely lucky or extremely careful, and left no fingerprints or obvious trace evidence at the crime scene. Tiina Holopainen's autopsy, carried out during the night after a heart-rending formal identification by the parents, had provided none either; although bruising around the vaginal area indicated that this third victim had probably been raped. The use of a condom meant that no semen would be available for DNA testing.

"But, boss," said Miranda, letting her frustration show, "we've already worked hard on the connections. We've compared Liisa's and Christa's lives — their friends, their contacts, their daily routines. Nothing matches. They moved in different circles. No acquaintances in common. No indication they frequented the same pubs, restaurants or supermarkets. Both used the metro, but who doesn't at some time or another?"

"So compare them with this *new* victim. There *must* be something to give us a lead. What about the violin?"

Tero nodded. "Two might've been a coincidence, but *three*? No way!"

"But where do we go with it?" Miranda wanted to know. "Is the connection on the victims' side or on the murderer's? Did all three victims meet the murderer *through* their violins — at a music shop or a violin repairer's? Or did the killer just single them out because they were *carrying* violins? And, if *that's* the case, what's he got against violinists?"

"He could be a musician himself," suggested Ylenius. "He clearly knows something about Sibelius."

"But we followed up on the musician angle," Miranda protested. "We questioned every musician that Liisa and Christa knew without a single substantial lead. And, if we're looking for cross-victim links, Liisa's and Christa's musical spheres were totally different — the professional classical world and amateur Irish folk music. Anyway, it doesn't have to be a practising musician who's killing these women. He could just be a dilettante."

"A dilly-what?" asked Tero, squinting at Miranda down his long, rat-like nose.

"Of course, we'll have to keep trying, boss," she hurried on, "with the music aspect, I mean. Perhaps a connection will surface with this latest victim."

— * —

In fact, a surprising connection surfaced that very afternoon. A team of eight officers were taking advantage of a scheduled Tapiola Sinfonietta rehearsal to interview Tiina Holopainen's colleagues. Faced with the prospect of individual musicians drifting backwards and forwards between their seats and the practice rooms (now sequestered by the police), the conductor postponed the rehearsal until the evening. This caused disgruntlement amongst some of the musicians; but, as Tiina had been a popular member of the orchestra, most were willing to cooperate and patiently awaited their turns.

Towards four o'clock, one of the clarinettists reported that, after Saturday evening's performance, she'd spotted Tiina Holopainen in the car park getting into the passenger seat of a small red Fiat. She was almost certain it belonged to the principal player of the second violins: Zoltán Szervánszky.

When this titbit of information was relayed back to Pasila, Miranda and Tero abandoned their own lines of enquiry and descended on the rehearsal hall like two birds of prey. The Hungarian wasn't at all pleased to be the focus of police attention again: "First it is that Liisa Louhi girl," he complained. "Then last week one of your people... she comes to ask me why I am taking a metro train to my own home on a Friday evening. To my own home! And now this! How many times must I answer these stupid questions?"

"As often as we find you in the path of our investigation, Mr Szervánszky," said Miranda, with no trace of apology. "Will you tell us what you did after last Saturday evening's concert?"

"I went home."

"And how did you make the journey home?"

"That day I had my car with me."

"Did you travel alone?"

Szervánszky hesitated. He eyed the two detectives warily.

"Isn't it true, Mr Szervánszky, that you took Tiina Holopainen with you?"

The Hungarian remained silent.

"Someone saw her getting into your red Fiat."

"All right, so I took her to the city. But she got out near the Sibelius Academy in Pitäjänmäki. That is all I know. I have done nothing wrong. Why do you accuse me again?"

"We're not accusing you of anything... yet."

The Hungarian writhed in further annoyance at the implied threat. But, with persistent questioning, Szervánszky's story unfolded...

He'd dropped Tiina off at the bus stop beside the Academy P-block at approximately 10 pm. He'd actually offered to take her all the way home to Munkkivuori — something he'd done once before, a couple of weeks earlier — but, as she didn't have a computer of her own, she'd wanted to check her email at P-block's computer station. She was expecting a decision from the Amsterdam Concertgebouw Orchestra as to whether they'd accepted her for a job in the second violins. Szervánszky made it clear to Miranda and Tero how sceptical he was of her chances.

"I left her at the bus stop. Then I went home. But I bought petrol on the way," he added, "at the Shell station near my apartment. Certainly the assistant remembers me."

They could get nothing more from him. He kept repeating the same ideas. But there was something else Miranda wanted to check.

"By the way, Mr Szervánszky... " She waited for the Hungarian to make eye contact, and then shifted language from Finnish to Swedish: *"I heard you play in a recital a few weeks ago. You were terrible — like a cat with a sore throat. Maybe you should get back to school and find yourself a proper violin teacher!"*

Tero had spun round in astonishment, but Szervánszky's normal supercilious expression hardly changed.

"Why do you speak Swedish to me?" he said. "I do not understand Swedish."

"Is that so?" said Miranda, reverting to Finnish. In fact, she'd never heard Szervánszky play in public. But she was sure that, had he understood her provocative criticism, he would have been unable to hide some visible reflex of displeasure. His knowledge of Swedish therefore seemed minimal, perhaps non-existent... which was inconvenient in view of the language used for the Ainola letters — though certainly not enough to discount him from their list of suspects.

Further displays of outrage were forthcoming when Miranda told Szervánszky that he'd now be driven to Pasila HQ to have his fingerprints taken; then his car would be impounded for forensic tests and his flat searched. The clothing and shoes he'd been wearing last Saturday evening would also need inspection. In spite of Szervánszky's objections, both detectives knew they were within their rights to seek links between him and the Munkkivuori murder scene. There could be matching soil on the Hungarian's shoes or on the floor of his car; tape or rope might be discovered in the vehicle's boot; his flat might reveal that he'd somehow managed to write the Ainola letters; and, lurking in a kitchen drawer, might be a pair of bloodstained, finely-serrated garden secateurs with a distinctive nick along one of its blades.

Meanwhile Szervánszky would remain in custody.

On their own drive back to Pasila, Miranda and Tero dropped by the Sibelius Academy building in Pitäjänmäki to pick up the security videos for the previous Saturday evening. On inspection, these showed Tiina Holopainen letting herself in through the outer door with an electronic key at 10.03 pm, then leaving again at 10.28. She was unaccompanied, and nobody else entered or left the building during that twenty-five minute period — or indeed for another hour before or afterwards. This verified Szervánszky's story. But could he have been waiting for her outside in his car? The security cameras gave no coverage of the parking area. He claimed he'd refuelled at a petrol station near his home at least fifteen minutes' drive away in Herttoniemi. If that were so, would he still have had time to return to Pitäjänmäki and meet or follow Tiina when she left the Academy building?

Miranda was acutely aware that Szervánszky's trump card was his opera orchestra alibi for the evening of Liisa Louhi's murder. Another problem was the flimsy circumstantial connection between him and Christa Bäckström's death — no more than his presence at the Siilitie metro station ten minutes before Christa's. Even so, this new and more convincing link with the *third* victim demanded their fullest investigation. Nobody seemed to have seen or heard anything of Tiina Holopainen since Saturday evening, and it wasn't as if there were a lot of other leads to follow up.

Staring at a grainy, blank TV screen — all of the security videos now scrutinized — Miranda realized it was Wednesday, and she still had time to reach her father's lecture. Dumping the videos on her desk, she ran for the car park.

Tero had meanwhile volunteered to check out Szervánszky's petrol-station alibi.

Entering the shop at the Herttoniemi Shell, he almost fell over a middle-aged man kneeling on the floor emptying the contents of a large cardboard box onto the confectionery shelves. This turned out to be the same assistant who'd been on duty the previous Saturday evening, so Tero showed him a blow-up of Szervánszky's driving licence photo.

"He would've been wearing evening dress. He'd just been playing at a concert."

The assistant gave the picture a cursory glance and turned back to his work. "Okay, so I know him," he said casually. "Comes in here from time to time. Cocky bastard. Foreign, isn't he?"

"When was the last time you saw him?"

"Don't know." There was a long pause. "A few days ago, I suppose."

"Which day? What time of day? Can you be more precise?"

The answer was so long coming Tero had to ask again.

"A bit before half past ten," the assistant decided at last. "I was just closing up — bringing the stuff in off the forecourt." Another pause. "He got annoyed with me. Thought I wasn't serving him fast enough."

For once, Tero found himself sympathizing with Szervánszky.

"But maybe that wasn't the *last* time," the assistant reconsidered. "It could've been the time before. His sort's always annoyed about something or other."

"And which day of the week are we talking about here?"

"Definitely not Sunday. I was on early shift, Sunday. Could've been Saturday — Friday perhaps. Can't be sure."

"Think harder!" Tero was getting annoyed. "The day is *very* important."

But the assistant wasn't impressed. "Look, I get a lot of customers in here. Don't expect me to remember every little thing every one of them does. You should've asked sooner."

"What about security videos?"

"The tapes are recycled every three days. You're too late."

Tero gave up. He'd met this type often enough: refusing to commit themselves to anything definite, even their own names, it sometimes seemed. And their kind of evidence was a liability in court. The only alternative was to crosscheck with what Szervánszky had been doing at 10.30 pm on the Friday. If they could prove the Hungarian was elsewhere *that* evening, by elimination he must have been at the petrol station on *Saturday*. More legwork for someone! Fortunately, there were enough new constables on the team he could delegate the job to. Chances were it would only lead to more uncertainty and frustration.

"Always nice to meet a public-spirited citizen," Tero commented, on his way out of the shop. The assistant shrugged and went back to stacking chocolate bars on the shelves.

As Tero eased himself into his car and revved up the engine noisily, the digital clock on his dashboard displayed 7.30 pm. Back in the city centre, Miranda, Rosie, Phillip and Adrian were already seated in the Wegelius Hall, and Nick was climbing onto the dais. . .

II

Allegro molto vivace

"At the American premiere in New York, the conductor, Walter Damrosch, felt it necessary to explain to the audience that the symphony they were about to hear had been placed on the programme out of a sense of duty towards a distinguished musician whose other beautiful and important works had won such admiration. He did, however, wish to make it clear that, in this case, the music was of an anomalous character and its performance under his baton should not be taken as any kind of personal affirmation of its merit. A few years later, another American conductor — this time of the Boston Symphony Orchestra — was heard to comment that he'd rehearsed the symphony nine times and given eight performances, but he still hadn't the faintest idea what the composer meant! The work in question, as you've probably guessed, is the subject of this evening's lecture: Jean Sibelius's Symphony No 4 in A minor, opus 63."

Dr Lewis leant forward over the lectern for a few moments. Then, apparently feeling obstructed by its size, he abandoned both the lectern and his notes to approach the front of the platform and engage his audience on a more intimate and informal basis.

"So there were some puzzled reactions across the Atlantic, but what of the composer's *own* countrymen? The world premiere was conducted by the composer in Helsinki on April 3rd, 1911. The audience was so bewildered by the stark and reticent closing phrases of the symphony that nobody knew whether or not it was time to applaud. This uncomfortable silence was broken by the customary arrival on stage of flowers to garland the composer. And then a suitable enough ovation followed. After all, this was a significant event in the life of the Finnish public: a major new work from their

180

national idol. What else could they do?

"Many years later in her old age, Aino Sibelius recalled that, after the concert, people avoided making eye contact with the composer and his wife; that their smiles were *embarrassed or ironic* and that, contrary to the normal practice, very few ventured backstage to pay their respects.

"Only four years had elapsed since the premiere of the Third Symphony. What was so shockingly different about this fourth one? The answer would have to be: Practically everything! As the audience settled down in their seats with expectant curiosity, nothing could have prepared them for the morose, introverted opening bars of the Fourth Symphony that foreshadow more than thirty minutes of almost unbroken bleakness and austerity. One influential commentator later dubbed it *The Barkbread Symphony*, referring to a period of Nordic history when famine drove the desperate population to experiment with ground tree bark as a substitute for flour.

"So how was the Finnish public to come to terms with this disturbing and enigmatic statement from their revered national hero — their champion of the indomitable Finnish spirit?

"The contemporary spin-doctors of the press were quick to respond. For example, a *Hufvudstadsbladet* music critic explained how a couple of years earlier, Sibelius had made a trip to Karelia in the company of his talented painter brother-in-law and close friend, Eero Järnefelt. They'd hiked together to the top of Koli hill which affords magnificent views of the surrounding forests and lakes. According to the newspaper columnist, the Fourth Symphony was a musical impression of this event, describing the composer's feelings: *as he looks down upon Lake Pielisjärvi, the sun touching it with gold and its sparkling waves glistening in the sun's rays.* It's certainly true that Sibelius referred to this trip as one of his life's greatest experiences. And he did begin work on the Fourth at about the same time. But the composer was so outraged at seeing this simplistic appraisal of his symphony that he sent a written rebuff to the newspaper denying categorically that the work possessed any such pictorial or programmatic underpinning.

"And there were other attempts to give the symphony a recognizably 'national' twist. Finland was suffering new and seriously repressive measures under the Russian Czar designed to strip it of its already limited autonomy. Could the Fourth be a reflection of these troubling events? Well, I believe, if we're determined to attribute the symphony's character to some contemporaneous aspect of Sibelius's life, we'd do better to consider his recent brush with death.

"In 1908, at the age of forty-two, the composer underwent surgery to remove a tumour from his throat. The medical prognosis was gloomy, but Sibelius, as we know, survived for almost another half century; though without the benefit of our hindsight, he must have long felt under mortal treat. And doctor's orders obliged him to abstain from alcohol and cigars — a regimen he kept up for several years despite the misery it caused him. *Life is not easy!* he wrote. *If I could only empty my glass and smoke my cigar, ah! then, believe me, my youth would be recaptured!*

"Meanwhile, worries of a different nature continued to plague him. *I would advise no one to be a composer unless they have private means*, he said, in a letter to his friend Baron Axel Carpelan. Not for the first time, Sibelius had allowed himself to get into serious debt. He was habitually careless with money — driving his poor wife to distraction. But again Carpelan bailed him out by appealing to various rich patrons to sponsor their 'struggling' national artist. The financial pressures were eased — at least, until next time! — but Sibelius's diaries still testify to almost manic-depressive swings of mood. One day he writes: *Light, expectant, hopeful thoughts.* Another day: *In the deepest depression.* Or then: *Yesterday a wonderful day. Youth, joy and warmth.* Contrasted a week later by: *Everything stagnant... In the grip of a depression...* These are typical of the period when Sibelius was working on his Fourth Symphony: *Everything causes me endless suffering*, he complains. *When one is forty-five, the future begins to pale.* Making allowances for some self-indulgent melodrama — let's remember, he was only communing with himself — the picture emerges of a person clinging to his highs as he slips continually back into despondent lows. Should it really surprise us that Sibelius now writes a symphony revealing the darker side of his nature?"

* [Dr Lewis crossed the platform to the piano and sat down to reface his audience, leaning casually sideways with one arm along the back of the music stand.

"In actual fact, there's a more substantial and purely musical side to the Fourth Symphony's sudden change of style. In a letter to an English patroness, Sibelius explained that the Fourth Symphony *stands as a protest against present-day music. It has nothing, absolutely nothing of the circus about it.* And we may imagine that Baron Axel Carpelan was privy to 'insider' information, when he expressed the following view in a Gothenburg newspaper article: *The symphony*, Carpelan wrote, *can be regarded as a protest against prevalent musical tendencies... where orchestral music is becoming a mere technical operation, a kind of musical civil engineering.* One contemporary Finnish musicologist shared these sentiments, adding that the Fourth Symphony was *the most modern of the modern and, in terms of both counterpoint and harmony, the boldest work yet written.* Retrospectively, we can admire such insight. The Fourth stands, in its historical context, as a towering lonely monolith, without equal or imitation — a fearlessly uncompromising statement of 'modernity' which retains to this day its status as one of the least-approachable — one might even say 'difficult' — masterpieces of the early twentieth century."] *

Dr Lewis now undertook a detailed musical analysis of the symphony and, as in the three previous lectures, guided and beguiled his audience with numerous illustrative examples.

* [Here are a few highlights:
"A striking feature of this symphony is its chamber ensemble use of the orchestra. Instrumental timbres are less typically mixed than in the composer's other works. The texture is sparse, sometimes combining extreme high and low registers with a yawning void between. Many important thematic ideas are carried by solo instruments — perhaps a single woodwind, or an isolated viola or cello. Trumpets and trombones are used sparingly, and the rare occasions when they're allowed to reach *forte* dynamics are short-lived.
"Let us consider the opening moments of the work." Swivelling round on the piano stool to properly face the instrument, Dr Lewis focused his attention on the bass register of the keyboard and played, in low octaves and with a steady, dragging *rallentando*, the symphony's first eight notes — C D F# E F# E F# E — beginning *fortissimo*, but soon dying away to *piano*. "Now listen again," he said, "to the first and third notes. " With his left hand only, he picked out the C and the F#, rocking slowly backwards and forwards between them

several times. "This is the interval of the 'tritone', the interval that medieval music theorists called 'diabolus in musica' — 'the devil in music'. It is an ambiguous interval: restless, unsettling; and throughout this symphony it plays a pivotal thematic role, undermining the traditional sense of key relationships — repeatedly edging the fabric of the music towards the brink of atonality.
. . . .

"The second movement is, in my opinion, one of the most un-*scherzo*-like *scherzos* ever written. The perception of speed in music, although hard to explain physiologically, is a very real subjective phenomenon. If we survey the period from Haydn onwards, we may notice a steady historical deceleration. Many of Haydn's finales move lightly but with breathtaking speed. Beethoven, although still energetic, has forfeited some of this speed in favour of weight and power. By the time we reach Brahms and Bruckner, their so-called fast movements are sounding ponderous. The *scherzo* of Sibelius's Fourth Symphony, in its turn, could almost be categorized as 'static'! Repeated attempts to pick up speed prove to be false starts. Although there is an underlying pulse, much of the time we're obliged to count it in our heads — it's seldom overt in the musical texture. What's more, the score is booby-trapped with brief but numerous *ritardandos* — impeding any momentum that might otherwise accumulate. Looking at the symphony as a whole, it's this prevailing static quality that seems to me to contribute so much to the work's 'modern' feel. Later avant-garde styles of composition were frequently intent on jettisoning musical momentum in favour of an aphoristic language that obliged the listener to perceive sound as a painting on a wall rather than as a temporal sequence akin to watching a movie. The Fourth Symphony could well be considered an early twentieth-century precursor of this compositional approach.
. . . .

"The third movement, marked *Il tempo largo*, is the emotional core of the symphony: introspective, unrelentingly serious, one of Sibelius's most deeply felt utterances — a fact endorsed by the composer's request that it should be played at his own funeral. Sibelius here employs one of his most important structural devices: a recurring, clearly recognizable theme, which gains in significance at each successive appearance. This *particular* theme climbs from the bass, initially in large confident intervals but with steadily dwindling progress, as if it were reaching for some exalted but unattainable goal. The motif's first appearances are sketchy — mere tentative gropings towards the light — at quiet dynamic levels, and often on solo instruments. Not until two-thirds of the way through the movement does the whole string section unite to take up the theme and, with the support of a gently rocking figure in the oboes, build it towards a solemnly majestic, though brief, *forte*. One more listless passage of quiet rumination must intervene before we reach the final impressive *fortissimo* statement — the brass section providing powerful backup at the peak of the phrase. Yet even *this* expression of defiant anguish is momentary and subsides into a grim, taciturn coda reiterating disjointed and dispirited fragments of the theme that fade into stillness and shadow.

. . . .

"The finale is the only movement which achieves an extended sensation of ongoing movement with those undercurrents of surging energy that we would normally expect from Sibelius. But this belated recovery will also falter as we reach the closing pages of the symphony. There are two schools of thought about how to perform the coda of this fourth movement. The majority of conductors apply a slackening of tempo towards the end. This tradition is authorized by a letter that Sibelius wrote to Serge Koussevitsky condoning such deviations from the printed score. But other conductors prefer to take the score literally, and maintain the same tempo throughout, avoiding romantic pathos in favour of a simple and understated resignation. In the words of that famous Sibelius interpreter, Sir Colin Davis: *A brusque hand smoothes the earth over the grave.*

. . . .

"In many ways, the Fourth Symphony is an extremist work — almost self-consciously so. We see Sibelius turning his back on what he felt to be the virtuoso excesses of a Strauss or a Mahler, with their dense sonorities and inflated ensembles.

"Amongst music professionals and specialists, it is a widely held feeling that the Fourth Symphony represents the 'quintessential' Sibelius. Personally, I don't subscribe to such a view. Much as I respect the symphony's courage in the face of fashion, its unique personality, its skill and restraint, its strangely prophetic qualities with regard to trends that were to surface later in the century; and, above all else, its severe and remote beauty... Yes, much as I admire these qualities, I feel the symphony lacks too many aspects of Sibelius's musical personality to be seen as central to his life's work. It is predominantly static, withdrawn, lacking the resilience and energy of much of his other work. *Of course,* you may say, *that is exactly what Sibelius intended here!* Granted, but I still view it, like the Third Symphony, as a 'one-off' experiment."] *

Then the speaker returned to the lectern to make his final comments:

"The Fourth Symphony certainly achieves a lot more than its predecessor in originality of language and in psychological depth. Sibelius himself once referred to the Fourth as *a psychological symphony.* But the quintessential Sibelius — as far as one may attempt to define such a thing — is, in my opinion, yet to come."

Closing his notes, which he'd scarcely referred to for the last hour and a half, Dr Lewis scooped them up from the lectern, tucked them under his arm and, with a smile and a tip of the head, stepped from the platform.

Miranda and the others made their way down to the front to congratulate Nick, but Rosie soon turned the conversation to the Tallinn excursion. She'd made all the arrangements, including boat and hotel bookings. Miranda said she still wasn't sure she could get away, so attempts were made to persuade her: She needed the break; she deserved it; she'd come back refreshed and better able to do her job; in any case, they'd miss her terribly. Rosie and Phillip did all the talking. Adrian seemed not to pay much attention.

Miranda agreed to put her decision on hold a little longer. If forced to cancel, she'd only lose the booking fee.

When Nick left for a reunion with some university colleagues, the other four tried prolonging their evening with a visit to the local pub. It wasn't a success. Adrian averted his eyes from Miranda's throughout, and said almost nothing. Even Phillip's efforts to lighten the mood were a failure. By unspoken consent, they abandoned the idea after a single drink. The sisters returned to their flat and spent the rest of the evening watching a Humphrey Bogart rerun.

Szervánszky was released on Thursday morning, complaining bitterly about his night in a cell. Miranda would have liked to hold him longer, but the forensic tests and searches of his car and flat had failed to uncover anything incriminating. There was simply no case — just a persistent gut feeling that Miranda couldn't back up with hard evidence.

Meanwhile the Sibelius Academy webmaster had granted access to Tiina Holopainen's email. Szervánszky's story about a message from the Concertgebouw was confirmed, although he'd been mistaken in doubting Tiina's qualifications. The prestigious Dutch orchestra had offered her a job. At 10.22 that final evening, she'd sent an excited email to somebody in Holland — clearly a boyfriend — telling him the wonderful news.

Miranda emailed this Hans van der Waag herself, and he replied within the hour, telephoning directly from Amsterdam. His shock at the news was palpable — even over the phone — but Miranda eventually learned that Hans had been expecting a call from Tiina on the Saturday evening which never came. He'd called her himself, at about 11.30 Finnish time, and then repeatedly through the night. For four days she'd neither answered her phone nor his email messages. Miranda offered some words of comfort, but there was little she could do — especially from such a distance.

The boyfriend's story supported the scenario the team had already constructed. After dealing with her email messages, Tiina had left the Academy building at a couple of minutes before half past ten. She'd then set out to walk home, taking a short cut across the Tali playing fields; but, some time between 10.35 and 10.45, she was dragged into the trees, where her assailant raped and murdered her.

"Hey, Miranda!" Tero said, from the adjacent desk. "How many symphonies did this Haydn bloke write?" He was leaning back, perched precariously on two legs of his chair.

"What are you reading?" Miranda asked, seeing some kind of brochure propped open on Tero's stomach.

"Concert programme I picked up at the opera house. I thought they only did operas, but they've got some kind of orchestra concert there as well — on May Day. Says they're going to play Haydn's Symphony No 48. Forty-eight?! I just asked you: how many of these symphony things did he write?"

"A hundred and four," said Miranda.

"You're kidding!"

Miranda shook her head.

"Who the hell would want to listen to that many?" Tero seemed genuinely puzzled. "All I can say is thank God our Freako doesn't think he's Haydn!"

"Can I have a look when you've finished with it?" Miranda asked, and Tero tossed the concert programme across the gap between their desks.

"What was that ballet Szervánszky was playing in?" she wondered aloud, turning the pages "...the night of Liisa's murder? Ah, here it is: *String Serenade* for string orchestra only... Interesting collection of pieces: Elgar's *Introduction and Allegro*, Barber's *Adagio,* Bach's *6th Brandenburg*, Vaughan Williams's *Thomas Tallis Fantasia*, Tchaikovsky's *Serenade*..."

Tero wasn't paying much attention until Miranda jerked violently upright in her seat, clutching the programme in front of her face as if it were a winning pools coupon.

"Oh, my God," she moaned, in seeming ecstasy. "The *6th Brandenburg*. That's it! That's got to be it! Tero, for heaven's sake, get a bit of culture into your life!" She scrambled out of her seat and bore down on him, blazing with excitement. He actually cringed, as if expecting her to grab him by the collar and shake him.

"Who's the contact person at the opera house?" she demanded. "Who told you about the performance times? Find the number for me!"

Tero was bewildered, but did as he was told. A few minutes later, Miranda had the desk phone clamped to her ear: "So which item is performed just before the interval?" she asked. "And do all of the musicians keep their seats?" The answers seemed to please her. Completing the call she swivelled back to Tero.

"The final piece in the first half of the programme," she said, "was Bach's *Brandenburg Concerto No 6*, and that would've accounted for the last twenty minutes before the nine o'clock interval. But the 6th *Brandenburg* is very unusual because it's for the lower strings only. No violins are needed and the violinists all left the orchestra pit during the applause for the *previous* piece. Szervánszky's alibi for Liisa's murder is bogus. He had nearly twenty minutes to get to the

Sibelius Monument and twenty to get back again. Still a bit tight, and he couldn't have made it on foot, but by car...? Yes, dear Zoltán's right back in the frame!"

Miranda sent two officers to his flat in Herttoniemi and two to the rehearsal hall of the Tapiola Sinfonietta. A third two-man sortie failed to turn up Szervánszky at the opera house, but they did talk to a violinist who'd shared a desk with him on the evening of the Sibelius Monument murder. She described how Szervánszky had disappeared without trace for the whole of the forty-minute break. She'd wanted to discuss his taking part in a performance of Schubert's *Octet* at a provincial summer festival, but he was nowhere to be found. At the end of the interval, he'd squeezed back into his place only seconds before the return of the conductor and was, in the words of his colleague, looking *overheated and a bit dishevelled.*

This news was passed on to Miranda; and moments later, a call came in that Szervánszky had been plucked from the end of the afternoon's Sinfonietta rehearsal and was already on his way to Pasila under escort.

"So how do you reckon he knew Christa Bäckström?" Tero asked.

"We'll prise it out of him this afternoon."

"But he wasn't even on the same train," Tero pointed out. "He was on the one *before* Christa's."

"I've been thinking about that," said Miranda. "He caught his train at Kamppi, didn't he?... one stop earlier than where Christa caught hers. So, imagine this... Szervánszky's train pulls in and stops at Central Station. He's sitting there, looking out of the window, when who should come running onto the platform but Christa Bäckström. Well, she's too late. The doors shut in her face and she's left standing there to wait for the next one. But Szervánszky's seen her. He knows she'll be on the *following* train. So, when he gets off at Siilitie, he hurries on ahead to the murder scene and positions himself ready."

"It fits! You're right. Shall we have another look at the metro videos?"

"I've already done it," said Miranda complacently. "Christa *did* just miss that earlier train."

"But it's still only circumstantial."

"Stop worrying, Tero! We'll nail him in the interrogation room."

To Miranda's surprise, Szervánszky waived his right to a lawyer. He seemed not to appreciate the seriousness of his situation — even though, at this stage, they weren't officially charging him. He adopted an attitude of disdainful annoyance that they should be wasting yet more of his time.

"It must not take long," he declared, as they sat down. "I am to play one of the solos in *Le quattro stagioni* this evening. I must be back before six-thirty."

Neither Miranda nor Tero reacted. Tero merely switched on the tape recorder.

"In our earlier discussions," Miranda began, "you told us that you spent the whole evening of Friday the twenty-fourth of March at the National Opera House."

"That is right. Why do you ask me again?"

"Because, Mr Szervánszky, you weren't playing in the *Brandenburg Concerto* — the last item before the interval. This means you had from twenty to nine until twenty past nine completely free." Although Miranda had interviewed the Hungarian on two previous occasions, this was the first time she'd seen any signs of uncertainty. His confidence was visibly fraying, and she gave him no time to recover: "Will you tell us where you were during that forty-minute break?"

"I was in the musicians' lounge," he said unconvincingly.

"A colleague of yours was looking for you. She couldn't find you anywhere in the building."

Szervánszky hesitated. "Ah, yes... now I remember. I went to walk."

Miranda was openly sceptical: "Where, Mr Szervánszky? Where was it you 'went to walk'?"

"Outside. In the park."

"It was a raw twelve degrees below freezing that evening — and you went for a walk in the park?"

"The opera house — it is very hot sometimes. I needed clean air. That is not against Finnish law, I think. Even in my country, in the bad time of the communism, it was allowed us to walk outside in cold weather."

"Did you have your car at the opera house that evening?" asked Tero, ignoring Szervánszky's attempt at sarcasm.

The Hungarian nodded.

"Where did you park it?" Miranda wanted to know.

"Across the road in the big car park."

"And did you take it for a drive during the interval?" Tero suggested. "Go for a little spin round the block?"

Szervánszky clearly had some difficulty unravelling the idiomatic complexities of Tero's question, but he got the main idea and was adamant: "I *walked*. I did *not* drive my car."

"And this walk you took..." persisted Miranda. "Did you go by yourself?"

"Yes, I was alone."

"Did anybody else see you while you were outside?" Tero demanded.

"It is not possible to remember such things. Your question... it is insensible."

"You'd better try anyway, Mr Szervánszky!" said Miranda.

"Perhaps someone saw me. Perhaps a stranger. I cannot say."

Szervánszky was getting rattled — which, of course, was Miranda's and Tero's intention. They quizzed him in fast succession about his dealings with Liisa Louhi; then about his journey to Siilitie metro station the evening that Christa Bäckström died. Where was he coming from? Did he know Christa? Did he see her on the Central Station platform? And what about the lift he gave Tiina Holopainen on the night of *her* death? Backwards and forwards, trying to catch him out with inconsistencies. As the afternoon drew to a close, Szervánszky became ever more agitated, glancing frequently at his watch.

"My concert," he said, on several occasions. "I must return for my concert."

But Miranda made it clear they had no intention of letting him go anywhere until he gave them some satisfactory answers.

"All right! All right!" he finally burst out. "I will tell you what you want to know. I will tell you what really was happening on the evening of the ballet. And that other time — when I went home on the metro."

Miranda and Tero fell expectantly silent. Their tactics had paid off. But what they learned wasn't what they'd hoped for.

"I was with a woman," said Szervánszky. "I could not tell you because she is a married woman. It is very difficult for her."

The two detectives stared at him.

"What do you mean," asked Miranda at last, "you were *with* a woman? Where? At the opera house? During the interval?"

"We found an empty practice room. We made sex there."

Miranda had trouble grasping this new concept. "What woman are you talking about? Do you mean one of the musicians?"

"She is a musician, yes. But not a string player. She did not play that evening. She was in the audience. She came backstage to meet me after the Barber *Adagio*. I am good to satisfy her," he said with some resurgence of his earlier swagger. "She is always wanting more. We went to an empty room. That is why nobody saw me."

Szervánszky's interrogators were struck dumb.

"And the other time you ask about — when I took the metro to my home — we met at my flat. She already was waiting for me there. She has a key. She stayed with me until midnight. I did not follow this Christa you talk about. I do not know any Christa."

Miranda and Tero exchanged glances. Could Szervánszky be telling the truth?

"Who is this woman?" demanded Tero. "Has she got a name and address?"

"I cannot tell you her name. I have explained. She is married. Her husband must not know."

"Come on!" Miranda exclaimed angrily. "You don't expect us to take your word for all this, do you?" Much of her anger sprang from the fact that their most promising suspect so far seemed, like the earlier ones, to be slipping through their fingers. "Give us her name or we'll have to hold you overnight again."

"But I must play this evening! It is an important concert for me!"

"Tell us her name, and we'll let you go."

Szervánszky struggled with this dilemma for a few moments... but decided in favour of his evening performance rather than his lady friend's honour.

"Her name is Sinikka Matikainen. She plays the oboe in the opera orchestra. But the husband — if he learns about this, it is a terrible thing! You must promise that nobody tells him!"

Miranda responded with icy calm. "Your duty was to inform us about this oboist friend of yours from the start. You've wasted a considerable amount of police time with lies and evasions. And that, Mr Szervánszky, is a criminal offence which could earn you a fine or a prison sentence. Our superiors may find it appropriate to press charges."

"No, please, please!" Szervánszky was beside himself. "You must try to understand. I could not tell. The situation... it is very difficult. Her husband, he is a composer and a music professor, and I hear surely that he is to be on the jury next November — the jury of the Sibelius Violin Competition. If he is knowing about me and his wife, I will have no chance. He is doing everything he can to stop me from winning. I will be lucky if I go even to the finals."

Tero gazed back with a mocking sneer, so Szervánszky focused all his powers of persuasion on Miranda: "Please, please, you must try to understand," he begged again. "I know it is difficult. You are not a musician. Music means nothing to you. But for an artist like me, it is all. It is my life!"

Well, well, thought Miranda, with grim satisfaction, *don't expect any sympathy from me, Mr Szervánszky. Serves you right for sailing too close to the woodwind.*

III

Il tempo largo

But Miranda was having problems with her disappointment. Of course, she'd hoped Szervánszky would turn out to be the killer — and not only because of her natural aversion to him. Adrian hadn't yet been properly vindicated, and she wanted to escape the doubts that still tormented her whenever she was alone: at her desk, in her car, in her own room at home, jogging round Töölönlahti bay — doubts which conflicted with her instinctive feeling that Adrian could never be a murderer. But was it possible he'd got hold of someone else's mobile phone? Had he, in fact, made that nine o'clock call from the Sibelius Monument? Why couldn't he just have left his flat straight after Liisa herself stormed off into the night? He would've arrived a bit sooner at the *Ateljé*, and then she and Phillip could have provided him with an unassailable alibi. He would never have been considered as a suspect in the first place!

Remembering that euphoric night when she'd allowed Adrian into her bed, she craved his company and his touch. She was sleeping badly. Even physical exercise failed to give the release it had generally provided in her life. And what if this doubt was never resolved? What if they *never* caught the monster who'd destroyed these young women's lives?

Once Szervánszky had hurried off for his solo spot in the Sinfonietta concert, Tero suggested they try finding Sinikka Matikainen. Miranda was equally curious to meet this lady oboist who'd supposedly shared in Szervánszky's backstage exploits. They tracked her down at the opera house as she was arriving for the evening's performance.

'Glamorous' was the word that came instantly to mind: voluptuous

194

in all the right places, and wearing suitable clothes to display the right places; scarcely past the thirty mark; convincingly blonde hair; bold but expertly applied make-up and expensive-looking jewellery.

Oh, yes, Miranda concluded, Mrs Matikainen possessed all the right qualities to bolster Szervánszky's vanity. He must've felt bitter at being unable to flaunt himself with this woman in public. It was easy to understand why he'd succumbed to temptation again and again — even at risk to his career.

The oboist ushered them to a quieter spot away from the comings and goings of her colleagues and, with much annoyance, verified Szervánszky's assertions that they'd been together at the time of both Liisa Louhi's and Christa Bäckström's deaths. She was outraged at being drawn into *this whole sordid murder business*, and left no doubt that she would never forgive her erstwhile (and obviously soon to be spurned) lover for such cowardly behaviour. Nonetheless, she promised to make a formal statement at Pasila police station the next day, after Miranda's reassurance that the information was unlikely ever to reach a courtroom. Fuming with indignation, the woman turned on her high heels, and stamped off down the corridor.

"How about an anonymous phone call to the husband?" Tero suggested, as they were leaving the building. "Stir things up a bit."

"That would be most unprofessional," was Miranda's response, although she had to admit the idea held considerable charm.

Next morning in Ylenius's office, Miranda vented her frustration: "Adrian Gamble and Martti Hakala, then Sirén and Szervánszky! This is getting us nowhere! We're chasing our own tails looking for a clear personal connection and motive. But it's probably not like that. The murderer doesn't need to know the victims as such. It's enough for him to see them somewhere — in a restaurant, in a shop, or getting out of a taxi. He marks them, stalks them and, sooner or later, he kills them. No personal motive required. Just an opportunistic and random selection."

"Apart from the violin," said Tero.

"Okay, so there's the violin motif, which presumably has some special significance for the killer. But what is it? We still don't know. Isn't it time we got a profiler in? A professional psychologist?

Someone who can tell us the kind of predator we're dealing with here? We need a clearer idea of what to look for."

The Chief Inspector's face had become guarded. The attentive gaze he typically offered when subordinates put forward an opinion was conspicuously missing. Instead he scrutinized his own hands clasped heavily on the desk before him.

This reaction didn't surprise Miranda. Everyone knew Ylenius's stubbornness in such matters. And Miranda had to admit her own views on 'offender profiling' were ambiguous. She'd found the psychology courses at university interesting and rewarding, but she realized that psychology could in no way be considered a hard science like physics or chemistry. In some cases, its practice seemed to border on pseudoscience or unabashed flakiness. Ylenius, however, was inclined to view psychology and psychiatry as little more than charlatanism. Although fashionable amongst some of his colleagues to recruit the occasional services of a forensic psychologist, in his own investigations Ylenius had consistently refused such support.

"Boss, three women have died already," Miranda persisted. "We've got nothing to lose by getting a profiler's opinion. If it turns out of no help... well, okay! But we don't know till we've tried."

The Chief Inspector continued to avoid Miranda's eyes, and seemed to be struggling with himself. When he did look up, it wasn't at Miranda.

"Tero," he said, "what's your opinion on this?"

Tero shrugged. "I'm inclined to agree with Miranda. It might give us some new ideas."

With a sigh, Ylenius came to a decision. "All right," he said, "go ahead and locate somebody. We'll see what he or she has to offer."

Miranda's respect for Ylenius rose a further notch. He could so easily have quashed her proposal outright. Again he'd shown regard for the opinions of his subordinates and determination to place the success of the investigation above his own personal feelings.

Miranda wasted no time. On the recommendation of a colleague, she selected Panu Marski — a psychologist working for the Helsinki prison service — and tapped his number into her desk phone.

"Doctor Marski is presently at a meeting," an officious-sounding secretary informed her, "but I shall pass on your request at the first opportunity."

Within ten minutes, the secretary phoned back. Although Doctor Marski was unable to return her call in person — due to another pressing engagement — he *was* prepared to take on the case. Would Inspector Lewis be so kind as to courier all the relevant material to his office: reports, witness statements, photographs, etc?

Miranda readily complied.

It was still fairly early when Miranda let herself into the flat. Rosie came rushing out of her bedroom.

"Perfect timing, Miranda! Now you can play the Evolution Game with us at Niall's. He invented it, and he's a friend of Phillip and Adrian's, and we're supposed to be there at seven-thirty, so you've just got time to get ready. Well, you can't stay here by yourself, can you? It's Friday evening and there's... "

"Rosie, Rosie! Slow down! What on earth are you talking about?"

Miranda eventually grasped that Phillip and Adrian had invited Rosie to a board-game evening at the home of an Irish friend living on the northeasterly branch of the metro line.

Miranda put up a token resistance. "It's a bit short notice, Rosie. I haven't eaten anything since midday."

"There'll be plenty to eat and drink. We're taking stuff with us. And I've got a bottle of wine you can share."

Miranda capitulated. It beat sitting at home alone with the telly!

"But not by metro," she stipulated. "I'll drive us there, and skip the wine. That way I can leave early on my own."

Rosie accepted this condition; so, when Phillip and Adrian arrived ten minutes later, all four of them squeezed into Miranda's Corsa and headed east.

Niall MacLaverty was bald and bespectacled. He welcomed them into the small kitchen-dinette area of his flat where the game was ready laid out on a spacious white table. Hovering either side of the host in their pyjamas were two young children, gazing up at the guests with friendly eyes.

"This is Esme. She's eight," explained Niall, "and Robbie had his sixth birthday last week, didn't you, Rob?"

Rosie knelt down to engage the two children in conversation.

Miranda looked on, intrigued to notice how they spoke with the same distinctive Belfast accent as their father.

"Were they born in Northern Ireland?" she asked.

"No, Helsinki Maternity Hospital. Their mum's Finnish. She hasn't lived with us for a couple of years. Had other things to do. But the kids see her quite often."

"So you're pretty much a single parent."

"Wouldn't have it any other way. Love them being round on a daily basis. Okay, it's bedtime, kids!"

Esme and Robert did a circuit of the visitors, giving each a goodnight hug and a kiss.

Rosie was enchanted by this universally dispensed affection: "Such sweet children you have, Niall," she sighed, waving as the youngsters pattered barefoot into their bedroom.

But now the adults turned their attention to the game. It was designed for a maximum of four players and, since they'd be five this evening, Phillip asked Rosie to double up as his partner. Then Adrian suggested Miranda sit beside him, so he could guide her through the initial stages of play. He did this with such deference that Miranda felt it would be churlish to refuse.

The numerous components of the Evolution Game — boards, cards, counters and dice — had obviously been hand-made with loving care. Miranda was familiar with many commercially produced games, but the layout of this one, with its central octagonal board, resembled nothing she'd ever seen.

"You invented this yourself?" she asked Niall.

"Yes, it's based on the concept of biological evolution."

"So you're a biologist?"

"No, no!" grinned Niall. "Only as a hobby. I did music history at university with musicology as a subsid."

"And now he's another of us learned blokes wot teaches the English as a foreign lingo," Phillip explained.

"Suppose I'm still applying my education," Niall said. "My teaching's at the Sibelius Academy: special English courses for music students — professional terminology and so on. Lots of fun. Been doing it for years."

Miranda wondered if Niall had known the latest murder victim,

Tiina Holopainen. Had he been questioned yet in the general sweep of students and personnel? *Oh, for godssake, Miranda! Stop it! You're here to unwind!* She took a deep breath, resolving to concentrate on the game.

At first, it was bewildering, with so many things to consider at the same time: the changing conditions of the environment, the adaptation of one's gene pool, the placing of colonies. There were ecological niches, and cards for natural selection and mutation. Adrian patiently explained everything and, before long, Miranda was getting the hang of it. The cards and counters were colourful and changed their patterns and combinations so frequently it reminded her of a slow-motion kaleidoscope.

Meanwhile Rosie was succumbing to regular giggling attacks, complaining it was all much too complicated and she'd never figure out what was going on. Phillip jollied her along.

For Miranda the evening turned out refreshing and fun. Only once did the discussion take a more serious turn, triggered by a story of Phillip's about a female colleague at the School of Economics planning to file a complaint of sexual harassment against one of her male colleagues.

"Men *can* be a bit unkind sometimes," Rosie admitted. "I hate how they eye you up and down in the street as if you were a piece of meat!"

"You'd like it even less if men *never* looked at you," Phillip said quietly.

"But Rosie," appealed Niall, with a kindly smile, "don't be too hard on us. Evolution's programmed us that way. When you think about it, a woman has to invest nine months of resource-draining pregnancy and years of nursing into every child so she can pass her DNA on to the next generation. A man only needs a couple of minutes and a millilitre of sperm. And then a woman's limited to producing a dozen or so kids max during her lifetime. A man can potentially father hundreds. That's why men and women's sexual behaviour is different. It makes sense for a woman to limit her promiscuity. Sex with lots of men doesn't change the number of children she can bear. Much better tactics to focus on one partner who'll stick around and provide protection for her and the child —

someone who'll come up with the resources she hasn't got time to gather herself: prehistorically speaking, like protein-rich meat. And men are more or less ready to comply, though they're still inclined to dally elsewhere and impregnate other women. Those who do inevitably pass on more copies of their DNA to the next generation."

"Are you suggesting," Miranda cut in, "that men are somehow justified in behaving like total slime towards women, and they can't help themselves when they cheat on their wives and girlfriends, have sex with all and sundry — even underage girls — or go and commit incest and rape?"

"No, no!" Niall seemed upset, and Miranda regretted the discordant note she'd brought to the discussion. She well knew it was prompted by guilt over her failure to track down and stop the present serial killer.

"I'm not *justifying* anything," Niall insisted. "I'm only saying it's why men tend to behave the way they do. But there's another side, because we've also evolved as *social* animals, and we've had to learn how to make complex choices between alternative and conflicting behaviours. In a sense, it's like the gift of 'free will'. We've evolved an in-built and sophisticated sense of empathy, and it's our natural birthright to be able to choose between right and wrong. There can never be a *genetic* justification for inflicting pain on another human being — physical *or* mental. Social responsibility's an intrinsic part of our evolution — a big part of what makes us *Homo sapiens*."

"Are you saying," asked Adrian, "that we've evolved an instinctive knowledge of the difference between good and evil?"

"Yes, why not?" Niall rolled the dice, and played his next move before returning to the subject. "But we need to realize that men and women have always been subjected to different selection pressures. It explains why men are so preoccupied with women's looks, and women are relatively more interested in a man's personality or social status."

"You mean," proposed Miranda, "why dating agencies say their women customers read carefully through all the information, but the men only look at the pictures."

"Yes, it's enough if a man's desire to mate is triggered by a woman's appearance: that'll ensure he mates as often as possible. And we all know that men are prepared to pay for sex with a total stranger, while women almost never are. From an evolutionary viewpoint, a woman needs to be more discerning, and assess each man as a potential long-term support for her children. Men favour younger-looking women, probably because a young woman has fewer children in tow from previous liaisons. In evolutionary terms, it makes her a better bet as a DNA-transmitter for any man who can get there early enough. Women, on the other hand, are often drawn to men with power and status — even much older and physically less attractive men."

"Apparently, Henry Kissinger was a successful womanizer," said Phillip.

Niall nodded: "And nobody's very surprised if a younger woman goes to bed with a dumpy, middle-aged statesman wearing heavy-framed spectacles — not if he's charismatic. Kissinger said himself: for a woman, power is one of the great aphrodisiacs. But imagine it happening the other way round! All right, so a young man might feel admiration for a senior female politician. That doesn't mean he'll want to bed her down. But a powerful partner's always meant a safer environment for a woman's children. The corollary is men often seek power and status so they can have access to more women. Aristotle Onassis said, if women didn't exist, all the money in the world would have no meaning."

"Suppose he was in a position to know!" said Phillip.

"But, Niall, do you honestly think women are such goody-goodies?" challenged Miranda... "that they never cheat on their husbands?"

"Of course, they do!" grinned Niall. "Though rather more circumspectly. If they're reasonably sure they can get away with it, they might try importing some high quality sperm for hubby to take care of."

"But where's the romance in all this?" Rosie complained. "You make everything sound so calculated."

"None of this happens consciously," said Niall. "It's just, over the millennia, men and women adopting certain strategies leave more of their genes in the gene pool. That doesn't preclude romance as such."

"And what about love at first sight? How do you explain that?"

Rosie asked.

Miranda rallied behind her sister: "Yes, explain why we find some people more attractive than others! What constitutes good looks in an evolutionary sense?"

"That's a tricky one," Niall admitted, "why each species favours one set of characteristics over another: like the peacock's tail or the lion's mane. I suspect it's a sort of genetic drift. Once it happens that a line of peahens is turned on by a slightly longer and more colourful tail, the trait gets exaggerated with each successive generation. Perhaps human tastes in beauty developed the same way — though something occurred to me the other day. You'd expect to be attracted to a partner resembling your own parent, wouldn't you? I mean, if my father found my mother attractive, I should've inherited his tastes and be looking for a woman with the same looks as my mother. Makes sense, doesn't it?"

"I do declare," exclaimed Phillip, "you've hit on a universal truth. At last I comprehend why I've always been so irresistibly drawn to women who resemble my father."

Niall sighed: "Trust you to make a mockery of my theories."

"Yes," laughed Adrian, "Phillip loves to go for the jocular vein."

The mood lightened. And during the long, nail-biting endgame — with each player struggling to reach the Pleistocene first — humour and backchat flew across the table. Miranda was having fun, and her interaction with Adrian, sitting close beside her, felt natural and cosy. Wasn't this how it ought to feel? If only she could find some way to join them on the Tallinn trip tomorrow.

Tero entered the main office at 10.30 am with a message for Miranda: "That psychologist bloke you contacted — Marski, wasn't it? — he's on his way here. Rang to say he wants a look at the three murder sites. The boss wants *you* to take care of it."

Till then, Miranda had been toying with the idea of asking for her last two days of winter leave, and catching the afternoon hydrofoil with Adrian and the others. But she'd known all along it was impractical. How could she abandon her colleagues at a time like this? And chaperoning Marski around Helsinki would take up most of the remaining day. Of course, it was her own fault; she'd suggested they brought a psychologist on board. With a quick phone call she broke the news to a very disappointed Rosie, and went downstairs to meet the criminal profiler. She was momentarily thrown off balance by the man's stunning good looks: having somehow visualized him with an intense, bookish face, narrow shoulders and spectacles.

Doctor Panu Marski was a vigorous forty-year-old (or thereabouts) with a luxuriant head of dark hair and a closely cropped beard. Touches of grey at his temples added distinction to striking, masculine features; and his grey, confident eyes engaged Miranda's own. She hesitated, recovering from her surprise; but Marski extended his hand with an easy smile, and she shook it gratefully.

"Generous of you to spare me the time," he said, in a velvety bass-baritone. "I've had a prelim glance through the material, but a look at the murder sites would be extremely useful before I go into any greater depth and detail. I need some personal experience of the physical environment so my instincts can come properly into play. I'm sure you understand."

"It's the same for me," said Miranda.

She took the psychologist for a brief meeting upstairs with Tero, and then tried to introduce him to Ylenius. The boss was nowhere to be found.

So they set out in Miranda's Corsa and, on the way, Marski explained how he liked to approach a new case.

"Please tell me your personal feelings as well," he said. "Not just the official material. Whatever comes to mind — anything that might help me get the feel of the crimes. Some workers in the profiling field restrict themselves to the cold facts — to the written reports — so they can avoid having their thoughts coloured by other people's preconceptions. But I think a more personal viewpoint from someone deeply involved in the case can be extremely valuable. I still have to stand back afterwards and form my own opinions, of course."

Miranda parked the car beside Töölö library — just opposite Adrian's building. She'd never been in Adrian's flat but glanced instinctively up at the second-floor windows where she assumed it would be.

Walking Panu Marski through the route that Liisa Louhi had probably taken to the Sibelius Monument, Miranda followed the psychologist's request and described her own impressions of the crime scene that bitterly cold morning three weeks ago. She also showed him the path walked by the two teenagers who'd seen the murderer as he crouched over his victim.

Panu spent a further ten minutes wandering around the area. Miranda sat on a park bench and allowed him his own space.

"Thanks," he said, at last. "Shall we go on to the second site?"

But, as they came alongside Miranda's car, Marski spotted the café on the opposite corner — the same café Liisa had visited on the afternoon of her death. He proposed a short break for coffee and a sandwich and, over their snacks, they politely probed each other's professional backgrounds.

"It's lucky you contacted me when you did," Marski said. "I'm leaving for the States next Thursday. I'll be gone almost a fortnight. There's a three-day criminal profiling conference in Boston and, afterwards, I'm touring New England with my family. Been wanting to see it for a long time."

"You have children?" Miranda asked.

"Two girls. Nine and seven." He then drew a vivid picture of each of his daughters — their personalities and their hobbies — before returning his attention to the sandwich.

"And your wife?" Miranda heard herself asking.

He looked up. "Oh, I won't bore you with any of *that* stuff," he said dismissively — though continuing to hold Miranda's gaze.

She laughed into the ensuing silence. "This isn't leading up to one of those 'my wife doesn't understand me' lines, is it?" Her voice was playful, but Panu didn't respond in kind.

"My wife and I understand each other only too well," he said blandly. "Shall we change the subject?"

And soon he had Miranda laughing at his description of an eccentric American colleague expected at the Boston conference. They were still laughing as they rose to leave.

Miranda turned to find Adrian standing directly in front of her. He must have just entered the café, and he looked puzzled. His eyes flicked back and forth between herself and Marski.

To hide a sudden inexplicable sensation of guilt, Miranda hurriedly introduced the men to each other, adding an unnecessary —

and professionally indiscreet — explanation of how Marski was helping them with the murder enquiry.

"What about Tallinn?" Adrian asked quietly, directing his question exclusively to her.

"Sorry, it's quite impossible," Miranda murmured, and then made an abrupt and clumsy exit with Marski trailing behind her. The last thing she wanted was to draw the psychologist's attention to the fact she was still in social contact with Adrian Gamble.

"So that was your initial suspect, was it?" Marski commented, as they recrossed the road to Miranda's car. "Struck me as the anally retentive type."

"Bit of a snap judgment, don't you think?" Miranda said, a shade too sharply. "You only exchanged a few words."

"One gets a feel for these things after interviewing several hundred of them. Anyway," he gave her a conciliatory smile, "I wasn't being serious. In a job like this, an occasional touch of flippancy helps keep you sane."

The next three hours were spent criss-crossing the city: first driving east to Herttoniemi, and later cutting back westwards to Pitäjänmäki. Marski also wanted to retrace the second and third victims' final footsteps. So they left Miranda's car beside Siilitie metro station and walked the third of a mile to the wooded track where Christa Bäckström was attacked. Similarly, at Pitäjänmäki, they parked in front of the Sibelius Academy P-block and took the footpath across the Tali playing fields to where Tiina Holopainen's body had been found.

It was almost three o'clock when Miranda dropped Panu Marski beside his Volvo at the back of Pasila HQ. He promised to study the murder case files in depth over the rest of the weekend, and proposed a meeting with the whole team for the following Monday afternoon.

"I should have a report ready by then," he said.

Miranda made her way back to the office, and worked on until well after 10 pm, being in no hurry to return to an empty flat.

Rosie, of course, was already in Tallinn.

The capital of Estonia is positioned strategically on the southern shore of the Gulf of Finland. The Danish king, Waldemar II, founded its stone fortress in 1219, marking out the city walls and the basic street plan that remain to the present day. Over the centuries, this thriving merchant city attracted the covetous graspings of neighbouring nations — the Swedes, the Germans, and the Russians — who took turns incorporating it into their own empires. Apart from a brief period of sovereignty in the 1920s and 30s, it wasn't until 1991 that Estonia was finally able to declare independence — breaking from the unravelling Soviet Union to elect its own president and create its own currency.

Estonia and Finland are more than just neighbours: they are cousins, sharing the same ancient ethnic origins, and speaking two non-Indo-European languages so similar that they seem to hover just beyond mutual comprehension. During the days of the Soviet Union, tourism between the two countries functioned almost exclusively in one direction. A steady stream of Finns made the fifty-five-mile crossing in creaky, aging Russian ships — drawn by the prospect of cheap alcohol and the exotic, rather sinister experience of stepping behind the Iron Curtain into the lair of the communist Bear. Nowadays, of course, Estonians are equally free to make the voyage.

Disembarking at Tallinn harbour, Rosie, Phillip and Adrian took a courtesy coach to the Viru Hotel, a tall Finnish-built tower block in the centre of the city. They checked in, unpacked and almost immediately set off on foot to explore the Old Town. This was Adrian's first visit, so Rosie and Phillip were bubbling over with evangelical zeal to show him — as Phillip put it — all of the *sights and sounds of the citadel.*

The next morning was devoted to Mustamäe: a vast market, oddly situated in a dilapidated outer suburb of jerry-built, Soviet-period apartment blocks. Adrian was struck by how many Russian voices he heard around him.

"One of old Joe Stalin's legacies," Phillip explained. "Pulled the same stunt with all the Baltic States. Forcibly deported large numbers of the original inhabitants to the east and brought in train-loads of Russians to replace them — presumably to even out the demographic mix and undermine any sense of national identity. Nowadays a third of Tallinn's population is Russian-speaking."

The market was a sprawling affair with acres of outdoor stalls and an enormous covered market hall. The three of them roamed around together until it became clear they were interested in different things. They agreed to split up and reconvene after an hour.

It was several minutes before the rendezvous time when Adrian ambled out of the front entrance of the hall with an armful of (probably bootleg) classical CDs. He found Phillip waiting on a battered wooden bench, talking to a young man with slicked-back hair and the local *de rigueur* zip-fronted leather jacket. As Adrian approached, the stranger gave Phillip a shrug and moved off.

"Getting yourself accosted again?" asked Adrian.

"Yes, another of those charming young Russian entrepreneurs. Crossed the border from St. Pete's-burg last week — so he said — intent on a bit of creative enterprise with the Finnish tourists. Assured me though he's got plenty of useful contacts here in Tallinn. Cousins by the dozen! Well, you know how the conversation goes: *You like sleep with my sister?* I'm sure she's charming but no, thank you! *My brother then?* Pass on that too. *So you want drugs? I get you cannabis? Ecstasy? Crack?* Sorry, wasn't planning to abuse any substances this morning. *Guns then? I arrange for you Kalashnikovs? I bring you Semtex? How'bout Russian tank? Neutron bomb? Intercontinental ballistic missile?'* Seems no limit to their resourcefulness. I truly believe, for a suitable sum in dollars, you could acquire Boris Yeltsin, stuffed in a glass case, to adorn your hallway and dance a little motorized jig for the amusement of your guests... Ah, here comes Rosie."

The three had fun showing off their purchases and, after a plastic mug of watery coffee in a small café tent, they caught the trolley bus back to the city centre. Most of the afternoon was spent wandering the corridors of the Estonian National Art Gallery. But weariness set in and they returned to their own hotel rooms to shower and recharge their batteries ready for the evening.

Just before 7 pm, Rosie travelled up to the twelfth floor to fetch Phillip and Adrian. Emerging from the lift, she almost bumped into a swarthy man in black leather coming along the corridor. Rosie gave a bright greeting of "Tere!" ("Hello!") — one of the few words she knew in Estonian — but the man ignored her and squeezed into the lift she'd vacated.

The door of Adrian's room was already open with Adrian's head peering out.

"Rosie!" he said. "Thought you'd be arriving about now."

"Did you know that man?" she asked, glancing over her shoulder. "The one who just got into the lift?"

"He was coming from your direction."

"Think I saw him earlier hanging round in the corridor."

"He seemed a bit creepy."

The door beyond Adrian's was also open, and Phillip drifted out trailing his jacket in one hand. "Hotel security, I'd imagine," he said. "Probably ex-KGB. Looked suitably cloak-and-dagger, did he?"

"More Mafioso," was Adrian's assessment. "Perhaps he was casing out the corridor with a view to turning over our rooms."

"So please don't leave anything valuable in them," said Rosie, looking worried.

"No problem," said Phillip. "Neither of us owns anything valuable. Hey, I was just reading a tourist brochure about this 'medieval' restaurant in the Old Town. Whole pigs roasting on spits, jugglers, minstrels, dancing bears, warm mead overflowing from wooden tankards served by buxom medieval wenches with daring décolletage."

"Did it say that in the brochure?" asked Rosie.

"I am embellishing somewhat. But they definitely mentioned minstrels. I can guarantee the minstrels. Aren't you tempted by the idea of live medieval musicians? Or am I being oxymoronic? Don't say it, Adrian! Much too obvious!"

Adrian seemed to agree, and shut his mouth again.

Phillip's proposal was taken up, and the meal turned out to be a great success — the main attraction being a lively atmosphere and the bonus of a sixty-minute performance by the locally acclaimed group of medieval music specialists *Hortus Musicus*.

It was eleven o'clock when Phillip and Adrian escorted Rosie to her room. She declined an invitation to join them for a nightcap, reminding them about tomorrow's early start back to Helsinki. But Phillip wasn't to be deterred. He dragged Adrian downstairs to the hotel cellar bar for *a companionable chat over just one more drink*. In Adrian's case the 'one more' stretched to four; and Phillip lost count completely. They were still there at three in the morning.

"Pity Miranda couldn't make it," said Phillip, for the umpteenth time. Adrian hadn't reacted earlier, and didn't look like reacting now.

"Probably got too much work going on," added Phillip, refusing to give up. He was nevertheless surprised when Adrian at last took the bait: "That's not *all* she seems to have going on," he mumbled.

It took another prompt from Phillip before Adrian recounted the story of his brief meeting with Miranda and Panu Marski.

"Self-satisfied bastard," he complained. "Some kind of psychologist. Criminal profiler, Miranda said. Nobody in real life should be that good-looking. Could've walked straight off a Hollywood film set. So I had to be polite, and shake hands with the smug bugger."

"Something going on between them, you reckon?"

"Wouldn't be surprised. She looked guilty as hell!"

"Expect you're overreacting. She was friendly enough at Niall's place."

"Yes, things seemed to be looking up for a while."

"But women are so damned unpredictable, aren't they? Never know where you stand with them. Of course, you'll always have me."

"What the hell does that mean?"

"I'm not making a pass, you idiot! I mean, I'll never let you down," explained Phillip. "Always be there for you."

"For godssake! Please, don't get maudlin on me!"

"We all need a bit of sentimentality in our lives." Phillip was getting steadily louder and more excitable. "I've been thinking a lot about our friendship recently. Been through a lot together, you and I — home *and* abroad. That's what it's all about, isn't it? Shared experiences, shared outlook. Seen each other at our best. *And* our worst. No place for secrets between two old travellers like us — co-travellers in life's rich and perilous journey."

"Are you journeying your way round to my confession again?"

Phillip stared back with bloodshot eyes. He seemed to be having trouble maintaining an upright posture on his bar stool. "No secrets, Adrian. Just not appropriate. If there was something you wanted to tell me, I wouldn't be judgmental. Doesn't matter what it was. You could always rely on me to take your part. And you'd do the same for me, wouldn't you?" His voice had taken on an almost pleading tone, but Adrian offered nothing in reply.

"It's all about the nature of friendship, isn't it?" Phillip maundered on. "True friendship, I mean. Sometimes I think I could risk everything for friendship — jump off a cliff, break any laws. Shouldn't be limits to what one's ready to do for a friend. Surely you agree with me? All that unrealistic crap about blood being thicker than water. Often doesn't work out. Brothers at each others' throats. Cain and Abel, etcetera."

"I get on perfectly well with my sister," said Adrian.

"Well, of course, you do. *You've* got the magnificent Theresa! But that's a special case. It's because of *her*... because of your *friendship*... not because she's your biological sister. I'm not saying brothers and sisters can't share a friendship. Any two people can. But it doesn't depend on whether you're blood relatives, does it?"

"Where's all this leading, Phillip? Isn't it time we hit the sack?" Adrian downed the last dregs of gin and tonic and stood up.

"I just want you to know I'd stick my neck out for you," Phillip persisted. "Swallow my pride, throw caution to the wind, betray my own grandmother — both of 'em dead for years, mind you... Yes, I'd tear down the whole moral house of cards, if necessary. Even act against my own conscience. All in the name of friendship."

Phillip's speech was slurring, and Adrian — though far from sober himself — managed to persuade his 'co-traveller in life's perilous journey' to leave the bar and ride the lift back to their rooms. Phillip needed some help getting his key in the lock, but staggered successfully over to the bed where he spread-eagled himself face-down and passed out. Adrian threw a quilt over his comatose friend and left him to it — no doubt already wondering about the hangover they'd be suffering on the return voyage to Helsinki.

* *

~ *And you were playing the cards close to your chest again... because that Rapier business wasn't the end of the Sally Primrose affair, was it?*

~ For Rapier it was. All the police attention sowed enough seeds of doubt. She started avoiding him.

~ *So you thought you could step back in to fill the vacuum.*

~ Of course! We were doing very nicely, thank you, until *he* turned up.

~ *But she didn't want you back, did she?*

~ That wasn't obvious at first...

~ *Not to you it seems! You started pestering her for dates, following her around everywhere, hovering outside her flat, phoning her in the middle of the night.*

~ Where the hell did you hear all this stuff?

~ *Not from you, that's for sure! But rumours were going round, so I pieced it together by myself. And, in the end, she got so fed up with your attentions she had the police put a restraining order on you.*

~ That was *so* unnecessary! I was losing interest by then *any*way.

~ *And throughout this whole crazy mess, you left me completely in the dark.*

~ You don't tell me *every*thing about *your* business either.

~ *True, but I'm surprised you never once brought it up.*

~ Didn't seem any point. Wasn't your problem, was it?

* *

IV

Allegro

The scheduled Monday meeting with the forensic psychologist, Panu Marski, was held at 2.30 pm in a meeting room on the third floor of Pasila HQ. Only the three core members of the investigative team (Ylenius, Miranda and Tero) were present. The Chief Inspector had opposed the idea that the whole team should be witness to Marski's verbal report. He felt it sufficient to distribute a printed summary later in the day.

Mindful of her boss's scepticism towards offender profiling, Miranda began by asking Panu to outline the overall objectives of the forensic psychologist in an investigation of the present type.

Marski took some time extracting his notes from a calfskin briefcase and laying them out on the table before him. He slipped an elegant pair of reading glasses from a pouch in his jacket pocket and positioned them carefully on the bridge of his nose.

"Applying a psychological approach to the analysis of a crime," he replied, at last, "is mainly aimed at narrowing down the number of potential suspects — thus allowing the police investigation to focus its resources better. It's often possible to reconstruct a crime from the viewpoint of the motivations which led to it and which drove it. That way we can gain insight into the background of the offender and predict such factors as age, marital status, living and working environments, etcetera."

"And upon what do you base such leaps of imaginative reconstruction?" asked Ylenius.

"The basis, Chief Inspector, lies in thousands of case studies of convicted serial rapists and murderers made in the United States, Canada, Europe and Australasia. Sexual predators have been interviewed about their pasts, their backgrounds and their obsessions — about their physical, mental and emotional states before, during and after their crimes. They've been encouraged to reveal details of their childhood, schooling, employment, hobbies, accommodation, relationships and sexuality. The exact sequencing of their crimes is probed again and again. They lie to the interviewers and they lie to themselves. But, by careful crosschecking with other sources like families, friends, teachers, social workers, the court and medical records, it's possible to build up a fairly reliable picture of the person's life, deeds and desires. There are thousands of deviant personality patterns. So, as a psychologist, I approach each case as unique. A crime needn't fit into clear, tidy boundaries, and neither the criminal who committed it. But we can identify clear core elements, tendencies, likelihoods, and so on. These are what allow us to construct a working profile of the offender."

Marski paused to gauge the effect he was having on the three detectives. Ylenius's face was noncommittal; Tero seemed genuinely interested, and Miranda encouraging. None made any comment, so Marski continued.

"I'd like to begin by reviewing the three murders and attempting a reconstruction of the crime sequence for each of them. I believe, by a process of analysis and comparison, we can learn a lot about the nature of the crimes and of the perpetrator himself. Let's first consider the attack in Sibelius Park. The sequence of events, as you noticed yourselves, was rather puzzling. The separate elements of the crime were clear enough: the strangulation by means of a ligature applied from behind with an upward pulling action; the partial removal of the victim's clothing to expose her breasts, and presumably to allow penetration — although its occurrence still remains unproven."

"I have, over the years," Ylenius said suddenly, "come across more than one crime scene where there's been an attempt by the husband or lover to conceal his own domestic murder by faking a break-in. He arranges the victim's clothes to make it look as if a fictitious intruder has committed the crime."

"Yes, the falsified simulation of an intruder-rape that went wrong," Marski conceded. "Of course, that's a well-documented stratagem. But the three murders we're now considering are not in domestic settings. They are out in the open, and they involve three quite separate and unrelated individuals."

There was an uneasy silence while Marski waited for a rejoinder, but Ylenius only stared back, his expression neutral.

"So we have the strangulation and the disturbed clothes," resumed Marski, "but also the removal of the finger and the visual staging of the scene. These are the four main elements. But how do we reconstruct the order? How do we arrange them in a convincing continuity? The pathologist's report indicates that the severing of the finger occurred after death, so this sets at least two items clearly in sequence. I believe the rest will fall into place if we assume one single event — an event unintended by the murderer, and one which broke the expected continuity. That event was premature ejaculation. The noose was in place. The victim was threatened verbally with strangulation if she refused to comply. She was instructed to open her jacket, to pull up her jumper and bra, and then to remove her jeans and panties. Meanwhile the murderer was standing behind, maintaining tension on the ligature with one hand, possibly fondling her body with the other, and pressing his erection into her back. It was all too much for him. Before she could do more than partially lower her jeans, he was reaching orgasm and had no alternative but to complete the strangulation immediately. Whereas a normally motivated male might try to time his orgasm with his partner's own, I believe for this kind of sexual offender the aim is to intensify his own orgasm by synchronizing it with his victim's death throes. That was the way he'd imagined it in his fantasies and that was what he now attempted to achieve in reality.

"This scenario accounts for the position of the girl's jeans and panties — still around her buttocks. We no longer need resort to explanations about why her trousers were pulled up *after* sexual intercourse, either by herself or by the killer. Nor do we need consider an attempt at sexual penetration *after* death that was interrupted by the young couple passing nearby. Penetration never occurred. Orgasm, yes. But penetration, no.

"Then came the staging of the scene — the placing of the girl in a sitting position against the rock face, the standing of the violin case beside her, under the relief of Sibelius's head. And finally the removal of the trophy — the fourth finger of the victim's right hand. This was presumably when the two teenagers arrived, just as he was severing the finger. It's possible that he never noticed them. Even if he did, his main business was over. In their absence, he might've stayed a little longer to survey his handiwork, to add a few finishing touches. Perhaps he would've removed the victim's lower clothing more completely to give the impression that sexual conquest had been fully accomplished. One thing he would almost certainly have learned from the interruption was the value of avoiding such a public place in future. There was, however, nothing more he could do to improve on his current performance, so he left with his trophy.

"When we come to the second killing, I believe he failed again in the same manner. This time he chose a more private spot, but ultimately with no greater success. We know he pinned Christa Bäckström face-first against a tree. The scratch marks on her face indicate this. But, apart from a couple of additional abrasions on her midriff, they were the only scratch marks the victim sustained anywhere on her body. Our conclusion must be that, at this point, she was fully dressed with only her stomach exposed. Her jumper could, of course, have ridden up in the struggle, but I suggest an alternative scenario. He applies the noose and forces his victim against the tree with the full weight of his own body. While he pulls on the ligature with his right hand, he slides his other hand under her jumper to fondle her breasts. Again the pressure of his genitals rubbing against her back overstimulates him. He loses control and ejaculates, simultaneously completing the strangulation.

"Allowing himself a few moments to recover, he then drags the girl's body further into the trees, away from the track — to reduce the likelihood of his being disturbed. There are tasks to be performed. First of all, he needs time to prepare the tableau — to place her in a seated position similar to the one used at the Sibelius Monument with the violin case standing upright against a nearby tree. At some point he severs the finger from the right hand. But he also adjusts her clothing to match the earlier attack... except that, on this occasion, he removes her tights and panties completely from one leg, and then spreads her legs wide to prove his power of access. Even if, as I believe, he once more failed in that respect, it's important to convince everyone else that he succeeded."

"To keep up his image," Tero suggested.

"Yes, indeed, the graphic exposure of her breasts and vulva serve exactly this purpose. Now the scenario I've drawn for you here may not be the correct one. It's possible that he did actually perform penetration, with the same kind of strawberry-flavoured condom as used earlier by Christa Bäckström's casual partner in the pub. But I'm very much inclined to doubt it. A second occurrence of premature ejaculation is in many ways consistent with the progressive development that we perceive in the modus operandi across these three murders as a whole."

Marski removed the folder containing his notes from the table and, leaning back in his chair to cross one leg comfortably over the other, rested the file across his lap. Miranda recognized this as a conscious effort to lighten the formal atmosphere of the meeting. In response, she reached for the thermos flask and began pouring coffee for everyone.

"Let's now survey," Marski said, "how the MO develops. For the first murder he needed only two pieces of equipment: the ready-made ligature and the cutting tool for removing the finger. The second murder introduces no new tools, but there's definitely more control in terms of his selection of the venue. To make an attack in a public place like the Sibelius Monument at nine o'clock on a Friday evening implies a serious lack of forethought. I see the killer on that first occasion finding himself unexpectedly alone with his intended victim and acting upon an uncontrollable impulse to take her at once — to hell with the consequences! Very risky — in fact, *reckless* behaviour on his part. For this reason, I suspect the Sibelius Park murder was his very first time. In a homicidal sense he was an inexperienced 'virgin'. We have no knowledge of any previous killings that fit this MO, do we?"

The others didn't contradict him, so Panu carried on...

"It has to be said, however, that this predator has proven himself a quick learner. He doesn't make the same mistake again. He takes possession of his second victim in a location where he's much less likely to be disturbed. We can further guess that, when he followed Christa Bäckström into the trees that evening, he was already familiar with the location. He knew she used that track as a short cut and had scouted out and familiarized himself with the terrain. Quite possibly he was lying in wait for her. But, in spite of all this, things didn't work out as he'd hoped. His sexual gratification was once more compromised.

"So he sets out to rectify his disappointment on the third attempt. We could say that the third murder represents an almost quantum leap forward in terms of planning and control. He comes equipped with a range of materials to bind and control his victim. The noose is of a softer, silky texture that will allow him to prolong and savour the strangulation process. He's very cautious about leaving forensic evidence. He may have been wearing surgical gloves. He certainly takes the precaution of using a condom to eliminate the risk of leaving behind samples of his semen. I think we can assume that this time he had more success, that his gratification was of a higher order. It does not however mean he is satiated. I believe he will kill again — within a week or two, judging by the time intervals so far. I also think it likely that we'll see a further escalation in the degree of control he brings to bear on his chosen prey. He'll develop still more sophisticated means of drawing out and enhancing his pleasure, and simultaneously, I'm afraid, also his victim's suffering."

There was a heavy silence while everyone pondered this warning. Then Miranda dispelled the tension with a question: "Do you think the murderer knew his victims?"

"A very important point," Panu replied. "It's possible that he knew them to some extent. He may earlier have had some casual dealings with them. Words may have been exchanged in a shop or on a bus. He may have come into contact with one or other of them through his work. But I doubt whether his association was anything closer. This isn't the behaviour of an intimate. We're not investigating a *crime passionel* — the slaying of a wife or lover through anger or jealousy. This is a much more distant affair. As far as our killer is concerned, the victim isn't a genuine person at all. She's merely a warm fleshy object upon which he can act out his fantasies."

Miranda winced, but Panu pressed on: "It is, in fact, possible that the murderer had never set eyes on *any* of his victims until briefly before each attack. But that would be unusual for a killer of this type.

A more typical scenario is that he spots a victim in the course of his everyday life, and for some reason he's especially drawn to her: perhaps it's her hair, her figure, the clothes she wears, the way she walks... "

"Or the violin she's toting," Tero chipped in.

Marski nodded. "But, whatever the reason for his interest, he starts to follow her. He finds out where she lives and works, the shops and restaurants she frequents, her regular daily routines. In private he masturbates and fantasizes about her, about intercepting her, controlling her, of sexually dominating and, of course, strangling her. Eventually his fantasies no longer suffice. He must cross the line from imagination to action. The moment of transition — the point where social restraints are ignored and overridden... this is often linked to some trauma in the killer's own life, some destabilizing event, like the loss of a job, or the loss of a wife or girlfriend."

Tero interrupted in near disbelief. "Are you saying this 'freako' could have a girlfriend or even be married?"

"It's not out of the question," Panu assured him. "There are plenty of documented cases in the criminological literature. But I'd prefer to return to that a little later because, as yet, I've said nothing about the victims themselves...

"In fact, the choice of victim often tells us a good deal about the murderer. First of all, we can ask ourselves, what do these three women have in common? All of them were small and lightly built. This, as I'm sure you've realized, broadens the field to an unfortunate degree. Their attacker needn't have been an especially large man. Strength would be an advantage for overpowering them — particularly, I believe, in the case of the second victim — but we should never underestimate the persuasiveness of fear. Even a less powerfully built man is capable of control and domination with the help of suitably conveyed threats, perhaps with the help of a knife, and especially if he possesses what could be termed an 'evil charisma'.

"Next — as you pointed out, Tero — there's the common factor of the musical instrument. That all three victims were carrying a violin obliges us to assume that it was a critical element in their selection. But in what way exactly? Does it relate to some important event in the killer's past? Perhaps he formed a fixation on a girl who played the violin, a girl who then cruelly rejected him. Or does the violinist originate in his own family — a domineering mother or sister whose years of bullying and mistreatment he now wishes to pay back on a surrogate figure? Actually, these two explanations seem unsatisfactory to me. The murderer's fascination with his victims' immediate *physical* sexuality suggests another kind of motive: one which I shall shortly delineate for you. So, although we can't entirely rule out 'historical' or biographical associations, I feel the presence of the violin is better explained in terms of how the murderer first encountered his victims. His job may involve the sale or repair of violins. He could himself be a professional violinist or violin teacher."

"We've already explored those avenues," said Miranda, disappointed that Marski was stating the obvious.

"Of course," he nodded, "you have the expertise and experience — the well-practised routines — to follow up such leads. My domain, however, is the psychological motivation. So I suggest we put the violin question aside and consider what else could have singled out these three girls and made them the focus of this particular predator's fantasies? The most obvious similarity is they were all young and attractive. This may seem altogether *too* obvious, but it tells us that the sexual component in the killer's psyche still lies near the surface. Some killers are much less discriminating. They are equally happy attacking old women and very young girls — even small children. This doesn't mean their violence is non-sexual. It simply shows that the sexual dysfunction has become fully integrated with their feelings of anger and hatred towards women in general — if not towards the whole of mankind. Such a person is unable to function successfully in society and will find it difficult to form relationships — even with members of his own sex. But that doesn't seem to be the case with our present offender. There's nothing to suggest he'd stand out as anything strange or perverted. He could almost certainly hold down a job, enjoy a circle of friends. And, yes, he may even have a female partner — although I'd expect their relationship to be stormy and precarious. Perhaps he's married. More probably he's worked his way through a succession of shorter-term partners. His problem is that the *reality* of sex never matches up to the intensity he experiences in his sexual fantasies. The women he meets are too independent. They have wills of their own and he is unable to exert as much control over them as he craves. His sexuality is self-centred. It's focused on his own gratification. He views a woman's body as an object for satisfying his own desires, not as the vehicle of another thinking, feeling entity. And yet he adores those bodies. It's notable that in none of these three murders are there any signs of extraneous cruelty or sadism. This is *especially* significant in the case of the third murder where he had plenty of time and freedom to do exactly what he wanted. But he hasn't beaten any of his victims. He hasn't torn, cut or burnt their flesh. Their bodies seem in some way sacrosanct, to be cherished and enjoyed — not to be disfigured or mutilated."

"What about the ligature?" asked Tero.

"And the amputation of the finger?" Ylenius added smoothly. "Isn't that disfigurement and mutilation?"

"Indeed it is," said Marski, totally unfazed, "at least, from our point of view. But we can reconcile these apparent contradictions. The way to view the ligature is as a means of control. It's relatively simple to apply. It provides an effective threat, which immobilizes the victim's attempts at retaliation, and it gives the potential for that special moment of control — that moment when he will choose to wield his power over life and death... perhaps I should say of death over life. He could, for example, have used a knife at this point, but that is a much messier alternative. His choice is the noose because it causes less external damage. As an aside: we also know that the noose is associated with extreme forms of auto-eroticism. It's possible he has himself experimented in such directions, which could account for his interest in the strangulation element: it may well hold some fetishist significance for him. However, that is only surmise. What seems clearer is that he's moved away from the initial ligature of thin speaker wire — which, that first time, may simply have been the most convenient material to hand — and, for the second murder, he uses a broader, less incisive cable, with less of a tendency to cut and scar the throat. By the third victim, he's progressed to a much softer material. His aim is to control, not to mutilate."

"And the finger?" prompted Ylenius again.

"Well, at first sight, this is an act of mutilation. But mutilation is not the offender's *motive*. He's following a quite different agenda. He seeks a trophy, a souvenir of this special event in his life. He needs to take away proof that *this* time it's for real, that he hasn't just imagined it all — that, at last, he's succeeded in living out his fantasies."

Marski paused briefly to take a sip of coffee.

"The predilections of trophy-takers are legion. Most common would be something extrinsic: an article of jewellery or underwear. But sometimes a genuine part of the victim's body is desired: an ear lobe, a segment of skin, a piece of a sexual organ, in very rare cases even an internal organ. Although the present killer is averse to disfiguring the outward sexual beauty of the female form, he allows himself something relatively discreet. He takes the smallest of the fingers from one of the victim's hands."

"That's still gruesome," insisted Miranda. "If he's so squeamish about marring the perfection of his victim's body, how come he's ready to use a pair of secateurs to cut into and break open the joint, then tear and sever the muscles and the ligaments apart in such a brutal way? Surely that takes a lot of determination and a distinct lack of squeamishness."

"I agree with you." Marski spoke quietly, and without condescension. "You have, Miranda, pointed out the very crux of the matter. He *was* quite obviously determined, and that's exactly why I feel this particular trophy must be of considerable importance to him. He could have taken a lock of hair. But no, he takes the fourth finger of the right hand. That he should go to such lengths to acquire it indicates its extraordinary significance. What could that significance be? As with the violin, I can only ask tentative questions. Does it relate to the disfigurement of some previous girlfriend? Does he lack this finger himself? It's impossible to say at this stage, but I suggest you make this a major line of enquiry. Check the medical files of past offenders, especially sexual offenders. See if anything turns up. Or widen the search to anyone on record for any crime whatsoever. This is an important factor to bear in mind. The person we're looking for may well have an existing criminal record. The most likely offences will be of a sexual nature — if not rape, then voyeurism or exposure. I imagine you've already been screening such people. But don't discount *non*-sexual offences. This is somebody ready to take risks, to cross the normally accepted boundaries of society. He's certainly capable of other crimes as well."

"Shouldn't we be checking the psychiatric records?" said Tero. "Our killer's obviously a total fruitcake. He must've had dealings with shrinks of one sort or another in the past. Maybe he's had a few holidays on some funny farm somewhere."

Panu paused, as if to collect his thoughts and appraise the suggestion. There was nothing to indicate that he'd taken offence at Tero's terminology. "Well," he began carefully, "that's a common though very understandable misconception, Tero... but it's by no means automatically true that a person committing crimes of this nature is classifiable as mentally ill — I mean, in the clinical sense — that he's suffering from schizophrenia or manic depression or some other kind of illness where personal control has been genuinely lost. Suitable medication may make it possible for a schizophrenic to lead a normal life in society, but there's no drug known to medical science that will allow the typical sexual predator to return to normal patterns of behaviour and give up his predation. The reason is that he does it through choice. He rapes or kills or both because he enjoys it. And there are other things we should notice. He plans. He assesses the risk factors. He follows through with control and calculation. He takes precautions to avoid being caught. These aren't the behavioural characteristics of a crazed mind. They're the same things you and I might do if we, for example, were preparing a surprise birthday party for our wife or husband. It's unwise to assume that the person committing these crimes will stand out from the crowd. We can't expect a comic-book villain. His day-to-day existence will resemble anyone else's. He'll watch his favourite TV programmes. He'll go to the hairdresser and the local supermarket. He'll have his own tastes in food and clothes. Occasionally he'll come down with a cold or a bout of flu. But he'll also have strong psychological defences, which make it possible to see himself in the best possible light. If he admits that blame should be apportioned for his crimes, he'll tend to direct it outwards. He'll blame his upbringing, the society he lives in, even his victims. Self-justification can take bizarre turns. A man convicted of serial rape may also be on record as having rushed to the aid of a woman he saw being beaten by another man intent on subduing and raping her. When questioned about this apparent inconsistency, he's offended, and says he'd never stoop to beating a woman — in spite of the fact that he has *himself* sexually violated many: controlling and terrorizing them with threats and mental intimidation. He may even describe himself as a 'gentleman', as someone who 'treats women well' in everyday life. He'll tell us how he holds doors open for ladies, gives up his seat to them on buses, how he reminds his sisters and girlfriends to lock their doors and windows every evening against intruders. He seems oblivious to the irony! The extent to which such people can apply double standards to themselves is amazing. Even a sadistic killer who indulges in raping, mutilating and murdering women may refer to a child molester as 'despicably sick'. And, because they feel blameless in their own minds, they can conceal their guilt from us as well. Such people aren't easy to spot. So please note again that, although the examples I've just mentioned are extreme, we can't reassure ourselves by falling back on the expedient of mental illness. Double standards are typical of humanity at large. We *all* rely on a degree of self-delusion to bolster our feelings of personal esteem. The sexual predator is no different — even if his leaps of self-justification are greater than most of us would need. But to return to your earlier suggestion, Tero... Yes, it would be worthwhile crosschecking with mental hospitals and clinics — as far as they'll be ready to share privileged patient information. You could certainly enquire about the finger angle."

"Do you have any comments," asked Miranda, "about the geographical distribution of the three murders?"

"Well, serial attacks often fit neatly into one or two specific areas that coincide with the offender's home or work locations or both — what we might call his geographic 'comfort zones' — where he's familiar with his surroundings, and feels confident to negotiate a route through the successive stages of stalking, possession and escape. But it's difficult to see any pattern like that here. The choice of venue has, in every case, been close to the victim's own home. I think we must assume that the killer spotted them somewhere else — perhaps somewhere more central — and was drawn out to the murder sites by the victims themselves. He may have the use of a car to be so wide-ranging. But public transport's frequent and serves all three areas well. A car isn't a necessary prerequisite.

"One interesting detail is the incorrect designation for the third crime scene in the follow-up Ainola letter — his choice of Pitäjänmäki rather than Munkkivuori. It suggests the perpetrator isn't entirely local — that he's only lived in Helsinki for a few years or even less."

"Something else has been bothering us about the victims' homes," said Tero. "It's whether the killer visited Christa Bäckström's flat after he'd garrotted her in the woods. Could he have been on some kind of extra trophy-hunting spree?"

"Was there something missing?"

"Difficult to tell," Tero admitted. "Nothing obvious."

"What about the other victims' flats? Had they been visited too?"

Tero shrugged. "We're not sure."

Miranda could see this was leading nowhere. "A moment ago, Panu," she said, "you talked about self-justification. How do you think this serial killer justifies his actions?"

"I believe what we're seeing here is an expression of a deep-seated resentment originating in the offender's feelings of thwarted sexuality. His anger isn't as violent as it could be, falling far short of frenzied rage. Instead it's a slowly smouldering emotion which has festered within him, perhaps over a period of many years. Now it's finally breached the surface...

"You see, a sense of bitterness and resentment towards women can develop early, when a lonely and highly sexually driven young man — perhaps still in his teens — is unable to find a meaningful way of fulfilling his needs. He may discover that he lacks the social skills or appearance to make girls take an interest in him. His feelings of rejection are turned around. He starts to blame women for his frustration and loneliness. With time, bitterness can distort his sexuality. In masturbatory fantasies he's able to make women do what he wants and punish them for their reluctance to do it of their own volition. Once this pattern's established, even if he eventually finds a sexual partner in the real world, he may — as I mentioned earlier — feel a shortfall between his imagination and what he can actually achieve. His partners aren't prepared to indulge him in what they see as extreme and unnatural demands. Perhaps they fail to match up to his fantasies in terms of sexual attractiveness. All around he sees desirable women, some of them dressed provocatively and excitingly, taunting him with what he desperately craves, but — as he interprets it — perversely and cruelly denying him access. He convinces himself that *they* are the blameworthy ones for taking delight in his perpetual suffering. They have no right to torture him in this way. So he'll have to take what they consistently refuse to bestow. At the same time, he'll exact the punishment he's so often imagined in his fantasies."

"Aren't you prepared to consider," Ylenius cut in, "the simple pragmatic explanation that a dead person tells no tales? Killing the victim removes the sole witness of his sexual attack."

"Certainly the element of self-preservation mustn't be ignored, but I believe that, even if he could find a way to commit these sexual assaults in total anonymity and with no risk of being caught, he'd still need to kill his victims."

"As an integral part of his sexual fulfilment?" Miranda offered.

"Precisely," said Panu, holding her gaze for a few moments, "and the personalities of the three victims provide some substantiation for the view that their deaths were inevitable. The way in which a woman reacts to an attack of this nature can sometimes determine whether she lives or dies. Does she try to escape? Does she get angry? Is she passive? Does she try to reason with him? Does she beg for mercy? Does she insult him? The personalities of the three murdered women are extremely diverse. Liisa Louhi is intelligent but young and impulsive. She never seems quite in control of her own destiny. Christa Bäckström, on the other hand, is self-seeking, calculating, unscrupulous. We'd expect her to respond to aggression in matching kind. And then there's Tiina Holopainen: level-headed, likeable, hard-working. Three different women, three different personalities; and yet they all died."

"You've drawn us an impressive and graphic picture," said Ylenius dryly, "of how the first two murders — in particular the second — were carried out at speed. Would there really have been time for the victims' personalities to affect the outcome?"

"That's actually my point. In every case, *death* was the outcome, *regardless* of the personalities. Liisa Louhi succumbed to threats and began to undress herself. She was compliant, but it didn't save her.

Christa Bäckström probably put up a fight. The murderer was obliged to press her face-first against a tree to control her. If she had any opportunity to voice her anger and fear, it was most likely abusive and at a high level of decibels. That didn't save her either. The third victim, Tiina Holopainen, was apparently kept alive much longer and doesn't seem to have been gagged. She was presumably frightened into not screaming or shouting for help. And this is perfectly plausible. Intruder rapists routinely persuade their victims to keep silent, even with a sleeping flatmate, or a sibling or parent in the next room. But Tiina may still have tried to talk to her attacker... to appeal to his better nature and dissuade him from harming her. If that was the case, we know she failed. As you've pointed out, Chief Inspector, we can't be sure to what extent these three women confronted the murderer with the force of their own personalities — or the lack of it — but we do know it availed them nothing. He was intent on killing them anyway — for his own sexual gratification — and that's how it ended every time. I continue to say for his sexual gratification rather than merely silencing his victims because of the ritualistic element in his *means* of killing them, which is implied by the clear progressive refinement of the ligature from a brutal strand of wire to an immaculately knotted noose of softly textured rope. The MO — by which I refer to the *practical* details — has certainly changed. But what we could call the killer's 'signature': the factors which fulfil his emotional needs — they've remained consistent throughout."

There was a pause while Marski reached out for what, by now, must have been tepid coffee, and drained it in a single draught. Grimacing slightly, he returned the cup to its saucer.

"As yet, you've only mentioned in passing one of the three letters the killer's sent us," Miranda pointed out.

"Ah, yes, the Ainola letters," said Panu, running his tongue around his lips as if searching for the last remnants of caffeine. "Here we find one of the most revealing aspects of the case 'syndrome'. We might ask ourselves: Why quotes from Sibelius? Does he somehow think he is *himself* Jean Sibelius?" Marski shook his head dismissively. "No, I don't believe so. First of all, this component of the crime is the most calculated of all. It's put into effect entirely after the event. The hyped-up, adrenaline-releasing sequence of the stalking, acquisition and overpowering of the victim is long over. The body has been abandoned at the crime scene, and the killer's now back home in a reassuringly safe environment. His only physical connection to the crime and to his victim is the severed finger — his trophy — which upholds his sense of achievement, his feeling that in this world he can make a difference, that people are sitting up and taking notice. But, in itself, that knowledge isn't enough. He wants to reinforce it and intensify the link with those others in the world who have come to fear and respect him. He wishes to remind them of how clever he's been, and that they are unable to reach him. The letters satisfy this need and proclaim his power over us all. They humiliate us in our impotence.

"But again we must return to the question: why Sibelius quotations? An association with the site of the first murder — the Sibelius Monument — is immediately obvious. But there are two ways to interpret that association. Firstly, we can assume the choice of venue was pre-planned, that the murderer already had the Sibelius concept in mind and knew, in advance, the form his taunting letters would take. Such an interpretation strikes me as far-fetched. We've seen how features of that first murder suggest a spontaneous, only partially premeditated attack in an absurdly public place. The alternative explanation is not that the letter motif suggested the crime scene, but vice versa."

"You mean he dreamed up the letters as an afterthought?" said Miranda.

"Yes, I do believe that's what happened. For him it's now a form of game-playing, and he's manipulating us by drawing us into that game. But, at the same time, he's revealed a great deal about himself — whether unwittingly or out of a sense of bravado is hard to say. Very few people would have the capability or even the inclination to seek out and make capital of such arcane material as the Sibelius diaries. This indicates a person of well-above-average intelligence and with a solid educational background. He has a deep interest in music, and may even be a musician himself. Then there's the choice of language. Sibelius, of course, wrote his diaries in Swedish — his own mother tongue. But they're also freely available in Finnish translation. Why did the murderer use the original language? We should beware of misdirection from such an intelligent opponent, but I'm still inclined to believe that the killer is himself Swedish-speaking. That immediately reduces the number of suspects by a factor of ninety-six percent.

"But there's more to be gleaned from the letters. Sibelius's diaries span many decades. Why did the killer select these particular extracts? They must surely reflect his own thoughts. So let's consider the quotations in this light..."

Marski shuffled through his papers for a moment.

"In the first of the letters we're told: *Let the voice of my inner being and the spectres of dream and fantasy direct me. There are things to be done that cannot be delayed. Life is so very fleeting!* The implication is clear. He's discovered a new direction in his life: the physical realization and enactment of his fantasy world. And, having made this discovery, he intends to follow through with further deeds of self-revelation. Then comes the second quotation: *Such a vision of wonder: the slow movement of a symphony — malaise, mould and maggots — fortissimo strings muted and fading to silence. Oh, but the godlike power of it all! To be carried away in joy by the surging rush of strings.* The reference to death with *mould* and *maggots* is obvious, and we also sense his exhilaration, his feelings of *godlike power*. Is it going too far to interpret the *muted fortissimo strings* as the silencing of Christa Bäckström's final screams? Anyway, let's now look at the third quotation: *A symphony is always more than a musical composition in the generally accepted meaning of the word. In a very important sense it is also a personal confession relating to a specific point in the composer's life.* This is altogether more philosophical and quietly confident. I believe the first two letters help to confirm my appraisal of the processes involved in unleashing this serial killer on the city of Helsinki. But I fear the third informs us that he's only just getting into his stride."

Marski fell silent — perhaps for dramatic effect — and Ylenius used the opportunity to look pointedly at his watch: "So, if that's all you have for us, Dr Marski, we should be preparing ourselves for the afternoon debriefing."

"Might I beg a further five minutes, Chief Inspector," said Marski deferentially, "for a few final points?"

Ylenius had already made a move to stand up; but with no detectable rancour, resettled himself in his chair.

"Estimating the offender's age has been problematic," Marski explained. "There are contradictory factors involved. Premature ejaculation would normally be associated with a younger man — even a teenager — but the steep learning curve in the development of the MO, and the intellectual content of the Ainola letters would suggest a more mature person in his late twenties or early thirties. Ultimately I favour the older age group and attribute the premature ejaculation to the novelty of the situation — the fact that the attacker had never before lived out what may have been a long history of corresponding fantasies.

"So, to summarize: The person you're looking for is of high intelligence, with a good education to university level — either completed or ongoing. If not a full-time student, he's employed in a fairly well-paid professional job. He may even be a practising musician. His mother tongue is likely to be Swedish rather than Finnish. He's probably unmarried, but will have had a series of short-term girlfriends. His social life may, in fact, be extensive — supported by his intelligence and initiative. His main motive is revenge for the thwarting of unsatisfied sexual desires. He need have no history of psychiatric illness, but may have been guilty of earlier crimes, especially of a sexual nature — though not necessarily 'serious' ones. The violin and the finger are of considerable importance — the latter figuring significantly somewhere in the background of the killer. Both should be investigated and explored in every way conceivable. He'll almost certainly kill again, probably at similar intervals, and with steadily increasing levels of sophistication in the means of controlling his victims."

"One final point: I believe this killer is by nature also a stalker. He kindles his excitement by familiarizing himself with his victims before he strikes. That he stalked Liisa Louhi is, I think, confirmed by the finding of the Mozart score in the bushes opposite Adrian Gamble's flat. Presence of that score implies the presence of Liisa's handbag, because we know it's where she placed the score when she borrowed it a few hours prior to her death. I therefore conclude that it was the killer himself who stole the handbag at the Forum shopping centre — that he was already stalking her at that point. He afterwards followed Liisa to Gamble's flat, waited outside for her to re-emerge, and took his chance when she wandered alone into Sibelius Park. I strongly advise you not to consider the theft of the handbag as an unrelated event. Find Liisa's handbag, or any of its contents — the credit cards or the telephone, for example — and they could lead you directly to her killer."

It was Marski who now stood up. "Here, Chief Inspector, is a full copy of my report." He handed over a thick sheaf of stapled A4 pages. "Please, feel free to copy as many as you need and distribute them amongst the members of your team. I hope my efforts will prove useful, and don't hesitate to contact me if you have any further questions."

Ylenius thanked the psychologist politely — if not profusely — and they all filed out of the meeting room. With a quick round of handshakes, Marski left the three detectives standing in the corridor.

"I found his reconstruction of the murder sequences rather convincing," Miranda ventured at last, watching for her colleagues reactions.

"Yes, a virtuoso piece of story-telling," Ylenius agreed, without obvious enthusiasm. "He did leave out one thing though. He forgot to mention the weather."

With that, the Chief Inspector strode off, leaving Tero and Miranda exchanging mystified shrugs.

On the drive home, Miranda surveyed the day's work — especially the meeting with Panu Marski. Overall, she felt the psychologist's report had been worthwhile. Her vision of the killer had taken on more substance. She also allowed herself an appraisal of the psychologist. There was no denying she found him attractive. Marski had a striking charisma... though that could easily have been a turn-off. Miranda was inclined to take charisma as an affront, especially when combined with good looks. Such overendowment, she felt, gave an unfair advantage in the social arena — an excessive power to dominate and manipulate. Surprisingly, Marski hadn't evoked in her any such competitive reaction. Some hint of human weakness tempered the sense of challenge. Was it that touch of vanity? A glimpse of vulnerability just below the surface? She realized how, strangely enough, this increased rather than diminished his attractiveness. *Oh, for godssake, Miranda! Stop it! He's a married man with two darling daughters! Haven't you got enough problems with Adrian?*

It was a relief to find Rosie at home. They sat down at the kitchen table for a glass of wine and a résumé of the Tallinn trip. Rosie enthused about the weekend, with one reservation...

"Phillip and Adrian were a bit the worse for wear on the journey back. Seems they overdid it last night in the hotel bar. Both said they'd have to call in sick and spend the rest of the day sleeping it off. But, otherwise, we had so much fun. They were fabulous company. Oh, I really wish you could've come with us!"

*   *   *

[9.26 pm; Monday, 17th April]

Mall! My darling little Mall! You can't possibly know how much I miss you. It's so hard to leave you behind. I hate us being separated even for one day. But I'm doing it for you, of course — for both of us. And it won't be much longer. Soon I can give up these trips to Helsinki. Another year and I'll be ready to earn a proper living. We can have our own little home, just like we've dreamed together. A little blue-painted wooden house with a garden. Lots of apple trees, and a swing for you to play on. In the summer we'll sit on the grass and pick clover and weave it into necklaces and crowns. Then I'll read you stories under one of the apple trees. Maybe we'll have a cat to sit with us. Or should it be a dog? Let's have both! And, on Sundays, Granny will come for coffee and cakes. We'll bake them together before she arrives, and she'll be so happy to eat what little Mall's made for her. I wish we could be there already. Almost any place would be better than this. In some ways the job gets easier — more routine — but in other ways it's harder every time. I want it to end. And you must never find out, Mall. Nor your grandmother. It would break her heart.

Why are things so slow this evening? The weather's warm enough.

Symphony No 4

Well, it's getting darker. That should improve matters. Ah, what did I say? Definite signs of interest. Yes, here we go again!

Very few words were spoken. The extent to which they shared a common language was anyway rather limiting. He asked her name. She told him: "Anna." Then, with a quick laugh, she added: "Anna Karenina" — supposedly in jest. *So this one's well-read, is she?* The thought was momentary. He was primarily concerned with controlling his nerves. He felt nervous to a point where he might make a mistake. The previous occasion had required speed and an unbroken sequence of snap decisions. There was little time to dwell on his own courage, or the lack of it. He'd simply been carried along in the heat of the chase and he remembered the experience as almost pure 'buzz'. He hoped to recapture that feeling later but, for now, it was all about calculation and correct timing. He couldn't afford to get it wrong. Meanwhile he'd try to hide his nervousness. Until it occurred to him that she was used to such things — that she'd be half expecting it. This insight relaxed him slightly.

And there were directions to follow. Turn left here, turn to the right. He cast frequent glances to where she sat beside him. She looked so composed, so in control. And, yes, she was attractive enough. She had all the necessary attributes. Not his first choice, of course, but she'd do... for now. At last the adrenalin levels were working in his favour. Nervousness was transforming into excitement and anticipation. Her composure was starting to irritate him, but she wouldn't be so self-satisfied when she found out what this was really about. They'd be going somewhere discreet, some seldom used piece of wasteland — behind the railway sidings or bordering on the yards where the containers were off-loaded. It would suit his purposes admirably. A few seconds was all he needed to subdue her. Then they could head for their true destination, the one *he* had planned and prepared: a palace of delights in which he could take all the time he needed to enact so many details of his personal fantasy world.

*　　　*　　　*

232

Symphony No 5
in E-flat major

I

Tempo molto moderato—Allegro moderato—Presto

"**M**aking any progress?" asked Miranda, hovering beside Tero's desk. It was now Tuesday, a little after midday. She was on her way back from an uninspiring lunch in the police canteen with an uncomfortable sensation in her stomach and a reluctance to return to her own desk and its mountain of paperwork that she never seemed able to diminish. Tero looked up from his computer work station.

"I've been following up on Marski's suggestions about the freako's interest in liberating little fingers. Been doing a 'pinkie probe'... typing a few keywords into the city search engine to see what it throws up." He raised his eyes in Miranda's direction. "So far, nothing to point the *finger* of suspicion. No obvious *finger* posts. Still it beats the old method of hunting through rows of filing cabinets *manually*. All you need's a bit of *dexterity* with a computer keyboard. Thank heavens for the *digital* age, eh?"

Miranda supposed he'd been entertaining himself thinking up all this nonsense in advance. Even worse was how, with every laboured pun, Tero fluttered his eyelashes: a mannerism he typically combined with a foolish smirk. On this occasion, Miranda felt an almost overwhelming urge to give his face a slap. She was saved from a serious professional indiscretion by the timely entrance of Chief Inspector Ylenius.

"Miranda, Tero... my office, please," he called, in his usual avuncular manner.

First they reviewed the updated postmortem and forensic reports on Tiina Holopainen. The most interesting new items referred to the killer's equipment. The microscopic marks left at the fourth-finger amputation once again revealed the presence of a small nick along one of the blades. But this time the traces were so distinct that, not only could the forensic team guarantee the same cutting tool had been used, they could specify the exact nature of the tool itself. Comparing the size and curvature of the blades' serrations with a wide range of domestic and industrial alternatives had given a match to a specific pair of medium-sized garden secateurs: *Jardine 360s*. Also, in a similar way, the make of rope used to strangle the third victim had been successfully identified.

"You know what follows..." said Ylenius. "Scouring every hardware and gardening shop in the Helsinki area that might've sold such items over the last few weeks — or, if necessary, months. Hopefully the killer used a credit card. Not much chance of tracing him otherwise."

Tero had something else to discuss: "I've been thinking," he said, "about those Ainola letters the freako's been sending. The first envelope had *our* address on it: *Helsinki City Police, Homicide Unit* with *c/o The Ainola Residence*. But the second and third letters left *our* bit out. They were addressed directly to Ainola, as if the killer knew for sure we'd received the first one and was confident the others would reach us anyway."

"What's your point?" asked Miranda. "Are you suggesting a leak to the press?"

"Not necessarily to the press. Perhaps you mentioned it to your friend Gamble?"

Miranda exploded. "Of course, I didn't! Give me some credit, Tero!" But it was a defensive reflex. She was already trying to remember. Were there any occasions when she could have let something slip to Adrian? At Mama Rosa's, for instance? That was three weeks ago. (God, it seemed much longer!) Phillip had turned up with an email from Adrian's sister announcing the new baby. But, before that, she'd had some time alone with Adrian. She certainly remembered discussing the murder with him. She also remembered behaving like a love-struck teenager. Could she have blurted out something important? Damn it! She wasn't sure. But hang on! The first Ainola letter didn't show up until two days *later* — the same day she and Adrian went for that Indian meal and he'd ended up staying the night? She'd felt so close to him lying entwined there on her bed. They'd talked quietly, intimately. He'd dropped his guard to a surprising degree. Had she also dropped hers and told him something she shouldn't?

Tero and Ylenius were still waiting... to see if she had anything to add.

She shook her head. "I *absolutely* did *not* tell him!"

"What about when you showed your dad the quotation from that first letter — to get his opinion?" Tero persisted. "Was Gamble around then?"

Yes, Miranda was certain of that much. She'd given her father the Ainola text just after the Second Symphony lecture. She'd turned away from Adrian and left him talking to Phillip. Could Adrian have realized what was going on? Did her father actually read the sentences out loud? He might've done. She'd suggested a quote from Sibelius and her father had promised to hunt for it. Did Adrian overhear their conversation?

"Look, Tero," she said impatiently, to hide her own confusion, "you're reading way too much into this change of address. What we should be trying to do is figure out some way of locating where the letters are coming from — where they're getting posted." This was, of course, a diversionary tactic. But it worked surprisingly well.

"That," said Ylenius, "was one of the things I wanted to discuss with you both. I've been in touch with the post office this morning. They confirmed what we knew already. The mail from every post box round the city's brought to the central sorting office in Pasila. The bags are emptied into a franking machine, which stamps them with 'HELSINKI' and the date. From there they pass on to a sorting machine that reads the addresses and redirects the letters accordingly. That means there's no way of telling where the three letters we've already received were posted. But I'm inclined to agree with your Dr Marski. It's not over yet. Naturally, we all hope the murderer won't strike again, but we'd better be ready to catch him out if he posts another of these letters. I've suggested labelling the incoming bags, so the origin of each batch can be checked before it goes through the sorting machine. If another letter pops up for The Ainola Residence, we'll know exactly which postbox it came from. That in itself won't catch us the killer, but it might suggest where he lives or works."

"Is the post office ready to cooperate?" asked Miranda.

"I spoke to the boss of the sorting office. He's got two teenage daughters of his own and wants this killer off the streets as much as we do. I'd like you to pop over there, Miranda, and liaise with him this afternoon. I've already stressed the need for secrecy. Only a tiny handful of post-office employees can be told why the bags are being labelled. If any of this gets out to the press, it'll tip off the killer and the whole exercise will've been in vain."

Aleksi Ylenius had expressed a guarded hope that the killer wouldn't strike again. In fact, the next victim was already dead, although her body wouldn't be discovered until six o'clock the following morning...

An early-rising, seventy-year-old retired school teacher had just set out for a walk with her three excited King Charles spaniels — taking them, as usual, along a footpath that threaded through a quiet wooded area near her house — when she saw the naked body of a young woman propped against a tree. The pensioner dragged her mystified and thoroughly disappointed animals straight back home, and phoned the police.

Miranda drove directly from her flat to the crime scene in Käpylä, a suburb three miles north of the city centre. She arrived at the same time as Aleksi Ylenius, only to find that Tero had beaten them both to it and was standing beside the body in conversation with the police pathologist.

Scanning the scene, Miranda observed that, although the murdered girl was completely naked, not a stitch of clothing could be seen anywhere in the vicinity. This was something new! Had the killer taken the clothes away with him? But a few yards to the victim's right — resting against a tree like a provisional tombstone — was the signature violin case. Miranda had no doubt this was the work of the same predator.

At Ylenius's request, the pathologist summarized his findings: "Cause of death: strangulation," he said. "As you can see, the rope ligature's still in place. It looks identical to the one used in the previous murder — although I'm not paid, of course, to do the forensic people's job for them. She's been dead at least twenty-four hours, not more than thirty-six. Rigor is complete, but there's some reslackening detectable in the eyelids and jaw. I'll give you a more precise time of death when we've checked the potassium levels in her ocular fluid. One thing I *am* certain about is she didn't die here. She's been dumped. And within the last three or four hours."

"How do you deduce that, doctor?" Ylenius asked deferentially.

"First of all there's the direct visual evidence. I'll show you." He squatted down beside the body. "The position we find her in — kneeling and leaning sideways against the tree — is totally unnatural and defies the laws of gravity. Her arms and legs are fixed by rigor mortis in poses that don't make proper contact with the ground as they should if the body had been placed here soon after death. What we see is consistent with a quite *different* position for the onset of rigor. She was lying on her right side turned slightly face-downwards. Her arms were straight and taped at the wrists behind her. The knees were drawn up at differing angles, a little above and below the level of the navel. The body's posture already testifies strongly to this interpretation, but there's more: the hypostatic evidence."

This was a reference to the fact that, when the heart stops beating, blood gravitates to the lowest parts of the body and darkens them by leaking into the surface vessels and capillaries. The pathologist indicated how the right shoulder and upper arm, the right breast, the right hip and thigh (those places that would have been pressed against the ground by the body's own weight) had been unable to accept any additional blood and therefore remained paler than the surrounding tissue.

"You mentioned a moment ago," Miranda said, "that her wrists were taped. They aren't taped now!"

"No, the tape's been removed. But the indentations are characteristic, and there are traces of adhesive left on the skin. I expect Forensics will be able to match it to the gaffer tape the killer used last time. And, while we're discussing the hands, you've probably noticed that the right little finger's missing again — the same three joints."

"Why do you believe the body was brought here no more than a few hours ago?" Ylenius enquired.

"Ah, that's very interesting, Chief Inspector. It's all to do with the body temperature. You see, it's been rather cool during the night — a low of seven or eight degrees Celsius. Even now, the ambient temperature's only eleven degrees, but the body itself is significantly warmer. I found the skin surface temperature to be fifteen degrees and the internal temperature eighteen degrees. The point is, if the body had been lying here for twenty-four hours or more, its surface temperature should by now be tracking the air around it. In other words, it should also be at about eleven degrees — certainly not fifteen. Meanwhile the rectal temperature falls about two-and-a-half times as slowly. So, although it might conceivably still be a few degrees higher than the air, eighteen is really stretching it. What I'm saying is that both values are too high. When I get back to the office computer, I'll put the figures into the relevant algorithm, but I can already offer a viable scenario. For *at least* the first twenty hours after death, the body cooled in an ambient temperature of around twenty degrees Celsius — in other words, a typical indoor, centrally-heated environment. Having reached that temperature both externally and internally, the body was brought out here, where it began to cool again. The surface temperature had time to fall by about five degrees, but the internal only by a couple — hence my estimate that she's been here since about three o'clock this morning." The pathologist paused for a moment, looking rather pleased with himself. "And there's something else I can show you," he added. "Puncture marks on her upper thighs — quite a lot of them — one displaying clear bruising, as if the needle were applied clumsily or with excessive force."

"A drug user?" asked Tero.

"No, these aren't intravenous, they're intramuscular. She might've been a diabetic, but I seriously doubt that's the explanation. I suspect our killer's been using something to keep her quiet."

"Part of his foreplay strategy?" suggested Tero.

The pathologist shrugged. "The toxicology tests should tell us more." He stood up and peeled off his latex gloves. "I'll make myself scarce for now, but I'll be doing the PM this afternoon. By the way, one other minor point of interest: did you notice she's been shaved — the whole of her pubic area shaved clean? Recently too. There's no sign of regrowth. Just a few hours before death, I'd say."

— * —

240

As with the very first victim at the Sibelius Monument, they were faced with a problem of identification. A naked body with no jewellery, no clothes, no handbag... little to give a clue as to who this latest young woman might have been. Nothing except for the body itself... and, of course, the violin. Again Miranda asked to inspect it.

"I think this could help us, boss," she said, carefully turning the instrument in her latex gloves, viewing it from various angles. "It's a rather nice fiddle. Italian made. Not tremendously expensive — no Stradivarius or anything — but a serious instrument. And quite unusual for this part of the world. I could check it out with some violin dealers and repairers. One of them might recognize it."

"All right, we'll leave that to you, Miranda," said Ylenius. "And, Tero, since it seems the body was dumped here in the early hours of the morning, call in all the local traffic-flow video-tapes. Let's see who was on the move at that time and heading to and from this direction. Another thing," he added thoughtfully, "is whether we'll get another follow-up letter to Ainola. What did you decide at the sorting office, Miranda? Has the postbag labelling come into effect yet?"

"Afraid not. The first labelled bags won't be installed in the postboxes until the post vans do their collections this afternoon."

"So, if the pathologist's right," Ylenius calculated, "that this latest victim died the night before last, we may be too late. The killer could've posted his letter yesterday."

"But what if he does do it today," brooded Miranda, "before the new labelled bags are in place? I'll get over to the sorting office, and see if there's some way to save the situation. Identifying the violin will have to wait."

Miranda arrived at the Pasila sorting office a few minutes after 8 am, glad to find that the manager had just started his shift.

"If the letter was picked up in yesterday's batch," he frowned, "it's already been processed and slipped through the net. But, if it gets posted before the afternoon collection today, there's still something we can do. When the vans start arriving, we can ask the drivers which districts they've come from and process each van load separately. That won't tell us the exact postboxes. But it'll narrow things down to a specific area. I'd better stay on this evening and make sure the job gets done properly."

Miranda gratefully accepted the manager's offer of breakfast in the post office canteen, and then set out on her tour of Helsinki's violin specialists. It was little more than a couple of hours before she struck gold.

"Yes, I know this instrument," said an elderly, white-haired craftsman, as he sat in his tiny workshop perusing the Polaroid photos Miranda had brought. "A very respectable example of Torini's work. I was trimming it up for its new owner just a few weeks ago."

"Are you absolutely sure — that it's the same violin?" asked Miranda, hardly daring to believe her luck.

"Oh, the colour and grain of the wood are unmistakable. Look at the beautiful flaming there on the back. It was a young woman who brought it in. About twenty, I suppose. What was her name now? Jaakkola, if I'm not mistaken. Do you want her address? I've got it somewhere."

Miranda phoned the information to Tero. By the time she'd reached the office herself, he'd done a preliminary check on the computer.

"Anneli Jaakkola: Nineteen years old. Lived with her parents. Another music student at the Sibelius Academy. Getting predictable, isn't it? But, that's all we know so far. No criminal record. Didn't have a driving licence... but maybe a mobile phone. I'll check that next."

"Nineteen?" mused Miranda. "I'd've guessed a bit older. Never easy, is it — estimating age after a violent death? I'd better go and talk to the family. Break the news." Tero glanced up enquiringly, but Miranda shook her head. "No, you've got other things to do. I'll take a uniform with me." She had in mind her young protégée, Riitta — the constable she'd taken to that initial interview with Szervánszky. At Miranda's request, Riitta had been one of the extra staff seconded to the investigation a couple of weeks ago.

The Jaakkola home was located in a neat but not especially up-market row of small, two-storey town houses in the eastern suburb of Laajasalo. As Miranda and Riitta approached the front-garden gate, they saw a boy of about ten with a colourful school-satchel ringing the doorbell. A woman, dressed to match her tidy, conventional-looking home, opened the door and gave the boy a weary, welcoming smile. She looked up in mild surprise at the two strangers entering her tiny front garden. As she took in Riitta's uniform, her eyes became anxious. Then almost instantly her expression changed, her face lighting up in a way that, given the nature of the visit, Miranda found unnerving.

"Wonderful," said the woman. "Have you found it? Oh, please say you have!"

Miranda and Riitta exchanged worried glances, neither sure how to proceed. The woman was looking at them expectantly, and Miranda knew she'd have to take the initiative.

"Mrs Jaakkola...? There's something we need to discuss with you. May we come in? Much better to talk inside. Can we sit down somewhere?"

Looking less elated, Mrs Jaakkola led them into the sitting room. The boy hovered.

"We'd prefer to discuss this with you personally," Miranda said, flicking a quick glance at the child. Mrs Jaakkola took the hint.

"Jonni," she said, "go and do your homework at the kitchen table. I'll come and help you soon." Jonni left the room reluctantly. "And close the door behind you, dear!"

The three adults sat around the coffee table, Riitta and Miranda on armchairs, Mrs Jaakkola perched on the edge of the sofa. She didn't look especially worried.

"So what's this all about?" she asked, her eyes drifting back and forth between the visitors.

"The situation is..." Miranda began slowly. "There's no easy way to tell you this but..."

Mrs Jaakkola's face blanched. "What is it? What's happened?" Her fingers dug into the sofa.

"We've found the body of a young woman..." Miranda forced herself to continue. "And we fear that it could be your daughter, Anneli."

"It can't be! She went down the shops. Has she been in an accident?" Panic now consumed her.

"Mrs Jaakkola, this is a terrible thing for you to consider, but no — the young woman in question didn't meet with an accident. I regret to tell you that she was murdered."

"Murdered? My Anneli murdered...?" Her voice faded away in horror and shock as she struggled with this appalling concept.

And then a key turned in the front door lock. Mrs Jaakkola's attention shifted, all of her senses now focused on the unseen person entering the hallway. Like a somnambulist, she raised herself from the sofa and moved haltingly towards the connecting door. It opened before she could reach it, and a young woman of about twenty came quietly into the room, arms laden with plastic shopping bags.

"Mummy," she began, "I managed to find a nice dress for Saturday's..." She broke off, realizing something was wrong. Mrs Jaakkola managed to stagger the last couple of yards and crumpled, sobbing, into the girl's arms. The shopping had fallen to the floor.

"Oh, Anneli! Anneli! They said... They told me..."

The girl stared over her mother's shoulder at the two strangers, who had risen to their feet. As fear ebbed from the older woman it seemed to transfer itself to the daughter.

"What are the police doing here, Mummy? Has something happened to Jonni?"

Miranda stepped forward, determined to clear up the confusion: "No, Jonni's just fine. He's in the kitchen. Are you Anneli Jaakkola?"

The girl nodded.

So who the hell, Miranda wondered, was that other girl lying cold and violated in a body bag at the city morgue?

"I'm afraid, Anneli, there's been an unfortunate misunderstanding."

"They said you were dead!" stammered Mrs Jaakkola, easing back at arm's length to study her daughter's face.

Miranda did her best to apologize for the scare: "I really am sorry about this, but there are some questions we need to ask you, Anneli."

Trying to set an example, Miranda lowered herself back into her seat. The other three eventually followed suit, Mrs Jaakkola pulling her daughter gently onto the sofa beside her, clutching the girl's hand in her own.

"Are you the owner of a Torini violin?"

"Have you found it?" cried Anneli, and again the two policewomen witnessed a violent pendulum swing of emotion, this time from incomprehension to delight.

"We believe we have," Miranda replied.

"That's marvellous! Where did it turn up?"

Then Miranda sensed a hint of caution — even nervousness — colouring the girl's happiness. Was she afraid her instrument had been damaged?

"Your violin's perfectly all right," Miranda assured her, "although it was discovered in connection with a serious crime. I don't want to go into details, but we'd be grateful, Anneli, if you could tell us how it went missing."

"Stolen," the girl said, a fraction hastily. She glanced at her mother, who stopped dabbing at her eyes with a tissue and took up the story on her daughter's behalf: "Somebody stole it off a tram. Right from under your nose, wasn't it, darling? It's been a terrible week, Inspector. First my husband's mother died last Thursday. A lovely person. We were all so fond of her. Then on Monday afternoon Anneli's violin was stolen. A very expensive instrument. What a relief it's been found. Her father had to take out another loan for it. Wanted Anneli to have the very best violin possible now she's getting on so well with her playing. But that wasn't the end of it. Next night, Myrsky — that's my son-in-law, my other daughter's husband — he had his Honda stolen. A couple of joy riders drove off with it at four o'clock in the morning and ran it straight into a tree. Wrote it off! High on drugs, the police said. Under twenty both of them! The world doesn't seem a nice place to live in sometimes, does it, Inspector?"

Miranda felt she wasn't learning anything useful here. "It's the exact circumstances of the violin theft that we need to know," she explained to Anneli patiently.

The girl still seemed reluctant to speak, so again Mrs Jaakkola took over: "Anneli had to go to Stockholm for an audition. She's hoping to study in Sweden next year, and she was taking a tram to the harbour to catch the night ferry. Her father would've given her a lift. Fetches and carries her all over the place. But the rest of us... well, we'd already left for my mother-in-law's funeral — that's me and my husband, and Jonni and Anneli's big sister, Sonja. The funeral was on Tuesday morning in Kuopio so we drove up the day before and stayed overnight. Anneli wanted to come too, but her father said she mustn't miss the audition. This violin teacher in Stockholm... he's very famous, you see... and it's a wonderful chance for Anneli."

"Mrs Jaakkola," Miranda broke in, as gently as possible — although guilt over the horror she'd subjected the woman to earlier was fading fast. "We'd really prefer to hear this from your daughter first-hand."

The mother blinked a couple of times, nodded, and then turned to her daughter with an encouraging smile.

"So when and where was it, Anneli," asked Miranda, "that you caught this tram?"

"On Monday afternoon..." the girl began hesitantly... "at about five o'clock. It was a 3B. I got on at Arkadiankatu." She didn't volunteer any more and Miranda had to prompt her again: "Can you describe the exact sequence of events that led up to the theft?"

Anneli cleared her throat, and gave another sideways glance at her mother. "I had a big rucksack as well as my violin. I got on the tram in the middle. There weren't any free seats, so I put my stuff on the floor by the window. Then I realized my travel pass had run out. I had to go to the front to pay the driver. It was really crowded. I didn't see how I could squeeze up the aisle with all my luggage, so I left it where it was. Silly of me, but it's what I did anyway." As Anneli got further into her story she gained confidence. "But a drunk had got on at the front and was making a bit of a scene with the driver. So it was ages before I could pay. And by the time I got back to my luggage, the violin was gone!"

"Had the tram doors been open all this time?" asked Miranda.

"The driver was too busy with the drunk to close them. Somebody must've picked up my violin and jumped off. I was in a panic. By then we were already halfway to the next stop. I asked all the other passengers, but nobody had seen anything. I got off as soon as the tram stopped and ran back to the museum. But there was no sign of the violin, of course."

"Did you report it to the police?"

"I wasn't thinking clearly. The boat left at six, so when another tram came along I just jumped on. I thought I'd better catch the boat anyway."

"But how were you going to play your audition without an instrument?"

"A friend of mine was going too, and she was the one who bought my previous violin when I got the Torini. I knew she'd lend me the old one."

"When was it you finally told the police?"

"This morning, after I got back to Helsinki."

"Why wait so long?"

"I thought I had to report it to the insurance company first, but I didn't see how I could do that from the boat or from Stockholm. I suppose I was hoping it would all turn out to be a mistake — that someone had picked the violin up thinking it was theirs and would've returned it by the time I got home. And I was ashamed to tell my Dad what had happened. I didn't want to upset him. But when I got back, I told Mum and then I phoned the insurance company. They said I had to make an official report to the police. So then I called the police station, and they told me to go in and make a proper statement — to have it all written down."

"She was so miserable," said Mrs Jaakkola. "I sent her off to the shops to take her mind off it all, and then wait till her father got home from work so she could go to the police station with him. He doesn't know about it yet."

"And now we won't have to tell him, will we, Mum? Not now the violin's turned up."

On the return journey to Pasila, Miranda asked Riitta to drive, and phoned in with the latest news.

"I'm not surprised this Anneli Jaakkola's alive and kicking," Tero said. "We found out who the victim *really* is a few minutes ago. Her fingerprints are on file. She's Estonian and her name's Anna Orav. Twenty-five years old. Noticed soliciting on the street in Helsinki last autumn without a residence or work permit. Sent back to Tallinn with a slap on the bottom. She must've sneaked over again."

"So how does Anneli Jaakkola's violin fit into all this?"

"Obvious, isn't it?" said Tero. "The Orav woman stole it. Big mistake! Turned her into Freako's next target."

A very useful titbit was scrawled on the margin of Anna Orav's police report: the name and address of a friend she'd been staying with in

Finland. This Signe Laan was another Estonian girl, presently an exchange student at Helsinki University. Miranda and Tero paid her a visit.

The petite brunette with close-cropped hair let them into her student apartment. She sat on the bed and offered her visitors the only two chairs available.

"I suppose this is about Anna," the girl said quietly, in excellent, almost unaccented Finnish. "Is she in trouble again?"

Miranda paused, wondering how to reply. "I'm afraid, Signe, it's worse than that."

Signe didn't react violently when told about her friend's death. She sat very still, seeming to shrink in upon herself, tears forming in the corners of her eyes.

"When did Anna return to Finland?" Miranda asked gently.

Signe nerved herself to reply: "A week ago."

"And when did you last see her?"

"On Monday afternoon. She left here about three o'clock. I think she was visiting a regular client. I suppose you know about Anna's..."

Miranda nodded.

"Sometimes I get calls from men," Signe continued, "asking to speak to Anna. I hate that. It wasn't fair to give out *my* phone number. She apologized but the calls kept coming anyway."

"Do you know who any of her regular clients were?"

"We never discussed them. Anna was a dear friend. It's why I let her stay. But I didn't want to know about this other life she was leading."

"Do you think Anna was still working the streets, as well as visiting her regulars?"

"A few nights ago she said she'd been down to Kallio. That's where the prostitutes go, isn't it? She complained all the 'eligible men' were out of town on other business, so she'd have to find some 'new recruits'. That's how she put it, like it was some kind of joke."

Tero brought up the subject of the stolen violin, and Signe's reaction took them by surprise.

"No! No!" she burst out. "Anna would never steal anything!" Her face writhed in reproach. "She wasn't a thief!"

"She was a hooker," said Tero, unimpressed. "Are you saying she was too morally minded to lift the occasional item when the chance came her way?"

"It's true she worked as a prostitute, but she was only selling what was hers to sell. She'd never steal anything!"

"And what about yourself?" asked Tero. "Ever felt the need for a bit of extra income? Ever thought of selling what's yours?"

"You cannot understand, you Finns! Everything is so easy here. Not long ago we were still part of the Soviet Union. We've come a long way. We've made progress. But we cannot work miracles. There's only so much to share around. I was one of the lucky ones. I got a scholarship. Anna wasn't so lucky. She couldn't get money to support her, and she had a little child. Poor Mall! She's only four. What will happen to her now? The father... he's gone... much too young. Young men can't even look after themselves."

"And where's the child now?" asked Miranda.

"With her grandmother in Narva. But Anna's mother is old and not in good health. How long can she manage? It's all so terrible!"

The tears were flowing now, but Signe seemed determined not to let that defeat her: "Some of you Finns think Estonians are all prostitutes and criminals. That's so stupid. We're like everyone else. We're honest and we work hard. We want to make the most of our lives. Anna was very special. She was strong. She was brave. She thought only of little Mall's future. I could never have done what she did. I was so afraid for her. I begged her not to go, but she was stubborn. It was her biggest fault. She always thought she could handle everything. She said it was the quickest way to get money — to finish her education and find a teaching job. And now — now she..." Signe broke off and gave full rein to her misery. Miranda moved across to the bed and sat beside her.

"Signe, I believe you that Anna wasn't a bad person. And whatever she might've done, she didn't deserve to die in that awful way. I promise you we'll do everything we can to catch whoever did this to her. But we need all the help you can give us — to stop him ever doing such a thing again."

II

Andante mosso, quasi allegretto

As Miranda stepped into the Pasila office, the phone was ringing on her desk. It was Panu Marski.

"Just heard on the radio about the latest murder. Am I right in assuming it's part of the same series?"

"Yes, you are."

"Would you like my input again? I'm very willing to help. The problem is I'm off to Boston with the family first thing tomorrow. I mentioned this criminal profilers' conference to you, didn't I? And afterwards we're taking the kids round New England. I'll be gone ten days, so if we're going to meet before that it's got to be today. And my window of opportunity's very narrow, I'm afraid. Lots of last-minute stuff to deal with. But I could probably drop by your office about an hour from now — in transit, so to speak — and take a look at what you've got so far on this fourth one — give some feedback. Is that a viable idea?"

"I can shuffle things to fit you in. I'll meet you downstairs at reception."

Miranda and Tero then went to update Ylenius on their Signe Laan interview.

"She's giving us access to her phone records," Miranda reported. "Any callers' names she doesn't recognize will presumably be Anna Orav's clients."

"And what about the violin theft, Tero?"

"The team's located all three drivers taking 3B trams through Töölö on Monday evening. One of them thinks a drunk could've tried to board at one point but — as he said — it happens all the time. He doesn't remember a girl losing her violin. The tram's crowded at that time of day. Suppose we could have someone travel 3Bs and interview the regular passengers — see if anyone witnessed the theft. But there doesn't seem much point. We already know it was the Orav woman who pinched the violin."

"Perhaps," said Ylenius, "but follow it up anyway — for completeness sake. Has the next Ainola letter turned up, Miranda?"

"No, the vans'll be bringing the mail to the sorting office from about six-thirty onwards. If it's in this batch, at least we'll find out which part of town it was posted in."

"Good. And it's time to give a more detailed release to the media. We can't go on withholding so many features of the MO. The press picked up early on two of the victims being music students, which seemed enough to put the city's young women on their guard. But now we need to warn the public that walking around after dark with a violin is potentially lethal. It's too late to catch the evening tabloids. But we can make sure it reaches today's TV news and the morning papers."

Miranda was about to go down to reception when she got a second call from Panu Marski.

"Look, I'm sorry to mess you about, Miranda, but something unforeseen's cropped up, and I've had to reschedule at the last moment. No way I can meet you now before seven. But I've got a suggestion, and I hope it'll work for you. How about if we do the job over dinner? My treat, naturally. I could meet you at the Savoy on Esplanadi. I expect you know the place."

Miranda's eyebrows rose. Not the class of restaurant she usually got to eat in.

"We could go over the stuff at the same time," Panu continued. "What do you say?"

Miranda said, yes.

It was twenty past seven, and Rosie and Adrian were waiting for Phillip downstairs in the foyer of the Sibelius Academy. By now Adrian knew that Miranda wouldn't be coming to the evening's Sibelius lecture.

"She's tied up at work," Rosie had explained, "meeting some high-powered psychologist. He's helping her with these terrible murders the newspapers are so full of. I understand he's a bit of a dish," she added with an ingenuous smile, and wondered why Adrian winced. Rosie wasn't privy to Miranda's one-night romance with Adrian. It had happened while she was still in London. As far as Rosie understood, relations between herself, her sister and the two Englishmen were entirely Platonic.

Suddenly Rosie's phone rang in her shoulder bag: Phillip offering regrets that he couldn't make the lecture either.

"Struck down with an attack of the Tallinn Tummies," he explained. "Is Adrian there with you, Rosie? Can I have a word?"

Adrian lifted her phone to his ear, and was rewarded with Phillip's baritone voice crooning: "*Diarrhoea! I just got a dose of diarrhoea! And suddenly that pain, will never be the...*"

Adrian was indignant: "Cut it out, Phillip! You're vandalizing my adolescence! I was fond of that song in my youth. I still think it's the best musical ever written."

"Apologies, my suddenly so-sentimental friend. No offence meant to you or Mr Bernstein, but I've got to keep my spirits up. Montezuma's taking his terrible revenge."

"Monty who?"

"It's the 'running trots', dear fellow — the 'galloping geysers', the 'raging rivers of Babylon'. Verily, even as I speak, I'm encamped on the carzey, awaiting life's next gut-wrenching emergency. Pity about the lecture! I was really looking forward to this one. Very keen on the Fifth. Extraordinary stuff, even by our Jean's standards! Still, glad *you* won't be missing any of it. Turn on the mental tape-recorder and play it back to me later. Yes, my advice is sit tight and enjoy the ebb and flow of it all — which is exactly what *I'll* be doing *here*! Sorry, got to go. And I doubt you'd savour the sound effects." He rang off abruptly.

"Sibelius had managed to divide his audience in two: those who recognized the Fourth Symphony as the product of a unique and profoundly creative mind; and those who saw it as an incomprehensible aberration. At a performance in Gothenburg, polite attempts to applaud were drowned out by loud hissing. In Vienna, the work was withdrawn two days before its advertised performance: the reason being that the members of the orchestra had refused to rehearse it! True, there were occasional successes with audiences and critics — notably in Holland, England and the USA — but Sibelius was deeply upset, going so far as to comment in his diary that the best way out would be a bullet in the head. Ultimately he chose a more constructive solution. He began work on new compositions...

"Over the next couple of years, Sibelius produced three important, non-symphonic orchestral works. None of them exceeds a dozen minutes in duration, yet all three are masterpieces.

* [First came *The Bard*: an exquisite, though seldom performed tone poem which almost throughout holds the listener in a strange, contradictory state of stillness and tension — as if suspended motionless a few inches above the ground. The second was *Luonnotar* for soprano and orchestra: a powerful evocation of the Finnish creation myth as told by the epic poem *Kalevala*. Cruel demands are made here on the singer. The vocal line is successively mysterious, passionate, hypnotic, at times approaching atonality in its level of melodic chromaticism.

"If these first two works are recognizable companions to the Fourth Symphony, inhabiting a similarly rarified universe, the third work, *The Oceanides* strikes out in a newly confident and forthright direction: a vivid, iridescent depiction of the sea — with all its capricious and relentless power — and it builds to an awe-inspiring climax of tsunami proportions. Much has been said about this tone poem's impressionistic orchestral textures, but it remains an unmistakably Sibelian analogue to Debussy's *La Mer*. Sibelius himself was excited by what he'd achieved. *My new work*, he wrote, *is altogether superb... The Fourth Symphony was the beginning, but in this there is even more... There are moments that drive me mad. What poetry!*] *

"In terms of present day popularity, *The Oceanides* should be considered the most successful of these three new works. It was commissioned by Carl Stoeckel, a wealthy American businessman and patron of the arts. At Stoeckel's invitation, Sibelius set sail across the Atlantic in May, 1914 — probably with some trepidation, as *The Titanic* had sunk less than two years previously — his objective being to conduct the world premiere of *The Oceanides* at the Norfolk Festival in New England. Stoeckel, the festival's creator, entertained

Sibelius in his own mansion, pampering him with banquets and personal servants. The composer revelled in all this luxury, and in the admiring attention paid him by local musicians and music critics. He was especially delighted with the orchestra Stoeckel provided: an aggregate of some of the best players from Boston and New York. *The orchestra is wonderful!!* Jean wrote to Axel Carpelan. *It surpasses anything we have in Europe.*

"The Americans, in their turn, were much impressed by the Finn's conducting skills. Stoeckel described Sibelius on the podium as *both graceful and powerful*; seldom beating out a steady pulse, his gestures were *reminiscent of someone reciting a great poem.*

* [In *The Oceanides* he created an aethereal *pianissimo*, but was equally capable of whipping the players up into such an overwhelming *fortissimo* as the Norfolk audience would never forget. Meanwhile Olin Downes (later to become the chief music critic of *The New York Times*) felt himself to be in the presence of a genius of world class, comparable only to Richard Strauss and Toscanini. It's instructive to compare these comments with some counterparts in Europe. When Sibelius conducted his Fourth Symphony in Copenhagen, one critic described the composer's conducting technique as *far from virtuoso: not elegant or beautiful to watch, though completely at one with the music.* The Finn's large gestures and outstretched arms suggested to the writer a bird in flight — the music itself seeming to take wing. Another less sympathetic commentator felt Sibelius to be *an anxious, haunted creature whose baton hand trembled like an aspen leaf and whose left hand nervously flailed the air.*] *

In fact, Sibelius usually suffered from terrible stage nerves. At this particular time in his life, he was abstaining from alcohol, but it had earlier been his custom — as a preliminary to public performance — to consume half a bottle of champagne. In his own opinion, he could then conduct like a god!

"Anyway, after much fêting and adulation, Sibelius sailed back from his American visit with plans to return on a major and lucrative conducting tour. Sadly this was never to be. In mid-Atlantic, news arrived by telegraph of the assassination in Sarajevo of the Archduke Franz Ferdinand and, within months of the composer's arrival home, World War I had broken out.

* ["Sibelius was, of course, horrified at the prospect of war, and found his loyalties perplexingly divided. As a musician, he'd travelled much and made important contacts with people now forced to regard each other as enemies. How was he to take sides — either against the Germans or, for example, against his many friends and supporters in England? Although Germany was now officially Finland's enemy, Sibelius deeply admired German literary and artistic traditions. What's more, he would presumably not have been averse to seeing Finland's Russian oppressor under attack — from whatever quarter. If the Czar's regime were sufficiently weakened, might not the Finns seize their opportunity and achieve independence?

"The war also created a serious financial problem. Being cut off from his Berlin publisher robbed Sibelius of one of his main sources of income. He found himself obliged to write a whole series of minor potboilers for Finnish and Danish publishers — piano pieces, songs, choral works — just to make ends meet. This was an enormous frustration. What he really wanted was to get on with his next symphony...] *

"In the autumn of 1914, Sibelius jotted in his notebook: *I already dimly see the mountain I shall certainly ascend... God opens His door and His orchestra plays the Fifth Symphony.* However, the composer's mountain turned out to be steep and arduous. A version performed under the composer's baton at his fiftieth-birthday celebrations in 1915 was immediately withdrawn to be replaced a year later by a radically revised one. The final definitive score which we're familiar with today didn't appear until the autumn of 1919. Looking back over this five-year struggle, Sibelius later explained that the final form of a work is dependent on powers stronger than the composer himself. Although one may later try to justify this idea or another, on the whole one is merely a tool..."

*　　*　　*

[7.49 pm; Wednesday, 19th April]

Didn't it sound wonderful this afternoon? The acoustics in that room! It has to be the high ceilings. And the blending with the Steinway... Really, really beautiful! Her parents must be swimming in money.

255

Still, who's complaining? I've got a fantastic instrument of my own now. Yes! You're everything I could ever've wished for. And almost a giveaway at the price. Can't imagine I'll ever want to part with you... whatever the future might bring.

Oh, shit, not him *again! He seems to show up everywhere these days. I didn't notice him on the bus. Suppose he could've been sitting at the back. It's almost like he's following me around. I wouldn't normally care, but with all this stuff in the papers and music students being attacked. Everyone's getting jumpy. It couldn't possibly be* him *though. Surely not! Anyway it's not even dark yet. But he does seem to be trailing me. Oh, shit! I'm getting a really bad feeling about this. I'd better get home quick!*

She accelerated over the last twenty yards — was almost running when she reached the front door of the apartment block, fumbling with her key. She yanked the door open just enough to squeeze through the gap. Her instrument case got in the way and slowed her marginally. The delay was critical. He was also running up the path, determined not to be locked out. She tugged with all her force to reclose the door, fighting the pneumatic spring that resisted her efforts. Just as the lock should have clicked shut, he grabbed the handle and pulled from the other side. For a moment she tried to counter his pull with her own, but he was clearly going to be the stronger. Abandoning the attempt, she turned tail and stumbled up the stairs. Her instrument was again a handicap. She should have discarded it. Perhaps the joy she'd felt earlier over this new acquisition was impairing her judgment. Whatever the reason, the case remained clutched in her right hand. And she could sense him on the stairs below, gaining on her. Whimpering sounds came from her throat as she propelled herself upwards, step by frantic step. She could have called out for help but dared not waste her waning energy — or her labouring breath. Her flat was on the third floor. How would she open the door fast enough and get inside to safety? In the event, she never had the chance. He caught up with her on the second-floor landing, grasping her hair, dragging her to a stop. She spun round to face him. The instrument case might yet have been her salvation. She swung it with all her strength, aiming for his head. But, at such close quarters, she misjudged the distance. He brushed the blow aside with his upper arm, forcing her backwards into a corner of the hallway. The instrument crashed to the floor and bounced out of reach. She screamed three times as he wrenched the noose over her head. A fourth scream was cut short as he jerked it tight. Her eyes locked onto his, terrified, pleading. The gaze he offered in return was implacable.

She had, of course, been created as a thing of beauty: he recognized the fact. But he wouldn't allow that to deter him. Appearances were often deceptive. Nor would he be swayed by her youth. His duty was inescapable. He served an ideal greater than his own will or any considerations of pity. He was merely the tool of a higher authority; and this role, which he had courageously taken upon himself, was one that he would not — indeed could not — fail to perform.

*   *   *

"... although one may later try to justify this idea or another, on the whole one is merely a tool. And the wonderful logic — which Sibelius suggests we call God — the wonderful logic that governs a work is the *true* compelling power. On another occasion, Sibelius compared the compositional process to the Almighty throwing pieces of a mosaic down from the floor of heaven and telling the composer to put them together again. Reconstructing the mosaic for the Fifth Symphony turned out to be the most challenging task he had so far faced.

"And the pressures of the war and of continuing financial insecurity were telling on Sibelius in other ways. After a nine-year abstinence, he was slipping back into his old habits: smoking, drinking, extravagantly carousing till the early hours in the watering holes of Helsinki — putting himself and his family even further into debt. His diaries attest to the guilt and shame he felt over this backsliding, and to an awareness of the renewed misery it caused his wife, Aino. Nevertheless, his weakness prevailed.

"Meanwhile, in the world at large, monumental historic events were unfolding. As a knock-on effect of the Russian Revolution in October 1917, Finland declared its independence. Within three weeks, this bold opportunistic step had been ratified by Lenin himself. Statehood thus came to the Finns with surprising suddenness, but it was not to be a bloodless transition. Civil war swept the country. A 'red' faction, hoping to create Finland in the image of Russia's new Bolshevik model, took control of the south. Lawless armed bands roamed the countryside taking reprisals on 'white' nationalists. Sibelius's home, Ainola, was twice invaded by red militia claiming the right to search the premises for weapons. During one of these incidents, to quell his daughters' fears — and most probably his own — the composer sat down at the piano and started to play. One of the militiamen commented to a servant in the kitchen how pleasant it must be to work in a house filled with such music. But the safety of Ainola could no longer be guaranteed. Sibelius was persuaded to bring his family into Helsinki on a temporary basis. In fact, the national situation was a short while later normalized when a German expeditionary force routed the red supporters and handed Finland over to the whites.

"Throughout these troubled times, Sibelius had maintained a regular correspondence with his old friend Axel Carpelan. The baron had continued to provide support and encouragement, offering insightful advice on Jean's composition and penetrating appraisals of the unsettled political climate. But their long association was now to end. In March 1919, Axel succumbed to a worsening heart condition. His death left Sibelius devastated: *How alone I am with all my music*, he wrote in his diary. *Whom shall I compose for now?* Despite their long friendship, Sibelius persisted in an earlier resolution to attend no more funerals. He instead threw himself once and for all into the task of completing the Fifth Symphony. Perhaps he saw this as the best possible epitaph to a man who, for nearly twenty years, had so faithfully shared in his creative struggles."

* [*Further excerpts from Dr Lewis's fifth lecture:*
"In the Fifth Symphony, we shall find virtually every element of Sibelius's mature style. Let us review seven of the most important:

"ONE: Thematic unity. As we noticed in the earlier symphonies (from at least the Second onwards) the melodic material seems to evolve and mutate organically from a few short germinal ideas.

"TWO: Harmonically the music drifts backwards and forwards between a limited number of chords whose interrelationships are modal rather than complying with traditional major-minor progressions. These chords also have a tendency to overlap and blur at the edges.

"THREE: Much use of 'pedals' — that is, long held notes — which underpin the musical texture, and yet, paradoxically, generate a hovering sensation of suspense.

"FOUR: A calculated obscuring of the pulse. Melodies are often syncopated and dissociate themselves from the bar lines. At times, it seems that almost the only member of the orchestra observing the downbeats is the conductor!

"FIVE: An avoidance of modulating sequences. These were stock-in-trade for many Romantic-period composers, especially in their development sections. Instead of taking a melodic idea and transposing it into a succession of different keys, Sibelius drifts from one key to another by chromatically mutating the melodic fragments themselves.

"SIX: The use of two or more simultaneous layers of sound. These are generally distinguishable by their instrumentation (strings or brass or woodwind) but, more importantly, each is moving at a different speed. In a process perhaps akin to the mathematical concept of the 'lowest common denominator', the combined texture takes on such enormous metrical phrase lengths that the music seems to stop moving altogether — to be hovering in space. And yet there is an enormous amount of throbbing, pulsating potential energy generated as the layers collide internally.

"SEVEN: Frequent use of *tremolando* strings, in which the players agitate their bows rapidly back and forth. The resulting texture can be shimmering, murmuring, rustling, quivering or chattering. Typically Sibelius places the *tremolando* effect across intervals that are continuously and irregularly shifting, thus further serving to obscure the pulse. Textures of this kind can also generate enormous amounts of energy without contributing to a sense of clear forward motion.

. . . .

"The Fifth Symphony opens in a spacious tonal landscape, tentatively optimistic. But this mood is subtly transformed into something else: a restless groping towards some undefined goal. To me it suggests a disembodied soul wandering in a vast and viscous three-dimensional no-man's-land — although this state of limbo remains mysterious rather than fearful or despondent. The orchestral colours are translucent, sometimes vibrant; predominantly in pastel shades. The overall impression of these first eight minutes is one of slow-motion, even stasis. But Sibelius is able to generate enormous reserves of churning, seething power by means of the devices I described earlier: a blurring of the pulse and the harmony, long suspended pedals, overlaying of contrasting speeds; the whole effect frequently intensified by pulsating, irregularly shifting tremolando strings.

"And now comes one of the most fascinating moments in the whole of Western orchestral music: This state of churning potential energy is converted — over a period of eight bars — to one of pure kinetic energy. As if lovingly set free from the grinding turmoil, a lilting dance-like theme in a rocking triple metre emerges from the dissipating tension. Its onward coasting motion contrasts strikingly with everything that has gone before. The extraordinary magic of this passage lies in how the transitional process is achieved so smoothly and seamlessly. One is at a loss to say exactly where the transformation from potential to kinetic energy has occurred... Once released, however, the ongoing motion is nurtured and relentlessly intensified. A steady *accelerando* — both in terms of the written tempo and the subjective sensation of speed — makes the exhilarating close to this first movement the fastest music that Sibelius ever wrote.

. . . .

"I've sometimes wondered about the composer's original intention of supporting, with a background of tremolando strings, the famous hammer blows that conclude this symphony. I've even toyed with the idea that, in some ways, it might have been a more coherent way to round off the whole work. But, as we know, Sibelius, after many years of deliberation, thought otherwise. And there's no denying that separated — as they now are — between stark, pregnant silences, those six *staccato*, *fortissimo* chords provide a dramatic and unforgettable close to one of the greatest masterpieces of our symphonic literature."] *

When the lecture was over, Rosie and Adrian made their way to a locked rehearsal room on the fourth floor of the Academy where Rosie had stowed her cello. Their plan was to run through the first pages of Adrian's new sonata, addressing questions of notation, idiom and practicability.

But first Rosie wanted to phone Phillip to see how he was.

"He's not answering," she said. "He must've switched his mobile off. When did he start this tummy upset?"

"Don't know," answered Adrian. "Haven't talked to him since the Tallinn trip. Mind you, I've been busy the last couple of days. He's probably tried to call my flat. Lately he's been fussing over me like a mother hen. It gets a bit irritating."

"Oh, don't take it like that, Adrian. Phillip's a lovely person. I'm sure he does it with the best of intentions."

"Of course, Rosie. You're probably right."

* *

~ *I remember another rumour doing the rounds.*

~ *What rumour was that?*

~ *One evening you dated a girl from the French Department, went back to her place for coffee, and ended up forcing her to have sex with you.*

~ Are you suggesting I'm some kind of date rapist? Don't be absurd!

~ *If it's so absurd, tell me what* really *happened.*

~ I can't believe you'd take that crap seriously. She was up for it. No question! Invited me into her room... knew damn well what came next. We played it a bit rough, certainly. But she enjoyed every minute of it. I can vouch for it.

~ *Then why did she say otherwise later?*

~ Getting back at me probably. It was just a one-off as far as I was concerned. Probably ruffled her feathers. She never reported anything to the police, did she? Obvious now I look back on it. She spread the rumours out of spite.

~ *Then there was another occasion — a different girl a year later.*

~ Hey, leave it off, will you? Stop giving me the third degree!

~ *I just want the truth. Was there anything in it?*

~ Of course there bloody wasn't! Stop making such a fuss! There's always got to be some arsehole somewhere trying to defame one's character. I'm telling you, it was all exaggerated. Just foul loose tongues. Forget the whole thing!

~ *In the light of subsequent events, that's going to be very difficult.*

* *

261

Miranda and Panu had dealt with the Anna Orav files while sipping alcohol-free cocktails and picking occasionally at their hors d'oeuvres.

"It's just as you predicted," Miranda said. "He's still refining his MO. The basic elements are the same, but now he's added abduction and an anaesthetic drug to the spectrum."

"I would've preferred to be wrong," Panu admitted, "but, yes, he's finding new ways to increase his control and draw out his pleasure."

"He must've had a vehicle of some kind for this latest victim, although it's still guesswork where he picked her up. Tero thinks the killer selected Anna because of the violin she was carrying. Seems reasonable. So, if the poor woman was trawling for punters with a violin case in her hand, some third party must surely've noticed her. As Tero said, it's not your standard hooker's fashion accessory, is it? A couple of our own girls are asking around. Hopefully one of Anna's colleagues saw something that night."

"Prostitutes are always at risk," said Panu. "Their promise of instant availability's a powerful draw for many men — especially a man of the type we're considering here. It's so easy to lure a prostitute into a car, drive her to a secluded spot, and overpower her. But I suspect our killer's found his own secluded spot — a special hideaway where he can take his victim and enjoy her to the full."

"We wondered if the vehicle *itself* could've been a sort of 'mobile hideaway' — a windowless van, for example. But the pathologist's report seems to discount that. The body was stored in a warm temperature for the best part of twenty-four hours before it was finally dumped, so the engine would've had to be kept running the whole time. A more likely alternative's the murderer transported her to some indoor location on the Monday night, killed her in the early hours and waited until the *following* night to get rid of the body. Any ideas what kind of 'hideaway' he'd favour, Panu?"

"Somewhere private, of course — which rules out a flat. Too many neighbours. Too risky getting her in and out. A house with an adjoining garage would be more practical — assuming, of course, he lived there alone. But I suspect he's found somewhere completely separate — a new dedicated venue to match this new discovery he's made about himself. That'd be much more in character, though exactly what kind of place I couldn't say. A cottage in the forest? A lock-up cellar or garage? A residential caravan on a camping site?"

When the main course arrived, Panu insisted they put the files away and concentrate on their food. Miranda dutifully shifted the discussion from the present murders by asking Panu how he'd got into criminal profiling in the first place.

"Not by seeking it out," he replied. "I've been working in the prison service for the best part of ten years — psychiatric support and rehabilitation of prisoners. Some of them have violent histories. Some are rapists. Some murderers. In the day-to-day routine, I started meeting some of the police officers involved in putting the criminals away. Occasionally they'd ask me for informal advice on a case they were pursuing. After a while the requests became more official."

"Do you regret being drawn in?"

"Not exactly." Panu gave her a quick appreciative glance. "I'm glad you're not one of those who assume I enjoy the job. I even get asked whether I find it exciting. You must feel the same about your own work: studying brutal crime scenes and autopsy photographs, trying to penetrate the minds of people who are capable of committing appalling acts of violence on others. The day we find such things enjoyable or exciting is the day we should give it up forever."

Miranda nodded agreement. She realized how unconcerned she felt this evening about resisting Panu's natural charm. She could even admit to falling a little under the spell of his deeply mellow, soft-spoken voice. Should that worry her? Had it been wise to accept this invitation? Should she have insisted on more neutral, professional ground? *Oh, for heaven's sake, Miranda, don't be so tedious! The food's excellent. The milieu's opulent. Even the conversation's of interest.*

"But there's a definite need to make a contribution, isn't there?" Panu went on... "to help catch a violent criminal before he can harm again. I mean, if there's a small chance we might protect another potential victim from suffering, and his or her loved ones from horror and grief. Of course," he added wryly, "I've considered giving up this side of my life altogether, and starting up a lucrative private practice somewhere dealing with 'normal' people — tending troubled teenagers and bored housewives. Even my regular prison work lacks glamour. Sitting there with a sympathetic mask, while you listen to a sadistic rapist describing the life-enhancing thrill he experienced from subjecting some poor innocent woman to humiliation and torture. Criminal profiling's another slant on the same ugly picture: just viewing it from the opposite end."

"And *will* you eventually give up on it?"

Marski returned Miranda's gaze before answering: "It's difficult to refuse a new request for help when it comes. I have to make the attempt. It was the same when *you* called. Perhaps it always will be."

Throughout the meal, Miranda was aware of how the eyes of other women at neighbouring tables were drawn repeatedly and surreptitiously in Panu's direction. It was rather flattering to be the one sitting opposite him. Marski himself seemed oblivious to the attention, and showed no interest in anyone except his own table companion.

Miranda reflected on what Panu had just said. It resonated strongly with her own experience.

"Don't you find it difficult," she said, "to avoid carrying the horror around as permanent baggage? I'm especially finding that with this latest series of murders."

Marski understood at once. "Yes, it drives a wedge into your private life, and insinuates itself into your personal relationships — not only in what you say and do, but in what you find unable to say or do. It creates an unwelcome distance between yourself and those you should feel closest to."

They exchanged specific episodes from their parallel professions: comparing stresses and successes. And as they spoke, Miranda had the fanciful sensation — not unpleasant — that Panu was peeling back the layers of her self-imposed reserve, unwrapping her professional persona to discover the private woman beneath. Was it his professional couch-side manner on autopilot? Maybe. But she'd felt from their first meeting that his interest was of a more personal nature. Is that why she'd agreed to this unusual dinner arrangement? To test out her suspicions? And what did she intend doing with the knowledge if she acquired it?

The conversation drifted — or was it being steered? — until she found herself talking about the breakdown of her marriage, and analysing the causes.

Panu was sympathetic. "It's hard," he agreed, "for a partner to appreciate the intensity of what we have to do on a daily basis — impossible, in fact — unless that person's experienced it themselves. Unfair of us to expect it. But the isolation gets unbearable sometimes. A solution, of course, would be to have a partner who *does* know — someone who's able to share the pain."

But when Panu admitted that the family trip to New England had been a last-ditch effort to hold his marriage together, Miranda's guard came up. Where was this really leading?

Marski had been steadily displaying more intimacy — in the tone of his voice, in the way he held Miranda's eyes a fraction longer than necessary. Was it time to muster her defences... before things got out of hand?

Of course, it was her own fault. She'd stepped into this situation, in all probability anticipated it from the start, even dared it to happen. And now she'd have to deal with the consequences. Whatever Panu might disclose about a bankrupt relationship with his wife, there were two young children in the equation. Miranda wasn't about to take on the role of homebreaker.

Then, like a gift from heaven, her mobile phone rang... Although the 'gift' Tero Toivonen offered seemed more likely to have come from hell.

"Things are hotting up," he said. "Another one already — a fifth girl strangled!" His voice sounded far too zestful for Miranda's taste. "It's in Kuusitie. I'm heading that way right now. Can you meet me there?"

Miranda asked for the precise address and rang off.

"Sorry, Panu, there's an emergency." She was already on her feet. "I'll have to go. Many thanks for the delicious meal." She retrieved her bag from the back of the chair and hooked it over her shoulder. "And, of course, for the feedback on Anna Orav. Hope you have a marvellous trip with your family."

By now, Marski had also risen from his chair, gracefully resigned to the interruption. "I'll be in touch as soon as I get back," he said.

Miranda dashed for the door, relieved to be distancing herself from this hazardous rendezvous… which also explains why she failed to mention the reason for her hasty departure. Marski would certainly have offered to accompany her.

As things turned out, it might have been better if he had.

III

Allegro molto—
Misterioso—Un pochettino largamente

"**D**efinitely the same killer," announced Tero, as soon as Miranda joined him. Along with the two uniformed officers who'd answered the emergency call, they were still the only ones to have arrived at the crime scene. "Victim's been strangled with a length of electrical cable. Fourth finger of the right hand missing. But he's changed his instrumentation." Tero indicated a black, distinctively shaped case lying up against the wall of the landing.

"That's a French horn!" exclaimed Miranda, in astonishment.

"Even I didn't mistake it for a violin."

Miranda turned her attention back to the victim and squatted down beside the body. The light was dim on the stairs but, as before, this girl was very young: twenty, maybe less. Curly blonde hair. Pretty, delicate features. Miranda thought she looked familiar.

Tero was meanwhile providing the background: "Victim found just before eight o'clock by an old gent living on the floor above. Says he was up in his flat and heard some blood-curdling screams from the stairwell. Didn't do anything immediately. He's been down with the flu and was wandering around in his pyjamas. Anyway, he listened at the door a bit, and then decided to investigate. Found her here, already dead."

"No sign of the killer?"

"Not exactly. The old geezer heard someone running down the stairs, leaving by the front entrance in a hurry. Too late to see who it was though."

"I don't get it," Miranda said, standing up. "The victim's fully clothed. No sign of any sexual assault."

"Perhaps he wasn't in the mood," suggested Tero. "Perhaps he had a headache."

This was more than Miranda could bear: "For God's sake!" she exploded. "Show a bit of respect, will you?"

Tero stared back in wonder, obviously feeling she'd overreacted to such a harmless little remark. When he spoke again, it was with no hint of remorse: "Dear old Freako was interrupted, that's all. Didn't have time for the full works. Heard somebody coming and had to settle for the essentials."

Miranda shook her head. "No, Tero, the sequence is all wrong. The rape should've come *before* the amputation. He still made time for *that*, didn't he? And he hasn't staged her in the usual sitting position. She's sprawled on the floor, just as she fell."

"No use quibbling over details. The missing finger proves it's the same fruitcake."

"Yes, yes, all right. But the whole thing seems out of character. He abducted Anna Orav to give himself more time. Why didn't he do the same with *this* girl? Why the sudden reversion in MO?"

At that moment, her mobile phone rang. It was the manager at the postal sorting office. The fourth Ainola letter had arrived.

"Came in on a van from the Töölö area," the manager told her. "Narrows things down to just nine collection points."

"That's good," said Miranda, "but we've already got a fifth victim, so you can expect another letter at any time."

"Right, well, the postbag labelling's set up for tomorrow's collections. Next time we should be able to pinpoint the exact letterbox."

Miranda thanked him and pocketed her phone, just as Ylenius, the pathologist and the SOCO team arrived en masse, climbing noisily up the stairs. Powerful portable lights were set up to illuminate the scene. Highly trained personnel went about their disciplined business while Miranda hung back on the fringe, still puzzling over the inconsistencies and suffering from an ever more crippling sense of horror...

Yet another young woman viciously slaughtered! How many more before they caught the killer? If they ever did! And how much more could she take herself? She experienced a visual recall of Panu across the dinner table, reaching out with an understanding smile and placing his hand tenderly over her own. This wasn't genuine recall. She'd left the restaurant before anything of the sort could happen. But, for all that, the image was disconcerting. She dismissed it from her mind and picked her way to the landing below, where she could be out of earshot of her colleagues. Finding her phone again, she dialled Rosie's mobile.

"Rosie, I'm going to be in late tonight. We've had another murder — up on Kuusitie — and it's obviously in the same series. No way of knowing how long I'll be tied up at the scene. By the way, is Adrian with you?"

"Yes, right here. Do you want to speak to him?"

"No, I just wondered... has he been with you the whole evening?"

"Since quarter past seven."

"And he hasn't been out of your sight since then?"

"No, we sat together at Daddy's lecture, and the last half-hour we've been running through the new cello sonata."

"Thank God!" said Miranda, in an undertone.

"The sonata's wonderful, Miranda. So lyrical. I know you're going to love it."

"Yes, I'm sure I am, Rosie. But things are really busy here. I'll have to go. Bye!"

In the rehearsal room at T-building, Rosie put the phone away, and reached for her cello.

"Was that Miranda?" asked Adrian.

Rosie nodded. "She's been called away to Kuusitie for another of those awful murders. Done by the same man, she said. It's so revolting. I don't know how she can stand it."

"Was she asking about me?"

"She wanted to know if we'd been together the whole evening. Seemed to think it was important for some reason."

Adrian stared back thoughtfully.

"And she sounded really relieved when I said we had," Rosie added, with a slightly puzzled smile.

Just before one o'clock the next day, Phillip heard something drop on his doormat. Seeking a moment's distraction, he went to investigate.

Far too late to be a normal postal delivery, so he wasn't surprised to find just the usual bundle of advertising circulars and the free, district newspaper. The latter had been jammed so ham-fistedly into the letter box that it was caught in the sprung hinge of the outer metal flap. After tugging fruitlessly for a few moments, he realized his only recourse was to retrieve the newspaper from the other side. He opened the door... and there stood Rosie, smiling up at him brightly.

"Did you hear me coming?" she said. "I haven't rung the door bell yet."

"Good heavens! What are *you* doing here, Rosie?"

"I was at a friend's place round the corner, so I thought I'd find out how you're feeling today." Since Phillip looked rather dismayed, she added: "You did say drop in any time. Are you sorry to see me?"

"Oh, please forgive my hideous bad manners! What an atrocious lack of breeding!" Phillip reached around the door and struggled to pull the entangled newspaper from the outside of the letter box. "My dear Rosie, how could I ever be less than delighted — day or night — to receive your adorable person at my home."

Taking this as an invitation, Rosie squeezed past him into the flat's tiny hallway. Phillip continued to fumble in frustration at the letter box for a few moments and, at last extricating the shredded remains of the newspaper, followed her inside. He would have preferred her to turn left into the kitchen, but no, she'd taken the opposite direction into his only other room: a hybrid lounge, study and bedroom. When he caught up with her she was leaning over his desk casually flipping through the pages of one of several books lying there untidily open and surrounded by loose sheets of notepaper. She seemed impressed.

"Do you really read such difficult stuff in a foreign language? More than *I* could ever manage. Give me a nice romantic novel any day."

"I like to keep my hand in," said Phillip as he busily stacked the books into a neat pile and stowed the papers away in one of the desk drawers. He then rushed around the room, scooping up a few items of clothing, a discarded coffee mug and a plate from the floor; finally pulling the bedcovers as straight as he could manage with his remaining free hand.

"You've caught me off guard," he said, "in an embarrassing state of disarray!"

"Disarray?" laughed Rosie. "You should see *my* room six days out of seven. Miranda's always complaining about the mess I make around the flat. I try to do my share. I know it's not fair to leave it all to her. I suppose I'm just disorganized."

"*My* only excuse is yesterday's little indisposition," Phillip continued. "Really wasn't up to much, I have to admit."

"And are you feeling any better?" asked Rosie, suddenly solicitous.

"Yes, yes! Vast improvement. Shall we withdraw to the kitchen and partake of a steaming cup of the old char? Lapsang Souchong suit you?"

After the mild 'disarray' of the bedroom, the kitchen was immaculate: spotlessly clean, with every item in its allotted place. Phillip looked relieved to be there as he filled and plugged in the electric kettle.

"Take a seat, Rosie, do! Tell me *all* about *every*thing! Good lecture was it? How about your run-through with Adrian? Go according to plan?"

"Oh, the cello sonata, Phillip! It's beautiful! Adrian's fantastically talented, isn't he?"

"Yes, I have often noticed something fantastical about him."

Rosie laughed, and they continued in the same cosy fashion, sharing their tea across the kitchen table, until Phillip brought up the subject of the latest murder.

"Adrian told me about it last night," he said, pouring them a second cup. "Phoned me when he got home. It happened near here I understand."

"In Kuusitie," Rosie admitted reluctantly.

"Then I heard something on the radio this morning. Wasn't it another of those music student murders?"

"So Miranda said..." Rosie clearly didn't want to discuss the matter, but Phillip hadn't finished yet.

"And I suppose there was that business with the finger again."

He received a blank look. "What do you mean? Whose finger?"

"You know, the thing with the finger... that the killer always..." Phillip stopped and stared at her. "I heard it from..." He hesitated again, only to burst out: "What an imbecile! How could I be so indiscreet? Please, please, promise me, darling Rosie, that you won't mention anything about this to Miranda. It'll only cause *more* bad feeling in the wrong places. If she finds out he's been telling me stuff that she... Dear God! It's *me* who's the *real* blabbermouth! I sometimes think I should have my tongue surgically removed."

"Please, Phillip, don't! That really *is* a horrid thing to say. And all this murder stuff. It's something Miranda and I hardly ever talk about. I don't want to hear it, and she doesn't want to tell me. So there's no need to worry, is there?"

"Any further thoughts on the fourth letter?" asked Ylenius.

Tero and Miranda glanced again at the photocopy in their ever-thickening files:

Käpylä
Monday, 17th April

Symphony No 4 in A minor

Dear A.
I know you must find my fallibility and capriciousness almost intolerable. Well, of course, it's true: I shouldn't allow myself to give way to these impulses. Perhaps I can learn to govern them in future; although I very much fear the contrary.

"There's a clear shift of viewpoint," Miranda noted. "Now he seems to be admitting there's something reprehensible in his behaviour, and he should be trying to control himself."

"He hasn't done much of a job so far," said Tero. "He apologizes for abducting and killing his fourth victim on Monday night, and a couple of days later he's gone and garrotted another one."

Ylenius frowned. "Yes, the frequency of the attacks has suddenly escalated. But what about the letter's place and date headings? We know from the pathologist's report that Anna Orav's death occurred in the early hours of Tuesday morning. But the letter's dated Monday — the day before."

"He's referring to the abduction time," said Miranda, "not to when he actually killed her."

"And he specifies Käpylä as the location. Do we really believe he abducted her from the same place we found the body?"

"He's just muddying the waters," Tero said.

Miranda agreed: "Why should he make us a gift of where he picked Anna up? If we knew *that* we'd have a chance of finding a witness."

"And I don't think it was one of her regular johns," Tero went on. "I've been checking the names we got from Signe Laan's telephone log. None of the men admits to meeting Orav on Monday night. And, so far, their alibis check out."

"Any luck finding Anna's clothes?" asked Ylenius.

"No, we've trawled the area, and checked all the local rubbish bins. No result."

"Well," said Ylenius, "I heard something important from the lab this afternoon. The pathologist got it right. Anna Orav was injected with a drug called Comatin: an anaesthetic used regularly for operations. The first shot was probably designed to knock her out while he transferred her to somewhere private. But there were so many other puncture marks on the victim's thighs — eleven in all — the implication is that, afterwards, he used very low dosages at intervals of say fifteen or twenty minutes. That way he could've kept her in a state of compliant drowsiness for several hours."

"You mean she was semi-conscious the whole time?"

"Yes, Miranda. Compliant, but not completely unaware."

"So he could give himself the illusion she was a consenting party," Miranda concluded, frowning with distaste.

"But where did he lay his hands on this Comatin?" Tero wondered. "Do you think he's a doctor?"

"Possibly," Ylenius nodded. "But he could've just stolen the drug from somewhere. Better check if any's gone missing."

"But, boss," Miranda objected, "wouldn't it need specialist knowledge to administer this Comatin?"

"I asked the pathologist, and he reckons it wouldn't take much skill. Intramuscular injection. No need to even find a vein. Of course, you'd have to know the right dosage. But the killer could've looked that up in a medical library."

"Or on the internet," said Tero.

"It's true he's not against doing a bit of background research," Miranda conceded. "He's proved *that* with his Sibelius quotes. But I'm wondering where he got the Comatin idea in the first place. Not the layman's obvious choice for subduing a rape and murder victim, is it?"

Ylenius shrugged. "I suppose there's no harm adding a possible medical background to the profile. But we can't rule out that he heard of Comatin some other way. And something else they found in connection with Anna Orav: the killer used a different pair of secateurs to amputate her finger. The blades weren't serrated. The lab couldn't be specific about the model, but they suggested a larger, heavier-duty pair than the ones he's used on his earlier victims."

"Probably thought they'd be more serviceable for the job *on hand*," Tero suggested, with one of his irritating smirks.

Next they reviewed the facts so far about the *fifth* victim: Jaana Saari, twenty years old, and a second-year student at the Helsinki Conservatory; her instrument the French horn. The autopsy had confirmed death by strangulation with no indications of rape or recent intercourse. And there were no suspicious pinpricks on her body. Although the noose had been fashioned in a similar design to the ones they'd seen earlier, the cable itself was curious. It consisted of two separate plastic-coated wires, one red and one black, which spiralled around each other and were then fused at their line of contact.

"A cable like this can't be very common," Ylenius conjectured. "Find out who manufactures it and if there's any specific equipment it comes with as an accessory. That could give us something to follow up."

"You mean it could be a useful *lead*," Tero smirked again.

"I'm surprised," Miranda said, all her attention on Ylenius, "that the killer's reverted to electric cable. And what's happened to all the sophisticated planning? This looks like another rush job."

"Probably our Freako's version of a 'quickie'," said Tero.

Miranda flinched, but refused to be drawn, suspecting Tero of trying to goad her... as some kind of retaliation for her outburst at yesterday's crime scene.

"In fact, I'd seen her before," Miranda said, redirecting the conversation "...the victim, I mean. Though I didn't register it at first — not till the Conservatory connection cropped up again. She was in a group of students I chatted to in the Conservatory canteen — three or four weeks ago it must've been. Seems like months!"

Ylenius sighed. "Yes, Jaana Saari's the second victim from the Conservatory. So let's focus more of our attention there. It might turn out to be the source of the whole problem."

"You reckon, boss?" Tero asked doubtfully. "We've also had a press photographer, a Sibelius Academy student and an Estonian hooker. The only connection I can see is they were each carrying a musical instrument. Two Conservatory girls could just be a coincidence."

"And another coincidence turned up just before this meeting," Miranda cut in. "I got a call from a piano student at the Conservatory named Hanna Kettunen. She was really upset... thinks she must have a jinx on her, because Jaana Saari visited her flat in Mariankatu yesterday afternoon. They ran through a horn sonata together at Hanna's own Steinway. And that's the coincidence. Hanna's the same girl Liisa Louhi went to practise with a few hours before *she* was murdered!"

Ylenius shook his head. "I don't like coincidences. In Mariankatu, you say? Maybe the murderer lives in the same area, perhaps even in the same block. He could've picked up on Liisa and Jaana in a similar fashion — spotted them near this pianist's flat or coming out of her building — started following each of them from there. Put as much manpower as you can spare on checking out residents in that locality: anyone who might fit our profile. Cross-reference. See if somebody's figured earlier in our enquiries. I presume you're doing door-to-door in Jaana Saari's neighbourhood?"

Tero and Miranda nodded.

"There's one other thing," Ylenius said. "We need to modify our disclosure to the media: that not only carrying a violin can be dangerous, but carrying *any* musical instrument. We've got to warn every young female musician to avoid crossing the city alone — not until we catch up with this maniac. And it's no longer safe to specify 'after dark'. He's getting bolder. Potential victims will have to be on their guard at all times — even in broad daylight."

Adrian answered the door stripped to the waist, his face partially covered in shaving cream.

"Won't be long. Just finish this off."

Phillip drifted into the front room. Warm sensuous sounds from the CD player were filling the modestly sized space.

"What's this music you're playing?" called Phillip, loud enough to reach the bathroom. "Smells like Debussy."

"Full marks!" Adrian shouted back. "*Les Parfums de la Nuit*: from his *Images*."

"Rosie dropped in on me today."

"Sorry, can't hear you!" Adrian's voice was raised over the sound of running water. "Hang on a moment."

A few seconds later, he emerged with a towel draped round his neck, wiping the last traces of shaving cream from his jawline.

"Did you say something?"

"Rosie paid me a surprise visit this afternoon. She seemed suitably impressed by your new cello sonata. When do *I* get to hear it?"

"Don't know. Plenty to do still. And we'll have to mike the cello through all the special effects before my full intentions can be heard." He plumped himself down on an armchair.

Phillip remained standing, a vacant smile cast in Adrian's approximate direction.

"Recovered from yesterday's gut rot?" Adrian asked.

"Yes, all over."

"Perhaps a bug you picked up in Tallinn."

"Could've been."

Adrian gestured an invitation towards the other armchair, but Phillip shook his head and began wandering listlessly around the room, pulling books and CDs off the shelves, giving each a cursory examination before returning it.

"Been in touch with Miranda yet?" he asked.

"How do you mean?"

"Come on, Adrian. It's time to take the initiative — find out what her real feelings are. She hasn't got an excuse to hide behind any more."

"I can't afford to be pushy. She reacts badly to that kind of thing. Better to hold off a bit longer — give *her* a chance to make the running."

"Anyway, at last you've got an unassailable alibi. Even Mr Tero 'The Terrier' Toivonen won't be able to argue with a lecture hall full of people — not to mention your being accompanied by the sister of a superior officer!" He moved across to the window and gazed out beyond the library to Sibelius Park. Some of the birch trees were already displaying fresh pale-green leaves.

"Yes," Phillip added quietly, "it could hardly've worked out better if I'd organized it myself."

Symphony No 6

I

Allegro molto moderato

Seven o'clock in the evening, and Miranda was feeling restless again, unable to concentrate on reading and crosschecking the numerous reports left on her desk by other members of the murder team. Despite that, going home held little attraction, especially as Rosie wouldn't be there. She'd already left to spend the Easter holiday with a girlfriend in Stockholm.

On a whim, Miranda took a lift to the basement and drove her Corsa across Pasila to the postal sorting office. After yesterday's Kuusitie killing, another letter must surely be due.

The manager was overseeing the sifting and searching. He welcomed Miranda warmly, but with no encouraging news. She watched as the very last bags were processed.

"Sorry," said the manager, "and with the Easter break just starting, the next collection won't be for another five days."

"That's really bad timing," Miranda lamented. "The murderer's sent his covering letters within a day or two of each attack. Pity to have to wait so long."

"What about if we go it alone," the manager grinned, "tomorrow evening, for example? We could take a van round and check a few bags for ourselves."

"But tomorrow's Good Friday! You won't want to give up your holiday."

"Truth is I'd be glad of an excuse. The wife's sister's on a visit, and we've never hit it off. Of course, there's no way you and I could cover the whole of Helsinki. But the last letter was posted in Töölö, so it could be worth checking the nine collection points there. Who knows? We might strike lucky!"

Symphony No 6

— * —

The following twenty-four hours dragged unpleasantly for Miranda. She went home to sleep, but only briefly, and was back in the office again by 7.30 am. Being Good Friday and a national holiday, the building was sparsely populated. That reduced the external distractions from her paperwork, but the internal ones were giving her a lot more trouble. With all of the recent accumulating strain, she was in desperate need of an emotional outlet — some physical tenderness, a release of tension — and the memory of Adrian's touch three weeks ago was becoming an irresistible lure. There was no longer any official obstacle to renewing their relationship. He wasn't now considered a viable suspect. But she knew it was up to her to take the initiative. In fact, she'd tried to phone him the previous evening, but there'd been no reply.

It was a relief when the time came to meet the sorting office manager again, and they could set off on their semi-official, unscheduled postal collection. Miranda soon relaxed. The manager was excellent company, and he kept her entertained with amusing anecdotes from his thirty-year career in the postal service. They included all nine Töölö post boxes in their round and, for good measure, took in a few extra ones from Pasila and Kallio. It was 9.30 pm before they started emptying the labelled bags into the franking and sorting machines. Almost immediately, they found what they were looking for in a batch of letters posted at the Töölöntori market square. Having thanked the manager profusely, Miranda returned to the forensic lab where she found a 'skeleton staff' of one. Even he was just leaving for home, but Miranda persuaded him to open the letter first so they could read the killer's message:

Kuusitie
Wednesday, 19th April

Symphony No 5 in Eb major

Dear A.
Even composers of high integrity may sometimes feel obliged to
compromise and bow to the prevailing consensus of style and

idiom. Nevertheless, works that fail to reflect the genuine personality of the artist cannot hope to be taken seriously for all time.

"What the hell does that mean?" Miranda wondered aloud. The lab technician shrugged.

Half an hour later, Miranda was sitting at her desk. The time was 10.50 pm and the whole floor seemed deserted. She stared at the office phone for several minutes before picking up the receiver and dialling Adrian's number. It rang for a very long time. Eventually she was only listening to the ringing tone, too numb and weary to cancel the call. When Adrian suddenly picked up, it threw her off balance.

"Oh, hi... uh, this is Miranda... So you're there after all. Sorry, did I wake you up?"

"No, I wasn't asleep."

"Thought you must be out with Phillip or something... You took so long to answer." She felt she was losing her nerve. Why the hell had she called this late in the evening?

"We had a couple of beers in town yesterday," Adrian said, his voice lacking in warmth. "I haven't spoken to him today. Been too busy with the cello sonata. He hasn't called me either, so he's probably got a date with some girl or other."

"But, not you?"

"Not me what?"

"No date with some girl or other?" God! What was she saying? How absurdly school-girlish!

Adrian rebuffed her with silence.

Oh, hell! She'd been the one to initiate this call. She couldn't give up on it now!

"Look, Adrian, the reason I'm phoning is to apologize for the last few weeks. You know, it hasn't been easy for me either... keeping a professional distance."

"Oh, is *that* what it was? I thought you were afraid of becoming the next victim."

"Please, Adrian, don't! It was never like that. And now you're out of the loop. Thank God you were with Rosie on Wednesday evening.

Which also proves my point. Do you honestly believe I'd let you anywhere near my baby sister if I thought you were a serial killer?"

Adrian digested that for a moment.

"Even the rest of my colleagues'll have to cross you off their lists," Miranda went on. "Can't you understand? I didn't want things to turn out how they did. We'd only just passed the starting post when all this mess happened. And that night we spent together — it meant a lot to me..." When no response came, she burst out in exasperation: "For heaven's sake, don't you believe any of this?"

"I'm trying."

"What's it going to take to convince you?"

"Do you really need to ask?"

Miranda paused. "I suppose not," she acknowledged. "Expect me in about twenty minutes."

Next morning Ylenius stopped Tero and Miranda in the corridor.

"The lab checked the signature fingerprint on the fifth letter," he announced, "and they got a surprise. It's the wrong one."

Miranda frowned, mystified. "How can it be the wrong one?"

"It's not Jaana Saari's. It's Anna Orav's. He's used Orav's fingerprint twice — on the fourth letter and now again on this fifth one."

"But why? Has he made a mistake?"

"I suppose," said Tero, "one pretty little pinkie looks much like another. Perhaps he was browsing his collection out on the kitchen table and got them mixed up."

Miranda found the image of someone sitting down to inspect and count his digital trophies grotesque. But Tero could be right. The killer might somehow have lost track of which was which and reused the fourth victim's finger by mistake.

"Any other forensic evidence from the letter?" Miranda asked.

"No, I'm afraid he's been equally careful."

"You know, Boss," said Tero suddenly, "I've been thinking about those last two letters. Both of them were posted in Töölö. It suggests Freako's local to the area. If he gets round to a sixth victim — which seems likely — there's a good chance he'll mail his next letter in the same postal zone, perhaps even at the same postbox. He probably thinks there's no way we can trace him from the post mark, so he won't realize we're homing in on him. It's a long shot, but how about setting up video surveillance of the Töölö postboxes. Next time we might catch him on film."

Ylenius's eyes narrowed. "An interesting idea, Tero, but it sounds expensive... with nine collection points to consider. I suggest you have a word with the technical department. See if they think it's feasible."

Tero was keen to follow up immediately, so the Chief Inspector sent him off with a benedictory nod.

"The lab report's in my office," Ylenius said, turning to Miranda. "Why don't you come and have a look?"

Ylenius closed the door behind them, and then passed her the report across his desk.

One detail in particular caught Miranda's eye. The larger garden secateurs the killer had tried out on his fourth victim, Anna Orav, didn't seem to have matched up to his expectations. When amputating Jaana Saari's finger he'd reverted to the earlier serrated type. Although the microscope was unable to reveal any trace of the tiny nick on the blade, the lab felt it reasonable to assume these were the same secateurs as had been used on the first three victims.

Miranda placed the lab report back on the desk. "Did you know Panu Marski's in the States?" she ventured slowly.

Ylenius gave no reply either way.

"He won't be back till May Day. Do you think we should find another psychologist to show the case notes to?"

The Chief Inspector steepled his fingers to his lips for a moment before calmly shaking his head. "I think, Miranda, we'd better muddle through on our own for the time being." His tone was neutral and, try as she might, Miranda could detect no ironic edge to the remark. She began to rise from her seat, but Ylenius asked her to wait.

"There are a couple of things I've been meaning to bring up, Miranda. Things of a more personal nature. Now could be a good moment."

She sat down again, disconcerted. What on earth could *this* be about?

"I have to say, Miranda, you're looking extremely tired." There was genuine concern in his voice. "I fear you've been pushing yourself too hard."

Was it so obvious? The strain she'd been feeling? In fact, she felt calmer this morning than she had for a long time. The tiredness was real enough, but was mainly due to a restless night spent in Adrian's bed. Again and again he'd teased her awake, and each time she'd responded willingly. Abandonment in lovemaking provided a restorative vent to the last few weeks of pent-up horror and frustration.

"Of course," Ylenius went on, "this is a tough job, and we each have our own ways of dealing with the emotional pressures. Don't forget that Tero is no exception. It's clear that he sometimes causes you irritation. But I can't help feeling that might also have a beneficial side by redirecting some of your natural anger towards the crimes — giving you an immediate outlet, so to speak."

Miranda wasn't sure what she'd expected. Certainly not this. Tero cast as 'scapegoat'? And the boss had never earlier shown any awareness of the tension between herself and Tero.

"I don't think he feels any animosity towards *you*, Miranda. And it would be wise not to underestimate him. He may seem to lack sensitivity but, in his own way, he does a good job. Even the abrasive style he adopts with some of the suspects can occasionally bear fruit."

What did Ylenius have in mind now? Some kind of 'good-cop-bad-cop' tactics? There were Machiavellian depths to the Chief Inspector she'd never suspected.

"This case is taking its toll on every one of us," he continued. "Time to give yourself a little distance. After all, it's Easter weekend. Why not take a couple of days off? Perhaps get out of Helsinki altogether. The rest of us can hold the fort. Even *you* aren't indispensable, Miranda." His eyes creased in an amiable smile. "Make tomorrow a holiday. Monday too. It's what most of the population will be doing anyway. I'll expect you back on Tuesday morning."

A part of her resented the offer. Was Ylenius suggesting she couldn't take the pace?

"It's not that I think you can't cut it," he added, as if reading her thoughts. "I just feel you've earned yourself a break."

It would've been churlish to refuse. And it was true that the department could function perfectly well without her. If Adrian didn't have other plans, perhaps the two of them could make up some more lost time.

Miranda awoke on Sunday morning momentarily disoriented; until she realized she was in Adrian's bedroom again. This last night he'd been a little less insistent, and for several hours she'd fallen into a deep, revitalizing sleep. Sunlight was filtering through the window. She turned to curl herself against Adrian's naked body, and he responded with a contented grunt.

"It's a beautiful morning," she murmured close to his ear. "Shall we go for a walk? Down by the sea?"

They ate a leisurely breakfast and set off. By unspoken consent, they avoided the most obvious route beside the Sibelius Monument, skirting Sibelius Park altogether. The birch trees that lined the streets were now in full leaf, and the air was too warm for anything more than a T-shirt.

"I've never seen the spring start so early," Miranda marvelled, pulling off her cardigan and tying it round her waist. "It's not even May yet! All the warm weather we've had the last couple of months must've mixed up the plants' biological clocks."

"Just another symptom of global warming," Adrian proposed.

They soon reached the sea. At this place it was a large inlet completely circumscribed by low-lying, forested islands that obstructed any clear view of the open horizon. Alongside the marina jetties, there was a good deal of activity as part-time sailors prepared their boats and small yachts ready for lowering into the water. All such craft were routinely beached in September and stored under canvas for the duration of the winter to protect them from the clinging, crushing ice.

Miranda urged Adrian to tell her about his new sonata.

"Rosie keeps saying how beautifully lyrical the cello line is," she confided.

"I pirated a couple of the melodic ideas from some theatre music I did earlier this year. Phillip roped me in for a semi-pro production of Othello. We put it on in English — here in Helsinki. And it was surprisingly well attended. Seven nights, playing to a full house every time. The acting was a bit patchy... all done by native English speakers living in the Helsinki area — Brits, Americans, a couple of Aussies — though the main roles were covered by drama-school graduates. And the production and the lighting, the costumes and choreography... they were excellent — really imaginative and professional."

"As was the music, I presume," Miranda teased.

"I did it all live, sitting out in the audience with synths and samplers — controlled them directly from the Mac mouse, synchronizing everything to the action. A bit hairy! You can never rely on a computer to behave one hundred percent in a situation like that. But it was a lot of fun. And I was sitting there watching this fantastic Shakespeare play every evening. Got totally hooked. Learned everyone's lines by heart over the course of that week."

"What was Phillip doing in the production?"

"They cast him as Iago. Thoroughly enjoyed himself playing the arch-villain."

Miranda laughed. "That I can imagine!"

They were nearing Adrian's flat again, and Miranda made a proposal.

"What do you say to us driving out to our cottage — the 'Lewis family' cottage, I mean. We could stay overnight and come back tomorrow evening. Dad's already there, but I don't think he'd mind a bit of company over the holiday. It's only sixty miles from here, and in a beautiful spot. The cottage is called Tapiola — named after my grandfather, Tapio. He built the original structure back in the fifties with his own two hands. Of course, it's been renovated and extended since then. But it still bears his name. 'Tapiola' means Tapio's place, just like the Sibelius home 'Ainola' means Aino's place."

"I think it's a great idea, Miranda. In fact, Niall's already invited Phillip and me for an Easter meal at his place — *a day of domestic sanity in the bosom of my family*, he called it. But they'll manage without me. This cottage idea's too good to pass up... so how about if we drive there in *this*?"

Adrian had stopped beside a pale blue Renault saloon parked close into the kerb. He patted its roof solicitously with an open palm.

Miranda turned back quizzically, assuming he was making some kind of joke. "Planning to steal it, are you?" she asked.

"Don't need to." Adrian fished deep in his jacket pocket, and pulled out a bunch of keys. "This one's mine. I bought it off Phillip for a song back before Christmas. He wanted to invest in something more salubrious. Got himself a brand new VW. At the time it seemed like a good idea taking the old one off him. He had a teaching contract at Taurus Pharmaceuticals but he was having trouble fitting in all the lessons they needed. My scholarship wasn't stretching as far as I'd hoped so I agreed to take on some of the lessons myself."

"I didn't know you'd done English teaching?"

"Oh, plenty of it... before I started making my modest mark on the music world. Convenient way of earning a living. Gives a fair amount of spare time to compose, and a chance to see a bit of the world. Anyway, the problem with this Taurus drug company was its being way out in the sticks. Getting there and back was a pain. That's why I took up Phillip's offer of the car. It turned out to be a white elephant. As soon as I got offered some teaching at the Conservatory, I passed the Taurus job on to Niall. Hardly ever use the Renault nowadays. More trouble than it's worth in the city. Bus and Metro are a lot easier. So what do you think, Miranda? Take my limo, shall we? Out to this Tapiola place of yours?"

She eyed the vehicle with suspicion. It was at least fifteen years old, rusting visibly round the edges of the doors. There was a sizeable dent to the left of the off-side headlight and the windscreen was badly cracked. She wondered when it had last had a road test. "I think we'd be better off in mine," she said.

The drive westward out of the city was glorious under the crisp blue Nordic sky. Miranda avoided the main trunk roads, taking a more leisurely route of winding lanes. They passed through tiny villages and beside picturesque wooden farmhouses — mostly painted the traditional primrose yellow or brick red — each one proudly overseeing its domain of freshly ploughed fields. The terrain was, for Finland, unusually hilly, with views across cleared arable land to vertical, pinkish-granite outcrops and imposing stands of natural forest. The tall birch trees with their slender silvery trunks and freshly unfurled leaves were an incandescent yellowish green — *like giant candle flames*, Adrian suggested — and they stood dramatically against the darker backdrop of coniferous firs and pines. Occasionally a stretch of glittering water opened up beside the road. This was Finland, and a lake could never be far away.

Miranda had phoned ahead, so her father was expecting them. The first thing Nick wanted to do was give Adrian the grand tour. The property lay on an incline falling steeply to the edge of a lake which, although not as vast as the lake systems further north and east, could still offer a magnificent view — taking in numerous scattered islands — across to the opposite shore more than a mile away. The cottage, a single-storey log cabin of four rooms with a verandah, was perched near the top of the slope. In addition, there was a small outhouse with a cosy bedroom for guests and, on the shore itself, a boathouse and a sauna with its own small verandah and jetty.

"The sauna's irreplaceable," said Nick with pride, as Adrian peered in through the smoke-darkened door. "I mean that literally. If this ever burns down, we won't get planning permission for another one so close to the water. Of course, the modern legislation's to prevent any further spoiling of the natural shoreline. And that's fair enough. But it's still a pleasure when you can jump straight into the lake from your own sauna door."

"The way you carry on, Dad," Miranda grinned, "you'd have Adrian believe you were born right here in the sauna yourself, like a true-blue-and-white Finn" — she referred to the colours of the Finnish flag — "not in the shadow of some Rhondda Valley slag heap."

"Allow me my proprietary feelings, dear daughter. My claim to a Finnish soul lies in having spent more years in this country than I ever did in South Wales."

Nick led them back to the main building where he set about preparing a meal of smoked perch — "Netted them out of the lake myself this afternoon!" — and new potatoes served with dill and lavish helpings of butter. It was already five o'clock when they sat down on the verandah to eat. The conversation turned to Nick's previous Wednesday lecture on the Fifth Symphony.

"That transitional passage..." Adrian enthused between mouthfuls... "the one coming in the middle of the first movement. It was a sort of watershed in my own life. Just after I met Phillip at university, almost the first thing he did was sit me down in the Students' Union music library and play me some CDs of Sibelius's Second and Fifth. And that first movement of the Fifth completely blew me away. That was when I realized I wanted to be a composer — so I could create amazing stuff like that Sibelius transition. Till then I hadn't composed a thing."

"Phillip changed your life then," said Miranda.

"Him and Sibelius both. Mind you, later on I introduced Phillip to the Fourth and Sixth. A fair exchange, wouldn't you say?"

The conversation continued well into the evening, although they were forced indoors by the attentions of the summer's first mosquitoes. Miranda sat back and, for a change, let the men do most of the talking. She blessed Ylenius for her temporary banishment from the murder investigation.

"Adrian, wake up! It's so beautiful on the lake. You have to come and see."

"What on earth's the time?"

"Twenty past five, and the sun's about to rise. It's magical out there."

"It'd be magical in *here*, if you'd just come back to bed."

"No, you mustn't miss this. It's a special moment. I've already lit the sauna stove. Early morning saunas are even better than evening ones. I'll fetch you when it's up to temperature."

Twenty minutes later, she coaxed a complaining Adrian from under the covers of the guest-room bed and led him bleary-eyed down to the jetty. Miranda hadn't overrated the scene. A thin layer of mist hovered a yard or so above the perfectly still mirror-like surface of the lake. Not a leaf or an insect stirred. The silence seemed absolute.

Following Miranda's example, Adrian shed his borrowed bath-robe in the small anteroom, and accompanied her into the seventy-five Celsius degrees of the pine-wood scented sauna. They climbed up to the highest bench, and Miranda cast a ladleful of water onto the hot stones that topped the log-burning stove. With a crackling and a hissing, a wave of stinging, sweat-inducing steam engulfed them. Adrian had learned from past experience to breathe through his mouth, avoiding the more sensitive mucous membranes of the nose. Neither spoke as, bit by bit, the aromatic heat subsided — each content to focus on their own physical sensations. And Miranda realized that Adrian needed more time to surface from his interrupted sleep. Twice more she enveloped them in scalding steam before they re-emerged into the dawn light and slid into the bitingly chilly water of the lake — making as little noise as possible not to disturb the natural silence.

A few breast-strokes out and back were enough. Then it was a breathless, gasping clamber onto the jetty with droplets scattering all around them... ready again for the warm embrace of the sauna and a repeat of the whole cycle.

Two cycles and a ritual, mutual soaping and rinsing of their bodies later, they wrapped themselves in generous soft white towels and went outside to sit close together on the sauna's verandah bench. The early sun's rays were breaking through the pines and spruces set in close ranks to their left; and the mist was lifting slightly.

As if by sorcery, Miranda had produced two mugs and a thermos of fresh coffee she'd prepared in the main building while the sauna was heating up.

Adrian took a first sip and sighed in contentment. "In some strange way," he said, "this reminds me of Bolivia."

"Bolivia?" she asked, surprised. "Was that on one of your English-teaching expeditions?"

"Yes, I did do some teaching there to cover my expenses. But the place I'm talking about was two or three miles above sea-level. The nights were chilly. There was mist on the lake in the mornings. Of course, Finland doesn't have a backdrop of the Andes mountains. But, up here close to the Arctic Circle, there's such a special quality to the light — with the sun hovering just above the horizon. And the sunrise seems so drawn out... I love that. Especially in the winter. The whole day's like an extended sunrise merging into an extended sunset. Everything takes on that special pinky-orange hue and casts such long shadows. Yes, it is stunningly beautiful here this morning, Miranda. I'm glad you enticed me out of bed."

"Just trying to compensate for the times you've enticed me *into* bed."

"Call it quits then, shall we?"

"For me," she said, "this is the essence of Finland — of being Finnish — surrounded by all this natural beauty. I know Helsinki's a lightweight city by European standards, but even *there* — the traffic noise, being tied to inflexible timetables, the demands of other people pressed in around you... Until you get away from it, you don't realize the effect it's having on you. A place like this sort of peels off the layers of tension and stress — let's you rediscover how to simply 'exist'. Most Finns need a regular fix of peace and wilderness so they can get back in touch with their roots — with the primeval forest... a chance to sit out on a lake and listen to the water lapping against the bottom of a boat. This special morning silence... It's like listening to infinity. There's no other time when I have a stronger feeling there must be more to life than what we actually see."

"Do you mean, some kind of after-life?"

"No, I wouldn't put it that tangibly. But something immutable anyway — something which goes on beyond our three-score-and-ten. Dad calls me a 'closet Christian'," she laughed, "but he's exaggerating. It's just that I sense some kind of underlying permanence at a time like this, when you're confronted with so much beauty. Don't you think there has to be something, well... 'eternal'? — I suppose that's what I mean?"

"I do believe in 'eternal death'. Which is a pretty awesome concept in its own right, when you allow yourself to dwell on it. The upside, though, is how it can help you to concentrate on making the most of what you've got — Shakespeare's *little life rounded with a sleep* — one's own consciousness... a brief flame flickering in the vastness of space and time. Or am I being too melodramatic?"

"Go right ahead," Miranda smiled. She tipped her head against his shoulder.

"To me it's awe-inspiring," he continued, his quiet, controlled voice coming in sharp contrast to the intensity she sensed behind the words. "All those billions of little evolutionary steps leading to this sensation of being 'me'. I don't see why it needs any divine intervention. Theoretically you can figure out how each discrete step might've happened, but the totality is mind-boggling. This personal flame of consciousness... It's a tiny miracle. It deserves to be nurtured and treasured. Completely insignificant in the context of the universe as a whole, I admit. But for each of us it's uniquely 'mine'."

He slipped his arm around Miranda's waist, prising his fingers between the warmth of her thigh and the smooth, cool wooden bench.

"When Phillip and I were students, we did what most young students do, I suppose... we talked about whether there was any point to it all — any underlying truth or meaning. The heaviest of all this chitchat coincided with my first major heartbreak. This girl I'd been going out with for months had met some other bloke, and she was being painfully indecisive about which one of us she wanted. There came a point when I'd had enough. I couldn't eat. I couldn't sleep. I started thinking it might be better to just give up on everything. Why put up with all the misery? Then I had an experience which, for me, was pivotal. On the campus, there was a tall building every one called the Biology Block. And one evening I was waiting there on the eleventh floor landing for this same girl to come out of one of the physiology labs, convinced she was about to dump me in favour of the other bloke. The window on the landing was very large and reached down below knee level. I went and placed my palms on the glass — pressed my whole body against the pane. The illusion of being able to fall out into the void was powerful. Suddenly I imagined the glass had melted away, and I was doing exactly that. I say 'imagined', but the experience was so vivid — as if it were actually happening. My body edged forward into space... and a moment came when my centre of gravity was poised, neither one thing nor the other, neither safely anchored to life nor totally committed to the fall. Time stopped altogether. The moment seemed interminable. And then gradually I realized that I'd passed the point of no return. I was definitely tilting further and further outwards. I thrust my arms ahead, instinctively trying to save myself, but they only met emptiness — no resistance that could possibly halt me. I was accelerating steadily out of that initial ultraslow-motion. Fear and panic came flooding in like a wave. I was falling beyond help and hope. My legs were frantically treading air, trying to find a foothold in all that nothingness. I could see the concrete paving slabs at the foot of the building rising to meet me. And my mind was screaming: *You fool! You pathetic, weakwilled fool! You had so much, and you've thrown it all away. You've made the biggest mistake anyone can ever make. You've rejected something priceless that can never be retrieved. What an appalling, unforgivable waste!* I was overwhelmed with self-disgust and regret. I desperately wanted to reverse the choice I'd made and be given another chance."

Adrian fell silent, and gazed out over the lake... though presumably seeing a different place and time. Miranda remained quite still, her breathing shallow, waiting for him to continue, not wishing to break the spell he'd created. Somewhere in the forest a woodpecker hammered: two short bursts of sound that echoed and re-echoed across the expanse of water before them. It seemed to awaken Adrian to his immediate surroundings, and he went on with his story...

"It was then I found myself back on the landing, trembling with shock, a cold sweat breaking out all over my body. The whole thing had been some kind of hallucination. But I knew I'd been given a vision of how it would really be if I ever gave in to such self-pity and weakness of spirit. This time I'd got away with it. I'd been given that second chance. Since then I've always viewed suicide as the ultimate act of cowardice and folly. I've never considered taking that route again. It's no longer an option."

II

Allegretto moderato

Tero was running out of options. His ammunition was low. His energy resources were almost exhausted. His small reconnaissance party had been ambushed by an overwhelming force. They'd defended themselves valiantly, but one by one, Tero had seen his comrades fall. The plasma gun he still gripped tightly against his shoulder would be of little help now. He was virtually defenceless. No time to attempt nanobot repair of his peltast body armour. He must find a way to slip through the ever-tightening net and reunite with others of the Phoenix tribe. If he could only reach the one surviving Gyrfalcon flyer, there might still be a chance. But then he noticed something that drained him of every last hope. A tell-tale spot of red light glowed on his chest-cuirass. He was being 'painted' by a Delphi targeting laser. He should try to spin away, to escape the unwelcome attentions of this directional range-finding device. But he was already too late. A smoke trail spewing towards him from an Imperial grenade launcher was the last thing he saw before his computer screen exploded in flames. He'd failed in his mission. He'd been destroyed.

Should he re-register? Perhaps this time as a member of the Star Wolf tribe? Oh, well… he was getting peckish again. Probably a good moment to make himself a peanut butter and blue cheese sandwich: one of his more impressive inventions, he'd always thought. Logging off, he padded out to the kitchen, singing along to the last track of the *Nirvana* CD that had been a high-decibel background to his game-playing for the last hour. His sense of pitch would have failed to impress Miranda, but he made up for that with a gutsy rendering of the lyrics.

Of course, a day like this was enjoyable: internet games and chat rooms, a trip round the corner to McDonald's for lunch and dinner. But, in truth, he was already itching to get back to work. This case had him in its grip as strongly as anyone else on the team. Not quite in the same way as Miranda perhaps — though, like her, he very much wanted to catch the killer and put him away.

Tero wasn't ambitious in the sense of seeking promotion or a high salary. But he enjoyed his work, resented being bettered by any criminal, and always wanted to see the job through. It was these qualities that had won him his Sergeant's status. Recently he'd been putting in long hours, and that was why, on Sunday evening, Ylenius had prompted him to follow Miranda's example and take Easter Monday off.

The CD ended in the adjoining room, but Tero remained perched on the kitchen windowsill in the ear-ringing silence, clutching a mug of strong black coffee in one hand, the remains of his sandwich in the other. He watched a young couple shepherding their enthusiastic though wobbly toddler along the street below. But Tero's mind was somewhere else altogether. He was thinking about Adrian Gamble...

The Englishman's unbreakable alibi for the fifth murder had come as a surprise. Until that moment, Gamble had been top of Tero's unofficial suspect list. True, no material evidence connected Gamble directly to any of the murder scenes, and Phillip Burton had provided an alibi for the first two murders. But Burton's corroboration had never convinced Tero. He prided himself on having a sixth sense for liars. Those two Englishmen were so deep in each other's pockets, Burton could be relied on to stick up for his little buddy as far as the gates of hell.

Apart from all that obvious stuff, Tero had, from the very beginning, sensed an uncertainty in Burton — as if Burton himself was doubtful about his friend's innocence.

And then there was that business with Miranda...

When Gamble first turned up at Pasila to make his qualified confession about Liisa Louhi, Tero had spotted Miranda dropping the Englishman off fifty yards down the road. She'd later failed to mention anything about it. Why was that? Had she been trying to cover for Gamble in some way? Ultimately Tero hadn't ratted her out to the boss, persuading himself it would be a breach of loyalty to a close team-mate. The truth was probably more complicated.

Tero's respect for Miranda was genuine enough. He respected her intelligence and her professionalism, but it wasn't in his nature to demonstrate such sentiments openly. He was probably only vaguely aware of them himself. And parallel to this ran his success at suppressing any conscious recognition of Miranda's attractiveness as a woman. She was, of course, way out of his league. In fact, Tero had never had much success with the women he truly fancied. There'd been a few tepid affairs — mainly with girls he'd met via the internet. But when he'd dated them face to face, the physical reality was always a disappointment. Interest petered out with no obvious regret on either side.

Perhaps Tero's knowledge of Miranda's small act of professional duplicity afforded him a mild sense of power — that, in some way, he held her fate in his hands. But again these feelings would never have reached a conscious level. Tero was extremely sharp when interpreting other people's motives and hidden agendas, but seemed blissfully unaware of his own. The possibility of turning his analytical flair back upon himself had never occurred to him.

In any case, Adrian Gamble was now eliminated. Suspects for the serial killings were steadily falling by the wayside, even though the team had been following what Ylenius termed his 'double jeopardy' approach. A single alibi could feasibly be rigged. But if a suspect was covered for two or more of the murders, he could be safely struck off the list. For example, Jorma Mannila (the younger of the two Conservatory porters) was attending a Bible-study group at the time of the second killing. The journalist, Kai Sirén, was in Oslo at the time of the third. Martti Hakala — the ex-soldier, ex-dog-owner — had been sitting in a pub with three witnesses at the time of the fourth. And so on... Even Zoltán Szervánszky, whose previous elimination had depended on the sole testimony of his oboist lover, was now fully vindicated. Like Adrian Gamble, he had, at the time of Jaana Saari's murder, been attending the lecture on Sibelius's Fifth Symphony at the Wegelius Hall.

So where did that leave the investigation? Tero felt they were scratching around pursuing hours of routine questioning and accumulating a confusing mass of paperwork — all in the dubious hope of a chance breakthrough. Well, of course, that went with the territory! It was just part of the job. Meanwhile, there was one new direction he had high hopes for: covert video surveillance of the Töölö post boxes. A green light had been given for five of the most central ones. His first task tomorrow morning would be to help set them up.

The two-day break had done wonders for Miranda's concentration and resolve — Ylenius had got it right again! — although she'd had to spend a large part of Tuesday catching up on the backlog of paperwork. By midday most of the ground was covered, but one thing still bothered her. There'd been a security video recovered from a cashpoint situated on Jaana Saari's route home — between the number 18 bus stop and her flat in Kuusitie — but Miranda could find no follow-up report describing the video's contents, nor anyone in the office who'd actually watched it. In the end, she hunted down the video and viewed it herself.

The victim, Jaana Saari, only appeared partially on the recording. The camera was trained downwards at an angle to film customers withdrawing their money, so its field of view only took in the pavement and the nearest edge of the road. Nevertheless, at exactly the expected moment — a couple of minutes after the number 18 bus would have dropped off its passengers — a pair of legs from the knees downward could be seen passing over one corner of the screen. The owner was mounting the kerb, having just crossed from the other side of the street. It wasn't conclusive, but they could certainly be Jaana Saari's legs: the trousers and shoes looked right. Miranda waited. Not more than ten seconds later, someone else moved across the screen in the same direction, this time in full view of the camera. Miranda jolted forward; rewound and paused the tape. Good God! Here was an almost bird's eye image of the familiar balding head with its absurd decoration of combed-across strands: the younger porter at the Helsinki Conservatory. Mannila? Was that his name? Yes, Jorma Mannila. What in heaven's name was everyone playing at? How could they miss something this obvious? Tero, at least, should've spotted it. She rushed back to her desk fuming, and dialled his mobile number.

"What's up?" came Tero's voice.

"Where the hell are you?"

"Right behind you."

She turned, and there was Tero in the doorway, his phone pressed to one ear, another infuriating smirk stretched across his face. "Just got back," he said.

Miranda slammed the receiver down on the desk phone. "Do you realize who's on that video from the cashpoint in Kuusitie and can be clearly seen following Jaana Saari home? Didn't you even look at it?"

"Calm down, Miranda," his expression scarcely changed. "I know who you mean, but it doesn't work. He's got an alibi for the first two killings. Don't you remember? He was on late shift when the Louhi girl got topped at the Sibelius Monument. He didn't clock off till 9.15 pm, and she'd been dead a quarter of an hour by then. Same thing with Christa Bäckström's murder. He had a Bible-study session in Kallio. Ten more of God's chosen are ready to swear to the fact. Can't see they'd all jeopardize their immortal souls lying for Mr Mannila, can you?"

"Are you telling me you didn't even follow up on this?"

"Of course, I did. Interviewed darling Jorma myself on Sunday. He was well and truly peeved I'd barged in on his holy day! Anyway, when the camera caught him last Wednesday evening, he was on his way to his aunt's place. She lives right there on Kuusitie — a couple of hundred yards down the road from where Jaana Saari was strangled."

"And could the aunt verify this?"

"Seems he drops in uninvited every couple of weeks. She gives him a meal and off he goes again. Says she feels sorry for him since his mother died a few months back. Very attached to his mum was Jorma — or so Auntie would have us believe."

"What time did he get to his aunt's place?"

"Well, *she* arrived back from work at about quarter past eight, and he was already sitting in the kitchen. He's got his own key. Couldn't've arrived more than ten minutes before she did."

"Or *five* minutes, if he'd murdered Jaana Saari en route," Miranda pointed out acidly. "Did you ask his aunt if he was hyped-up or upset in any way?"

"I certainly *did*. But she hadn't noticed anything special. He's always the quiet type, she said. Not much of a conversationalist."

"And why didn't I read about all this in the reports today?"

"Well, you see, that was the very last thing I did before the boss sent me home on Sunday evening. I wrote up the last bits back at the flat. And today I've been completely tied up with this surveillance job. Sorry! Forgot to file the report when I passed through this morning. You can have it now," he said, and drew a folder out of his shoulder bag. "Anyway, it can't be Mannila. He's got a valid explanation for being in Kuusitie on Wednesday evening. Much more important, he's been eliminated from the suspect list with his earlier alibis. We can't do any more with him or he'll cry harassment. He's just the type, I reckon."

Miranda sighed, threw Tero's file on the desk, and slumped back in her seat.

"Cheer up!" he added breezily. "The post-box surveillance is set up now. If Freako posts another of his letters under one of our cameras, we'll get a beautiful mug-shot. We can frame it and put it up on the office wall."

"You're here then?"

"Did you think I wouldn't be?"

Beatrice only smiled, shaking a swathe of exotic black hair from her youthful face.

"Shall I carry one of those for you?" he offered.

"They aren't heavy."

But she let him ease the violin case from one hand, leaving her with the music file in the other.

"How about going for a walk somewhere?"

"Can't," she replied abruptly. "Have to go straight home."

This elicited the hoped for flash of disappointment in — as friend Lotta had described them — his 'scary-sexy' blue eyes.

"But you could come on the bus and walk the last bit with me," Beatrice added sweetly.

So they ambled down to the number 18 bus stop together.

Beatrice hid her nervousness quite well, although what felt like a hundred grass-hoppers were jumping around somewhere inside her. He was even more gorgeous than she remembered. So manly. To kick-start the conversation she said the first thing that came into her head: "Did you know, on an average day a woman speaks seven thousand words but a man only speaks two thousand? Why's that, do you think?"

"Maybe 'cause men only speak when they've got something worth saying."

"Could be. Well, it's not often men have anything worth saying, is it?"

He grinned and held up the violin case. "How long've you been playing this thing?"

"Since I was six."

"You must enjoy it, then."

"The practising's a pain. I don't seem to do much these days. Too many other things going on."

"So why don't you give it up?"

"Perhaps I will. Except I don't want to disappoint my mum."

"She can't force you to play, if you don't want to."

"She doesn't force me exactly."

The bus arrived, and they worked their way down the aisle to squeeze tightly together into a seat at the back.

"What about your dad? Does he agree with this violin thing?"

"Dad's dead. He died of cancer when I was thirteen."

"Sorry I brought it up. Must've been a tough one."

"I still miss him. Even if he wasn't my real father."

"Your mum had remarried, then?"

"No, she's not my real mum either. I was born in Nicaragua — somewhere on the edge of the jungle. They adopted me 'cause my real parents died of swamp fever. I was only three at the time."

"Suppose you don't remember the real ones."

"I sort of get flashes sometimes, like flashes of memory. Don't know if they're proper memories — if that's what my parents really looked like — or if I've just made it all up in my head. I tried to contact them once."

He looked puzzled. "I thought you said they were dead."

"They are. But we had a sort of séance thing — you know, candles, round table, glass in the middle."

"You believe in that kind of stuff?"

"Half believe... Well, it's always good for a laugh!"

"Any success?"

"Only Lotta mucking about trying to convince the rest of us we'd made contact with Countess Zelda von Nijinsky, mistress and confidante of Czar Peter the Great."

"And how's your Spanish?"

"What's that got to do with it?"

"Well, I don't suppose your Nicaraguan parents speak much Swedish, do they? Unless they've been taking language courses up in heaven."

Beatrice giggled. "In fact, I've been thinking of doing Spanish next year at school. Back to my roots kind of thing. And you're right. It could help with the séances too."

"Ever tried contacting your Finnish father?"

Beatrice's mood sobered. "No, I wouldn't want to. It's all right fooling around with someone you don't remember properly. But my Finnish dad... he's still too real for me. If I tried reaching him and didn't manage, I think I'd be disappointed. But I'd probably feel even worse if it *did* work. Anyway, we talked a lot at the end. And I can't bring him back, can I? I'd only end up missing him more."

"Yeah, right. Better just remember him as he was."

A new topic was needed, and Beatrice had one ready...

"It's sort of my birthday next Tuesday," she said.

"How can it be 'sort of' your birthday? Either it is or it isn't."

"No, it's 'sort of' my birthday. Nobody knows exactly when I was born. There weren't any proper records in Nicaragua. They had to guess something to put on the adoption papers."

"So how old will you 'sort of' be next Tuesday?"

"'Sixteen. And I'm having a 'sort of' party the Saturday after. Mum's promised to disappear until midnight."

"Cinderella in reverse?"

"You could come too," she added, with uncharacteristic shyness.

He considered the proposition for what Beatrice clearly felt was an excessive length of time.

"Okay," he nodded at last. "Don't see why not."

Boldly she slipped her hand over his and interlocked fingers with him. His response was to look casually away, taking a sudden interest in the street beyond the bus window. Nevertheless, he returned the pressure.

Soon they were jumping off the bus and picking their way across the traffic to follow Beatrice's habitual route home. They flanked the petrol station forecourt, keeping the burger restaurant to their left, and — again, hand in hand — climbed up onto the quiet stretch of road that overlooked the start of the Turku motorway.

Tight in against the kerb some thirty yards ahead and facing forwards away from them was a single parked car. A man squatting on the pavement beside the open rear passenger door glanced quickly in their direction, stood up, slammed the door shut and hurried round to slide into the driver's seat. As the two teenagers continued approaching, the car pulled away to make a U-turn at the top of the cul-de-sac and then sped back past them. The driver raised his left arm, as if to cover his face, but neither Beatrice nor 'Luscious' Lars were paying any attention. They were too interested in each other.

The following day was Wednesday: a week since the fifth murder, but with very little progress made. Door-to-door and other such routine enquiries had led to nothing but time-wasting dead ends.

Somebody on the team drew attention to how the number 18 bus figured in three of the five murders. Liisa Louhi, Tiina Holopainen, and Jaana Saari had all lived and died close to the 18 bus-route. Was that a coincidence? Or did the killer himself use it on a regular basis? Could that be how he'd come to target those three in the first place? Possibly... but no one had any suggestions about how to follow up on the idea. As Tero pointed out, they could hardly flag down every passing 18 bus and ask if any serial killers amongst the passengers would please raise their hands. It was just another factor to add to the mix... and not even one that worked across-the-board. There was no evidence that the murdered photojournalist, Christa Bäckström, or the Estonian girl, Anna Orav, had ever had reason to use the 18 route.

Meanwhile, a pressing personal matter occupied Miranda's thoughts. Not one of the last five nights had she spent in her own bed. The flat in Töölö had stood empty. But Rosie was due home from Stockholm today, and they'd be meeting at this evening's Sibelius lecture. The thought of explaining the new 'Adrian situation' to Rosie made her uncomfortable. Miranda wasn't sure why. There was no reason to feel ashamed. She couldn't tell where this relationship with Adrian might lead long-term, but it had already reawakened her responsiveness to physical tenderness and closeness: something she'd almost conditioned herself into believing she didn't need. Yes, it was high time to break out of her self-imposed celibacy! So why this reluctance to tell Rosie? One way or another, she'd have to deal with it by the end of the day.

"Five weeks ago, in the first lecture of this series, I discussed the concept of *Finnishness* in Sibelius's music. I'd now like to review the subject...

"We've seen how the composer's style — initially derived from the prevailing German and Russian models — steadily evolved into something altogether more personal and original. Was this evolution then an acquisition of greater degrees of Finnishness? Throughout his life, Sibelius categorically denied — although perhaps not with total honesty — having employed folk melodies in any of his compositions; and he clearly wished to be taken seriously as a player in the larger arena of Western musical civilization — not compartmentalized off into some parochial Nordic national school. Which begs a further question: if Sibelius was such a national composer, shouldn't there be a national school to accompany him? It's true that a handful of Finnish composers self-consciously attempted to create one. But their works affect a superficial imitation of some of the master's textural characteristics with an almost exclusive reliance on Kalevala mythology. They are seldom performed outside Finland.

"Sibelius's *modus operandi* was, in fact, such that his music is extremely difficult to imitate...

* [He would allow a composition to grow organically from a small amount of thematic material, and his orchestration was an integral part of that process. It's true that he made use of the piano to sketch out his preliminary ideas, but rarely did he draught the bare musical lines of his orchestral works at any length — intending to orchestrate them later. Much of the compositional process occurred in his own head over a long period of gestation until, at last, it could flow onto the page more or less in full score.

"Last Wednesday I endeavoured to outline some of the

composer's stylistic devices. It's important to realize that none of them can be easily separated from the music as a whole. We cannot graft them onto another piece to make a parody of Sibelius, as we might do successfully with, for example, Stravinsky's harmonic and rhythmic devices. Stravinsky's traits are skin-deep and easily imitated. Sibelius's lie at a more profound level of structure. They're fully integrated into the compositional process for each specific composition. This is why a convincing imitation of Sibelius's music would prove so difficult.] *

"It's a tempting yet ultimately simplistic stratagem in criticism and commentary to catalogue an artist according to his environment — to somehow attribute his genius to such geographical features as fjords or mountain ranges or idyllic rolling hillsides of agrarian greenery. But the well-springs of creativity will always lie in the artist's individuality as a human spirit, in his or her unique ability to transform the medium of choice — be it music, painting or literature — into a vehicle for universal human expression. We cannot limit the source of Sibelius's finest music to a single geographical location. It is the heritage of all mankind. It speaks to everyone everywhere, and at the most profound of human levels. What should be recognized is that Sibelius's music is not, in any very important sense, itself Finnish; rather that Finnish music has become, by definition and after the event, the music of Sibelius.

"And yet... "

Dr Lewis halted on a high peak of intonation. The audience waited expectantly, and the sudden silence achieved something that the last few minutes of Welshly lilting eloquence had failed to do: it snapped Miranda back from where she'd drifted at the earlier mention of Sibelius's *modus operandi* into a separate train of thought concerning garden secateurs, hypodermic syringes, and wire ligatures. With a shudder she resolved to keep her attention on the lecture — although her father was himself now heading off in a direction not obviously connected to the previous topic...

"Sibelius was endowed with the faculty of perfect pitch, and he also experienced a vivid synaesthetic connection between colours and musical sounds. In childhood, he attempted to match the bright hues of the living room carpet to particular keys on the family piano. In later life, he would describe B major, for example, as a glaring red; or explain that an especially favourite shade of green found rarely and exclusively in the sky at sunset time lay somewhere between D and E-flat. Colours could likewise affect his mood. The sight of venison soup mixed with blackcurrant juice is said to have depressed him, whereas a glimpse of scarlet silk could cheer him up for the rest of the day. Birdsong he found especially fascinating. The curlew sang between A and F. The bullfinch 'double-stopped' like two simultaneous strings on a violin. The composer even claimed that he could recognize which flocks of migrating starlings had wintered in noisy city environments by the timbre of their twittering. And then there was the call of the crane, which he referred to as the *leitmotiv* of his whole life. His favourite birds were, in fact, cranes and swans. Could there be some significance in the fact that Jean's only memory of the parent he lost so young was sitting on his father's lap being shown a picture of a huge swan?

"All this leads us to an important aspect of Sibelius's personality: his closeness to nature. He'd visited Niagara Falls; he'd revelled in the Moravian scenery of farmhouses and forested hills near Brno, once viewed from a railway carriage; and he'd never forgotten the majestic oak trees and bluebell woods of the English countryside. But his greatest love would remain for his home country.

"By overpopulated mainstream European standards, Finland is still blessed with large and relatively untouched areas of natural beauty. Respect for nature is a deep-seated component of the Finnish persona. Even the technologically savvy, mobile-phone-wielding, internet-exploiting, techno-music-designing younger generation of Finns hasn't entirely lost this traditional love for the forests and lakes of the national heartland. Should we then be asking ourselves whether this oh-so-Finnish love of nature, with all its associated world of rich visual and aural timbres... whether this has in some sense found its way into the music of Sibelius? Have we at last found that Finnish connection? The only answer I can offer is a subjective one. If I were sent alone to an isolated cottage on an island somewhere in the middle of the Finnish lake district, and was allowed just one piece of music to keep me company for the duration, I know exactly which piece it would have to be: Sibelius's Sixth Symphony, opus 104.

"Having categorized the Fourth as the least understood of

Sibelius's symphonies, we should, I believe, designate the Sixth as the most underestimated.

* [Like the Third, it's less frequently performed, and the impression made on the unfamiliar listener is likely to be that of a lightweight, insubstantial work. It is, in fact, that very insubstantiality which, after repeated listenings, makes the Sixth Symphony one of Sibelius's most rewarding creations. It floats, it glides, it drifts like gossamer on a predominantly gentle, though from time to time quirky and unpredictable wind. This lighter-than-air incorporeality is achieved, in part, by an underutilization of the bass instruments and a tendency towards quieter dynamic levels. The addition of a smooth-sounding bass clarinet to the low register — its only appearance in any of Sibelius's symphonies, by the way — and the delicate highlighting imparted by a single harp: these also contribute much to the individual colouring of the symphony.] *

"The orchestration is indisputably original, although it remains straightforward and unassuming, avoiding any unnecessary 'window dressing'. As Sibelius explained: in contrast to most of his contemporaries, he was not offering a colourfully concocted cocktail, but *pure spring water*."

Miranda's mind was wandering again...

The girl is found spread-eagled on the landing. She's fully clothed. The French horn lies untidily upended and forgotten in the corner. The finger has been removed, but where is the 'window dressing'? Where is the vanity of the set piece? The tableau? And what on earth happened to the sexual component? Of course, he was interrupted, but...

Phillip shifted in his chair beside her. She turned, and their eyes met. When he gave her a questioning look, Miranda made an effort to smooth the frown she must be wearing into something more appropriate. Phillip seemed reassured and his attention slipped back to the stage. Miranda's was proving more elusive.

* ["Although outwardly adopting the traditional four-part plan," her father was now saying, "the symphony lacks a genuine slow movement. In fact, the four movements seem strangely alike. The dramatic contrasts we expect in the large-scale architecture of a symphony have been subsumed and miniaturized into brief, elegantly delineated upsurges of more turbulent and strident energy. They

provide a minimal, though essential, amount of piquancy. Only in the finale is the calmly rippling textural stream allowed to expand for a while into a raging torrent. And yet even *this* outburst is counteracted by the serenity — one might almost say detached restraint — of the beautiful coda that concludes the movement and the whole work. The overall after-image one carries away from a performance of the Sixth symphony is that of pastoral tranquility and inner solitude; benign certainly but, as we would expect of Sibelius's important later works, entirely without sentimentality.] *

"Yes, this Sixth Symphony, like the Fourth, stands quite alone in the composer's output. Its atmosphere is unique, though bearing throughout Sibelius's unmistakable signature."

Another distraction for Miranda: What had Panu Marski said about the difference between *modus operandi* and 'signature'? Something about the 'signature' being less functional than the MO — that it revealed the emotional component of the crime rather than mere practicalities. Was that the point he'd been making? Damn, she couldn't remember! And damn the whole case! It interfered with everything she tried to do. She couldn't even listen to her father's lecture without drawing a parallel to those miserable serial killings!

Despite later recalling mention of Sibelius's *emphasis on the Dorian mode*, and the *organic, almost minimalistic development of his motivic material*, Miranda realized towards the end of the lecture how little she'd taken in of her father's detailed analysis. She was obliged to comfort herself with his closing comments...

"In conclusion," Nick had said, "we should surely pay heed to the composer's own advice that, although one may analyse, explain theoretically, and find various interesting things going on in the music, it's important not to forget that the Sixth Symphony is, beyond anything else, a poem."

As far as the investigation was concerned, the next few days were uneventful; although Miranda would later tend to think of them as the 'lull before the maelstrom'. She spent an hour or two with Adrian each evening — most of it in or around his bed — but insisted on returning home every night to sleep. The reason was her inability to tell Rosie about their escalated relationship. She tried rationalizing this puritanical behaviour as a fear of exposing her little sister to uncertainty about the future — uncertainty about their future together in the flat they'd so comfortably shared since Rosie was a teenager. The seven-year age difference had always made Miranda feel less like a sister than a substitute mother. Rosie had always brought out her protective instincts. Over-protective, perhaps? Her father thought so. He'd told Miranda to "stop shillyshallying. Go ahead and tell her, for heaven's sake!"

Adrian had shown some surprise when she left him cold after the Wednesday evening lecture to go straight home with Rosie. But he'd made no immediate complaint, perhaps assuming Miranda needed some space to bring her sister up to date. That still hadn't happened.

"I'm only waiting for the right moment," Miranda explained feebly; and then promised that at least May Day's Eve — the following Sunday — would be different. Rosie was playing a concert a hundred miles away in Tampere and would herself be spending the night away from home.

It was, in fact, late afternoon on May Day's Eve when the investigative team were rewarded with their first glimpse of a genuine crack in the murder-case. The curious red and black, spiralling cable found around the neck of the fifth victim had turned out to be an accessory supplied exclusively with an obscure brand of South Korean MiniDisc recorder. It had been imported in low numbers and had sold even fewer: just a couple of hundred units. The only purchasers traceable were those who had paid by credit card, or since applied for repairs on guarantee. Even they numbered more than eighty individuals, and all of them had to be interviewed and asked to produce their cable intact. Almost the very last to be located was a middle-aged woman returning from an extended Easter holiday in the Canary Isles. The interviewing officer was instantly alerted when he heard that she was a music history teacher at the Helsinki Conservatory. She, in turn, was equally surprised by the subject of the police enquiry because... Yes, the cable of her MiniDisc recorder had indeed gone missing! On the Wednesday before Easter — the very day of the fifth murder — she'd connected her machine up to the classroom amplifier to play examples of Renaissance church music to the students. Returning from her lunch break, she found the connecting cable had mysteriously vanished. Was the classroom left open in her absence? Yes, she'd forgotten to lock the door.

So, although it was impossible to prove with certainty that the history teacher's missing cable was the one used to strangle Jaana Saari, nobody really doubted it. Ylenius's hunch that the Conservatory would turn out to be the true source of the serial killings looked increasingly more likely. He urged his team to refocus their attention on every member of staff; on every student: "And double-check everything. No, *triple*-check everything! Every alibi, every possible link to the murder victims — especially those who weren't themselves Conservatory students. That's where we have the best chance of a breakthrough. An unexpected cross-reference could give exactly the pointer we need."

In that last respect, Chief Inspector Ylenius was mistaken.

When Miranda and Adrian arrived at *Molly Malone's* 'Irish' pub, the May Day's Eve ambience was rowdily in evidence. Only 8 pm, but voices were raised well above normal Sunday evening levels. Sidling through the tight press of revelling bodies, they found Phillip and Niall tucked away at a corner table with two tanned, athletic-looking males in their early twenties. All four were laughing uproariously. Miranda wondered how early they'd arrived to secure seats on this, the busiest evening of the year.

Phillip jumped up in welcome and introduced the new arrivals to "Mel'n'Sid", who, as he explained, were Californian visitors to Helsinki attending an international gay-rights conference. The Americans rose formally to their feet and, before long, were offering their seats to Miranda and Adrian: "No, no, ma'am," insisted Mel, with courteous American charm, "we're on our way out. Some serious clubbing ahead, you understand." He turned back to Phillip and Niall. "A real pleasure meeting you two gentlemen. Much obliged for the company." There were beaming smiles and handshakes all round.

As soon as the Americans had left, the others reoccupied the four precious seats, and Phillip drawled in a laboured John Wayne impersonation: "Oh, brave New World that has such critters in it..." adding immediately in his own voice: "Sorry, to rip you off so outrageously, Miranda!"

"She that's robb'd, not wanting what is stol'n," Adrian also recited, "better not let her know't, then she's not robb'd at all."

Phillip clapped his hands in mock delight.

"Hey," said Adrian, a touch defensively, "you don't have a monopoly on Shakespearean quotes!"

"Or misquotes," murmured Miranda.

"Since Adrian met *you*, fair Miranda," Phillip now confided, "he hath suffered a sea-change into something rich and strange."

Just then a white-bloused member of the bar staff leant over their table to empty ashtrays and whisk away abandoned glasses. Young and pretty, her height was stunningly Amazonian and her girth Falstaffian. Not ideal proportions for working in these crowded conditions, Miranda felt. The ungracious thought crossed her mind that the girl might be better off at the door employed as a bouncer. Phillip meanwhile watched the barmaid in undisguised admiration as she moved off to the next table.

"I love big women like that," he enthused. "They bring out the mountaineering instinct in me. Crampons and ice picks. Pitch your tent on the windswept slopes. Magnificent!" He was obviously succumbing to a generous intake of alcohol. This far it was still amusing; but the evening was young, Miranda reminded herself uneasily.

"Come on, don't you agree?" Phillip now targeted Niall. "It's time to sweep the cobwebs off your Y-fronts, young man — pass the torch to some other poor Guinness Book record-holder. And when better than on May Day's Eve? Bacchus weaves his spell. Inhibitions evaporate. Best scoring night of the year!"

"I'm not looking for a casual sexual encounter," replied Niall mildly.

Phillip scratched his head in ostentatious bewilderment. "Well, then, whatever shall we do with you? Have you considered contact ads? How about a computer dating service?"

"Twice shy with that one. It's how I met my ex-wife!"

"Ignore him, Niall," said Adrian. "Phillip's always trying to organize other people's love lives."

"Well, yes, I'd prefer to stick with what I've got for now," Niall admitted. "The trouble is, Phillip, a childless couple like you and

Adrian" — he gave them both a broad grin — "you miss out on one of the most meaningful experiences of all. Having kids of your own shifts the focus from egocentric whims of the moment to the well-being of another separate, living, breathing bundle of humanity — one that's dependent on you for its survival. Okay, so you're forced to be less selfish and give up some independence. But the payback's enormous: a solid foundation to life, a sense there's something beyond yourself, something less petty."

"Aren't you getting oversentimental?" Miranda cautioned, finding the topic unsettling. "It doesn't work for everybody. I've seen the consequences too often. Parenting's seriously demanding stuff. Some mums and dads end up resenting the whole thing and resort to violent abuse."

Niall shrugged. "All I know is when I was single and childless, I'd wake up sometimes in the middle of the night with a sense of crippling emptiness. What the hell was I doing on this earth? Why was I bothering? It never happens now."

"Nowadays when you wake up in the middle of the night," Adrian gibed, "it's because little Esme wants Daddy to fetch her a glass of water."

"It's still worth it," grinned Niall.

Phillip was sceptical: "This tight-knit family-unit thing, this blissful married state... It all sounds fine in theory, but what about in practice? Divorce statistics are rampant! Your monogamania's all very commendable, Niall, but the number of married men I've seen gagging pitifully for something on the side... letching after the receptionist, drooling over the typing pool, panting for the canteen cutie as she dishes out their 'spotted dick'. Whatever happened to *their* sense of fulfilment? They don't look blessedly fulfilled to me. They look desperate! They look plain bloody trapped!"

"Screwing around only screws up everything else that's good in a relationship," objected Niall. "Better to desensitize yourself to other women around you. Even unmarried men have to do that. There'll always be beautiful women you can't have — women out of your reach. Better not to dwell on it. Find something else to think about."

"Sublimation, you mean?" Phillip was derisive. "That's what I call the ostrich approach. Hide your wimpy piece of head in the sand and hope it'll wither away. Well, well, each to his own," he concluded, more philosophically. "Whatever turns you off!"

"But if you reckon you can't get it anyway," persisted Niall, "why torment yourself?"

Phillip shook his head in disgust. "So it's all jolly hockey sticks down the pub with the lads. Pats on the back. *Must be my round this time, Reginald.* Endless discussions about Manchester United's chances in the Premier League Cup. Meanwhile no one's putting it in the back of the net." He twisted away in his chair, as if to dissociate himself from present company. "No, thank *you!* The day I give in to that's the day they nail me in my coffin."

"The way you tell it," said Miranda primly, "they'll need a hacksaw before they can get the lid shut."

Phillip looked pained. "An appalling thought! That they should break my staff to bury it certain fathoms in the earth. But, if you'll excuse me, I have to go and 'drown my book', etcetera in the little boys' room." He stood up and began insinuating his way through the crowd.

Miranda watched him vanish before turning to Adrian: "Not so much Prospero as Mercutio, I'd say."

"You aren't the first to make the comparison."

She traced a finger across the back of Adrian's hand. "Perhaps he's playing Mercutio to your Romeo."

"I've heard that one before as well."

Phillip returned some fifteen minutes later, puffing on a small dark cheroot.

Miranda was surprised. "I didn't know you smoked," she said.

"An old skill I've recently rediscovered," Phillip boasted. "Anyone else fancy one?"

Adrian looked tempted... but, registering Miranda's disapproval, declined the offer.

"I'd no idea you'd ever smoked, either," she frowned.

"There's a lot you don't know about me," Adrian said, with a touch of defiance.

Then Niall decided to tell everyone about his summer plans: taking Esme and Robbie to Greece for their first real beach holiday... which led Miranda on to describing her long-standing ambition of visiting Egypt.

"Want to come too?" she invited Adrian. "The pyramids? A cruise down the Nile? Abu Simbel?"

"Don't much care for Arabia," he said dismissively.

As the evening proceeded, the alcohol intake Miranda witnessed around her began to grate. And dialogue between Adrian and Phillip was growing steadily more contentious.

"Honestly, Adrian," she said at one point, "you and Phillip bicker like an old married couple."

"Oh, Miranda," complained Phillip theatrically, "I've asked him dozens of times! He's always got some excuse or other: *We're still too young... I don't feel I should tie you down... I'm not sure I love you enough to make a total commitment...* Been putting me off for years. Alas, fool that I am," he added, despondently, "I'll never give up hope."

Adrian shook his head in exasperation. "Could we *please* try to elevate the tone of this conversation?"

"Elevation you want, is it? What do you suggest? Quadrofoil kite flying? Hot-air ballooning? Moon rocketry? Maybe Miranda could oblige us with something uplifting. How about an introduction to forensic psychologists — sorry, I meant forensic psychology."

Miranda was suddenly very angry: "Didn't you notice? I'm off-duty! Niall, you're the only other sober person round here. Can't you save the evening, and talk about something intelligent?"

"How about a lecture on music history?" suggested Adrian, with undisguised sarcasm.

"Who needs Niall for that?" exclaimed Phillip. "Look no further! I'm your man. Yes, roll up, roll up for Burton's *Magical 'Istory Tour!*" He'd slipped effortlessly into the accent of a sassy East London market vendor: "And where better to begin, ladies and gen'lemen, than dear old Pope Gregory 'izself, who — as well as dishin' out the usual Papal bull — told the church it was time to cut out the fancy stuff and stick to a bit of plain song. Not that anyone took a blind bit of notice! Not for 'undreds of years. Not even Landini. And before long they was all goin' supersonic... or p'raps I mean polyphonic. True, there was still a few 'iccups on the way but, in the end, this bloke Josquin decided 'e'd 'ad enough and it was time for a bit of a

Renaissance... Trouble was he was just an imitator. Used imitation all over the place. Soon they was all at it — imitating everythin', each other, even themselves. Got really borin'. Till along comes Montgomery Verdi — great-great-grandpapa of the famous Giuseppe. Well, Montgomery — known to all 'iz mates as 'Monty' — it was 'im wot invented opera. (Probably so as 'iz great-great-grandkiddie could get famous later on!) And Monty soon 'ad the 'ole of Europe baroquin'n'a-rollin'. There was Johnny S. Bach airin' 'iz G-string, George Freddie 'Andel servin' largos for largo louts, and the one'n'only Albinoni doin' 'iz slow smoochy stuff."

Phillip seemed to be working himself into a frenzy. Miranda and Niall followed his performance in astonishment. Adrian had clearly heard something similar before.

"If you don't mind," Phillip careered on, "I'll give the *Coffee Cantata* and the Ro-Cocoa a total miss. Let's go straight on to the Classical period, which gave us all a damn' good Haydn. Yes, Granpappy Joe was very free'n'easy wiv 'iz symphonies — more than an 'undred of 'em. And every one a winnin' number, ladies and gen'lemen! Not that 'iz buddy Mozart did so well for 'izself. No, 'e was bullied by 'iz dad, bullied by 'iz wife, bullied by 'iz bosses. And, in the end, 'e got sick, wrote 'iz own requiem and fell into a pauper's grave. Which, of course, brings us on to lonely old Ludwig van B. — anuvver loser. 'Ammered 'iz klavier so 'ard 'e ended up goin' deaf, poor bloke. Needless to say, when Schubert went an' died of a social disease, they all reckoned as they needed a touch more romance in their lives... though it 'az to be said, this so-called Romantic period was a bit of a washout too. I've 'eard tell some geezer named Berlioz wrote at least *one* fantastic symphony, but when Tchaikovsky 'ad a go, 'iz turned out plain pathetic. Of course, there was Wagner and all the uvvers, but they spent most of their time down the local tavern gettin' totally Brahms'n'Liszt. Fings really didn't get any better till Debussy comes on the scene. Now that bloke — 'e was a truly amazin' impressionist. 'E could mimic Ravel and Satie to a 'tee' — voices, facial expressions, the lot! And sometimes 'e did a bit'v composin' as well. 'E was very fond of 'is muvver, so 'e did this lovely piece called *La Mère*."

Everyone groaned, but Phillip was undaunted...

"*And* 'e was keen on the sea an' all. Wrote anuvver little number about these gorgeous bits of stuff wot sat scantily dressed on the rocks and lured all the sailors to their doom. Every time a ship went by, they'd go 'Yoo-hoo!' — *tiddley-tiddley-pom* — 'Yoo-hoo! Yoo-hoo! Oooh!'"

The 'yoo-hoos' Phillip sang in a flirtatious *falsetto*, and the *tiddley-pom* was his rendering of an orchestral woodwind phrase. With each 'yoo-hoo', he gave a lascivious smile and briefly pulled the left lapel of his corduroy jacket to one side.

Adrian's patience ran out: "For God's sake, stop, stop! No more of this school-boy lunacy, Phillip! And you could've spared us the musical vandalism. I'll never be able to listen to Debussy's *Sirènes* again without seeing you obscenely flashing your left tit. The number of masterpieces you've ruined for me over the years!"

"Sorry, your 'onour. Fings just get out of hand sometimes." By degrees he was returning to his normal RP. "It's like I go into overdrive. All this stuff's coming out of my mouth, but I'm not sure who's saying any of it."

A short while later, Miranda complained to Adrian: "My God, Phillip's completely over the top this evening."

"Just drowning his sorrows. He lost a big teaching contract last week. Means a huge drop in salary."

"So he's spending the little he's got left down the pub, is that the idea? What's *your* excuse? You're doing your utmost to keep up with him."

"Hey, everyone has a few jars on a May Day's Eve! Finnish tradition, so I'm told! In fact, I'm just getting some more in — one for you, of course."

"I don't want any more. I've got an eight o'clock start tomorrow."

"Don't be such a killjoy, Miranda! Enter into the seasonal spirit! Live life on the vernal edge!"

* *

~ *Tell me more about this 'risk-taking' thing of yours.*

~ How do you mean?

~ *This need you have of placing yourself in danger at regular intervals.*

~ Still following up on your enquiries?

~ *What else can you expect? I'm trying to piece everything together. That crazy stunt of climbing into the stairwell wasn't the only example I've seen of your recklessness. What about Saudi Arabia?*

~ Do we have to drag that up again?

~ *There you were in Addis Ababa, ostensibly teaching English to the Saudi air force but, as a sideline, running a still in your bathroom — manufacturing pure alcohol and selling it to other European expats.*

~ I blame the Glaswegian living in the house before me. He left the still behind. I found it stashed away in a cupboard. Seemed a pity to smash the thing up and dump it. Such a lovingly constructed piece of apparatus! But I wasn't in the hooch business for the money. The teaching salary was sizeable enough. Not much to spend it on out there anyway. No, I saw myself more as providing a public service.

~ *And you thought you could get away with it? That you were bloody untouchable?*

~ Oh, you know the setup. Shut away in a compound with a load of other foreigners. High fences and security guards. Hermetically sealed off from the rest of the country.

~ *You must've been aware of their alcohol laws!*

~ Those were for the locals, weren't they? Not for infidels like you and me. Anyway, it wasn't the still I got clobbered for. I'd got rid of it by then. That busybody, Bible-bashing American civil engineer's wife next door was getting overcurious about all the water flowing out of my bathroom in the early hours of the morning. Didn't feel I could depend on her solidarity, so I jettisoned the lot. Off-loaded it on some madcap Aussie. He was well pleased, as you can imagine.

~ *You've got a nerve calling* him *mad. It was you who crashed a hire car into a tree a couple of weeks later with an overdose of alcohol in your bloodstream.*

~ That *was* rather unfortunate. I'd've been all right if a police car hadn't shown up at the wrong moment. Never there when you need 'em, etc.

~ *So you got sentenced to fifty lashes.*

~ Seemed a bit excessive. Didn't think I'd live through it. And the whole legal process dragging on forever — the trial, appeals by embassy lawyers, all the rest of the shit. Left in that hellhole prison for months. So I just told them to get on with it. Send me home in an ambulance or a body bag — whichever turned out more appropriate.

~ *Scary stuff!*

~ They took me out into the prison yard and tied me to a stake. Yes, it was pretty damn scary! They read me a long diatribe in Arabic, of which I understood not a word — in all likelihood telling me what a naughty boy I'd been. Then, after all that build-up and bowel-loosening suspense, the bastard executioner just tapped me forty-five times on the back with the handle of his whip.

~ *An act of mercy — carrying out the sentence in principle rather than in earnest.*

~ That was the first forty-five. Forty-six to fifty were for real. And, by God, did they sting. Couldn't sleep on my back for a week.

~ *So when they packed you off on a plane back to Heathrow, I hope you'd learned your lesson.*

~ What lesson would that be?

~ *Not to take such bloody insane risks!*

~ Well, I learned never to go near an Arab country again.

* *

III

Poco vivace

Tero rushed exultantly into the open-plan office and yelled to anyone within earshot: "Liisa Louhi's telephone's come back to life!"

Miranda leapt up from her desk. "What do you mean? *How* come back to life?"

"The telephone company says her missing phone was used yesterday evening to make seven calls."

"Who to? Who were the calls to?"

Ylenius followed Tero into the room, and read her the answer from a faxed print-out: "One to 'Everyone's Top-40 Chart Selection', four to 'The Facts About Your Ice-hockey Heroes', and a couple to live sex-chat numbers."

"At least, the last two fit our killer's profile," said Miranda. "The others are a bit odd."

Panu Marski had seemed sure it was the killer who'd stolen Liisa's handbag. Since the phone was probably inside the bag at the time, it could very well now be in the murderer's possession.

"Is there some way we can trace back to the person who made the calls?" wondered Miranda. "Perhaps the sex-chat girls would remember something useful?"

Ylenius shook his head. "They must get dozens of clients in a single shift."

"But there's *something* we can use," Tero cut in. "The telephone company's given us info about where the phone was located for each of the calls. Some urban zones are only a couple of hundred yards across, so that gives a reasonable fix. Most of the calls were in the city central area, between 7 and 10 pm. One near the railway station, another on the Esplanade, and three over at the harbour market square. Suggests he was moving around on foot."

"Celebrating on the streets with the rest of the May Day's Eve crowd," Miranda frowned. "No way to pin-point him under those circumstances."

"The last call of the evening was made from Ruoholahti," Ylenius pointed out, "quite near the Conservatory. Could be where he lives."

"Unless he went to party at someone else's place," said Tero.

"What next then?" Miranda asked. "Even if he makes more calls, the phone company will only tell us long after the event which zone he was in. How can we actually nab him?"

"We could always ring him up and ask him where he is," Tero proposed facetiously. "But no, I've got another idea that might *really* help. There's this guy I know on the internet. We've played on-line game sessions together, and he's really hot stuff — really difficult to beat. Calls himself 's Gan... Gan d'Alvinci. That's his *histrionym* — his role-playing name, if you like. But I know his real name too. We've even met face-to-face once over a pint. He does R & D for Nokia. Some kind of whiz kid. Told me he'd devised a system some years back for tracking the real-time positions of individual phones inside Helsinki. Don't know the details, but I could ask him!"

Within minutes Tero had reached the Nokia engineer, and 'Gan' — as Tero addressed him — got the point immediately. He offered to drive into work and set up the tracking system at once. On the journey, he was already giving Tero a rundown, by phone, of how the equipment worked.

"Very simple really," Tero relayed to the others afterwards: "The city's divided up into zones — well, 'cells' is the technical term. Every time a mobile phone's carried across a cell boundary, it locks onto a different radio mast. The central computer records the cell along with the time and duration of every call the mobile makes — for billing purposes, of course. Now, what Gan's monitoring device does is it sends very short calls to the phone you're trying to track. They're just little blips — not long enough to trigger the mobile's ringing tone, but enough to locate where it is. That way the owner doesn't know what's happening. The phone has to be switched on, of course. And then Gan's got this map of Helsinki on his computer screen that shows the phone's movements. Every time it crosses a boundary, a new cell lights up."

"So we can't know the *exact* location?" Miranda asked. "Just the zone."

"Afraid so. It's just something Gan put together a few years ago for his own amusement. New phones are coming that'll give more accurate info for triangulating position, but Liisa's mobile's too primitive — although we can track whoever's carrying her phone in real time as he crosses from cell to cell and follow his movements round the city. Hopefully it'll give us some way to isolate him."

In less than an hour, Gan was at his computer terminal ready to operate. He and Tero would stay in contact via their own mobile phones.

"We're in luck!" exclaimed Tero, almost at once. "Liisa's phone's switched on. Gan says it's ID code identifies it as a Nokia model 3110. And right now it's situated in the centre — somewhere near the Swedish Theatre. Better get ourselves over there if we want any chance of grabbing him."

But this was one o'clock in the afternoon on the First of May: a national holiday; the Nordic equivalent of a carnival; the only day of the year when half the population seems to be out on the streets celebrating the official transition from long dark winter to the brief, heady months of warmth and light. May Day often turns out a chilly travesty. It has even been known to snow! But not this year. The sun was pouring down from an almost cloudless sky, and shirt-sleeved crowds filled the pavements and were spilling onto the streets.

Every generation was represented. Both teenage and elderly couples walked hand-in-hand. Young parents pushed prams. Small boys and girls clung to giant, helium-filled, purse-emptying balloons fashioned in the likenesses of animals, cartoon characters and other profitable children's icons. 'Kids' of every age from eighteen months to eighty licked at ice-creams or blew noisy toy trumpets. Some had adorned themselves with colourful paper streamers. Many wore discoloured white caps commemorating their school matriculation ceremonies of years, perhaps decades ago. And a few — including well-dressed middle-aged men and women — were noticeably drunk.

Miranda and Tero took an unmarked car downtown and parked close to the Swedish Theatre. Two similar teams positioned themselves strategically on other sides of the building. Ylenius had insisted on a discreet approach with no obvious presence of uniforms to scare the target off.

"How the hell are we going to find him in all *this* lot?" Miranda complained, surveying the teeming streets.

"Don't worry," said Tero, quite unperturbed. "We'll wait till he makes a move."

The first move came within twenty minutes. Gan informed Tero that Liisa Louhi's phone had crossed northwards into a cell bordering on the city's Central Railway Station.

"So what now?" Miranda still sounded exasperated. "The crowd's even worse in that direction."

"Have patience," said Tero, obviously enjoying himself. "Sooner or later Freako'll do something we can use against him. Only three routes he can be taking towards the station: Mannerheimintie, Keskuskatu or Mikonkatu. Let's try and keep up with him."

Miranda edged their car a hundred and fifty yards along Mikonkatu, while Tero radioed their associate teams to cover the other two streets.

Almost at once Gan was back in contact...

"He's reached Kaivokatu," Tero said. "He seems to be heading for the railway station."

"But we don't know what he looks like."

Tero ignored Miranda's griping, and Gan soon had news of a different sort. The signal strength from Liisa's mobile had significantly decreased over the last thirty seconds.

"He could've entered a large building. Something with several storeys," Tero said, looking around for a contender.

But Miranda had another explanation: "Perhaps he's gone underground. Down to the Metro line."

"My God, that's it!" Tero burst out, excited. "He's catching a Metro train!"

"But which direction? East or west?"

"Hope for east! It'll take him out to the suburbs — away from all this mess."

"Whichever it is," Miranda said, "we'll need an escort." But before she could radio a request to HQ, she spotted a blue and white vehicle approaching in her wing-mirror. Jumping out to wave the patrol car down, she flashed her ID, and explained the situation to the two uniformed officers inside.

"It's west!" Tero shouted from behind her. "Go! Go! Go!"

"Kamppi Metro station! Now!" she commanded the other driver, and leapt back into her own seat.

The marked vehicle set off, blue light flashing and siren clamouring for a path through the holiday crowds. Miranda followed as tight in its wake as she dared. Kamppi, the next Metro station westwards, was half a mile 'as the mole digs' — a little further on the surface through the network of streets. The underground train had a head start, but whoever was in possession of Liisa's phone would have to ride the escalator up to the station exit. So they were in with a chance.

Tero was holding his mobile to one ear — not to break contact with Gan — at the same time clutching white-knuckled to the dashboard. He called in on the car radio for backup: "We need uniforms at Kamppi Metro station! We have to seal it off!"

"What if he doesn't get off there?" Miranda managed as she took a right-angled turn too fast, back wheels sliding out in a precarious arc.

"Then God help us! Ruoholahti station's another mile and a half down the line."

Seconds later the leading patrol car came squealing to a halt alongside one of the Kamppi station exits. Throwing their doors wide, the two uniformed occupants burst out. Miranda was still tearing herself free from her seat belt when Tero restrained her.

"Don't bother! He didn't get off! He's on his way to Ruoholahti!"

"Oh, shit!" hissed Miranda, and leant out of the window to warn their escorts.

Then they were off again — at an even more breakneck speed now they'd cleared the worst of the crowds.

"Ruoholahti's the end of the line!" yelled Tero, competing with the engine. "So he *has to* get off there!"

"But we'll never make it!" Miranda moaned through clenched teeth. "Can't we stop the train? Get through to Metro traffic-control. Tell them to raise a red light. Halt the train in the tunnel!"

Tero did his best. He got HQ to patch the car radio straight through to the Metro authorities, but the phone just rang... and kept ringing.

"For fucksake!" Tero exploded.

Despite her other preoccupations, Miranda registered having never heard Tero swear before. This might have come as a startling revelation. Right now she could only sympathize.

"What the hell are they playing at?" Tero raged on. "Answer the phone, damn it!"

"National holiday," gasped Miranda, pursuing the patrol car full tilt through a red light and narrowly missing a slow-witted cyclist. "Skeleton staff!"

And still the phone rang.

They were more than half way to Ruoholahti — with Tero more than half way to an apoplectic fit — when somebody picked up at the other end. Tero didn't waste time complaining. He got straight to the point.

"Sorry mate, you're too late!" came the reply. "The train's already at Ruoholahti."

"Tell the driver not to open the doors!"

"Can't! They're already open."

HQ suddenly came back on the line: "Backup units awaiting your instructions at Kamppi Metro station."

"Kamppi? Oh, Christ, we forgot to redirect them! Send them to Ruoholahti! We need them at Ruoholahti!"

Another thirty seconds and Miranda, Tero and their escort skidded to a halt outside the Metro terminus. But the floodgates had already opened. Passengers were streaming out from both exits, some heading south towards the Conservatory and the residential blocks beyond, others fanning out onto the main road to catch trams or buses.

Miranda and Tero tried to turn the tide and stop any more passengers escaping from the station, but it was hopeless. No one took them seriously. Everybody assumed it was some silly — probably drunken — practical joke, and pushed past with expressions ranging from solicitous amusement to downright annoyance. No one even bothered to look at the police warrant cards.

The uniformed officers were having a little more success, but there was too much humanity moving too relentlessly.

Miranda abandoned the attempt and rushed over to Tero.

"Give me your mobile!" she demanded, practically tearing it from his fingers. "Gan, this is Miranda. Tero's colleague. What's the number of the phone we're tracking? Dictate it to me!" As Gan did so, she grasped her own phone in the other hand and clumsily punched the keys with her thumb.

"What are you doing?" demanded Tero, suspicious. "Hey, Miranda...?"

She ignored him, handing back his mobile as she pressed the 'CALL' button on her own. There was a slight delay. Then, to their left, came a chirruping version of the *William Tell* Overture. They pushed across the stream towards the sound and the melody suddenly grew in volume as a blond, stocky man in his mid-thirties pulled a telephone out of his pocket. Miranda and Tero positioned themselves close on either side — in case he tried to make a break for it.

"Detective Inspector Lewis," she announced, showing her ID. "May I take a look at your mobile phone?"

The man seemed bemused by this suggestion. He also appeared rather drunk.

"What for?" he asked. "Can't I answer it first?"

"I'll do that for you."

Miranda took his handset, selected 'ANSWER', and placed it to her ear. She expected nothing more than a processed duplication of the station noise around her, and almost recoiled when a woman's voice said sharply: "Christ, Mikko, you took your time! Look, I'm going to be late. Mum's none too well. I'll stay on another hour."

Miranda drew the phone down to eye-level. It wasn't even the right make, for heaven's sake! An Ericsson, not a Nokia!

"Sorry," she said flatly, and gave the mobile back. "My mistake." Turning away, she checked her own telephone. It was still ringing Liisa's number. Nobody had answered. And no ringing tone could be heard from any other handset in the vicinity. She cancelled the call. Tero was right. Much too hit-and-miss.

Meanwhile the station hall had practically emptied. She followed the last stragglers out onto the street, furious with herself and with the foul-up she'd made of the operation.

Tero joined her, looking unusually docile. He decided to update

Gan. "The chicken's flown the coop," he began. "we tried to..."

But Gan cut in with a question: "Are you outside the station?"

"Yes."

"Look south. See the footbridge on the other side of the square? It crosses a canal that coincides with the boundary to another cell. A few seconds ago, our phone crossed into that cell. Somebody's just carried the phone across the bridge."

"My God! Come on, Miranda!" Tero broke into a run. The distance was less than two hundred yards, and he was already surveying the other side of the canal. He could make out only three possibilities: a woman pushing a small child in a buggy with two older kids in tow, a grey-haired man of about sixty, and a much younger and more vigorously moving male clutching a bag close to his chest.

Tero had no doubt which to go for. He hammered across the wooden boards of the footbridge and caught up with his quarry about fifty yards further on. Restraining the man by the arm, Tero tried to catch his breath, all the time fumbling for his warrant card. The suspect turned in shock and horror; then, tearing himself free, darted off like a hare.

Tero was already winded, but definitely not ready to give up. He set off in pursuit again, aware that Miranda was now close at his heels, but it was another three hundred yards between tall blocks of flats before they brought the man down. He kicked and cursed and wriggled as Tero and Miranda tried to pin him to the ground. He didn't give up until their two escorts from the patrol car also arrived on the scene. The sight of police uniforms seemed to calm him. He cast his eyes from one face to another and finally realized that all four of them were on the same team.

"What the hell's this about?" he demanded, in anger.

"Are you carrying a mobile phone?" Miranda asked, still breathing hard.

"Yes, I bloody am! So what?"

"We'd like to see it."

After a few more curses and complaints he pulled a small, bright blue telephone from his pocket. Miranda saw instantly that it couldn't be Liisa's — again it was the wrong model. But what if there'd been a

327

second phone and he'd jettisoned it during the chase? No, she'd had him in clear view the whole time. And he was only wearing a T-shirt and thin khaki shorts. Nowhere to conceal another phone — unless, of course...

"Can we have a look in your bag?"

Miranda found no second telephone. But she did find a thick bundle of bank notes.

"A very large sum to be carrying around with you, isn't it?" Her voice now carried a different kind of accusation.

"That's the bloody point, isn't it?"

"Meaning?"

"Meaning, it's why I ran! What would you have done, for Chrissake — with that much cash in your bag? I just drew it out at the Metro cash-point to pay for my neighbour's old Nissan before he changes his mind! He's finally agreed to sell it to me. I thought you were bloody muggers!"

Tero looked deflated. And Miranda didn't doubt the man's story. They'd screwed up and grabbed the wrong person again. She glanced at her watch. This whole wild-goose chase from the city centre had taken no more than eleven minutes! It felt like the longest eleven minutes of her life.

They checked the prospective Nissan-buyer's details from his driving licence and let him go.

Tero recontacted Gan: "Where's the phone now?"

"Same place. Same cell."

"He's probably gone to ground in one of the apartment blocks," Tero conjectured.

"Well, you've got him boxed off. This cell lies on a peninsula, and the canal effectively turns it into an island with only four ways off again. Stake each of them out along the boundaries of the cell, and you can wait for him to walk back into the trap."

"That's brilliant, Gan. Ever considered a career in the police force?"

"Reckon I'll settle for being a deputized member of the posse, thanks. There's one thing though. This could be a long process, and sooner or later I'll have to answer nature's call. How about some backup here?"

"Right, I'll send someone over to sit in with you."

"Ask him to bring a family-sized tuna-fish pizza and a large bottle of Coke, will you?"

Back at the Metro station, Miranda and Tero's *own* backup had arrived. An armada of police patrol vehicles had pulled up on the pavements. Blue lights were flashing everywhere. The two plain-clothes teams abandoned at the railway station had also found their way here. The uniformed officers were standing around in groups, unsure why they'd been summoned. It was Ylenius, working out of Pasila HQ, who deployed this loose assembly of personnel into a coordinated stakeout operation.

Within a short time, all four of the exits specified by Gan had been unobtrusively cordoned off: the original canal footbridge crossing to the north, and three other streets to the north-east that bordered on a quite separate cell. The footbridge seemed the most likely return route since it led straight back to the Metro station. Miranda and Tero claimed that one for themselves, feeling they were entitled to the best chance of finishing off the job. Well, they'd been the ones to start it, hadn't they?

This whole Ruoholahti area was a recent redevelopment of a run-down and defunct tract of dockland. From Miranda and Tero's chosen vantage point — with the canal and footbridge to their immediate left — a spacious cobbled square stretched out before them surrounded on three sides by smart modern buildings of concrete and glass. The fourth side offered a limited south-westerly view of the sea.

The Helsinki Conservatory stood at their backs. When viewed from the sides, it was a nondescript white three storeys — inset with windows. But the facade was of rather more interest, alternating large horizontal areas of glass with a warm, pale-brown texture of finely slatted wood; the whole overhung by a forward projection of the flat eaveless roof. Six black-painted, metal girders supported this overhang and thrust vertically down to ground level, hinting at a classical colonnade.

Miranda and Tero now sat within this colonnade, perched on a window-ledge outside the Conservatory cafeteria. Since this was a national holiday, the whole building was locked up and deserted.

329

Elsewhere around the square, three uniformed officers were positioned out of sight, ready for action. Two more lurked in a doorway on the far side of the bridge, in case the target tried to double back. All were linked to headquarters, to Gan, and to each other with personal radios.

Miranda viewed stakeouts as a tedious though necessary evil; but she'd noticed on earlier surveillance operations how Tero responded positively to the task. He seemed able to hold himself in a state of pleasurable suspense, regardless of how long the wait. Today he appeared even more upbeat than usual — almost euphoric.

"Good teamwork earlier on," he remarked.

"We haven't caught anyone yet," she reminded him.

"Oh, we will. No question." Nothing could spoil his mellow mood. "It's just a matter of time."

By 8 pm they were getting hungry and thirsty, but neither was prepared to leave the scene in search of refreshment for fear of missing the critical moment.

"We could be here all night," brooded Miranda.

"If we have to," Tero replied.

Whether it was the effect of sitting for so many hours beneath the portals of the Helsinki Conservatory, Miranda would never know, but Tero astounded her when he suddenly said: "All this classical music — the stuff *you* do, Miranda — there must be something to it, I suppose."

"Yes, Tero. Probably."

"I mean, I've been thinking about it... since we had this case going on... sort of wondering what this classical stuff's all about." He watched a middle-aged couple cross the footbridge and walk towards the Metro station. "Your mum and dad... musicians, right?"

"My father, yes."

"So you were brought up to it, weren't you? You had music all around when you were a kid."

"That's true."

"It was different for me, you see. My parents didn't like music. We only ever had news and discussions — boring stuff like that — on the radio. Any kind of music programme came on telly and they changed channel. But, when I was ten, I asked Dad if I could have a guitar for

Christmas. I'd tried one at school... thought I'd like one of my own. In the end they gave me a Lego construction kit. Well, that was all right too. It was enormous. But I never bothered asking for a guitar again."

"You listen to music nowadays though, don't you?"

"Yeah, mainly *Nirvana* and *Foo Fighters*."

"So how did *that* happen?"

He considered Miranda's question for a while. "At school, I was mainly into computers... and sport — volleyball, a bit of football. Didn't get my first CD player till I moved away from home... when I started at police college. I met this other cadet there and he was the one got me going on *Nirvana*. It was the lyrics grabbed me first. But then I started to get what the music was about too. I reckon they're the ultimate. Pity Kurt Cobain topped himself. You know their stuff?"

"Can't say I do," Miranda admitted. To her further amazement, Tero now became almost bashful: "I was thinking," he said, "wondering really... could you maybe lend me a couple of your CDs — classical ones, I mean? Choose something for me? A sort of 'starter pack'?"

Miranda studied his face, trying to appraise his sincerity — to convince herself he wasn't just winding her up again.

"All right," she said at last. "I can do that for you. But on one condition... You lend me a couple of your *Nirvana* albums in exchange."

For once, Miranda found the smirk that spread across Tero's face quite inoffensive.

Suddenly Gan's voice cut into their ear-pieces: "Breakthrough! Breakthrough!"

This was the code agreed on if Liisa's phone crossed north into Tero and Miranda's cell. Both leapt up from the window-ledge... but stopped dead in their tracks. Crossing the bridge towards them were two undersized figures — two boys aged about nine and eleven with no one accompanying them and no one else in sight.

Miranda frowned. "Gan must've got the code words mixed up." Damn it! Now one of the other teams would get the collar!

But Tero was already stepping forward on an interception course. He'd seen these two before — standing there gawking in fascination beside the woman with a buggy — as he'd tried to grab that earlier

331

bogus suspect and then given chase again. Thrown off-balance by his adversary, Tero had stumbled and almost run these two children down.

"Can I have a word, lads?" he said, holding out his warrant card. "We're police officers, and we'd like to... " He got no further. The older boy bolted off across the square throwing worried glances over his shoulder. The smaller boy's flight-reflexes seemed less highly developed. He froze to the spot like a frightened rabbit in headlights. Tero took a firm hold of his arm — just in case. The boy flinched, half-heartedly trying to pull loose.

"Relax, kid! We're not going to hurt you."

Miranda was at their side. "You're not in any trouble," she said. "But have either of you got a mobile phone?"

"No!" the boy blurted out, obviously meaning 'yes'.

"Is it your friend? Has he got one?"

"He's not my friend. He's my brother!"

"All right. Why don't you call your brother over here so we can talk to him?"

"Ah, now what's this?" Tero exclaimed, and lifted a black Nokia 3110 from the child's back pocket. The right model at last! But was it the actual phone? Tero held it out between forefinger and thumb while Miranda extracted a pair of latex evidence gloves from her shoulder bag. Then she summoned the 3110's internal 'phone book' onto the small LCD screen and didn't even need to scroll down the alphabetic list. The very first entry read: *ADRIAN (A.!)*, followed by a number that Miranda knew by heart.

She nodded to Tero. "This is the one."

"Somebody gave it to me!" the boy broke in, anticipating their next question.

"And who was that?" coaxed Miranda, trying to keep calm and not give away how much rode on the answer.

The boy's eyes flicked towards his brother; but, realizing the betrayal, immediately in the opposite direction.

"Your brother, was it? Did your brother give it to you?"

The youngster was on the verge of tears. "Aki said it'd be all right," he wailed.

"And it will be," Miranda assured him. "Aki's your brother, is he?

Shall we call Aki over here?"

By patient cajoling and repeated promises that he wasn't in any trouble, they persuaded the older boy to venture back within speaking distance, although still well out of arm's reach.

"All we want to know is where this phone came from," Miranda tried again.

"We found it!" pleaded the younger one, and received a warning glare from his brother. But that came too late... "We found it in there, "the small boy went on, and pointed to the building beside them. Miranda and Tero exchanged astonished glances.

"You found it in *this* building?" asked Miranda. "In the Helsinki Conservatory?"

"I dunno what it's called. But it was in there anyway. Inside the back door."

"Okay," Miranda said slowly, trying to take in this new development. "Can you show us which door you mean?"

The boys led them round to the other side of the building, and pointed down some steps to a heavy steel door set at basement level.

"How did you get in?" queried Tero. "Wasn't it locked?"

It certainly was now.

"Somebody'd left it open," said Aki. "Maybe 'cause it was a hot day. We only went in for a look. It's the back of a sort of stage place. Like behind a theatre. All kinds of junk there. We found the handbag in the corner."

"Handbag?"

"Yeah, the phone was in the handbag."

Miranda and Tero were visibly stunned. Liisa Louhi's missing handbag?

"No one else wanted it!" said Aki defiantly, misreading their expressions. "It was chucked down the back of an old cupboard."

"Where's the handbag now?" Miranda asked, reining in her excitement.

The brothers looked at each other, obviously wondering if it was in their best interests to answer.

"At home in our bedroom," Aki admitted.

Their mother answered the sixth-storey apartment door with a cigarette dangling from her lower lip. Somewhere in the background a small child was howling in rebellious frustration. The woman took in the group on her doorstep — two small, two large — and grasped the situation at once.

"Got themselves in trouble again, have they?" She seemed neither surprised nor much interested, and led the way into a shabbily furnished sitting-room. Toys, clothes, used coffee mugs and dirty plates were scattered about on the floor and on every other available horizontal surface. A small girl seated in the middle of the room looked up amazed at the two strangers and, to everyone's relief, was struck dumb.

"Aki's the problem," the woman said, drawing hard on her cigarette, and looking around vaguely for somewhere to seat the visitors. "Takes after his dad. Little Matti's not so bad. Well, *his* dad was the quiet type. Buggered off just the same though, didn't he? All *three* did in the end. Men don't hang about with kids underfoot. None of the men I've met anyway."

This cheerless summary of the woman's single-parent status wasn't what Miranda and Tero had come for. Without attempting to sit down, they explained about the handbag, and five minutes later were leaving with it. The boys agreed that tomorrow they'd show the exact spot where they'd found the bag, and then have their fingerprints taken at Pasila for elimination purposes. The prospect obviously excited them — not least perhaps as an excuse to skip school.

The stakeout was over. Since the Conservatory backstage site could be considered forensically 'cold', Ylenius decided to wait till morning to send in the SOCOs. Then there'd be no need to have the building opened specially.

Meanwhile, they had the handbag itself...

In the forensic lab, Tero and Miranda watched the Chief Inspector — with latex-gloves and a contented smile — open the tasselled, calfskin bag to make a preliminary inspection of its contents.

"When exactly did the boys find this?" he asked.

"Saturday afternoon," replied Miranda.

"And how did they get the phone working? The battery must've run down ages ago."

"It was switched off when the boys found it, so there was still some charge left. Of course, to switch the thing back on they needed the PIN code, but Liisa had scribbled it on the inside cover of her address book. That was in the bag as well."

"Have all the original contents of the bag been replaced?"

"The boys claim it's all in there, and I'm inclined to believe them."

Ylenius now laid everything out on a plastic sheet: purse, keys, make-up, a student identity card, the small address book that Miranda had just mentioned; and, most interestingly, a coiled-up length of cat-chewed speaker cable with one end cut cleanly off.

"All right," Ylenius said, surveying the items before him, "I think the chain of events is getting clearer. Early that Friday evening — after Liisa had been for a practice session with her accompanist in Mariankatu — the killer spots her at Forum shopping centre. Maybe he's already followed her there. Anyway, while she's busy looking at coats, he steals her handbag. My guess is he just wanted to find out something more personal about her — pure curiosity, if you like. But then Liisa rushes off in a panic to Adrian Gamble's place. The killer trails her there and waits on the other side of the road... which is where he drops the Mozart symphony score — by mistake, or perhaps he just discards it. When Liisa comes out again, he follows her into the park and strangles her with a piece of the speaker cable he's found in her bag. Presumably she took the cable with her as a model, intending to get a replacement at the Forum shops."

"So you're saying this first murder wasn't premeditated?" asked Miranda... "at least, not in any long-term sense?"

"I think the crime was more or less opportunistic. That was Marski's view as well, wasn't it?... that the killing showed a lack of organization and could almost be described as reckless. I visualize the murderer coming to a decision in the park opposite Gamble's flat. He cuts off a length of the cable with his secateurs and fashions the noose right there and then while he's waiting and hoping Liisa will reappear."

"But why," challenged Miranda, "would he be carrying secateurs in the first place if he hadn't planned the killing in advance?"

"Perhaps we need to look at it the other way round. A pair of secateurs being available at that critical moment could itself have been the trigger."

Miranda pondered this for a while. "You mean, the secateurs were the reason he decided to go ahead with the sexual attack? Because then he'd be able to take his fourth-finger trophy afterwards?"

"Exactly."

Miranda nodded slowly, half-persuaded already. "It still leaves us trying to explain why he had the secateurs with him in the first place."

"What if he found them in Liisa's handbag too?" volunteered Tero. "She had loads of plants at her flat. Perhaps she'd just bought some secateurs for herself."

The Chief Inspector was dubious. "Her plants aren't the kind you'd need secateurs for. No, I think it's more likely the killer bought them... maybe quite innocently, before he even spotted Liisa at the shopping centre."

"Something we've forgotten," Tero ventured cautiously. "We still only have Gamble's word for it that Liisa arrived at his place without the handbag — that it wasn't stolen later at the murder site."

Miranda drew in a sharp breath. "Why on earth, Tero, would Adrian bother to lie about that? Haven't we been over this before?"

Tero shrugged.

"In any case," Ylenius was now pulling off his latex gloves, "there's nothing more we can do here tonight. First thing tomorrow, let's have all this stuff of Liisa's checked by Forensics, and we'll get ourselves down to the Conservatory for some serious digging."

Miranda didn't immediately accompany the others to Ruoholahti the next morning. On arrival at Pasila she found an email from Panu Marski. He was back from the States and requesting an update on the latest developments. Miranda called him.

"Look, sorry, Miranda... I know I asked *you* to contact *me*, but I need to be at a parole board meeting in Töölö — less than an hour from now. And I'll probably be tied up there the rest of the day. I wonder, though, could we meet up briefly beforehand? I'm keen to get the latest data. And a quick re-orientation from you would be useful as well."

Töölö was on Miranda's route to the Conservatory, so she proposed the corner café opposite the library — the same café they'd visited once before.

Miranda adopted a business-like manner as soon as they'd sat down: laying out copies on the table of the files related to the fifth murder.

"Yes, good," said Marski. "I'll go over it as soon as I can. There's a lot of other stuff to catch up on first, of course, after a fortnight away. But I'll get back to you in a couple of days. Aim for Thursday, shall we?"

Miranda then gave him a brief account of yesterday's frantic chase across the city, and the recovery of Liisa's phone and handbag. Marski agreed with Ylenius's conclusions about the killer's state of mind during the hour or so leading up to the Sibelius Monument attack, and also that the secateurs could have been the final trigger. But, when the waitress arrived with their cappuccinos, he cleared the papers away into his briefcase.

"How was your tour of New England?" Miranda enquired conversationally.

"The kids enjoyed it," he said flatly.

Miranda had no wish to be drawn in this direction. She'd heard enough transparent hints about Panu's marital problems.

"And the conference?" she asked, trying a safer alternative.

Marski accepted the diversion. "Yes, quite stimulating. Two days and two topics: stalkers and date rapists. Not especially uplifting subjects," he admitted dryly, "but there were a lot of good minds present and plenty of worthwhile ideas."

"Any examples for me?" Miranda smiled neutrally.

"We had some interesting discussions on how to convey the true nature of date rape to lay workers in the field, law-enforcement personnel, and so on. More specifically how to convince the doubting Thomases — male police officers with residual chauvinist tendencies — those prone to assume it's usually the girl's own fault."

While Panu went into specifics, Miranda noticed with relief how detached she felt compared to their last meeting at the Savoy. Of course, the circumstances were different: morning rather than evening; no soft lighting and romantic ambience; just Formica table-tops and tubular steel chairs. And now there was another man more decisively in the picture. Not that she'd spoken to Adrian since that fiasco of May Day's Eve when she'd virtually had to carry him up to his flat and drop him semi-conscious on the bed. She hadn't even bothered to take off her shoes. She'd just walked out without a word, and without leaving a note. True, she'd never seen him so drunk before. Perhaps they'd be able to patch things up. One thing was certain: she had no intention of turning to Panu for comfort.

However, Panu's perception of their last meeting seemed unchanged. "I thoroughly enjoyed our dinner together," he was suddenly saying. "Mightn't we do the same again? Some evening next week, for example?"

The directness of his approach caught Miranda off guard, and she gave herself plenty of time to answer.

"Am I to take this as a non-professional invitation?" she said at last.

"You've been much in my thoughts, Miranda." His tone was muted enough, though carrying an undercurrent of intensity. And then his eyes were smiling as he added: "I hope you don't find my conduct too *un*professional?"

Pointedly, Miranda left this question unanswered. Placing her cup back in its saucer, she sat up a little straighter.

"It's very flattering, of course," she began, and Panu's expression sobered at the ominous platitude. "The situation, though, is you're married — however unsatisfactorily. You already have two small children in your life that depend on you. I'm not prepared to get involved in all that. The benefits are never worth the indignity. I made that mistake once years ago when I was a teenager. I'd prefer to think of myself as older and wiser. Sorry, Panu. It's too late for us this time around. Maybe in the next life."

He gazed back for a while, as if assessing the finality of her refusal. "You mean when we're reincarnated as a couple of pigs in the same pigsty?"

"For example."

"Knowing my luck, we'll be black widow spiders and you'll gobble me up after our first romantic encounter... but, okay — " he gave a wry grin " — I suppose I could settle for that."

Miranda laughed and stood up to leave. On a sudden impulse she leant forward and gave him a peck on the cheek. "Be in touch

Thursday, then," she said, wiggled a few fingers and walked briskly towards the door. She'd just emerged into the bright sunshine when Adrian appeared at her elbow.

"You startled me," she said. "Where were *you* hiding?"

"I wasn't hiding anywhere," he replied acidly. "I'm simply visiting my local café for a coffee and a sandwich. How was I to know I'd stumble on another of your little assignations?"

"Assignations? What the hell are you talking about, Adrian?"

"I understood your relationship with the glamorous psychologist was purely professional."

"Of course, it is. I've been handing over some documents."

"I saw you kissing him!"

Her anger came in an uncontrollable rush.

"For God's sake, don't be so childish, Adrian! You don't own me! I'll kiss anyone I please!" Spinning away, she stalked off towards her car.

Miranda drove straight to the Conservatory, where she located Tero in the auditorium at the back of the stage. A team of SOCOs were conducting a thorough search.

"Found anything?" she asked.

"Plenty of wooden swords and daggers splashed with blood. Some papier-mâché fruit. Nothing useful."

Miranda also spent some time poking around amongst the debris of past productions, but soon got bored and made her way back to the lobby. There she found the Chief Inspector in conversation with Jorma Mannila, the younger of the two porters — the one with the balding head. Ylenius was admiring the contents of a large vase on a stand beside the porter's cubicle.

"Cherry and lilac," he said to Mannila, "and in full bloom already. How beautiful!"

Miranda recalled seeing a similar vase of blossoming twigs on her visit to the Conservatory the Monday after Liisa Louhi's death. She studied Mannila with interest. Tero had overseen most of the earlier questioning of the Conservatory staff and students, so she'd only crossed paths with Mannila a couple of times, and then briefly. He was large and clumsy-looking: shoulders stooped and too narrow for his height; hips too wide. His face was heavily jowled, his eyes pale and watery — dead-pan, uncommunicative, lacking any trace of humour. How had Tero described him? Ponderous... Yes, that fit very well. She was surprised when the porter gave a significant response to the Chief Inspector's comment about the blossom-laden cuttings.

"All you have to do is bring them into the warm," Mannila explained, with something akin to animation, "and place them in water. In a few weeks the buds open."

"And was it you who brought these in here?" Ylenius asked, intrigued.

"A few weeks ago," the porter nodded. "It can work as early as January or February, but only with trees and bushes that produce their buds ready the previous autumn — cherry, plum, lilac, forsythia, horse chestnut."

"I gather this is a hobby of yours," continued Ylenius, in the same friendly tone.

"I suppose so," answered Mannila, his voice suddenly more wooden.

"I imagine you'd need a good quality pair of secateurs for the job. May I ask what kind you use?"

Mannila looked wary. "Why do you want to know?"

"Just interested," Ylenius persisted.

"Quite ordinary ones. *Jardine 360s.*"

"And do you have them in the building?"

Mannila gave a minimal nod.

"Could I see them, please?"

Begrudgingly, but without further comment, Mannila went and opened a drawer inside the porter's cubicle, and returned moments later with a pair of yellow-handled garden secateurs.

"Drop them in here for me, would you?" said Ylenius, holding out a clear-plastic evidence bag. "We'll need to take them over to Pasila police station for a few tests. I'd appreciate you coming along too, Mr Mannila, so we can take your fingerprints and ask you a few questions."

Jorma Mannila stared stony-faced at the Chief Inspector.

"Can I refuse?" he asked.

"Under the circumstances, I'm afraid that's not an option."

IV

Allegro molto

"So, Mr Mannila, can you *really* give us no explanation as to how your fingerprints got onto Liisa Louhi's handbag?"

At last they had a genuine lead. Fingerprints lifted from the recovered handbag had turned out a positive match to Jorma Mannila's. Enough to hold him for questioning, and justification for sending a SOCO team round to his flat.

"Well, Mr Mannila?" Ylenius prompted again. His tone was inquisitive rather than threatening. "Your fingerprints? The handbag?"

"I've told you. I cannot give you an explanation. Perhaps Liisa asked me to hold it for her... while she fetched her coat."

Ylenius seemed charmed by this suggestion. "And would that also account for your fingerprints *inside* the handbag?"

Impervious to the irony, Mannila tried again: "Perhaps she left it somewhere and I found it. I would have looked inside to see who the owner was."

The Chief Inspector moved on: "What was your relationship with Liisa Louhi?"

"I don't understand your question."

"Were you friends?" asked Ylenius patiently. "Did you chat together sometimes?"

"She was a student. She asked me to help her with things. That's my job."

"What kind of things?"

"Reserving practice rooms. Passing on messages. Once I repaired her shoe. The heel had broken off. I glued it back on."

"And did you like her?"

"Perhaps I did. I don't remember. Why is that important? I'd like to go home now."

Ylenius ignored the proposal. "And what about Jaana Saari? I suppose you knew her too?"

"I know all the students. I knew Liisa Louhi and I knew Jaana Saari. It's a pity they had to die."

Tero picked up on this at once. "What do you mean — they *had* to die?

Jorma gave him a superior look. "I mean that it was God's will to take their souls to judgment. They were very young, but the Almighty cannot be denied. His will must be done — here on earth, as it is in Heaven."

This was by no means Jorma's first reference during the interrogation to Heaven and the Almighty. They'd established early on that he was a zealous, perhaps a zealot, member of an obscure Christian sect, self-styled the Church of the Steadfast Pilgrim. Many of his responses were accompanied by declarations of God's will or, at least, Jorma's interpretation of it. Specific answers were hard to obtain on any important issue. He resorted to evasions and hypothetical generalities. Frequently he parried questions with his own. Whether he had something to hide or whether it was just an expression of his overall personality Miranda found difficult to assess. When asked about the three non-Conservatory victims — Christa Bäckström, Tiina Holopainen and Anna Orav — Mannila denied all knowledge of them: "I don't know these names. I don't know these women. I cannot understand why you mention them to me."

The straight answers he did give were never the ones his interrogators had hoped for.

"You're not registered as owning a motor vehicle," the Chief Inspector pointed out.

"That's because I don't."

"Nor a driving license. Have you never taken lessons?"

"No."

"Not even a few?"

"None."

"Is that because God hasn't built any motorways to the Pearly Gates yet?" asked Tero.

Mannila was outraged. "He that mocks the Lord shall be sorely punished."

"I'll take my chances," Tero countered.

Ylenius headed off this collision of mindsets: "Mr Mannila, we'd all be very interested to hear about how you spend your free time. Do you like to read, for example?"

"I read the Bible."

"Nothing else?"

"There are books recommended by our church founder, books revealing God's works and the path he has set for us."

"No novels? No biographies of famous people?"

Mannila tossed his head in contempt at such a suggestion.

"But you do have music at your church meetings," suggested Miranda.

"We sing hymns."

"Ah, hymns, yes!" Tero cut in again. "I expect you're fond of music."

Mannila looked blank.

"Like to settle down of an evening, do you? After a hard day's portering?" Tero's tone was wheedling. "Put on a CD? Sit back and relax? Nice bit of classical music, I shouldn't wonder. Sibelius even. Partial to a bit of Sibelius, are we?"

"I don't waste my time on trivial, Godless pursuits."

Miranda wondered what Sibelius would've thought of such an uncompromising dismissal.

"But you've got at least one hobby," Tero persisted. "This branch-cutting thing of yours."

"*That* is different. Blossoms and leaves are God's own creations. I merely bring their beauty, the bounteous work of the Almighty's own hands to other people's notice — to adorn the buildings of this spiritually barren man-made desert that we inhabit."

The others could only stare back at this barrage of what sounded like a hotchpotch of rote-learned phrases.

"I'd like to go home now," Mannila said again.

"I enjoy stonewallers like him," Tero commented, during one of their breaks from the interrogation room. "Usually some way of winding them up — some chink in the armour — if you can only find it."

Miranda drained her second cup of coffee and stretched her arms full length above her head. "Wonder how the SOCOs are getting on at his flat," she mused. "Hopefully they'll turn up something we can use as a lever — something damning."

Ylenius had just suggested they get back to Mannila for another go, when Miranda's mobile rang. It was Adrian. He seemed to be leading into some kind of apology, but Miranda cut him dead: "Look, I haven't got time for this right now. There's a lot going on here. I'll have to hang up." She terminated the call without waiting for his response. Well, it was true, wasn't it? This really wasn't the right moment! Although the fact that she still needed to punish him for yesterday's ridiculous scene outside the café didn't escape her notice.

'Luscious' Lars was once more escorting Beatrice Gröndahl home from her violin lesson. In the present climate of fear, Beatrice's mother had insisted she didn't make the journey alone. "I'll ask the matron if I can get away a bit early and pick you up in the car," Mrs Gröndahl proposed.

But Beatrice had been very convincing that everything would be all right. "Lars'll bring me home," she said. "He'll come right to the door." Unfortunately, that wasn't how things turned out. The trouble started soon after they got on the bus.

"I can't ask you in this week," she told Lars, with distinct coolness. She'd been throwing him suspicious looks ever since they met at the music school gates. "I'm going out with Mum tonight — as soon as she gets back from work. We're going to a film."

"With your *Mum*?" Lars marvelled.

"We do stuff together sometimes. She's good fun. And anyway, we're celebrating, aren't we?" she added pointedly.

"Celebrating? Oh, shit! It's your birthday!" Lars looked penitent. He even blushed. "God, I'm sorry, Bea! I thought of it yesterday, but a lot's happened since then. Damn! I was going to get you a present."

"Were you?" She made an effort to smile.

"I'd already decided what to give you."

Beatrice waited for him to elaborate, but he didn't.

"Well," she said, softening a little, "you can bring it on Saturday when you come to my party."

Now Lars looked even more uncomfortable.

"You *are* coming, aren't you?" There was a dangerous edge of hurt in her voice.

"It's my floor-ball team, you see. I didn't think we had a hope in hell of reaching the semifinals. Then we won the match yesterday. A fantastic fight! We've never come *close* to beating that team before." His eyes glowed, reliving the experience.

But Beatrice was getting impatient: "What's that got to do with my party?" she demanded.

"The semis are on Sunday morning. If we get through *them* the final's the same evening. God, it'd be great to get that far!"

"So it's on Sunday," Beatrice said, with growing resentment. "What's the big deal? My party's on Saturday."

"But the matches aren't in Helsinki, Bea. They're in Tampere. We'll be travelling up on Saturday evening and staying overnight in a hostel."

"Tell them you don't want to go. Say you've got something else on."

"I can't! I've been training with these guys for over a year!"

"So tell them you're ill. Duck out at the last moment."

"You don't understand. I'm their best forward. They need me. I can't let them down."

"What about letting *me* down? You *promised*, Lars!" Her infamous Latin-American temperament was taking over, and she didn't care.

"Come on, Bea, it's not fair to lay heavy stuff like this on me!" Lars was getting annoyed too. The bus halted to let off passengers and the rear automatic doors opened. "I'd come to your damn party if I could. But it's impossible. That's all I can say!"

"Well, I don't want you at my 'damn' party! I don't want you on this bus, either! Get off and leave me alone!"

"Suit yourself!" he said, and leapt between the doors just as they were reclosing. A spontaneous and understandable action given the circumstances, but one he would very soon regret.

345

Symphony No 6

*   *   *

[6.42 pm; Tuesday, 2nd May]

I've done it again, Daddy! You always warned me how my stupid temper would get me in trouble. Of course, Mum's taken over the job now. But it doesn't stop me missing you... and remembering those last talks we had together — holding your hand for hours beside the bed. You looked so weak, so ill. But your voice never changed. Just as lovely and strong as ever. And you sounded so close, so real — like you'd always be there for me and nothing could ever take you away. If they knew how often I talk to you, they'd think I'm a total loony — that I'd finally flipped. But you've got to be out there somewhere, listening to me, watching over me, keeping me from harm...

And now I've messed everything up again. But you heard Lars promise me, didn't you? He said he'd come. I know it's just I wanted to show him off to everybody — have everyone see us together. Well, he is gorgeous, isn't he? All the girls say he is. And now he'll never speak to me again. How could I be so childish? Like a stupid twelve-year-old!

She saw the car parked alongside the pavement. One of the doors was open, and somebody was squatting down, reaching inside. He seemed to be fiddling with something on the rear seat. This should perhaps have made her suspicious, but she was too engrossed in self-recriminations to make any conscious connection with the identical set of circumstances she'd witnessed a week earlier.

The procedure he planned was indeed like last Tuesday's aborted attempt — if that had, in fact, been a genuine attempt. He wasn't sure then whether he'd follow through, and he wasn't sure now either. When it actually started, he felt again as if somebody outside himself were pulling the strings.

He'd known from the first — when he saw her on the bus with her two friends — that she was a Swedish-speaker. That's why he'd decided to make his initial approach in her own language. There was a solidarity amongst the Swedish-speaking minority in Finland that could help him breach her natural caution. Even *his* modest skills in the language were adequate for the purpose. As she drew level with the vehicle, he turned and gave her an embarrassed smile. His tone was apologetic: *Ursäkta att jag stör, men kan du hjälpa mig ett ögonblick?* (Sorry to be a nuisance, but could you help me for a moment?) She hesitated and leant forward to see what he was doing. That was all he needed. With a quick glance up and down the street to verify they were still unobserved, he grabbed her round the waist and wrenched her forcibly into the car. He'd expected her to put up a spirited resistance, but nothing would deter him now. And he was much stronger than her. In the struggle, his earlier sense of detachment receded — became easier to ignore. The texture of her soft, warm flesh beneath the skimpy summer clothing fired his ardour. Especially when she began to relax under the influence of the anaesthetic. This was the moment he'd imagined. To have her so close, so available. But not yet! Not here! The priority was to get far away.

Pulling a dark woollen blanket from the floor of the car, he arranged it irregularly across her body, hiding her from casual view. Then he backed out through the door in a state of urgency and excitement, almost stumbling over the violin where it lay on the pavement. He'd forgotten the violin! What if he'd left without it? Throwing the instrument onto the back seat beside the inert, shapeless form, he slammed the door and stepped purposefully round to the driver's side.

*   *   *

The search of Jorma Mannila's flat was completed by 6 pm, but the initial report the team brought back seemed disappointing. Although the micro-evidence would take time to process, they'd found nothing to indicate that Mannila had any connection at all to the five murders: no gruesome collections of wire nooses or amputated fingers; no additional pairs of secateurs, *Jardine 360s* or otherwise; not even any books about Sibelius, or CDs of Sibelius's music. Mannila didn't even own a CD player or a computer. Could he really have been the one responsible for the Ainola letters?

"But he *feels* so guilty!" complained Miranda. They'd left Mannila

347

in a holding cell while they reviewed the situation. "I've got a powerful gut feeling about him."

"Gut feelings are all very well," brooded Ylenius, "but we need hard evidence. And what do we actually have on him? That he was in Kuusitie at the time of Jaana Saari's murder and he owns a pair of Jardine 360 secateurs — though apparently not the pair used to sever the fingers from the first three victims." The lab had been unable to detect any tell-tale nick in either of the blades. "And there's no forensic proof he used them on the *latest* victim either. The only concrete thing we have are his fingerprints on the outside and inside of Liisa Louhi's handbag. Hardly enough to charge him with! Even a novice defence lawyer could come up with some feasible explanation. There may actually *be* a feasible explanation." He shook his head in frustration. "And what about all the other non-starters? He appears to know nothing about Sibelius. He doesn't own a car or hold a driving licence. And we can't place him at more than one of the five crime scenes."

"In fact," Tero added, "we've already established his alibis for the first and second murders."

"So what about this Bible-study session?" Miranda continued to probe… "The one he's supposed to have attended at the time Christa Bäckström was killed? That's a pretty tight, exclusive sect he belongs to. Wouldn't they close ranks to protect their own?"

"Not out of the question," Tero conceded, "but it doesn't feel right. That's *my* gut reaction, if you like? And then there's his computerized work-log for the evening of Liisa Louhi's death. That clearly states he clocked off at 9.15 pm: a quarter of an hour after she died, and a mile and a half's journey from the Sibelius Monument!"

"Is there any way he could've faked the time?"

"The company that installed the equipment doesn't think so. It works the same way as the electronic system we've got here for the admin staff. You punch in your personal code when you arrive for work, and do it again when you leave. There's no way to doctor the times — not without a degree in computer science."

"Maybe he left earlier and somebody *else* punched in his clocking-off code," suggested Ylenius.

"Possible, I suppose," Tero frowned, "but who would've been

ready to do that for him? There could only've been a few students left in the building by then. Why would any of *them* want to fake his working hours? And what about the burglar alarms? They'd have to be armed when the place was locked up for the night by someone who knew the codes. If somebody unofficial did all that lot, I reckon we'd've heard about it by now."

"Perhaps we've been asking the wrong questions," said Ylenius.

"Boss, sorry to interrupt you..." It was Miranda's protégée, Riitta "...but a call's come in from Munkkiniemi. A teenage girl's gone missing on her way home from a violin lesson. She had her instrument with her. So we're afraid..."

"How long's she overdue?" Ylenius cut in.

"Over an hour. Not long under normal circumstances, but the mother's distraught — says she hurried home from work so they could head straight out to the cinema... for a special night out. It's the girl's birthday."

"Has she contacted all her daughter's friends?"

"That's another reason she's so worried. A boy named Lars Johansson was supposed to escort the girl home. But he says they had a row on the bus, and he got off early. The girl would've had to walk from the bus stop alone."

"It sounds ominous," Ylenius agreed, "but, even if she is the next victim, she could still be alive. Let's do everything possible to keep it that way. If he's abducted her like he did Anna Orav, that could give us several hours to trace where he's taken her. Find out what route she would've taken home and cover it with a fine-tooth comb. If her body doesn't turn up straight away, we're in with a chance."

It took only twenty minutes to find evidence of the girl's abduction. On a quiet stretch of road overlooking the start of the Turku motorway, her buff-coloured music file was found lying in the gutter. A dusty tyre print ran across it, too close to the kerb to have been made by the wheels of passing traffic. The implication was plain. The girl had been dragged in through the side-door of a car where she was presumably subdued by an injection of Comatin. The music file fell underneath the vehicle during the struggle and was subsequently run over by the back wheel as the killer drove away. The fact that the violin had vanished with the victim gave further credence to this being the same predator. Unfortunately, the tyre-print was from a very common Michelin model found on tens of thousands of vehicles in the Helsinki area; although it did indicate a medium-sized family car rather than a van.

Ylenius moved decisively into action, launching a mammoth operation which involved practically every branch of the police force. Ylenius called in favours from every direction he could think of in a desperate attempt to save this sixth young woman's life.

From the boyfriend's information, it was possible to narrow down the girl's time of arrival at the abduction site to between 6.40 and 6.45 pm. This in turn enabled the traffic surveillance team to estimate a time window for each of several cameras situated on escape routes the killer might have used. The relevant video sequences were scrutinized for vehicles of a suitable size driven by lone males. In those cases where registration numbers could be extracted directly or enhanced by computer from the grainy image, every effort was made to locate the drivers and interview them. Most were already harmlessly tucked up at home with their families. Others were more difficult to trace. The task was time-consuming and made enormous demands on the city's reserves of uniformed personnel. Many officers volunteered to extend their shifts to continue in the search.

Members of the Liaison Office were simultaneously busy contacting TV and radio stations — both national and local. Programme after programme was interrupted with an appeal for anyone who'd been in the Munkkiniemi area between half past six and seven, and who might have seen something significant, to contact the police immediately on a free-phone number requisitioned for the purpose. Most of the calls that began to flood in were of little value, but two independent sightings were reported of a white Volvo departing the scene at high speed and at the appropriate time. Given a more definite focus, traffic surveillance were able to identify three contenders for the Volvo. One was soon spotted parked in a northern suburb of the city where the owner was visiting his daughter. The driver of the second Volvo was eliminated in a similar fashion. The third evaded discovery for several hours but, after much wastage of time and manpower, was located a hundred miles away in Turku. The owner had driven directly along the motorway to visit his girlfriend.

Meanwhile the clock was ticking.

Further appeals went on air, and every possible lead, however improbable, aggressively followed up: reports of suspicious-looking bundles on the back seats of cars; reports of suspicious-looking bundles being carried into buildings; reports of girls' screams from neighbouring flats; and so on. Several hundred men and women laboured into the early hours of Wednesday morning. By 3 am even tenuous leads were drying up. The night faded and dawn was breaking. Ylenius instructed that any vehicle found on the move was to be stopped and searched. Those at the centre of the operation recognized his grim purpose. The only reason for the killer to be out on the road again was to find a dumping ground for his already dead victim. And when the streets started to fill with workbound commuters, even this measure became impractical.

Nevertheless, it was earlier than anyone anticipated that the decisive call came in. Both Miranda and Tero had worked through the night. They'd been first at the abduction site — the ones who'd found the music file in the gutter — and they'd personally followed up on some of the most promising leads, each time facing disappointment and frustration. By 8.15 am, like most of the core team, they were back in the Pasila office at a loss to know what could usefully be done next. Tero had adopted a near-horizontal position on his swivel chair, feet straight out on his desk, the latest of an uncountable succession of coffee-automat mugs nursed on his stomach. His eyes seemed more or less open but, at the neighbouring desk, Miranda's clearly weren't. Slumped forward with her head resting on her arms, she could have been asleep — except that, when the phone on Tero's desk rang, her head lifted instantly.

Fielding the call, Tero conveyed no obvious shift of emotion, but Miranda was forewarned by how he gradually drew himself into a more upright position on his chair, as if to steel himself for action. He replaced the receiver and, battling weariness, stood up from the desk.

"Okay, everyone," he called, loud enough to reach those at the far end of the room. "She's been found."

From the centre of Helsinki stretches a northbound ribbon of forest and open grassland popularly known as Central Park. Although it is, of necessity, criss-crossed at intervals by roads connecting the east and west sides of the city, one may, on foot or bicycle, completely exit the urban precincts — via an ingenious system of paths, subways and footbridges — without needing to negotiate one's way across a single stream of traffic. On the southern edge of the east-west road linking the suburbs of Käpylä and Haaga, and encroaching slightly upon the parkland, lies a gravelled area sometimes used by long-distance lorry drivers for overnight parking of their articulated vehicles. Shortly before 8 am, just such a driver emerged from his cab, having snatched a few hours rest in the integrated bunk compartment, and strolled around his sixteen-wheeler on a routine inspection. He made an unpleasant discovery that prompted him to phone the emergency services. Within fifteen minutes a small convoy of police vehicles arrived and arranged itself in an untidy circle around the lorry. The real focus of attention however lay on the lorry's blind side, away from the road.

The tableau this time lacked its usual precision — one might even say conviction — as if constructed in a hurry. The solitary figure was propped unceremoniously against a four-foot-high metal-framed rubbish bin. The head flopped forward, long black hair providing a modicum of decency in its partial covering of the young girl's nakedness. The violin case was positioned uncharacteristically far off, against the next available vertical object: a sapling rowan tree scarcely rigid enough to support even *that* nominal weight.

The ragged team of detectives and SOCOs gathered around, disconsolate. Their sense of failure was total: much worse than at any of the earlier crime scenes. Nobody spoke or made a move to commence their duties. Every face expressed defeat and exhaustion. Perhaps that's why Tero also kept his thoughts to himself; unless it signified a belated, awakening sensitivity towards his work partner's feelings. Because, as she knelt in the long grass a few yards from the lifeless body of Beatrice Gröndahl, tears could be seen rolling down Inspector Miranda Lewis's face.

Symphony No 7

Single Movement
Adagio—Vivacissimo—Adagio—
Allegro moderato—Adagio

It was 10.45 am before anyone on the investigative team remembered their suspect of the previous evening. Having received no instructions to the contrary, the officer in charge of the holding cells had detained Jorma Mannila overnight. But now a solicitor claiming to represent the interests of the Church of the Steadfast Pilgrim had arrived to demand why a respected member of their flock was still in police custody.

Aleksi Ylenius had only just returned from the Haaga crime scene, with scarcely enough time to lower himself behind his desk, before the telephone started ringing. He listened wearily for a moment, screwing his eyes into a tight knot and massaging the closed lids with forefinger and thumb.

"Yes, yes, release him," he said, with uncharacteristic impatience. "If he's been locked up in a cell all night, he can hardly be the killer, can he? And give him his secateurs, if he's making such a fuss about them. The lab says they're clean."

Slumped with Tero on the visitors' side of the desk, Miranda noted how the Chief Inspector seemed to have aged ten years in a single night. She suspected an independent observer would pass a similar judgment on herself: numbed by exhaustion, emotionally drained, throat raw and dehydrated from too much coffee; and still so much to do before she could think of going home.

The autopsy on Beatrice Gröndahl was scheduled for 2 pm. Perhaps Miranda should attend, but she'd find some excuse.

355

Symphony No 7

Witnessing any further violation of that young girl's body — however essential for the investigation — was more than she could bear. Reading the pathologist's report afterwards would just have to suffice.

And then she remembered it was Wednesday. Her father would give his concluding lecture in the Sibelius series this evening. If only she could be there: a chance to dwell on something humane, on something sublime. But when she finally escaped this building and walked away from the horror of the last twenty-four hours, her priority would be the oblivion of sleep.

*   *   *

[12.22 pm; Wednesday, 3rd May]

For godssake, can't you ever get it right? Try again, you cretin!... Okay, a bit better... Not much, but in the right direction. You've got to think it through first. Sing along mentally. If you can't hear it, you can't bloody play it, can you? How many times have I told you? Your fingers should be an extension of your musical thought and instinct — and your emotions, of course. It's all those sodding notes in the treble that screw everything up. Fine for a freak like Liszt — with six fingers on every hand! But for a normal human being... Oh, shit! Who's that now? God, I hate these fucking interruptions. I'll have to get a switch on that doorbell so I can turn the damn thing off when I'm practising. All right! I'm coming, aren't I?

She peered through the spyhole and was mystified. What the hell was *he* doing here? Must be something important to come round in person. Could it be that Brahms score she needed so urgently? Had the library got it from the publisher at last?

She released the catch, and he was immediately pushing his way in. No word of explanation. The door slammed behind him and the fevered fixation of his eyes struck her with instant, though uncomprehending, alarm. She retreated into the living room, her stare fixed in growing panic on his, and he followed her step for step, drawing something from his pocket, something of wire shaped into a loop. As he backed her up to the piano and pinned her against it to pull the noose over her head, she screamed hysterically. But these cries for help were absorbed by thick, impassive stone walls of an earlier and sturdier building tradition: walls that she'd always been so grateful for — that had allowed her to play her Steinway many hours a day and even into the night without fear of the neighbours' ire. Those same neighbours would again hear nothing.

*   *   *

"And so, ladies and gentlemen, it's time to embark on the final stage of our journey, and fill in the last important pieces of the puzzle. My intention this evening will be to focus not on a single work, but on three."

Miranda hadn't, of course, made it to her father's lecture. She was sleeping off her exhaustion. Rosie had explained this to Phillip and Adrian, and gone on to express her concern about how tired and drawn they looked themselves. Phillip admitted, shamefaced, to a lingering hangover. Adrian blamed *his* weariness on having stayed up half the night to work on the cello sonata.

"Just don't start snoring during Daddy's lecture!" she'd warned.

"The Seventh Symphony," Nick now continued, "followed hot on the heels of the Sixth with little more than a year between their completion dates. In fact, they bear consecutive opus numbers. On the twenty-fourth of March, 1924, Sibelius conducted the premiere performance of his new symphony in Stockholm. Aino refused to accompany him after the acute embarrassment she'd suffered at the premiere of the Sixth. On that occasion, her husband's customary pre-concert intake of alcohol had resulted in a highly unprofessional false start, with the composer halting the orchestra only a few bars into the work to demand they begin again — as if they were still at a rehearsal. The Swedish audience had been inclined to forgive the *maestro* this misdemeanour, but not Aino. Her near-saintly patience had finally run its course. Tension at home was at an extreme level, and would remain so for a considerable time, with Aino speaking to her husband rarely or not at all.

* ["There's been much dispute about the structure of the Seventh

357

Symphony. Some deny it's a symphony at all. And it's true that Sibelius originally conceived of the work as a 'symphonic fantasia' or 'sinfonia continua' — not giving the full designation 'symphony' until well after its first performance. On the other hand, there are many who consider it the very distillation of traditional four-part symphonic form, perfectly condensed into a single unbroken movement.

"Whichever way one chooses to define or analyse this masterpiece, the work we now know as the Seventh Symphony is unique. It moves with a free-flowing spontaneity through numerous sections that together build a formidable structure of strength and coherence."

Nick then sat at the piano to illustrate his analysis of the symphony with numerous keyboard examples.

"The symphony opens with a slow, stepwise ascent of an octave and a half, solely on the 'white notes' of an A minor scale. This I feel is an extraordinary way to begin a work composed in the years 1923 and '24 — making it historically synchronous with Arnold Schoenberg's invention of the twelve-tone technique! But Sibelius's deceptively simple scale is brought to an unnerving standstill on the tritone Eb, compromised further by a harmonic shift to distant Ab minor. After presenting and mutating a couple of important germinal motifs, Sibelius then leads us into an extended passage of almost Palestrina-like counterpoint — initiated in divided violas and cellos, joined later by the violins, and eventually drawing in the woodwinds and the brass. This highly charged mixture of solemnity and passion culminates in a majestic solo trombone theme which seems to float indomitably alone, far beyond the reach of the accompanying orchestral texture. This trombone theme is a crucial structural element. Its three C-tonic-centred appearances — each building to a climactic peak — articulate the symphony into clear, though seamlessly linked sections. Some commentators feel that the attractive, lilting interludes preceding the second and third peaks function as separate *Andante* and *Scherzando* movements...

"In any case, the second climax is an imposing multivelocity, multilayered affair — a premonition of which was heard in the fourth movement of the Second Symphony. Then, as we are drawn inexorably into the slowly mounting third climactic section, we confront one of the most — perhaps *the* most — awesome and terrifying of passages in all music literature. The energetic string texture seems to carry the main pulse but shifts it slightly from the 'official' downbeat, rendering the densely packed, slower-moving woodwind and brass lines anchorless — adrift in a Herculean limbo. This is, in fact, another version of Sibelius's multispeed-layering effect. The anguish accumulates and intensifies, but is suddenly cut off, leaving the impassioned high strings painfully, chromatically exposed... until a gentle supportive reminder of the trombone theme brings a softening and a filling-out, resolving thread by thread — first trombones, then violins, finally horns — onto a consoling D minor harmony. The distressing, traumatic effect of the preceding climax lingers however, as a calmer, objectively detached section concludes the whole symphony, leading us to that final determined cadence on the chord of C major.] *

"Back in 1891, after a painful operation in Vienna to combat throat cancer, Sibelius wrote to his wife: *One must not expect too much of life. One must face it boldly and look it straight in the eye.* This is exactly how we experience the closing minutes of the Seventh Symphony. There is no flinching, most decidedly no self-pity: instead, a stoic determination to accept and embrace the essence of — if I may borrow Bertrand Russell's expression? — our human *cosmic loneliness.*"

* [Nick abandoned the limitations of the piano to play a full orchestral version on CD of these last, harrowing, though cathartic minutes of the symphony. When the wrenching resolution of the final superimposed leading tone had died away, he allowed a long and respectful silence before stepping to the front of the stage.

"The incidental music," he ventured, at last — almost *sotto voce,* though gradually gaining in tone — "for a Copenhagen production of Shakespeare's *The Tempest* offers us a fascinating collection of pieces with some of Sibelius's most experimental adventures into the realms of atonality and dissonance. This, however, is not the second of the works I wish to discuss this evening. For inspiration we turn not to Copenhagen but, as the composer did himself, to New York.] *

"Early in 1926, the American conductor Walter Damrosch telegraphed a request for a symphonic poem, the choice of subject to be left entirely to the composer. The outcome of this second American commission, like its predecessor *The Oceanides,* would be a masterpiece: the tone poem *Tapiola.*

"On request, Sibelius provided a loose verbal sketch which the German publisher worked up into an almost programmatic description of the work's mythological subject: the realm of the forest god Tapio. This four-line stanza now appears at the beginning of the printed score:

Widespread they stand, the Northland's dusky forests,
Ancient, mysterious, brooding savage dreams;
Within them dwells the Forest's mighty God,
And wood-sprites in the gloom weave magic secrets.

* ["Sibelius once commented that his themes were, in a sense, tyrants and he was obliged to submit to their demands. We've seen earlier how he could draw enormous capital from the smallest of motivic resources. The tone poem *Tapiola* can be considered Sibelius's ultimate manifestation of this minimalist thinking. Everything here is derived from a single short motive stated in the strings at the very beginning of the work — a stepwise figure resembling an ornamental turn which employs just five different tones. Not only is the thematic sequence of notes prodigiously exploited, but even the stepwise feature itself — to the near exclusion of any larger interval. Whether melodic or textural, almost every instrumental line moves in minor or major seconds. Considering the jagged intervallic extremes that many other composers of the period were exploring, Sibelius's approach is nothing less than radical... Or should we say reactionary? Was this the mark of an aging artist with one foot stuck in the nineteenth century refusing to accept the realities of the contemporary world? My answer is categorically no! Sibelius reminds us in this extraordinary tone poem that the vagaries of fashion are irrelevant to producing art of originality and power. With sufficient talent, one may achieve a masterpiece from the simplest of materials. *Tapiola* is, in fact, one of the most stunningly original works of the twentieth century — it might even be argued of Western music history, and Cecil Gray, Sibelius's first biographer in the English language, did exactly that. He claimed: had the Finnish composer written nothing else, *Tapiola* would guarantee his place among the greatest composers of all time. I am tempted to agree. From its minutiae of detail upwards, drifting for much of its twenty-minute duration between a pedal B and a pedal D (implying the harmonies G# minor and B minor), this hypnotic work generates an eerie, dehumanized landscape of stark beauty and frightening power. There is nothing remotely like it anywhere in the orchestral literature.] *

"*Tapiola* received its first performance in New York shortly after Sibelius's sixty-first birthday.

"And then came silence...

"For the remaining thirty years of the composer's life, very little new music would reach the public ear. Certainly no large-scale works. Nothing at all for full orchestra, the medium in which the master had for so long excelled. What on earth was Sibelius doing during these final three decades? Had he simply 'retired'? Part of the answer seems to be that he was struggling unsuccessfully with an eighth symphony.

"We have documentary evidence that in 1933 a manuscript for at least the first movement of a new symphony was sent to a professional copyist who was subsequently paid for his work. So what happened to that copy of the score? Does it still exist somewhere? Towards the end of her life, Aino Sibelius recalled 'a great *auto da fé*' held at Ainola during the 1940s, in which her husband burnt a laundry basket's worth of manuscripts on the open fire. At the time, it upset her so much she was compelled to leave the room. However, she noted that, as a result of this appalling conflagration, Jean became calmer and lighter in mood; and the event heralded a happier period in their life together.

"We are bound to wonder if the Eighth Symphony suffered a similar fate. Was it burnt on that same occasion? Many years later, the composer confided to his secretary, Santeri Levas, that indeed he *had* destroyed his Eighth — that, although it had been *ready* several times over, he had eventually *put it in the fire*. He also admitted to thinking a great deal about the work, especially in the night hours. He even dreamt of conducting its first two movements in his sleep, at which times they were vividly clear in his mind. All we know with certainty is that, during the last twenty years of Sibelius's life, when Levas visited Ainola regularly to handle the composer's correspondence, not once did he catch sight of any such score (incomplete or otherwise)... and that, after the composer's death, no score for an eighth symphony has ever been discovered.

* ["Why did the task of adding another major opus to his already long list of works prove so impossible? When asked about her

husband's thirty years of silence, Aino replied tersely: *Rigorous self-criticism.* Jean himself had said, even before his sixtieth birthday: *How dreadful old age is for a composer! Things don't go as quickly as they used to, and self-criticism grows to impossible proportions.* He complained that his environment was now too restless, that his family made it difficult to concentrate. He had five married daughters and a tribe of grandchildren — before long, great-grandchildren too. There was always someone paying a visit.

"Indeed — Eighth Symphony or no — life continued around him... Sibelius lived through the horrors of the Second World War. He abhorred Nazi Aryanism with its so-called 'racial purity' and its anti-Semitism. In his diary, he bemoaned Finland's 'tragic fate' — that it should be forced to side with *Nazi barbarism* in order to resist the spreading mantle of Communism. And yet, in the same day's diary entry, he refers touchingly to an experience *like a caress from a sunnier world* — a performance heard on the radio of Ralph Vaughan Williams's Fifth Symphony. *Civilized and humane!* wrote Sibelius of this work, which the English composer had especially dedicated to his Finnish colleague. *I am deeply grateful. Vaughan Williams gives me more than anyone could imagine.*

"In later life, Sibelius rarely stirred from Ainola or its close environs — although, in a sense, we could say the world came to *him*; in the form of radio broadcasts and gramophone records; and in the continuous stream of visitors that crossed his threshold — international musical dignitaries and admirers of all kinds — a circumstance he found both wearing and gratifying. The familiar photographic portraits of Sibelius taken towards the end of his life, with their severe lines and uncompromising demeanour, offer a wholly misleading view of the composer's personality. In company he was engaging and amiable, always immaculately and dapperly dressed, playing the role of perfect host even to the most tiresome of his visitors. He once prided himself that he had for several hours held successful audience with a Danish publisher and his wife, neither of whom realized that throughout he was suffering from excruciating toothache. His biographer, Cecil Gray provides us with an excellent description of the 'social' Sibelius. I here paraphrase... *Most musicians,* Gray said, *have one-track minds, speaking mainly of themselves and their own achievements. Sibelius exhibits precisely the opposite tendency — speaking diffidently and unwillingly about his own work; preferring to discuss almost every other subject on earth — literature, philosophy, psychology, painting, politics, science*

— *and with enigmatic, gnomic, aphoristic, paradoxical wisdom and wit.*] *

"Jean Sibelius died on September 20th, 1957 at the venerable age of ninety one. He suffered a stroke at the lunch table and passed away quietly at 9.35 pm in the presence of his family. Some twenty miles away in Helsinki, Sir Malcolm Sargent was that same evening conducting the Fifth Symphony.

"Finland's revered composer received a state funeral, and seventeen thousand mourners filed past his coffin to pay their last respects. His body was buried in the grounds of his beloved Ainola where, twelve years later, he would be joined by his long-suffering but devoted Aino.

* ["How then should we appraise Sibelius's position in music history? Was he a great composer? It has to be admitted that the popularity and respect he enjoys in the Anglo-Saxon and Nordic countries has never been matched elsewhere. The composer complained that the only people in Germany who admired his music were conductors — of whom we could cite such important figures as Weingartner, Furtwängler, Klemperer and Karajan. Richard Strauss, famous both as a conductor *and* a composer, once said of Sibelius: *I can do more, but he is greater.* By this, I believe he meant to contrast his own unquestionable virtuosity in all things musical with the Finn's more introspective temperament that could probe the darkest and most forbidding territory of the human soul. (Although I should, in fairness, add that Strauss would achieve something comparable at the end of his own life with those wonderful and imposing *Four Last Songs*.)

"If we review the complete cycle of Sibelius symphonies, we are struck by its diversity. Although there could be some ironic justification in claiming that Mahler or Bruckner wrote the same symphony many times over, this cannot be said of Sibelius. Each symphony presents us with an individual atmosphere and a refreshing viewpoint...

"The First is planted firmly in the nineteenth century; the Second dispenses with most of its predecessor's Romantic, Tchaikovskian gestures, and achieves a cooler, more streamlined objectivity; the Third is overtly neoclassical — concise and supple; the Fourth follows, sparse, morose, introverted; the Fifth, in contrast, commands our attention with its broad sweep and imaginative power; the Sixth is subdued, rippling and sparkling with pastoral eccentricity; and the single movement of the Seventh plumbs disturbing philosophical and psychological depths.

"Aside from the seven symphonies, Sibelius composed an enormous amount of other attractive and well-crafted music. Regrettably, it's often the less serious works that are associated with his name by the general public and even by many music 'specialists' in Central and Southern Europe. *Valse Triste*, for example — charming as it may be within its own modest context — bears scarcely more resemblance to Sibelius's mature masterpieces than does *Für Elise* to Beethoven's last piano sonatas. Even the oft played and enormously popular Violin Concerto — a fine and original example of the form from a Romantic period perspective... even *this* is a relatively early work predating the Third Symphony, and it gives little indication of the uniquely 'modern' directions that Sibelius would later come to explore. I use the term 'modern' not to bracket Sibelius's achievements with, for example, Stravinsky's neoclassicism or Schoenberg's dodecaphony, but rather to indicate how he withdrew from Romantic values into a more austere and objective world of expression. All of his most important works are intellectually unimpeachable and devoid of sentimentality. No attempt to gauge Sibelius's significance within the larger context of Western musical culture can succeed without taking into account his last four symphonies and the four tone poems: *The Bard*, *Luonnotar*, *The Oceanides* and *Tapiola*. These are the works that confirm Sibelius's claim to greatness.

"And now I would like to close this lecture series with an observation concerning the composer's religious sensibility. Although Sibelius writes the word 'God' rather often in his diaries, he appears to be using it as a metaphor for something else: Destiny, the Artistic Muse, the Forces of Nature. On numerous occasions he made it clear how he held no expectation of an afterlife. This being one of the fundamental tenets of Christianity, we cannot expect the composer's concept of God to closely resemble the Christian one with its additional trappings of love and redemption. Was Sibelius then a religious man at all? I think we should answer yes, but in a more abstract, pantheistic sense. His sensitivity to the beauty and power of nature is legendary. His spirituality could thus be equated to an awareness of the enormity of the natural forces that surround us and to a sense of our insignificant yet magical place in the universe. His last two major works express the human condition with such overwhelming intensity and power: the Seventh Symphony from an internal, subjective point of view — the psychological pressures from within; and *Tapiola* the pressures from without — the terrifying external, non-human forces of nature, the belittling vastness of Time and Space. Perhaps Sibelius remained silent for the last thirty years of his life not so much because his creativity had deserted him, but because after two such masterpieces there was little more that *anyone* could have said."] *

On Thursday morning Miranda faxed a preliminary report of the latest murder to Panu Marski. She'd heard nothing from him since their café meeting two days earlier. Presumably he was busy catching up after his week abroad.

Further tests had confirmed the crime-scene estimate that the sixth victim, Beatrice Gröndahl, had died on Wednesday morning between 4 and 5 am. The killer had apparently kept her in a state of semiconsciousness for anything up to ten hours; this time without taping her wrists. No fewer than twenty-three puncture marks were found on the girl's thighs and buttocks, and toxicological screening of her blood revealed the same anaesthetic drug as used on the fourth victim, Anna Orav. Further equivalencies to that earlier murder were: the use of a condom to exclude traceable DNA; a noose of silky-textured rope pulled tightly and fatally around the victim's throat; the application — for the second time only — of a larger, non-serrated pair of secateurs; and the shaving of the girl's pubic area, performed a maximum of twelve hours previous to death — though probably less. Tero brought this last detail up with Miranda and Ylenius as they were sitting down for a late lunch.

"You know, this shaving thing...?" he said. "With the Estonian hooker it could've been a fashion statement — trick of the trade, so to speak. But a sixteen-year-old schoolgirl... doesn't seem so likely, does it? I reckon our Freako was the one wielding the razor — perhaps for the Orav woman as well."

"Another sexual component to the crime?" asked Miranda.

"Or a way to foil the forensic team."

"If that's the case," Ylenius said, eyeing his plate of canteen meatballs and mash with seasoned resignation, "he should've shaved their heads as well. I've just been on the phone to the lab. They found some interesting stuff in Beatrice Gröndahl's scalp hair. Esso W10/40 engine oil, for example."

"That's from the car he abducted her in," Miranda proposed, "off the floor or boot during transit."

"Perhaps, but the oil was thick with microscopic particles of iron," Ylenius went on, "so it must've spent a long time in some engine somewhere... which suggests a leak onto the floor of a garage or car servicing depot — perhaps during a routine oil-change."

"Could be where he's got his hidey-hole," said Tero. "Some kind of garage."

"And there was more unusual trace evidence: pigmented scales from a butterfly's wing. Not your common or garden cabbage white either. A consultant entomologist reckons it's a South-East Asian species."

"How the hell's *that* possible?"

"It isn't, Tero. Not naturally. Must be someone's personal *Lepidoptera* collection."

"Are you saying Freako's other hobby is sticking pins through butterflies?" marvelled Tero, and offered to follow up this intriguing new lead immediately after lunch...

The secretary of the Finnish Lepidoptera Society advised him that the only way to acquire such tropical species was to import them from foreign butterfly farms. She gave him the fax numbers of those that had been running adverts in the Finnish society's journal. By the end of the day, Tero had gathered faxes from Holland, Belgium, and the UK with the names and addresses of fourteen Finnish customers who'd purchased eggs of the relevant species during the last few years. Nine of them lived hundreds of miles from Helsinki. Of the remaining five, there was a middle-aged woman, a twelve-year-old schoolboy, two pensioners in their seventies; and the fifth customer had died six months ago."

"So another dead end," Tero complained to Miranda. But his hopes were still high for the video surveillance of the Töölö postboxes. In expectation of a sixth Ainola letter, the monitoring schedule had been stepped up. The contents of the boxes were being inspected in continuous hourly rotation. That way, if the letter was posted in view of one of the cameras, no more than an hour's worth of video tape would need processing. But by Thursday afternoon, the team was getting jittery. Would the killer cooperate? What if he used some other postbox? Or didn't bother at all this time? Thirty-six hours had passed since the dumping of Beatrice Gröndahl's body, and still there was no sign of a letter.

"Why can't he just get on and post the damn thing!" Miranda said.

"Perhaps he's run out of stamps," quipped Tero, but with a noticeable lack of enthusiasm.

Panu Marski phoned Miranda at five o'clock. At last he'd found time to review the material and confessed to being worried by what he'd read. Could she arrange an emergency meeting? This evening preferably? He'd also like the Chief Inspector and Tero to be present. Within two hours, all four were gathered in a meeting room on the fifth floor.

"I'll take this latest murder first," Marski said, without preamble, "the murder of Beatrice Gröndahl — provisionally designated as the sixth in the series. Here we find a clear continuity with the earlier killings. The development of the murderer's modus operandi — the intensification and refinement of his control over the victims — has already reached fruition with the Estonian woman, Anna Orav. The abduction and murder of Beatrice Gröndahl matches Orav's abduction and murder in practically every detail. One small enhancement is that he's now learned to calibrate the doses of anaesthetic sufficiently well to dispense with any form of taping or binding of his victim. To reach this level of 'perfection' — as the killer would certainly view it — he's developed the basic mechanics step by step until he's figured out exactly how to fulfil himself emotionally. This is a very important point. The modus operandi is not an end in itself: it's subservient to the emotional needs. So what *are* those emotional needs? Once we've determined them, we've found the killer's 'signature'. The modus operandi may change over time, but the signature will not, because it's the reason he commits the crimes in the first place."

Ylenius was fidgeting in his chair, and Miranda decided to speed things up: "Panu, you outlined the killer's emotional needs to us clearly at our first meeting. His obsession with the victim's beauty and his need to have complete control over her body; his desire to reach orgasm synchronously with her death throes; the musical instrument element in his choice of victim; the saving of the little finger as a trophy; and, in the aftermath, a display to the world of his self-perceived victory by visually arranging the crime scene and sending us the Ainola letters."

"Thank you, Miranda. Your summary highlights the main features, and the murder of the Gröndahl girl fits the pattern perfectly... except for the curiously slipshod way he prepared his final tableau at the lorry park — as if he'd lost interest, and was merely going through the motions."

"Or just in a hurry to get away," said Tero, "before anybody spotted him. It was rush hour by then."

"So why didn't he wait till the *following* night and transport her there under cover of darkness — like he did with Anna Orav?"

"Too exposed," said Ylenius. "A prostitute could go missing for a day or two without anyone raising the hue and cry. A young schoolgirl's a very different matter. He might've guessed we'd be sweeping the streets for him in the early hours. Waiting for the rush hour gave him more cover."

Marski nodded. "That could certainly be the explanation, Chief Inspector, although I can't help wondering if the half-hearted display at Beatrice Gröndahl's dump-site reflects something more personal — a failing commitment to the task, if you like — that he was dispirited by a realization that the execution of his fantasies had failed to bring the happiness he expected."

"Sort of post-coital depression?" asked Tero.

Marski shrugged. "It's not unusual for sexual offenders to experience such feelings. But perhaps I'm reading too much into the matter."

Ylenius's eyebrows lifted at this admission of fallibility.

"I'll be interested to see," Marski continued, "if there's any change of tone in the next Ainola letter. Incidentally, did you notice that Beatrice Gröndahl's eyes were closed? She's the first of the six victims to be found that way. An intriguing little detail, though probably not of significance. We'd better move onto something that I believe is *highly* significant. Let's consider the fifth murder: the murder of Jaana Saari on the stairs of her apartment block in Kuusitie. I find this scenario extremely problematic. The killer follows or accompanies his victim into the building, or gains access beforehand and waits for her there. He then brutally attacks her halfway up the stairs. Has he forgotten those earlier lessons that in such a location he'll have little chance to achieve gratification? Surely he knows by now that abduction and isolation of his victim is the only way that works for him? Why does he make this blitz-style attack on the girl in a more or less public place? He strangles her, amputates the finger and is gone, leaving her clothes undisturbed. We can find no overt indication of a sexual component to this crime."

"The old gent upstairs interrupted him," Tero pointed out. "No time for the killer to follow through."

"That's my point. Why didn't he give himself time? And where's the order of events we've come to expect: sexual assault culminating in strangulation followed by postmortem removal of the finger? The sexual element's been omitted. Compared to the earlier attacks, this one seems purely functional. Kill her quickly, take the finger, make your escape, and that's all. I find it inconceivable he'd be satisfied with so little — not after everything he's learned about himself. He's proved himself resourceful. He knows how to plan ahead. He's set up a secure and secret location where he can confine his victim and devote his full attention to her. He's even acquired a sophisticated drug and the knowledge of how to administer it, enabling him to stretch out his enjoyment over a period of several hours. No, no! In the case of Jaana Saari, I am not persuaded. Too much of the signature is missing. I fear the fifth attack is the work of a copycat."

Ylenius's frowned: "A copycat?"

"My God! Are you sure?" exclaimed Tero. "That would *really* move all the goal posts!"

Early next morning, Rosie turned up at Adrian's flat for another run-through of the cello sonata. She was just taking her coat off in the hallway when Phillip arrived as well. Several times he'd expressed a wish to hear the work in progress, so they'd invited him to sit in on this Friday morning session. Adrian ushered them both into his living room and gestured proudly towards one wall transformed by a new wood-framed bookcase that he'd already loaded to the ceiling with his extensive collection of books and music scores.

"Had the kit for weeks," he admitted. "It's been accusing me there in the corner. But this morning inspiration struck. Just this moment finished sticking the books on. Better than having them stacked round the walls."

"Vast improvement," agreed Phillip. "Should've done it sooner."

In readiness for the practice run-through, Adrian had rigged up a microphone and connected it to his music equipment. The special effects he'd planned could now be properly tested. At intervals he asked Rosie to repeat a phrase, tweaking the system until the sound was exactly as he'd envisaged it. Rosie and Phillip were fascinated by the results. Neither had heard anything remotely similar before. Rosie laughed outright at the startling, un-cellolike sounds her instrument was producing.

They only managed a couple of hours before Rosie had to leave for a cello lesson, and Phillip offered to accompany her to the city centre. He was helping her back into her coat when she spotted a pile of unposted letters on the hall table.

"Scholarships," explained Adrian. "I'm applying for new ones."

"I could post them for you," Rosie offered. "I'm passing a postbox."

"So am I for that matter," said Phillip.

A discussion followed on who could best take responsibility. The letters had already changed hands a couple of times when a cataclysmic crashing came from Adrian's living room. There were a few shocked moments of hesitation before all three rushed back to investigate.

"Good God, Adrian!" Phillip gasped, standing behind Rosie to survey the scene. "Your room's suffered an earthquake!"

The newly erected bookshelf had collapsed in a tangled heap. Paperbacks, scores, encyclopedias and dictionaries were scattered everywhere.

"How the hell could that've happened?" demanded Adrian.

Rosie was contrite that she couldn't stay to help clear up the mess. But her cello teacher was impossible, she explained. Once she'd arrived two minutes late for a lesson and he'd refused to teach her.

"Dearest Rosie, console yourself!" said Phillip. "I'll stay and provide the necessary assistance."

With a quick hug for each, Rosie abandoned them to the task and let herself out of the flat.

"Thank heavens none of my music equipment was involved," said Adrian, as he stared at the wreck of his short-lived domestic triumph.

Phillip was digging inside the cardboard package that had contained all of the shelf components. With an exasperated sigh he drew out two long strips of metal.

"Any inkling what these are for, Adrian?" he asked.

Adrian gave an embarrassed grimace.

"Exactly! The X-brace you should've fixed across the back. The whole thing's folded like a house of cards. My God, sometimes you can be such a totally helpless moron! Have I ever mentioned that?"

"On several occasions," Adrian answered humbly.

"We'd better take it as further vindication of your decision not to follow an engineering career. Try and sort out this bedlam, shall we?"

They worked together in silence for a while, tidying the chaos of books into the middle of the room before attempting to re-erect the shelf's wooden uprights and secure them with the metal cross-bracing.

Phillip was the first to speak: "Things all right with Miranda?" he asked matter-of-factly.

"Haven't seen her since May Day's Eve."

Phillip cast a suspicious eye. "Getting difficult again, is she?"

"Tried to phone her a couple of days ago. Wouldn't speak to me. Didn't turn up at Nick's lecture, either."

"Ah, well, Rosie explained that, didn't she? Miranda was up all night and had to catch up on her beauty sleep."

Adrian shrugged. "Could've been an excuse to avoid me."

"But I thought all that was sorted — once you'd got your fool-proof alibi."

"Apparently not."

Adrian held the shelf structure steady while Phillip screwed the second bracing strip into place.

"Actually," Adrian said, standing back to survey their handiwork, "in connection with that alibi..." He tailed off without finishing the sentence.

"Hundred percent," Phillip said after a pause, and bent down to retrieve some books from the floor. "At the lecture with Rosie, weren't you? Dozens of witnesses."

"Yes, yes, of course! *I* was!"

"This dictionary... do you want it on the top shelf?"

Adrian nodded impatiently. "Yes, if you like — next to the Swedish one. But a really bizarre thought occurred to me the other day..."

"Aren't they mandatory for you *every* day?"

"...that you might've popped out and killed that girl yourself."

Phillip stopped in mid-reach and turned to Adrian in astonishment.

"... so you could give me an alibi," Adrian hurried on. "Kuusitie's only just round the corner from your place. Maybe you decided to get me crossed off the suspect list once and for all... as a Byronic gesture of ultimate friendship."

Phillip stared at him curiously. He seemed to be struggling with the implications of this extraordinary suggestion — assessing how seriously it had been made. An ironic smile began to skew the corners of his mouth.

"That, Adrian," he said, "is definitely one of your sillier ideas."

"Is it?" Adrian sounded doubtful... but then changed the subject: "Got any of those cheroots about you?"

"Cheroots?" Phillip's head tipped quizzically. "Not falling to temptation, are you? Whatever would Miranda say?"

"Miranda doesn't say *anything* to me nowadays," Adrian reminded him.

They squeezed out onto the flat's miniscule balcony and lit up, leaning over the railings to gaze across Sibelius Park.

"What about your teaching?" Adrian asked. "Any improvement?"

"On the contrary! Had *another* contract cancelled yesterday. Now down to half my original income."

Adrian commiserated with a noisily exhaled plume of blue smoke.

"But I believe it's a sign," Phillip rallied. "A providential pointer to the future. Perhaps the same goes for your crumbling relationship with DI Miranda. Let's face it, she's been bad news from the start — playing her hot and cold routines. Seems to me we've outstayed our welcome. Time to move on. Plenty more countries where this one came from. Continents too, for that matter. What about Asia? Africa? Personally I'd opt for Latin America again."

"Been there, done that."

"No need to repeat Bolivia, is there?"

"In fact," Adrian continued more cautiously, "I've been thinking along similar lines myself — about moving on, I mean. Those letters I'm sending aren't all applying for scholarships. Some are for jobs — university posts in Britain. Thought I'd try my luck back in the home country."

Phillip raised an eyebrow, but refrained from any further comment. Stubbing out his cheroot, he stepped back into the living room. A couple of puffs later, Adrian did likewise.

"What happened to all those letters of yours?" Phillip called from the hallway.

"Don't worry, I'll deal with them," said Adrian, joining him. "Have to pass the post office anyway."

"My point is, where the hell *are* they? I dropped them in my jacket pocket when your shelves of Jericho came a-tumblin' down."

Phillip's jacket was still hanging on the hall coat-rack, and he seemed totally mystified. He went through every pocket... and then went through every one again.

"I suppose Rosie took them with her," Adrian concluded.

"Yes, she must've done," agreed Phillip.

* *

~ *You never explained why you left La Paz in such a hurry.*

~ Got fed up with the place.

~ *Come off it! You were up and out of there in twenty-four hours.*

~ Sudden impulse. Acted on it for once.

~ *As I recall, you'd been running around in unsavoury company.*

~ Had I?

~ *That playboy character, for example... Ramirez, wasn't it?*

~ Surely you aren't referring to Luis Rodrigo Ramirez de Castelar? Latest in a long line of influential aristocrats! Father a member of the Bolivian ruling élite! How the hell do you label someone with that sort of pedigree as 'unsavoury'?

~ *Word on the street, he was into some weird stuff.*

~ And what constitutes 'weird' in your expert opinion?

~ *Paying impoverished teenage girls large sums to indulge his degenerate peccadilloes.*

~ Paying for sex is 'weird', is it? Pastime dating back to Adam, I'd've thought.

~ *But Ramirez's special hobbies were bondage and sadism, staged as elaborate Satanic rites... or so the rumour went.*

~ Colourful characters like him always attract a level of gossip bordering on the mythological.

~ *Maybe it was exaggeration. But I've often wondered if there could've been a connection between Ramirez and your doing that sudden unceremonious runner.*

~ Not so 'unceremonious'! It wasn't even 'a runner'! And what possible connection could there've been?

~ *Don't know. I was hoping you'd tell me.*

* *

Friday morning at Pasila, and Miranda was trying to assimilate Panu's bombshell of the previous evening. Could he be right?

Six girls murdered: all strangled, all accompanied by a musical instrument, all missing their right-hand little fingers. What then made the fifth victim, Jaana Saari, different from the others?

Well, first of all, the finger amputations: The initial three had been carried out with a pair of *Jardine 360* secateurs. For the fourth and sixth, the killer had changed to a heavier-duty pair — a logical step, considering the difficulty of the task. But the fifth amputation seemed to break this pattern by employing the smaller type again — and moreover with a pair the lab couldn't verify was the *original Jardine 360s* because it appeared to lack the characteristic nick in its blade.

Next was the progressive modification of the noose from thin speaker wire to softly textured rope, already achieved by the third victim. Why had the killer reverted to that odd (and decidedly more brutal) spiral of red and black electrical wire only for the fifth victim?

Was there anything else that singled out Jaana Saari? Of course, she was the only one found with a horn rather than a violin. Could that somehow be significant? And she was the only victim not interfered with sexually. In Panu Marski's opinion, this was the crux of the matter: that Jaana Saari's killer had failed to plan ahead in a way that would ensure his sexual fulfilment.

It all seemed rather insubstantial to Miranda. Could this really be enough to warrant a conclusion that the fifth killing in Kuusitie was committed by a copycat? If so, the next question was how the second killer had learned about the finger amputations — information that had never been released to the public.

Tero seemed even more sceptical. But, to Miranda's surprise, Ylenius took Panu's idea seriously enough to suggest they consider the implications. That was why Miranda had spent the whole morning reviewing the facts: to see if they offered any alternative interpretations. Shortly before midday she realized something which might back up the copycat theory.

"You know," she said, turning to Tero at the adjacent desk, "we've been assuming the killer made a mistake when he used Anna Orav's fingerprint a second time. But there could be another explanation. What if he didn't have access to the..."

Her sentence was left incomplete. Riitta came rushing over with news that the sixth letter had at last been posted, and — to Tero's joy — at one of the postboxes under video surveillance. He dashed off to claim his prize in person and, within half an hour, he and Miranda were in the forensic lab studying the latest cryptic message:

Munkkivuori
Tuesday, 2nd May

Symphony No 6

Dear A.
It seems to me that amongst the most unfortunate persons on earth are composers who experience their work as an inner compulsion. My themes are tyrants. I must always surrender to their bidding.

"My heart bleeds!" sneered Tero.

"Yes, he seems to be looking for sympathy." Miranda's face was grim. "Let's nail him first, and worry about the sympathy bit afterwards!"

Leaving the letter with a lab technician, they found somewhere to view the fifty-five-minute surveillance video sequence that covered the period of its posting.

At first, Miranda was infected by Tero's excitement as he fast-forwarded through the dead moments, pausing only when someone approached the letter box. Miranda turned away for a moment to deposit a dead paper coffee cup in the rubbish bin, and Tero suddenly exclaimed: "Isn't that your sister?"

Miranda smiled as he re-ran the sequence. There was Rosie patiently sliding a large number of letters through the postbox flap.

"Who's she been writing all that lot to?" Miranda wondered aloud.

By the end of the segment they'd found thirteen males of a suitable age who'd posted letters between eleven-ten and twelve-fifteen that morning. Unfortunately, none were recognizable as previously interviewed suspects. Miranda was beginning to have doubts about the value of this whole exercise. Certainly it would provide corroborative evidence — once they had the killer in court — but what they needed right now was a way to catch him before he killed again. That's if they weren't already too late. She voiced her reservations to Tero.

"Hey, Miranda, this is a major breakthrough!" he said reproachfully. "One of the beauties on this action replay's our killer. We only have to figure out which one!"

And he had plenty of ideas about how to do that. They'd get the technical department to rush through some computer enhanced stills of the thirteen video suspects, and show them to the personnel of the Helsinki Conservatory and the Sibelius Academy. If that failed, they could broaden the search to other music establishments and organizations in the Greater Helsinki area: colleges, orchestras (both amateur and professional), even retailers specializing in classical CDs. Meanwhile, the team would scour mug shots of previous offenders and circulate copies of the thirteen suspects to every police station in the country.

"How about releasing the pictures to the press?" Miranda suggested.

Tero shook his head. "No, if he finds out we're getting this close, he'll destroy all the evidence. We need an element of surprise to build a case that'll stick."

But, as Tero and Miranda came to realize, this proposed labour-intensive operation was an irrelevance. In a sense, they already knew who had posted the sixth letter, and its posting would have a different, wholly unexpected consequence.

At 2 pm, the lab came back with surprising news. Although the killer had got the inked fingerprint on the letter correct this time — it definitely matched samples lifted from Beatrice Gröndahl's bedroom — the outside of the envelope bore three clear fingerprints of its own: two on the address side, and a thumbprint below. Unfortunately the lab couldn't match them to any existing set on record, and Miranda was at once suspicious about these windfall fingerprints. Could their adversary have really made such a rudimentary error after all his earlier caution?

She showed solidarity, however, by apportioning a few hours to the study of mug shots on the computer. Somebody in the office wondered if a face on the surveillance video might belong to a waiter working in a restaurant near her home. Tero whisked the young constable off to check. The connection seemed tenuous to Miranda, but now she wished she'd gone with them; she felt listless, and uninspired.

The sun shone invitingly outside the window. Unable to think of any legitimate pretext, Miranda decided to go AWOL. A junior member of the team looked up as she passed his desk.

"Popping out for a breath of fresh air," she said cheerily, and quite unnecessarily, considering the difference in their ranks. "Only be five minutes."

A hundred yards from the building, she realized her mobile phone lay upstairs on the desk. All the better! Now she could be sure of having some time to herself.

The wind had shifted to the north with a noticeable drop in temperature. Miranda enjoyed the refreshing coolness against her bare arms and face. Suddenly she craved the presence of trees. Central Park was only a short distance away, and she strode out towards it, trying to remember when she'd last had time for a proper run.

Being starved of vigorous exercise always made Miranda tetchy — although this present burden of distress could hardly be explained away that easily. Earlier in her career, she'd had no trouble facing the suffering and the death — had, in fact, shown herself up to handling anything the job could throw at her. Why then was she coming apart at the emotional seams this time? One difference, of course, was that violence and murder had previously arrived in discrete one-off packages: a drunken act of anger or of jealousy — a single crime to be investigated, and always after the event. Never before, had Miranda been in a position to anticipate the next killing — to know that she shared responsibility for preventing it by catching the perpetrator first. How many more deaths would there be? Could they rely on the murderer following Sibelius's symphonic lead and stopping at seven?

The team's consistent failure bore a millstone of guilt. Miranda's waking hours — occasionally even her dreams — were haunted by the image of Beatrice Gröndahl's abused, lifeless body propped against that lorry-park rubbish bin. If ever there were a time when Miranda needed physical comfort from another human being, this was it. So what the hell was Adrian playing at? Why hadn't he tried to contact her again? Of course, she'd snubbed his phone call last Tuesday. But surely he didn't expect her to come running again — the way she had a fortnight ago. This time *he* owed *her* an apology!

The intended five minutes had stretched to three quarters of an hour when Miranda re-entered the building. The duty sergeant beckoned her over. A plump, middle-aged woman standing at the reception desk turned uncertainly and introduced herself as Mrs Lea Linnamaa. Miranda made an effort to shake off her own concerns, responding with a bland, professional smile. *Linnamaa?* The name sounded familiar, but it took a few moments to make the connection. This must be Jorma Mannila's aunt — the one living in Kuusitie — the aunt that Jorma had visited on the evening of Jaana Saari's death. Miranda wondered, with only mild curiosity, why the woman had turned up now.

"You see," Mrs Linnamaa began, as if in answer to Miranda's silent query, "I found this message pushed through the door saying the police wanted to talk to me about my nephew. I thought they'd be coming back, and they never did." She hesitated, apparently expecting an explanation.

But Miranda gave no more than a vague nod. Because *that* had been on Tuesday, when Jorma Mannila was still a suspect. They'd sent a constable round to re-interview his aunt, with a view to gathering additional background. But Beatrice Gröndahl had been abducted and murdered while Jorma was still in custody, adding a third alibi to his previous two.

"So I thought I'd better come in myself," Mrs Linnamaa went on, "to see if I could help."

Miranda gazed back expressionlessly, wondering how best to turn the woman away, but ultimately took pity on her. After all, she'd taken the trouble to make the journey here. The least Miranda could do was offer her some coffee and a few minutes of conversation. More to the point, it was a way of avoiding the office a while longer. With a loaded thermos flask from the canteen, she bypassed the main office altogether, and took Lea Linnamaa up to the same conference room they'd used yesterday with Panu Marski.

"He's always been a strange boy," the aunt admitted conversationally as Miranda poured out the coffee. "What else can you expect — the way he was brought up? Though I can't imagine him hurting anyone. Really I can't."

Miranda had no reason to disagree. Nor did she have any particular line of questioning to follow up. The woman seemed to have lost her initial timidity, so Miranda let her natter on about her sister — Jorma's mother — and about Jorma's upbringing in the narrow confines of a claustrophobic religious sect.

"I suppose Elli was loving in her own way — touching and hugging him a lot — but she was bossy with it... always laying down the law. He had to do everything her way. And she had a cruel streak in her, too — even as a child. Knew exactly how to hurt us — me and my parents, I mean. Poor little Jorma had to put up with more than his fair share. Just little things, if you know what I mean, but..."

She paused to drop two sugar lumps into her cup and begin stirring them in.

"He never made any friends much of his own age. Well, she didn't encourage that. Wanted him to herself, I suppose. And he never moved out to get a place of his own. Seemed unnatural to me — a grown man like that. But one good thing: she got him started on his gardening. Crazy about it herself, she was. Surprising really! Not what you'd expect, somehow. No harm in it, of course. But she didn't have any garden of her own — living in a small flat like that — so she rented an allotment a couple of miles away. Spent hours there together in the summer months, they did. You could see Jorma loved it too. Still his main hobby... only hobby really, apart from his church-going. Though I suppose he turned out quite a handyman really — once he grew up — doing jobs round the house, mending things, that kind of stuff. Took over all the household chores. Did the cooking too. Seemed to me he was trying a bit too hard to please his mum. It didn't work anyway. She just took advantage, and got lazier and lazier herself. Never showed him any appreciation. Always criticizing. Even worse when she got the cancer. He nursed Elli as long as he could, but she had to go into hospital in the end. Hit him really hard when she passed away last autumn. And I'd say he's been even quieter since then... except when he's talking about God and all that kind of stuff. Mind you, I only listen with half an ear, like I did with his Mum."

As a token gesture, Miranda looked for a question relevant to the murder investigation: "Did Jorma's mother play the violin?"

Mrs Linnamaa was dumbfounded. "My goodness, no! Whatever gave you that idea? Nobody in our family's the slightest bit musical. Elli used to sing hymns round her flat when she was cleaning or doing the washing up... though, as far as I could tell, she never got them right — not sort of in tune, if you know what I mean?"

Miranda nodded. It confirmed Jorma's own alleged disinterest in things musical. Time to terminate this interview and do something more productive. But Miranda still didn't make any move. Was it just Friday afternoon inertia?

"Elli was such a beautiful child," Mrs Linnamaa continued, "to look at, I mean. Like an angel everybody used to say. Just the same when she grew up. Lots of lovely blonde hair. And the sweetest face. Butter wouldn't melt in her mouth, you'd think. Though what a trial to our poor parents! They never knew how to handle her. A bit overfond of the boys she was as well. Only nineteen when she got herself pregnant. Never told us who the father was. But she'd got mixed up with this religious sect — the Church of the Steadfast Pilgrim they call themselves. All kinds of rumours going round about how she was carrying on with the head of the group — the preacher or spiritual leader or whatever he was supposed to be. In his forties and married with two kids. Could've been Jorma's father, I suppose. Anyway all this religious stuff got worse after Jorma was born. Elli found herself a flat near the church, and it was only me in the family visited her after that. Never made Mum and Dad welcome, you see. But me... well, I was just a teenager — the baby sister — and I missed her, even if she kept going on about sin and hell's fire and God's judgment. Poor little Jorma had to grow up with all that nonsense. Got to make a difference, hasn't it? Hearing it day in day out. Like that business with the finger. I heard her say to Jorma more than once — he couldn't've been more than six at the time — she said: *God's taken my finger away to punish me for my sins. He's done it in this life so I can suffer here on Earth and go straight to Heaven in the next.* All a load of mumbo jumbo. It was just an accident at work — in the print shop. She wasn't taking the proper precautions. Guillotine came right down and chopped it off. Terrible thing, of course. But even *that* she had to turn into some kind of religious goings-on."

Miranda had been holding her breath. "Which finger?" she managed at last. "Which finger did the guillotine cut off?"

"Oh, this one," the woman answered, holding up her hand. "At least, I think it was." A moment's doubt crossed her face, but smoothed away again. "Yes, the little finger on her right hand."

Miranda was still in a state of shock at this extraordinary revelation when Tero burst into the room.

"My God, you were hard to find!" he said, feverish with excitement. "Been looking for you everywhere."

Miranda threw a hurried apology to Mrs Linnamaa and pushed Tero back into the corridor, anxious to pass on her latest discovery. Before she could even close the door, he preempted her.

"There's been a seventh killing!" he said. "It's another Conservatory student. On our way back through Kruununhaka we heard it called in over the radio and drove straight there. Remember that pianist girl — the one Liisa and Jaana both visited just before they got snuffed? It was *her*! The *pianist*! Family hadn't heard a thing for days. Phone wasn't answering. The brother goes round to Mariankatu to have a look and finds poor sis' strangled. Right beside the piano. Dead a couple of days the doctor reckons. Usual stuff otherwise. Wire noose. Finger missing. No sign of rape, but that's neither here nor there. I haven't told you the best bit. One of the neighbours saw a bloke letting himself out of the flat Wednesday lunchtime. Described him to a tee, right down to his fancy hairpiece. Our dear friend, Jorma Mannila! No doubt about it! Time to haul him in again!"

When Miranda told him her own news about the guillotined finger, Tero was jubilant.

And it was Tero who broke through Mannila's uncooperative resistance to interrogation by adopting his favourite belligerent and sarcastic approach with the suspect. The three detectives had questioned Mannila well into the night, taken a few hours rest on the premises, and then started again. On Saturday morning Tero touched a raw nerve with a brutal reference to the rumours concerning Jorma's mother and her affair with the leader of their church sect.

"Come on, Jorma, let's face it," he baited. "Your Mum... well, she used to spread herself around a bit, didn't she? All in all, I think we'd have to say she was a bit of a slut."

Mannila's reaction was immediate and violent. Two more officers were called in to help tear him away from Tero's throat and restrain him in his seat. But the floodgates had opened. Jorma's lawyer was helpless to keep his client silent.

"Wicked lies!" he screamed. "My mother was an angel! One of God's chosen! You dare insult her memory, you vile servant of the Serpent? No one could match her!"

"That's why you killed all those girls, is it?" Tero sneered. "Because they didn't match up? Is that why they had to die?"

"God created them perfect — in the image of my mother — destined for higher things, to serve the Lord in grace and light. But they chose to deny His will and follow the path of Satan into sin and impurity. God commanded I save them from eternal damnation — return them to His judgment before their sins could reach excess —

that they might yet be forgiven and save their eternal souls. Thus I fulfilled the wishes of the Lord my God." Jorma's eyes bulged. Spittle had formed in the corners of his mouth. A few drops flew in Tero's direction. Again Mannila fought — this time, unsuccessfully — to tear himself free and throw himself at his tormentor.

"But the other one," Jorma hissed. "She deserved to die. She was in the pay of the Devil. She it was who turned them from the paths of righteousness. Satan's tool! I could not allow her to corrupt again."

"So all this was God's will, was it?" Tero lashed out sarcastically. "God whispered in your ear: *Go strangle those pretty young women, dear Jorma. Tear off their clothes and rape them. Put a noose round their necks, and pull it nice and tight for me. That's what the Lord your God gets off on.*"

Now everyone seemed to be shouting at once. Mannila's lawyer was demanding the interview be terminated and Tero be removed from the room. Miranda was trying to persuade Tero he'd done enough and it was time to back off. The loudest voices were still Tero's and Jorma's, with Tero calling Jorma a vicious pervert who'd hated his mother and that was why he'd cut off the fingers — to convince himself it was his own mother he was raping and killing. Jorma was almost frothing at the mouth, railing against Tero in pulpit-hammering, fragmentary Biblical quotations: "Your lips have spoken lies! Your tongue hath muttered perverseness!" he raged. "But if I with the finger of God cast out devils, no doubt the kingdom of God is come upon you! Yea, my little finger shall be thicker than my father's loins, and the priest shall dip his finger in the blood and sprinkle of the blood seven times before the Lord, before the veil of the sanctuary — for your hands are defiled with blood and your fingers with iniquity!"

Ylenius had been the only one to remain silent; biding his time. But nothing more could be achieved in this anarchy. Tero had elicited what was effectively an admission of guilt, though nothing Mannila had said under such emotional duress could ever be used in evidence against him. It was time to defuse the situation. Ylenius ordered Tero to go and 'cool his heels in the office'. Mannila was removed to a restraining cell where he could be prevented from hurting himself or others, and a doctor was called in to decide if sedation would be advisable. Only then did the Chief Inspector and Miranda join Tero in the main office. A crowd had gathered round Tero — presumably for an unofficial debriefing — but it melted away when Ylenius and Miranda approached.

"*That*," said Tero, as they pulled two chairs up to his desk, "is a class-A weirdo. The genuine-article religious freaking fruitcake. Should've shut himself away in a monastery years ago: The Monastic Order of the Criminally Insane!"

Ylenius winced. Miranda knew the boss to be a serious, although undemonstrative churchgoer.

"Sets my teeth on edge to hear the Bible abused that way," he sighed.

"Well, now we definitely know it's him," said Tero, massaging the bruises on his neck. "As good as admitted it."

"Except his lawyer's going to have him retract every word," Ylenius said. "We need hard evidence to make this stick."

Miranda looked worried. "Can we really take all this ranting at face value? I agree there was a time earlier on when I thought he might've... " She broke off. Once upon a time, she'd been equally convinced that Zoltán Szervánszky was the killer, and Mannila was starting to look like another mistake. "The Ainola letters, for example," she went on. "It beggars belief that Mannila could've written them. Fire and brimstone verses from the Bible, maybe. But introspective quotations from our Finnish national composer? It's totally out of character! He wasn't caught on video posting the sixth letter, was he? And, for heaven's sake, he was locked up here the night Beatrice Gröndahl was abducted!"

"Perhaps he's got an accomplice," Tero suggested. "Someone to do the brainwork and occasionally help out with the manual labour."

Ylenius shook his head. "Mannila doesn't strike me as a team player. Anyway, first we have to break his other alibis. There's no doubt he could've killed Jaana Saari before going on to his aunt's place. The cash-point video categorically places him at the scene. But what about the other deaths? What about his Bible-study alibi for Christa's murder? And his computerized work log for the evening Liisa died?"

"As you once suggested," Tero said, "he could've got somebody else to clock him off that evening."

Suddenly a new possibility surfaced in Miranda's mind, triggered perhaps by a recent stray comment of Ylenius's. But before she could think the idea through, her mobile rang. The display told her it was Rosie. Oh, damn! She was supposed to be going shopping with Rosie this morning to find a birthday present for their father. She slid across to her own desk and answered the call, although it proved difficult to hold a conversation. Rosie's voice came through fragmented and distorted.

"You're breaking up," Miranda complained. "I can't hear you properly."

"And ... battery .... nearly flat .... forgot to recharge .... but I ...... to let .... know ..... wanted ... meet me ..... "

"It's no good, Rosie! I can't make out what you're saying. Look, sorry, I'm much too busy to go shopping today."

".... matter ... can't either .... on ... 32 bus .... way to Haaga .... try ..... text message ..... "

And that was it. The line went dead. Miranda shrugged, and tried to pick up her previous train of thought about Mannila's work-log... Yes, it was definitely a possibility... though she'd prefer to check the idea out before saying anything to the others. Flicking through her notebook, she picked up the desk-phone receiver and dialled a number at the Helsinki Conservatory.

"Mr Koskinen? This is DI Miranda Lewis — from Pasila police station. I'd like to ask you about that problem you had with your root filling..."

By then, Rosie was halfway through tapping out a message on the buttons of her handset — composing sentences in the abbreviated language of SMS writers everywhere:

... SO DONT TEL ANY 1 ELSE HE SED. MUST KEEP IT BIG SUPRIS 4 ALL & B SURE 2 BRING MY CELLO. VERY MYSTERIUS. BUT HAD 2 TEL U OF CORS. DADS PREZY MONDY INSTED? BYE!

Selecting Miranda's number from the internal directory, she pressed the SEND button. Almost immediately the battery gave up and the liquid crystal display went blank. Rosie wasn't sure if the message had got through. Now the phone was useless until she got home to recharge it. Dropping it in her handbag, she pulled the cello case a little closer to her body, and turned to look out of the bus window.

"... so, in fact, you were right, boss," Miranda explained, after completing her call to Mannila's older colleague at the Conservatory. "Someone else *did* punch in the code. And not just for clocking off — for clocking on as well."

Her mobile gave a bleep indicating the arrival of a text message. Miranda ignored it, but was anyway interrupted by a relentless ringing from her desk phone. She grabbed the receiver impatiently — having only moments ago put it down — and announced her name with unprofessional brusqueness.

The person on the other end soon had her attention. It was Britt-Marie Söderblom — Christa Bäckström's old school friend — now returned from her journalistic adventures in Madagascar.

"Heard you were trying to get in touch," Britt-Marie said, "about Christa's death. I may have something useful for you. Back in January, Christa gave me a small package sealed up with masses of tape. She told me to put it somewhere safe and only open it in dire circumstances. Never explained what she meant by 'dire'. Just called it her 'last will and testament', but then changed her mind, and said she'd prefer to think of it as her 'life insurance'. Well, I didn't give it much thought at the time. Christa always had a taste for melodrama. So I chucked it in a drawer and forgot about it... until now. When I opened the package, it turned out to be a CD-R. She must've burnt it herself. I tried it in the computer. There's only one file on it — a photographic image — but you'd better take a look. I'm wondering if it's connected to Christa's death. Pointless me trying to describe the image over the phone. Tell me your email address, and I'll send it as a file attachment."

Five minutes later, Ylenius, Tero and several other members of the team were crowded round Miranda's computer terminal watching a crisp photographic image appear on the screen...

It depicted a night-time scene. A road sloped downwards and curved away slightly from the camera's viewpoint. Street lamps shone over a bus shelter some fifteen yards down the hill, the bus route plainly displayed on a sign fixed to the roof: number 80, which served the Roihuvuori area where Christa Bäckström had lived. No buildings were visible. A dense growth of trees bordered the pavement as it stretched off into dimness. Despite the lack of snow, the impression was wintery — perhaps late November or early December. Most of the trees were deciduous and leafless. The outer and more distant fringes of the photographic image were poorly lit, but the foreground stood out sharp and bright, presumably illuminated by the camera's electronic flash. They could see the front view of a car stopped in the middle of the road, somewhat askew to the central line. Miranda recognized the vehicle with its dented off-side wing and its cracked windscreen. Yes, she'd seen it before. But something else drew her attention — something quite appalling...

An accident had just occurred. A crumpled body in a dark-blue jogging suit was piled untidily against the front bumper, the head pressed onto the pavement at an unnatural angle. One leg was draped vertically and improbably over the radiator. The victim had apparently been struck at some speed, spun upwards and forwards against the windscreen, and then slid back down the bonnet as the vehicle came to a halt. Both the driver and passenger doors were flung wide open, but only one other person could be seen in the frame: a man crouched over the broken body, a man in his early to mid-thirties, face horror-struck and raised towards the camera, caught in the flashlight as if he'd only that instant become aware of the photographer.

Tero breathed a long and gratified sigh.

A junior member of the team peered closer. "I know that place," he said. "It's down the road from Christa Bäckström's flat. They had a hit-and-run there last November. That very spot! Fifty-year-old jogger knocked down on a pedestrian crossing in the early hours of the morning. Killed outright. No witnesses. Never found out who did it."

Miranda sat immobile, hypnotized by that so familiar face, transfixed by those astonished eyes gazing up at her from the digital image, frozen in time and space, though seeming now to stare out beyond either — beyond the camera lens and the computer screen, locking involuntarily onto Miranda's own — exposing to her the depths of their guilt and depravity. Yes, the truth was unravelling fast before her rebellious mind. She now understood why Mannila's alibi for the second killing had been so solid. Although Panu's appraisal of the murder sequence had been flawed, he *had* been right about the copycat. The trouble was they'd been viewing it all the wrong way round. As the horrifying chain of events she desperately wished to deny clarified itself step by step to her rational self, her emotions — in a seemingly parallel universe — succumbed to the shock. How could she have allowed herself to get so close and fail to recognize him for the monster he was? How could she ever trust her own judgment again?

Ylenius was saying something beside her. She tried to focus on his words, to use them as a lifeline.

"... so I think it's better if Tero and I deal with it, Miranda? Can't see any need for you to be involved."

That wrenched her back to the immediate surroundings. No way would they exclude her now! Not after all these weeks of horror and hard work. She had to be there at the finish. They owed her that, and she told them so in forceful terms. Ylenius shrugged acceptance, and she rose to accompany them, grabbing her mobile phone from the desk, noticing the 'received text message' icon on the LCD. Mechanically — through mere force of habit — she pressed the READ button.

Rosie's message stopped her in her tracks.

"Oh, my God, no!" she shuddered. Her legs were giving way. She sank onto the edge of Tero's desk, and dialled her sister's number. But Rosie's battery obviously was now dead.

"Whatever's the matter, Miranda?" Ylenius was alerted by her sudden change in pallor.

"He's got Rosie! He's taken Rosie and..." She struggled to make her voice work normally. A stranger seemed to have taken control of it. She took a deep breath — forced herself to try again: "He's asked her to meet him. Said she mustn't tell anybody."

"Meet who?" asked Tero, getting impatient.

"Him! The killer!" She pointed at the image displayed on her computer screen, but couldn't bring herself to say the name — not the actual name.

Tero wasn't so squeamish. He wanted confirmation.

"Yes, yes!" she almost screamed back. "And she had to have her cello with her and not tell anybody where she was going. Dear God, what's he planning? Where's he taken her? We've got to find her! Before it's too late!"

Symphony No 8
(conjectured)

(Manuscript Unavailable)

*   *   *

*S**o what's all the mystery? And why so important I bring my cello?*

To try something out perhaps... something he wants me to play for the others... some kind of surprise at Daddy's birthday do next week. Yes, that could be it. Shame we couldn't get the present today. But there'll be time next week — if Miranda can only get away for a couple of hours. I know she thinks the bathrobe's boring, but his old one's falling apart. Or maybe he'd like another one of those things that you... Hey, isn't this the stop I'm supposed to get off at? Ah, there he is... parked round the corner. All a bit 'James Bond', isn't it? Wonder where we're going next...

"Just a few blocks from here," he told her. "Somewhere I'd like to show you. And I did get it right, didn't I? You haven't seen Miranda since we met yesterday?"

"No, she didn't come home last night. Something big on at work, I suppose. Perhaps they've caught that awful murderer."

"Doubtful," he said. And, as they pulled away from the kerb, he persisted: "Does that mean you haven't spoken to anyone at all about our little meeting this morning?"

Rosie shook her head, though not without a twinge of guilt. Well, she hadn't actually *spoken* to Miranda about it, had she? An SMS wasn't *speaking*.

A few minutes later, after they'd pulled into the squat, red-brick building and the cantilevered door had been relowered, he ushered her into an adjoining workshop.

"What's *this* place?" She looked around curiously.

"My little secret," he said. "And now it's yours too... for a while."

"Is that *your* butterfly collection?" she asked.

"I suppose you could say I've inherited it." He turned his back momentarily to remove something from the workbench drawer. "Why not sit down, Rosie? Perhaps I can help you."

He stepped over and eased her gently but masterfully into a faded-green armchair with leaky innards — kneeling on her legs and pinning her body with one arm while he injected the contents of a small hypodermic syringe straight through her dress into her thigh. She struggled uncertainly, protested weakly, gazing up into his face like a sacrificial lamb — incredulous rather than fearful — as if this were no more than a misguided joke: temporarily out of hand, it was true, but soon to be resolved and laughed over together. The anaesthetic took rapid effect, which wasn't surprising on a girl of such gracile fragility. Her muscles were relaxing, consciousness was fading from her eyes. He reached for the noose of silky, soft-textured rope and drew it slowly, almost tenderly over her head, placing it around her throat like a lover bestowing a gift: a necklace, perhaps, of silver or of gold — a declaration of his eternal devotion and respect. And, as he gently drew the noose tighter, he recited to himself — not to her, for she could no longer hear him — uttering the words quietly, but with an unmistakable edge of bitterness: *"Put out the light, and then put out the light. If I quench thee, I know not where is that Promethean heat that can thy light resume."*

*   *   *

++

How often I've whispered to you in the closed confessional of my own head. I've even tried to confide in the flesh — to pour out the whole sordid story. There've been plenty of opportunities, but every time I've held back and the moment has passed. It's all very well to talk about the bonds of friendship, of having the courage to unburden oneself. But how could I be sure of your reaction to an admission of this enormity? Were you capable of the necessary leap? Could you really forgive me such trespasses? Or would you feel compelled to turn me over to the Romans and the Pharisees? +++ There was a time when I thought you might be responsible for one of the deaths yourself. Absurd! I realize that now. But I'll ask you to indulge me yet again and cast your mind back to the night of Liisa Louhi's death. +++ It was a Friday evening at the end of March, and we had a sort of *ménage à trois* date arranged with Miranda at the Ateljé Restaurant. Of course, we'd met her a couple of days earlier at Nick's introductory lecture, but the Ateljé was our first chance to really find out something about her. She couldn't stay long. She had an early start the next day. So we walked her home at midnight, and later you and I ended up at Humalistonkatu for a nightcap and coffee. We must've parted company at around two o'clock, I suppose. But I knew I wouldn't be able to sleep. Too much on my mind, and too much caffeine in my bloodstream. So I decided to delay bed even longer — to go down to the sea and take a walk along the shore. I never got that far. Instead I stumbled on something at the Sibelius Monument that changed the whole direction of my life. +++ If you're going to understand any of this, I have to backtrack; and my first excursion into the past takes us twenty years or more. It concerns my Uncle Eric. I must've mentioned him to you. He was the one who made a serious miscalculation in his youth by marrying my Auntie Adelia. Adelia the Hun, he came to call her, though never to her face. Can't imagine why he didn't walk out on the whole deal. Nothing to hold him. No children involved. +++ Adelia and my mother were two of a kind. Tough, single-minded, under-educated... but definitely not the Ugly Sisters. Not to begin with at least. I've seen the teenage snapshots. A couple of crackers! But as soon as they'd achieved their goal of marrying above their stations, they shed their good looks like a superfluous disguise, revealing the tyrannical harpies beneath. Adelia was probably the worse of the two. And with no kids to absorb any of her spleen, poor Eric bore the full brunt. Most dogs had a better life than the one she led him. Bossed him around something awful. Couldn't do this, couldn't do that! "I'm not having that belly-ache music in my house!" she'd tell him about his beloved classical music. Eventually he found refuge in the shed at the bottom of the garden. Not as bad as you might imagine. He'd fitted it out comfortably enough: rug on the floor, a couple of old armchairs, an electric fire. More of a den than anything. And pride of place was given to his antique 'hi-fi' gramophone and his LP collection: trad jazz, a fair amount of big band, but most of it classical. +++ I spent a lot of my school breaks and holidays round there with Uncle Eric, bunkered down in his garden shed, playing cards and Monopoly or just chatting man to man. He called us 'the two garden gnomes'. And, of course, we listened to a lot of music: Dixieland, Glenn Miller, Tchaikovsky's *1812*. It was there I had my first taste of Sibelius: a scratchy old 10-inch LP with *The Karelia Suite* on one side, *En Saga* on the other. I suppose he came to think of me as his surrogate son. That's probably why he left everything to me when he died last autumn. +++ Poor devil only outlived his wife by a couple of years, but just before the end he won some money on the National Lottery. Underplayed the amount. Had a holiday on the Costa Brava. Bought himself a new car. And that seemed to be it. When the will came through at the end of November, was I gobsmacked!? The house was worth about fifty-thousand quid — well, I'd expected that — but stashed away in his bank account the executor found another cool half million! Every penny of it passing on to me! Not enough to retire on outright at the age of thirty-three, it's true — death duties, etc. — but enough to make one hell of a difference. Unfortunately, the very day I received news of my changed fortunes was the day I ran into Christa Bäckström. +++ You weren't around. You'd gone off to Sweden for something or other and were away at least a week. So that fateful evening I found myself celebrating alone in O'Malley's pub. Christa was playing her violin with a bunch of other Celtophiles. Not half badly either, to give her credit. Managed to get talking at the bar later on. A sexy piece of goods. Tight black leather skirt. Tight black jumper. Jet-black dyed hair. Stud in her nose. Told me she was a successful photojournalist. Mainly bullshit, I imagine. But she'd just got herself a new state-of-the-art digital camera. Cost her an arm and both legs on the never-never, so she claimed. Insisted on pulling it out of her bag and giving me the guided tour right there in the bar: high resolution, brilliant performance even at low light levels, saturation control, flash and exposure modes, megabytes of plug-in card memory, etcetera, etcetera. Naturally I showed an improper level of interest. The third pint of Guinness was kicking in and I had hopes of ingratiating my way into more than the mysteries of her fully automatic lens aperture. I suppose that's why I let slip about my sudden stunning inheritance. Probably trying to impress her. Shouldn't have done it, of course. A total stranger like that. +++ Come 1.30 am, we were turned out onto the street, and I offered to drive her home. Thought it'd give me a better chance of an invite when we got there. Another foolish move. I'd slowed down on the alcohol consumption the last couple of hours — didn't want to lose my wherewithal, did I? — but I was still way over the limit. And there we were speeding up through some trees somewhere out in the far east of the city, when some maniac nocturnal jogger comes bursting out of the undergrowth. No chance to avoid him. Flipped right over the bonnet into the windscreen. Must've snapped his neck there and then. When I jumped out to investigate, he was obviously dead. God knows why he didn't see us coming! Well, it's true I'd forgotten to switch on more than my sidelights. But he was wearing a personal CD-player on his belt. I could still hear the bass pumping away from the headphones, and that's probably what distracted him. But, Christ Almighty! Middle-aged man high on heavy metal, running out onto the road at two o'clock in the bloody morning! I call that deviant behaviour. The whole thing was ludicrous. He should never've died that easily. Just a freak accident. But who was going to believe me? +++ Anyway, there I was crouched over the body, when someone called my name. I turned round and was immediately blinded by a flash of light. Christa with her damned digital camera! By the time I could see anything again, she'd vanished — melted into the darkness — camera, violin, the lot. No idea where she lived, of course. Didn't know her surname — though it turned out I must've told her mine. +++ Meanwhile, I was left to handle the mess on my own. If I called the police, they were bound to breathalyse me, and the outcome of that was a foregone conclusion: I'd get banged up for years. There was no way to help the poor bugger any more. He'd well and truly popped his clogs. So you can guess what I did. I got the hell out. I took the car another mile into the eastern suburbs, left it in a side street and called a taxi on my mobile. Couldn't risk getting stopped behind the wheel of my own Renault, could I? Next day I went back to fetch it and, in full daylight, appraised the damage:

dented wing, cracked windscreen — minimal really, considering what had happened to the other half of the collision. +++ Just one day later I got my first email from Christa. She hadn't wasted much time figuring out how to reach me. Called herself *Camera Candida*, using a Hotmail address I had no way of tracing back to the genuine sender. Well, I knew it was her, of course. The email just said 'Hit and run!', and it had a *jpeg* image attachment of me squatting down beside the dead jogger: full-frontal face with the vehicle's registration number clear as crystal. A perfect endorsement for her new digital camera! +++ The second email came a couple of days later and — surprise, surprise — it was a demand for money, although couched in other terms. A request for sponsorship, she called it. The Finnish equivalent of a thousand pounds to be paid into a numbered bank account. The funds would be responsibly utilized, I was assured, to promote worldwide freedom of speech and expression — to expose the truth in even the darkest corners of the globe. Meaning the sarcastic bitch wanted me to pay off the outstanding debt on her digital camera. The irony bit hard, but I had no choice. Less than a month later another demand arrived: a couple of thousand this time. Then again and again, the interval diminishing and the sum increasing by alarming increments. +++ By the time you got back from Stockholm, this blackmailing thing was already underway. I suppose it's why I kept quiet about Uncle Eric's legacy. I didn't want to admit the stupid mess I'd got myself into, or involve you in any possible consequences. +++ The same day we met Miranda at the Ateljé, I'd just received Christa's latest and greediest request for sponsorship. Going on a field trip to Lapland, *Camera Candida* explained. Needed some new equipment. Felt sure I could accommodate her. Same bank account, thank you very much. All she asked was another ten thousand! How the hell long would my half million last at this rate? I'd never be rid of her. She'd hag-ride me till every last drop of my inheritance was squeezed out... unless I could find some radical solution to stop her. +++ With such thoughts, I headed off across Sibelius Park in the early hours of that bitterly cold Saturday morning, aiming for the seashore — only to stumble on Liisa Louhi at the Sibelius Monument. Not the first time I'd seen a dead body, but it took me aback. I removed one of my gloves and reached out to touch her cheek. It was icy. She was slumped back against the rock face — a little to the left of Sibelius's bust relief — more or less in a sitting position with her head flopped forward. She'd obviously been strangled. The wire noose was still around her throat. Her violin case was lying a few feet away, presumably where she'd dropped it during the attack. +++ I stood there for ages staring, until my own warmth seeped out through my clothing and I began to shiver. Gradually my earlier concerns about Christa intermingled with the scene before me. An extraordinary concept was taking shape. What if I used this murder as cover for one of my own? Could I somehow orchestrate two murders into a matching pair and make them look as if they'd been committed by the same person? The beauty of the idea was that I'd have a cast-iron alibi for this first one at Sibelius Park, which should automatically discount me for the second one I'd commit *myself* at a later date. As it turned out, I misjudged the time of Liisa's death. For no other reason than misguided instinct, I assumed Liisa had died a lot later than nine o'clock... by which time we'd both been sitting snugly in the Ateljé Restaurant with — for heaven's sake! — a Detective Inspector of the Helsinki City Police Force. Who could wish for a better alibi? But, as you very well know, my mistake about the time of death led to serious complications — complications that weren't properly resolved until almost four weeks later, when the French horn player was killed synchronously with Nick's fifth lecture. +++ Naturally I knew nothing of those future events as I stood viewing the murder scene at the Sibelius Monument. Instead I was considering what tricks I could use to generate a recognizable pattern between this murder and my own. +++ First there was the violin. Christa was a violinist too, so I could ensure she also had a violin at *her* demise. And the Sibelius Monument venue reinforced the musical motif. I picked up the violin case and propped it against the rock, just below Jean's frowning face. That was a genuine touch of theatre! But what else? How about adding a sexual component? Repeating it with Christa later would shift attention from my real motive of eliminating a blackmailer. Liisa was fully dressed when I found her, but I opened her jacket and pulled her jumper and bra up as far as her armpits. Undoing her jeans was trickier. I didn't want to take off my woollen gloves for fear of leaving fingerprints on the metal studs. My original intention of pulling her trousers and panties down to her ankles proved too difficult. Whether it was rigor mortis setting in or just the freezing effect of the sub-zero temperatures, I don't know, but her legs seemed more or less fixed in an open, splayed position. I couldn't get the clothes more than a couple of inches below her buttocks. Well, it already looked impressive, and vividly implied a sexual motive for the attack. +++ By then I'd noticed something else really bizarre. Her fourth finger had been partially severed from her right hand. It was hanging off with little more than skin and a strand of tendon holding it in place. The tool for this attempted amputation — a pair of garden secateurs — was still jammed there in the joint. The tendon had got caught right up in the hinge, rendering the secateurs both useless and impossible to remove. Liisa's killer must've given up the struggle and left without his trophy. But why shouldn't I take it myself? This was exactly what I needed! A weird and distinctive addition to the array of motifs — another one I could repeat with Christa. +++ As you know, I carry a Swiss army knife around with me — a throwback to my scouting days — various blades you can open out, a miniature screwdriver, and so on. Comes in useful — if only to open wine and beer bottles — but this was the most gruesome task I'd ever put it to: prising the tendon out of the secateur's hinge so I could complete the amputation. I stuck the finger in an old burger wrapper from a rubbish bin nearby, and pocketed it... along with the secateurs, which I'd need for later use. My idea at that stage was simply to get rid of the finger far from the crime scene. +++ Last of all, I studied the noose around Liisa's neck, and had a good look at the knot so I'd be able to attempt a fair imitation of it next time. The irony didn't escape me a couple of days later — when I was reading Theresa's email about the birth of baby Lily — that the very same night dear Theresa was struggling in a London maternity hospital to bring a new life into the world, I was plotting here in Helsinki how to destroy one! Anyway, hoping to avoid notice by anyone the police might question later, I took a roundabout route from the crime scene through the quietest back streets I could think of. +++ The Ainola letter idea didn't occur to me until I was already halfway home. Again the Sibelius Monument must've suggested it — that and Nick's first lecture still being fresh in my mind. I decided to send a letter to the police c/o The Ainola

Residence, Järvenpää, with some kind of quotation from Sibelius himself. And at the bottom I'd place an inked fingerprint from Liisa's fourth finger. Of course, I'd repeat the exercise with my follow-up victim. +++ After some research, the text I settled on for the first letter was as follows: *Let the voice of my inner being and the spectres of dream and fantasy direct me.* Yes, I was proud of the grand plan I'd devised to escape my tormentor's tyranny! *There are things to be done that cannot be delayed* — i.e. getting rid of Christa Bäckström! *Life is so very fleeting!* Well, hers certainly would be! +++ And the truth is I found the next week thoroughly exhilarating. The deed was still only a projection. Nothing had been finalized. The plan could be aborted at any time. Meanwhile I took pleasure in my preparations, purchasing electrical cable from a large hardware store at the busiest time of the day — paying cash, naturally. The same approach at a busy pharmacy to obtain surgical latex gloves. I also acquired a light-weight, one-piece skiing suit and elasticated plastic bags to cover my shoes. Most fun was the stalking. I'd already acquired a taste for it finding out who Christa really was. I'd trailed her unseen to her own door from one of the Friday *ceilidh* sessions at O'Malley's pub, and the rest had been easy. The residents' surnames and flat numbers were all listed on a board inside the front door. I checked the names later in a phone book, and bingo! — there she was: Bäckström, Christa; photojournalist. After that I learned something about her routines, the location of her main office, where she ate in the evenings, what route she took home, and I realized the only time I could rely on her having the violin with her was the weekly *ceilidh* night at O'Malley's. +++ Seeing no reason to delay, I decided to do the job the very next Friday. It was a little awkward when you suggested a late-night movie for that same evening. I wasn't sure I'd be able to get there. But as it might provide a partial alibi I provisionally agreed +++ Christa was in the habit of taking a short cut home from the Metro station through a dense clump of trees, and that would definitely be the best place to intercept her. Not far from there I found a suitably unremarkable spot to leave my car. I also scrutinized the alternative routes back into town, planning one that would avoid traffic surveillance cameras. +++ Come Friday, I was parked in viewing distance of O'Malley's waiting for her to turn up. She spent a surprisingly short time in the pub. No more than a couple of hours. I'd been worried she might leave with someone — that she'd find some other horny bloke hovering at the bar. But, no, she was alone. And she did exactly as expected. She headed for the closest Metro station. +++ It was easy reaching Herttoniemi before her. Metro trains travel at 50 mph and have to make frequent stops. I parked the car and positioned myself ready. The adrenaline was flowing in torrents, but an element of risk has always figured in my life. I've needed that kind of high from time to time. Things had been a bit sedate recently, so I was ready for the challenge. And throughout I held the main objective in mind: to stop that scheming parasite from robbing me of Uncle Eric's inheritance. +++ I took her more or less by surprise. Slammed her face-first against a tree to keep her still. Small woman — well within my ability to control — but she wriggled like a cat. Not for long. It was over amazingly fast. +++ The intensity of that experience is hard to convey to anyone who hasn't been through it. The ultimate sensation of power. I was surprised how natural it felt — as if my whole life had been waiting for this moment. Most unexpected was the intense sexual turn on. I actually orgasmed. +++ But, anyway, I didn't want her found before morning, so I dragged her deeper into the trees and prepared my piece of theatre. I sat her against a tree in a similar posture to Liisa's at the Sibelius Monument, propped her violin case against another tree nearby, lifted her top and bra to expose her breasts, pushed her skirt up to her waist, and left her tights and panties hooked over one ankle. Removing the finger was a grisly operation. Much harder than I'd expected. I got the hinge all jammed up, just like my anonymous mentor the week before, and had to resort to the trusty old Swiss knife again. Finally, I took her keys from her jacket pocket and headed back to the car. +++ Fortunately the traffic into town was light. I parked behind Kamppi Metro station, and just made it in time to meet you at Pizza Hut for ten thirty. The claim we agreed on making to the police that we'd met there half an hour earlier at ten o'clock was a perfect blind. It provided exactly the alibi I needed. +++ But my work wasn't over for that night. After the film, when we'd parted company, I doubled back to pick up my car, and drove over to Christa's place. I needed to locate and destroy every copy of that incriminating picture. That's why I'd taken her keys. +++ It was a bit eerie entering her flat in the early hours and creeping around with a torch. The place was relatively tidy, and that surprised me. I'd expected her to be more of a slattern. I went through all the drawers, especially those at her computer work-station. I didn't find any hard copies, so next I switched on the computer and checked her hard disk and CD-Rs. Eventually I found the right file. She'd made the job easier for me by naming it *hitnrun.jpg*. But I went through everything else to make sure there weren't any copies of it... spent ages previewing images from her hard disk — hundreds of them. And there was something else potentially worrying: her email records. She'd used Hotmail to contact me, so I didn't think there'd be anything damning on the computer's own hard-drive. But I had to check, and ended up erasing the whole of her 'sent-mail' folder by mistake. Stupid amateurish thing to do. Mind you, I was totally exhausted by then. I realized it was time to leave. +++ My intention had been to return to the body and put the keys back in Christa's pocket. But by now it was four o'clock and raining hard. The ground would be muddy out there in the trees, so I just left the keys on the hall table. Suppose I hoped the police would assume she'd left them at home by mistake the previous morning. Once outside the building, I regretted the move. Much better to have chucked them in a river or something. +++ The following day I had the Ainola letter to prepare. I took a short passage about *malaise, mould and maggots* which seemed appropriate. And then a bit about *fortissimo strings muted and fading to silence*. It reminded me of how I'd permanently muted Christa's clamouring for money. I especially liked the ending: *Oh, the godlike power of it all! To be carried away in joy by the surging rush of strings.* That matched my own sense of exhilaration. Yes, I'd actually had the courage to go through with the operation. What's more it had turned out a real turn on. +++ Of course, there was a darker side. It wasn't that I regretted my actions. Christa was an unscrupulous, grasping bitch and she deserved everything she got. But I knew I'd crossed a significant line. I was now a fugitive, a pariah hunted by society and all its self-righteous, judgmental members. I possessed a secret I could share with nobody, and one that I'd have to conceal forever. Of course, we're all actors to a certain extent. It's part of the social survival strategy. Most of the roles we play are the well-practised standard repertoire. Occasionally we have to improvise one on the spot, but now I needed to play a new and, in an ironic sense, unfamiliar role: that of a normal, non-homicidal human being. +++ Meanwhile I was carrying the images of that extraordinary moment around with me: the adrenaline rush, the sexual intensity. I began to fantasize how I might have gone still further and enjoyed her to the full... if I'd only known beforehand what to expect and prepared myself more carefully. +++ Nevertheless, that might've been it. I might've been able to compartmentalize the whole thing off — leave it in the past and reshut Pandora's box on my unhealthy imagination. That's if I hadn't been travelling home on a number 18 bus the following Tuesday evening and seen Juanita reincarnate. +++ Ah, Juanita! That lovely, youthful creature who had for so long haunted my dreams both wakeful and in sleep. I'd encountered her only the once and briefly, but still I found myself unable to relegate her to the past — to file her away as just another memory and move on. +++ In honour of Juanita, we must now embark on another excursion. I take you back to La Paz: that racy, vertiginous metropolis, where I had the misfortune to fall in with Luis Rodrigo Ramirez de Castelar, my very own Mephistopheles. +++ I'd only been in Bolivia a month when Ramirez sent me a letter on embossed, parchment-textured notepaper inviting me to provide him with weekly English lessons. Apparently I'd been recommended by a friend of his father at the Portuguese Embassy. Ramirez's lessons were to be held at the family mansion. A chauffeur-driven limousine would fetch me beforehand and return me home afterwards. As it turned out, he got bored almost immediately with the one-to-one teaching concept. His English was already excellent anyway, so he suggested: Why didn't we simply spend time together? A couple of evenings a week cruising the bars and nightclubs. A chance for him to practise his English under more recreational and diverting circumstances. Seemed okay to me. He was ready to pay handsomely. Plus, of course, he'd cover all the evening's expenses: drinks, meals, cabarets, casinos, whatever. Thus I found myself visiting a wide range of establishments from the most opulent to the decidedly seedy. His tastes were catholic. And everywhere we went, people fawned over him — the son of one of the richest and most influential men in the Bolivian government. We were both of an age — only a few months between us — and he seemed to enjoy showing me off like some kind of mascot: his tame English *gentilhombre*, I suppose! +++ After a few weeks, at the end of a harmless if extravagant evening, he proposed I accompany him to a more exotic location... *El Sombrero de Tres Picos* was an up-market knocking-shop, replete with every luxury and frill. The interior designer hadn't stinted himself either. Colonial-period wood panelling, crystal chandeliers and mirrors everywhere, El Greco-style frescos of erotically stimulating subjects. Way out of my financial league, naturally, but I wouldn't be paying. Possibly it was called *The Three-cornered Hat* because you could choose between female company, male company, or both at once. Ramirez courteously enquired after my predilections and seemed pleased when I selected the youngest-looking woman there — a dark-haired, brown-eyed, full-figured beauty of about eighteen. "Excellent choice, my friend! Truly exquisite!" +++ There were many other such visits, increasingly to less and less sophisticated establishments, involving younger and younger girls. I discovered that one of Ramirez's own predilections was the preliminary binding of his subjects with soft leather restraints and thongs. He also favoured the fourteen to sixteen age-group. *Look at their pretty, fresh faces, their enormous eyes, their pouting lips*, he would reassure me, *the unlined smoothness of their skin, their delightfully fragile shoulders. Ah, yes, my noble English friend, feast your eyes on those soft and succulent breasts, those berry-like nipples, on their little rounded bellies and plump firm buttocks. God designed them thus for one thing only. That we should seek coitus with them. That we should take our pleasure and procreate. Believe me, my friend, I know this with certainty. It is all part of God's magnificent plan!* And as I was led, much too compliantly, from one depravity to another, it must have been clear to me in some wilfully neglected corner of my mind that, if there truly were a supernatural agency at work behind all this, and Ramirez was its spokesperson, that agency wasn't God but the Devil.

+++

"Where's Rosie meeting him?" Ylenius asked urgently. "*Where*, Miranda? At his flat?" He gripped her by the shoulders. She was clearly on the verge of panic.

"I don't think so! I don't know!" She made an effort to overcome the crippling terror: "Rosie was on a bus. A number 32 to Haaga, but he doesn't live in Haaga."

"Perhaps his hideaway's there," said Tero, disconcerted by Miranda's uncharacteristic loss of control. "Has he ever mentioned a place in Haaga?"

"No! *No!*" Her fear was turning to anger, and she latched onto it as the more productive of the two — the one that might focus her thoughts and actions enough to save her sister. Though what if it was too late? Rosie might already be dead. *Don't, Miranda! For God's sake, concentrate!*

"Somebody must know where this place of his is," persisted Tero. "But who the hell do we ask?"

Miranda reached grimly for her mobile phone and selected a number.

"Who are you calling, Miranda?" Tero sounded suspicious.

She raised the phone to her ear, lips defiantly compressed.

"Miranda!" Ylenius warned. "Tell us who you're calling!"

Almost at once she cancelled the call. "Phillip Burton," she admitted belatedly, her voice deadpan, cheerless. "Number 'unavailable at this time'. His phone's switched off."

Her colleagues exchanged uneasy glances.

"All right, so we'll get no help that way," Ylenius said, firmly taking the lead. "Let's move as many mobile units into the area as possible. Circulate a description of both him and Rosie. Haaga seems most likely, but we can't be sure. Better warn the whole network to try and locate his car. And contact the bus company. Get us patched through to every driver out there with a number 32. One of them might remember where she got off."

"*I'll* do that," Miranda said, sounding more decisive. "I can give the best description."

Meanwhile Tero turned to his computer and started tapping keys furiously.

One of the bus drivers did recall a girl with long hair and a cello getting on at Töölö. But he wasn't sure where she'd got off. Somewhere in Haaga, he thought. Had there been a man waiting at any of the stops? Someone who hadn't got on, but might've been meeting the girl? Miranda described the man, but the driver was unable to help.

Tero suddenly beckoned Miranda over to his computer terminal. "You'd better have a look at this. The Haaga connection reminded me. I turned it up a couple of day's ago with the search engine. Meant to ask you at the time, but then all this stuff blew up with Mannila... Look, it's a report of a car theft at 4.15 am on the same night the Estonian hooker got abducted and murdered. The owner of the car, Myrsky Vaarela, dropped into a service station, parked his Honda Civic round the back, and went into the all-night café. Next thing some sleepless old biddy in a nearby block of flats spots two teenagers tampering with the vehicle. She calls the police, and a squad car arrives just as the kids are driving the Civic away. Turns into a Hollywood-style chase. More units called in. High speeds through the back streets. Ends up in Haaga with the kids trying to get round a roadblock and crashing the car into a lamppost. The driver fought like a madman. Took several officers to hold him down. The other kid did a runner, but a police dog caught up with him. Made a right mess of his leg apparently."

"What *is* all this, Tero?" Miranda was sounding hysterical again. "Car thieves in Haaga! How the hell does that help us find Rosie?"

"But, Miranda, it's the violin, you see."

"Violin? What the hell violin are you talking about, Tero?"

+++

Then one evening Ramirez took me to a shabby hotel in a run-down part of the capital. The night porter nodded as we passed, and quickly averted his eyes. As we climbed the stairs to room 27 — a room available to Ramirez on a full-time basis, so he informed me — I was promised something exceptional. Ramirez was right. The girl waiting for us was not more beautiful than other girls — though her face and figure were alluring — but she seemed to embody everything I had ever admired in a woman, with yet other qualities that I'd never before imagined. My desire for her was instant and acute. She smiled shyly, and told me her name was Juanita — a sweet-faced, native American girl, no more than sixteen years old, perhaps younger. Her hair was

407

thick and dark, her body curvaceously youthful. As I laid my hands on her for the first time, I shook with excitement and anticipation. But Ramirez wanted to draw out the enjoyment — to add piquancy, he said — and insisted on playing his little games. I helped prepare her, securing her wrists and ankles to a metal frame he'd had installed for the purpose. Incidental and irrelevant, I felt at first, until Ramirez produced the silk-cord noose and drew it firmly around Juanita's throat. I'm unable to explain why this excited me so much; but the throat, you see... It's such a delicate, beautiful part of a woman's body. It has always held a special fascination for me. Very soon I was adrift in the visual and tactile ferment of what seemed to me, at the time, a near-Nirvana state of euphoric arousal — though, in retrospect, more like untrammelled bestiality. +++ And when everything was over, it was Ramirez, not I, who noticed the excess to which our self-absorbed intemperance had driven us. I'm inclined to believe it a genuine accident. But I can't be sure. It may not have been his first time. And, although I could claim it wasn't my hand tightening the noose, I had certainly been complicit in the act. I couldn't absolve myself from responsibility. And, beyond that, I feared the repercussions. Ramirez assured me there would be none. The girl was fresh from the countryside, he said. She had few connections in the city. Everything would be taken care of. Nobody would miss her. "You must not trouble yourself, my friend. Go home. Leave everything to me." But I no longer trusted him. He had wealth and influence. I had neither. It was obvious who would be the fall guy if his cleanup operation failed. I packed my bags and left on the next available flight to Madrid. +++ And, you know, I'd like to think my subsequent migration to the European north, the land of blonde Brünnhildes and Sieglindes, was a subconscious attempt to turn my back on temptation — to keep myself pure in deed if not in thought. But, for heaven's sake! To rediscover Juanita on a number 18 bus in the middle of Helsinki! The same thick raven hair, the same pre-Columbian features, the same enticingly nubile body! And why the hell did she have to be carrying a violin? How could I fail to make the connection? +++ Over the next few days, my saner half must have been shocked by the powerful obsession that so quickly took hold. Not that I was listening to the voice of sanity any more. I could think only of Juanita — my Juanita reincarnate. +++ That first evening, I followed her from the bus to her home, and thereafter I hovered outside her apartment building in my car, hoping to catch a glimpse of her. Twice I escorted her unnoticed to school and, at school's end, chaperoned her home again. My work suffered. My regular duties were neglected. It was like falling off the edge of a precipice. Potential for this overwhelming obsession must have been festering in my subconscious since Bolivia, waiting for this chance encounter to trigger it off. And, whenever I could tear myself away from the hallowed ground of Munkkiniemi — the place where she lived and moved — I made further preparations; though very different from those with Christa Bäckström. I was like a sleep-walker. Each act seemed to occur of and by itself with me playing no genuine part. I acquired a decorative hunting knife — fierce-looking, though not in reality very sharp. I purchased two rolls of silver duct tape and found some silky-textured rope reminiscent of the type Ramirez had introduced me to nearly three years earlier. Adding a packet of common or garden condoms and my original supplies of latex gloves and elasticated shoe covers, I collected everything together in a small nylon backpack, and placed it in the boot of my car. I had no clear notion of how, when or where I intended to use this equipment — indeed, if I *ever* would. +++ Friday's dinner party at Miranda and Rosie's afforded a few hours escape to normality — especially the joy of Rosie's cello playing. But next evening, there I was again parked in sight of Juanita's home. Shortly before seven-thirty, she emerged alone from the front door, passing me on the other side of the road. It was a warm evening, and she'd obviously dressed up for a party with a thin lilac jacket tossed over one shoulder. She looked stunning. I left the car, donned my backpack, and followed at a safe distance. The plan, if I really had one, was open-ended: any action would be opportunistic. But even when she took a shortcut through an unpopulated patch of forest, I was at a loss how to proceed. Early April with the days lengthening fast up here at the sixtieth latitude meant almost an hour to sundown, and then another half hour until total darkness. Dare I attempt anything yet? What actually was it that I hoped to achieve? Would I dare do anything at all? Twice more she led me along secluded pathways; and still I was unmanned by indecision. When she met a girlfriend on a street corner and they walked on together, I cursed myself for not acting sooner. Several minutes later, they entered a block of flats and were gone. +++ I waited, of course — her image now vividly fresh and quickening my fantasies. I reminded myself how natural it had felt with Christa Bäckström. Why should tonight be different? Especially as, this time, I had genuine passion to carry me through. No, I wouldn't miss the next opportunity when it arose. I assured myself of that! +++ But when she reappeared an hour and a half later into a darkness that should have been my accomplice, it was with the same girlfriend. They retraced the whole route together as far as Juanita's home. Laughingly, casually they let themselves into the lobby — it was obvious with no intention of venturing forth again. And there on the outside I was left excluded, bereft, the adrenaline freezing into hard knots of frustration that I obstinately refused to relinquish or allow to fade. Returning to my car I drove — aimlessly — wallowing in my failure and disappointment. +++ Half an hour later, when a car pulled into the kerb ahead of me and a girl jumped out from the passenger side, it was the violin that I spotted first and that instantly fitted her into the paradigm. Whatever else followed would seem fated. And there was further confirmation in her similarities to Juanita. Older by a number of years — mid-twenties at a guess — but small in stature, long darkish hair, full-breasted. I caught a glimpse of her face as she turned to wave curtly at the driver. She was certainly pretty, in her own less exotic way. I overtook and watched in my wing-mirror as the girl ran lightly towards some steps flanking an impersonal four-story building that overlooked the road. I turned right and right again, wanting another look, aiming to intercept her on the other side, and I was just in time to see her disappear into a doorway at the far end of a courtyard. It surprised me to see the Sibelius Academy swan-and-music-stave logo on the wall beside the doorway. This must be the Pitäjänmäki building — or P-block, as I'd heard it called. I knew of its existence but I'd never had any reason to visit it. What on earth was the girl doing in there at ten o'clock at night? Surely she couldn't be staying long? I waited on the courtyard parking area and studied my city street map — getting my bearings. By the time she came back out of the building, I had a reasonable picture of the possible routes available to her. In fact, she headed south towards some playing fields. I left the car to follow her on foot, and she struck out along a footpath that crossed the open green. Half a mile in the distance I could make out a dense wall of trees — an ideal location for my purposes — perhaps the only chance before she was swallowed up by the tall residential blocks I could see lit up beyond. It was then I realized that my nylon backpack was still in the car. Had I left it there on purpose — as a last line of defence against my encroaching madness? To no avail; I wasn't ready to give up yet. I ran back to the car and, at high speed, drove the long detour around the parkland — the only route available by road — aiming to reach the trees from the other side. I didn't think I'd make it in time. A part of me hoped I wouldn't. And when I parked on the far side and set off with my backpack into the trees, I had no way of knowing if this was the path she'd be taking. There seemed to be several. It was a pure fluke that I actually met her coming the other way. I didn't doubt my ability to subdue her. I'd already proved once that I could muster enough physical will. But until the very last moment I doubted anything would happen. +++ Although the moon had sunk behind the trees, there was plenty of starlight. I should have concealed my face. That way she would have been unable to identify me: although it's doubtful I could, even then, have held back from the ultimate, lethal act of consummation. In that first astonishing moment, when I discovered myself turning and grabbing her from behind, I set in motion a process that I would seem helpless to control or curtail. +++ It's a human trait, wanting to be part of a recurrent ritual or routine. It gives one a sense of continuity and security. I've noticed the way students habitually take the same seat in the classroom. The places aren't labelled, but they establish their territory in the first lesson and return almost unfailingly. In some strange way I can equate my behaviour that night to the same blind following of a preordained sequence. A precedent had been set, both in reality with Christa, and thereafter in my fantasies. I did little more than act the sequence through: like following a computer program someone else had written for me. At first, I suppose her fear and her reluctant compliance were a turn on. But, ultimately, the whimpering and the perpetual pleading were a distraction I could well've done without. +++ There's something I'd like to stress here. Whatever you may think of me, I'm not a sadist. I get no pleasure from inflicting physical pain. The thought of torturing another human being disgusts me. Anyone who gets off on that kind of stuff... well, in my opinion, they're genuinely sick. All I sought was control: complete freedom to do what I wanted with her and enjoy her to the full. Can you understand that? +++ I realized afterwards that I hadn't properly fulfilled myself — not the way I'd expected to. Okay, so I was pretty well caught up in it all at the time — in a state of excitement even — but looking back I felt dissatisfied, and I blamed this on the fact that she was the wrong girl. With Juanita everything would be different. And now I was glad I had gained this extra self-knowledge and experience — that I hadn't rushed straight in unprepared for Juanita herself. +++ Not that there weren't contradictory thoughts and feelings at work within me... *A symphony is always more than a musical composition in the generally accepted meaning of the word. In a very important sense it is also a personal confession relating to a specific point in the composer's life.* I can't exactly say why I chose that quotation next, but from this point on, the concept of confession preoccupied me. I felt a growing need to confide in someone and, not surprisingly, that someone was you. +++ When we met the next afternoon at the street-side café, with so many regular, smiling citizens milling around enjoying the first summery weather, the whole scene somehow lacked reality, although I did maintain the necessary mask. I doubt you noticed anything unusual. In a way, of course, I was hiding the truth from myself. +++ That first time I saw Juanita travelling home on the number 18 bus with her violin, one of her friends was also carrying a guitar case. Had they been coming from some kind of music session? Lessons perhaps? If it were a regular weekly affair, devising a plan of action would be very much easier. I already knew the route she'd walked home alone that evening from the bus stop. The quiet stretch of road beyond the burger restaurant — that dead end overlooking the Turku motorway... It held definite possibilities. +++ When Tuesday came round again, I was parked at Töölöntori watching the bus stop where Juanita had got on the previous week. Sure enough, a little after six o'clock, I saw her crossing the road with one of her friends to board the number 18. I trailed the bus for a while but, reminiscent of the Big

Bad Wolf running on ahead to Grandma's cottage, I overtook and reached my chosen spot above the motorway some minutes before her... to observe her as she walked past and again devour every physical detail. My God, she was so beautiful! Yes, I had to find a way! +++ But it was time to reappraise my objectives. Thus far I'd been too haphazard in my approach and left too much to chance. I needed to be more in control of the variables. I needed a secure environment. So I rented a pair of old garages in a sleepy part of residential Haaga. They stood apart from the neighbouring five-storey blocks, more or less shielded by trees. And they were conveniently interconnected. I could drive my car into one half and carry my prize through to the other unobserved. In fact, the second garage had already been converted into a kind of workshop. The previous tenant had bricked in the outer doorway and installed electric heating. He was an amateur lepidopterist. His enormous collection of butterflies and moths was still displayed in glass cases around the walls. On the workbench were his killing jars, his mounting equipment, and — God knows where he got it! — an enormous industrial-sized demijohn of ether. At my initial viewing, the owner of the premises explained how the 'moth-man' had died suddenly of an aneurysm. Since there were no living relatives, all his equipment stood exactly where he'd left it. Would I like everything removed before taking occupancy? I declined the offer, unable to tolerate further delay. And perhaps I recognized the appropriateness of retaining these vestiges of an earlier history. This place had, after all, been the site of innumerable deaths... well, entymologically speaking. +++ There was another important refinement that I planned for the future: the use of an anaesthetic. I had one in mind. I'd learned about it during my teaching at Taurus Pharmaceuticals. One of the students there had made a detailed presentation in English to the rest of the class about *Comatin*: a drug used widely in operating theatres. Larger doses caused complete anaesthesia. But, when administered in small amounts subcutaneously, it induced a sleepy, euphoric state appropriate for local operations. It would also be appropriate for *my* purposes. Doubtless I could get details about exact dosages on the internet. More difficult would be obtaining the drug itself, and doing it without risk of exposure, either at the time or during any follow-up police investigation. +++ Suddenly the Tallinn trip Rosie was organizing offered more possibilities than mere tourism. Estonia was no longer as rife in black-market transactions as during its Soviet Union days, but it would still be a safer place to seek out what I needed than Finland. In the end, it turned out surprisingly easy, and I took the extortionate price in my stride. The same dealer also supplied me with hypodermic syringes. He brought everything to the hotel on our second evening, and I suspect Rosie saw him leaving my room as she got out of the lift. I wasn't too bothered. She wouldn't know what to make of it, would she?... although the things she found out later were more dangerously compromising.

++

"Violin? What the hell violin are you talking about, Tero?"

"Calm down, Miranda. I think it might be relevant."

She seemed about to walk off, so Tero pressed on urgently.

"An hour after the kids crashed the Civic into the tree, the owner was taken to Haaga to view the damage. He said a valuable violin was missing from the back seat. The police report describes it as a Torini."

"A Torini?" Suddenly Tero had Miranda's attention. "Like the one left with the Estonian girl."

"That's why I'm telling you."

"But they're extremely rare! Anneli Jaakkola's is probably the only one in Helsinki!"

"As rare as *that,* eh? Anyway, no violin turned up at the crash site in Haaga — although the dog handler thought the kid running off into the dark was carrying something sizeable in his arms. Could've been a violin. The kid denies it, of course. What's really strange is this bloke Myrsky Vaarela withdrew his claim the next day. Said it was a mistake. The violin had never been in his car after all."

"Myrsky..." Miranda was thinking back. "Unusual first name... And I've heard it recently. Check on the computer. Is he married? If so, what's his wife's maiden name?"

Tero had it in thirty seconds. "Jaakkola," he said in surprise. "Sonja Jaakkola."

"So he's married to Anneli's big sister, and it has to be the same instrument. But why would Myrsky think his sister-in-law's Torini was on the back seat of his car at 4 am that particular morning? Anneli claims she was on a ferry halfway to Stockholm by then and the Torini was stolen off a tram the previous afternoon."

"What if young Anneli never caught that boat, and the violin disappeared much later — *after* the Orav woman was abducted?"

"Yes, what the hell's the real story here? I reckon Anneli Jaakkola's been feeding us a pack of lies!"

+++

Late on Monday afternoon, having finally slept off the alcoholic extravagance of our night in the Tallinn Hotel bar, I awoke in my flat with a raging thirst and a need to see Juanita again. +++ But first I transported the new acquisitions I'd brought from Estonia to my garage-cum-workshop and laid everything out on the bench. I also rechecked the information I'd gathered on effective dosages of anaesthetic and how often to administer it. Tomorrow was Tuesday, the day of Juanita's weekly violin lesson. She'd be walking that quiet stretch of road from the bus stop alone. She'd even be carrying her instrument. Why then did I find myself, a day early, packing the small rucksack with everything necessary and driving across to the Munkkiniemi suburb where she lived? Could I really be so impatient? I hung about in sight of her home. I cruised everywhere in the area I'd seen her frequent with her friends. I spent hours without a single glimpse of her, experiencing a growing frustration and an icy numbing anger — probably directed as much at my subservience to this obsessional weakness as at Juanita for evading it. Clearly I was out of control. And had been for a long while. Though even now I seemed incapable of embracing the truth with all its hideous implications. +++ At nine o'clock, I abandoned my search and headed towards the city centre, gravitating to an industrial back street area of Kallio where one might occasionally find a lady of the night plying her trade. This early on a Monday evening business was far from brisk. I found a lone hooker anxious to draw my attention as I seemed to be the only punter available — a situation ideal for my purposes. What's more she looked unusually attractive for a common streetwalker. I made a second pass to convince myself it wasn't a trick of the light or a skilful cosmetic illusion before inviting her to slide into the passenger seat beside me. She flippantly gave her name as Anna Karenina, although I guessed she was Estonian rather than Russian. And, once we'd found somewhere secluded to park and engage in what she expected would be a simple trade of money for goods, I had no trouble overpowering her and injecting sufficient anaesthetic into her thigh to render her unconscious. Within half an hour she'd become an unconsenting yet acquiescent guest at my Haaga haven. +++ The feeling of control was sublime — the sense that she was available to my every whim. This woman was a prostitute. I could have paid to have sex with her, but that wouldn't have been the same thing at all. Prostitutes always managed to make me feel *they* were the ones in charge, regardless of what they let me do to them. Their compliance was a hypocritical sham. To possess a woman in *this* way was altogether different. Although, when everything was over, the anticlimax bit hard and with appalling speed. Post-coital paralysis I'd call it. I sat for an interminably long time — two hours, maybe three — just watching her from the other side of the room, both of us perfectly still. In her case, she would never perform a physical action of her own volition again. Such was the legacy of my aberrant hospitality. +++ I strove to keep my mind blank, aided by the physical exhaustion that had blessedly swept over me. At first, she lay there on her back, stretched diagonally across the mattress, twisted slightly at the waist, eyes staring at the ceiling. I turned her to the wall and hid the noose behind her hair, raising her legs into something resembling a foetal position. That way she looked almost natural, as if she were asleep... except for the wrists still bound together at her back. I now doubted that tying her had been necessary. The anaesthetic would almost certainly have been restraint enough. +++ And, when I reached my fourth cheroot, I went outside to smoke it — to escape this place of silent reproach — with no idea whether it was night or day. There were two windows in the workshop: a tiny one at the front, a full-sized one at the back above the workbench. But, for privacy's sake, I'd painted over them. In fact, sunrise must still have been an hour away. Raising the door of the adjoining garage that housed my car, I stepped out into the pre-dawn chill and received a massive jolt of adrenalin. Visible through the trees, little more than fifty yards down the street, a small convoy of police vehicles had gathered with blue lights flashing. My God! They're on to me, I thought! My instinct was to turn tail and run. But which way? Perhaps I was already surrounded! For the first time I considered the possibility of getting caught. Until that moment, I'd felt more or less invulnerable. Hadn't I been careful? Hadn't I planned ahead — as far as one could in such fluid, real-life situations? An element of risk was inevitable. It was even part of the buzz. But to actually get caught! No way could I let *that* happen! +++ In fact, it turned out to be a false alarm. The police weren't there for me. Peering between the trees, in the jagged, multi-layered, stroboscopic light, I could see that someone had piled their car into a lamppost. Perhaps I remembered hearing the muffled crunch from within my brick-walled sanctuary, absorbed there in my self-created universe, incurious about what might be happening to the rest of humanity. +++ I paid some attention now. A dog whined impatiently, and was silenced by a quiet command. A younger voice, on the verge of tears, uttered angry profanities. When an ambulance arrived, the complainant was ushered inside by two uniformed officers. +++ But as I turned away to re-enter the garage, the sight of something quite extraordinary stopped me short. I stared amazed into the long grass. How the hell did *that* get there? It was uncanny! Without really considering why, I picked up the rectangular, canvas-covered case and took it inside, propping it against the wall while I relowered the cantilevered door. But I didn't return to the workshop. I climbed onto the back seat of the car to envelope myself in the blanket that, the previous evening, had concealed the hooker's drugged body. I was aware how it still retained a hint of her perfume. +++ Hours later I awoke stiff and aching. Even with the blanket, I felt chilled. The workshop half of the building was comfortably heated, but I couldn't bring myself to go in there. I reversed the car out onto the gravelled track that led to the road, locked up the building and drove home. There I slept again, for the remainder of the day and well into the evening. Not the sleep of the righteous or the just; rather of cowardice and deliberate amnesia. +++ Eventually, of course, I had to return. And when I did, I realized my folly in putting off what should have been done at once. The girl had lain there alone far too long. Rigor mortis had transformed her young, desirable body into a rigid, unmanageable, skin-wrapped bundle of sticks. The next hour was gruesome, and too much under the censorious gaze of eyes that now proved impossible to close. Donning gloves and a plastic shower cap, I removed the tape from her inelastic wrists to get at the fourth finger more easily, and performed my butchering duties. I'd dumped the ineffectual garden secateurs inherited at the Sibelius Monument and replaced them with a new, heavier-duty pair. For that I was grateful. The job went a lot more smoothly. Next I dragged the uncooperative corpse onto a large plastic sheet where I endeavoured to vacuum it free of all trace evidence. Then, wrapping it in a fresh sheet, I manhandled it into the boot of the car. If I hadn't drawn both legs up to her chest the night before, she would never have fitted in. +++ Almost at the last moment, I spotted the violin case propped inside the garage door, exactly where I'd left it the previous night. Well, why not? It had, after all, appeared mystically and opportunely, as if its use were foreordained. I carried the case into the workshop and, with a damp cloth, meticulously wiped everything, both inside and out: the violin, the bow, the shoulder rest, even the rosin, and finally the case itself — removing any fingerprints that might disclose the instrument's ownership. A label on the underside of the lid bearing a name, address and telephone number I tore out and burnt. +++ Around 3 am I steeled myself to take the body to a preplanned site in Käpylä. In addition to the gloves and shower cap, I wore shoe covers and an ankle length plastic mac — all of which I disposed of later in a totally different suburb. +++ The following day, having gained some distance from the affair, I regretted leaving the violin with the Estonian woman. Of course, it had served to complete my tableau. But by whose design? I knew nothing of the violin's origins. It was hard to imagine some benevolent deity consorting with the likes of me, and stepping in to deliver an unsolicited gift of such appropriateness. A gnawing, superstitious doubt was whispering: *Betrayal!* Had the violin been left outside my garage fortress as a kind of Trojan horse? Would it ultimately be my downfall? +++ Meanwhile, I selected a quotation for the fourth Ainola letter: Originally an apology for Sibelius's persistent and excessive use of alcohol, it reflected my own present shift of mood: *I know you must find my fallibility and capriciousness almost intolerable. Well, of course, it's true: I shouldn't allow myself to give way to these impulses. Perhaps I can learn to govern them in future; although I very much fear the contrary.* Indeed I did! I'd stayed away from the vicinity of Juanita's home for forty-eight hours. I'd failed to be waiting for her above the motorway as she walked home from her Tuesday evening violin lesson. I'd even slept through those critical hours. But did I really persuade myself it was all over? That I was cured? How could I have been so naive? +++ Now it's time to consider a wholly separate event... The day after I'd deposited the Estonian woman's body in Käpylä, a young music student was strangled on the stairs of her apartment block in Kuusitie. Nothing to do with me, of course. But, as you're aware, its synchronization with Nick's fifth lecture would sort out a longstanding alibi problem — provided I could convincingly link her death to the earlier four. That presented me with a dilemma. Could I assume this to be the same unknown party who'd left Liisa Louhi's body at the Sibelius Monument? Could I also rely on him repeating his trick with the finger? Had he succeeded this time and taken the finger away with him? Miranda told Rosie that the Kuusitie murder was in the same series as the earlier ones. Surely that had to mean the finger was missing. But would it be the *same* finger? And would there be any kind of musical connection? I doubted it... until the newspapers proved me wrong: because, yes, the latest victim was another music student! Just what I needed to tie this fifth girl into the sequence! So now it definitely seemed worthwhile sending a message to The Ainola Residence on my unknown colleague's behalf. Fine in principle, but with one major drawback. I didn't have the latest victim's finger to provide the signature inked print. Well, I'd have to use someone else's, and the obvious choice was the Estonian hooker's. It would anyway offer some measure of authenticity. The trouble was I'd already dumped her finger the day before: wrapped in newspaper, tied up in a plastic supermarket bag and chucked in a rubbish bin at the back of a block of flats half a mile away. I had to go back in the middle of the night and burrow around in all that filth and stink to find the right bag again! +++ The quote I chose on this occasion was: *Even composers of high integrity may sometimes feel obliged to compromise, and bow to the prevailing consensus of style and idiom. Nevertheless, works that fail to reflect the genuine personality of the artist cannot hope to be taken seriously for all time.* It was an obscure reference to the fact that this fifth murder wasn't genuinely my own work. Naturally I couldn't be too transparent about that. +++ Over the next week, I managed to stay away from Juanita's neighbourhood. The emotional hangover from my encounter with the Estonian seemed to help. I slept as much as possible. I took advantage of every chance to distract myself. Sometimes I drank too much. The Easter holiday brought a temporary respite in the presence of good company. +++ But when Tuesday came round again, accompanied by that window of opportunity only Juanita's weekly violin lesson could offer, my thin veneer of resolve vanished... and with disconcerting ease. Mid-afternoon, in a state of perfect calm, as if it were the most natural thing in the world, I drove to Haaga and readied my garage playground for another visitor. I actually remember whistling to myself while I worked. All of the warning voices that should have been screaming in my head remained shamefully silent — as if there could never have been any doubt about returning to this unholy enterprise. Obviously I'd just been recouping my strength. +++ And so I gathered everything necessary into my backpack and took the car by a roundabout route to Munkkiniemi, parking at the quieter end of the burger restaurant forecourt to give myself a clear view of the bus stop where Juanita would get off. Even as the number 18 approached, I saw her on board, negotiating the aisle towards the exit doors, violin cradled tight against her chest. I pulled onto the dead end street overlooking the motorway, and positioned my car against the pavement in the shelter of some tall, dense maple trees that effectively concealed me from prying eyes at the windows of the computer research facility further up the hill. I got out and waited on the pavement beside the rear passenger door. My intention was to pull her onto the back-seat as she passed and sedate her with an injection of *Comatin*. A daring manoeuvre — certainly not without risk — but, I felt sure, a viable one. Imagine my dismay when Juanita came into view a mere twenty yards away accompanied by a teenage boy. Where in the Devil's name did *he* come from? With no choice but to abort the operation, I jumped back into the driving seat, made a U-turn and got the hell out of there. Once more I'd been thwarted! This time at the very last moment! +++ I drove around for several hours, burning up petrol and burning with resentment at my ill fortune. Dusk prematurely deepened into darkness as a bank of cloud, that matched my mood, spread a louring mantle over the city. I found myself entering Kallio's red-light district again. Perhaps I sought solace with another streetwalker, but the sky suddenly opened. A torrential downpour drove hooker and model citizen alike for cover. And at that point, I decided to accept no substitutes. Juanita was the true focus of my need. She was its very source. Only by fulfilling my destiny with *her* could I achieve closure and move on. At least, such was my absurd delusion. +++ Another week passed, another seven days of near delirium. I followed Juanita back and forth between school and home, and watched her with her friends in the evening — now at a more cautious distance, fearful of alerting her too early to my presence. In retrospect, I realize how I awaited our approaching union with a sense of dread — as if in anticipation of my *own* impending execution. But this was something I'd brooded over far too long. It was no longer undoable; and, in the doing, it would bring me only dry dust and ashes. +++ She got off the bus quite alone that following Tuesday evening and walked obediently and unguardedly into my unhallowed embrace. Many, many hours we shared that night in my workshop love-nest, and not one of them could consummate my fantasies. At close quarters, she was as beautiful as I had supposed — her silky skin, the wonderfully varied textures of her flesh. Yes, everything just as I'd imagined... everything, that is, except for myself. How was it that I could feel so detached? Why was I unable to let go and blissfully revel in this longed for experience? +++ Years ago and many thousands of miles away, on that night we spent with the first Juanita, my mentor Ramirez had suggested the preliminary diversion of shaving the young Indian girl's pubis clean — had actually asked *me* to do the honours. No doubt he saw it as an extra little treat for his English gentleman guest. And enjoy it I did: the intimacy of the act, the vulnerability of the subject and, throughout, Juanita's shy, nervous giggling. I had, in fact, already repeated the procedure with the Estonian girl, but expected to recapture the full pleasure of that earlier experience with my reincarnated Juanita. Even in this I was disappointed. And as the night unravelled, so did my misery and my bitter frustration. It wasn't supposed to be like this! It

421

should have been the most wonderful experience of my life! Where was the happy ending? And, despite the pacifying effects of the drug, Juanita kept whimpering for her Daddy to come and help her. Eventually I could stand no more of her pitiful sobbing. I had to finish it. +++ The Estonian woman taught me an important lesson: the consequences of delay. I wouldn't risk having to handle *this* girl when she was rigid and cold. I closed her eyes and performed all of the last rites and observances necessary to preserve my forensic anonymity. And, as I worked, I noticed that the whimpering and sobbing hadn't stopped after all. It continued in my own head. And the words *Hjälp mig!* — Help me! — were now mouthed repeatedly by my own lips. I won't try to overglorify the regret. Perhaps I did at last feel sympathy for this beautiful young woman whose life I had so pointlessly extinguished. But it was mixed with more than an equal amount of self-pity. +++ I drove her to a spot not far away on the edge of Haaga — a lorrypark set back from the road — normally deserted, but this morning occupied by a single articulated vehicle. I used it as a screen to hide my ministrations from the early rush-hour traffic. But then it occurred to me that the driver of the lorry might be asleep in his cab, so I ended up laying out my tableau in irreverent haste. All the while I was afraid I might start crying, and I didn't know for sure if the police could trace a person's DNA from tear drops. +++ Three days elapsed before I roused myself enough to send a follow-up letter. And then it came like a cry in the wilderness: *It seems to me that amongst the most unfortunate persons on earth are composers who experience their work as an inner compulsion. My themes are tyrants. I must always surrender to their bidding.*

++

Miranda needed to get to the physical vicinity where she thought her sister might be; if only to feel less helpless. They set off for Haaga, and she let Tero drive, knowing she was in no fit state herself. As soon as they emerged from the Pasila underground car park, Miranda dialled Anneli Jaakkola's number.

"Are you alone, Miss Jaakkola?"

"Yes, why do you ask?"

"Your mother's not in earshot?"

"No, there's only me in the house, but..."

"It's time for the truth," Miranda interrupted her. "Your lies have already led to another girl's death. You never actually caught that boat to Stockholm, did you? — any more than you lost your violin on the tram! You had quite different plans for that night with your brother-in-law, Myrsky."

The story came out amidst weeping and remorse, but Miranda had little sympathy for the young woman's protestations of hopeless, undying love for her sister's husband. Anneli admitted: Yes, she and Myrsky had become lovers — a dangerous game in such a tightknit family. Their plan was to spend Monday night together in a Helsinki motel room while everyone else drove north to her grandmother's funeral. Then Myrsky would take Anneli to the airport so she could catch the earliest flight to Stockholm and still be in time for her violin audition.

At around 4 am, Anneli suggested something almost as taboo as sharing semi-incestuous sex. She wanted them to shed their veil of secrecy and daringly have breakfast together in a public place: *Just like any normal couple.* Myrsky was persuaded, and they drove to an all-night service-station café. No time to return to the motel before catching the flight, so Anneli's luggage was now in the car. The last eight hours of euphoria had made her careless. When the Civic was stolen, the valuable violin was lying on the back seat.

"Try to understand!" pleaded Anneli. "I couldn't let my mother know. It's why I told her the violin was stolen from a tram. I would've told the truth at the police station... honestly, I would! But you turned up and said you'd already found it. And you made me tell everything in front of my mother. I *had* to carry on with the lie, didn't I? Think of all the grief I'd've caused otherwise."

Miranda didn't waste more time on Anneli Jaakkola. She cut the call with no words of forgiveness. *For Christ's sake, Anneli, what about Beatrice's mother's grief? What about mine?*

Yes, Rosie was in terrible danger, but the violin might yet help them locate her. The big question was how did the Torini get to be planted with the Estonian woman's body that following night?

At the flat in Haaga, which the younger car thief shared with his mother, they confronted him face to sullen face. He came to the door, bare-foot, lank-haired and uncooperative.

Miranda went straight on the offensive: "You're in deep shit when you get to court. No more community-service deals. They'll lock you up for sure. But help us and it could make things better for you. We want to know what happened to that violin you took?"

"I've told you lot, I didn't take no violin!"

But eventually he admitted to running off with it.

"Thought I'd cut my losses, didn't I? Get *something* away after all the hassle. But they sent that fucking dog after me, so I dumped it."

"*Where* did you dump it?"

"A bit off the road. Round the back of some trees — in the long grass. Next to a building."

"What sort of building?"

"Don't know. Red brick. Store rooms or something. Maybe it was garages."

Garages!!

"Get some shoes on!" commanded Miranda. "And show us where these garages are!"

+++

Remember that bloke in Chelsea, years ago? Malcolm Something-or-Other. Third-generation Afro-Brit with a Manchurian accent. Gay as a fruit bat. Used to hang around with our crowd when he wasn't cruising the 'boy-meets-boy' bars. Riotous sense of humour. Superb company. And I was enjoying some of it in the pub one evening — that and a few pints — when suddenly he gets all serious on me. *You know, mate*, he says, *you're always going on about women — about this gorgeous arse and that fabulous pair of tits, and all the rest of it. But it strikes me you don't really like women at all*. It wasn't a chat-up line. He wasn't trying to open my eyes to a latent homosexuality he could step in and exploit. He was simply making an observation. And I realized how well on target he'd been. When it comes down to it, I *don't* like women. In fact, I *resent* them. They've got something I desperately want, and most of the time they won't let me have it. What's more, they seem to take a perverse pleasure in withholding it from me and revelling in their power. +++ I'm not like *some* blokes — good-looking enough for women to perpetually throw themselves at my feet. Just the opposite. They make me jump through hoops for small pickings. Sometimes they give you a bit of a come-on and make you think you're in with a chance. But the moment they smell the need on you they lose interest. Trouble is: it's bloody difficult to act casual when your whole being's churning in desperation. The only really friendly type seem to be the 'wouldn't-you-fancy-a-semidetached-in-the-suburbs-with-a-double-garage-and-two-point-four-kids' brigade. I've tried playing ball with some of them — at least superficially — but I know they'd never let me do what I really want, even if I got round to suggesting it. +++ So, when I come to think about it, practically all my friendships — all the genuine relationships I've ever formed — they've been with other men, and *precisely* because men hold no physical attraction for me. With women it's almost impossible to see beyond the sexual signals their bodies are broadcasting. And now you'll ask me about Rosie. Well, she's an exception. Because basically she strikes me as asexual. Pretty, it's true, but simply not my type. I know some men get horny as hell and positively drool over skinny women. But not me. Theresa's in the same category. And with her and Rosie I've been grateful for my disinterest. A powerful sex-drive is no less than a scourge. That's something I've come to realize. In so many ways, life would be better without it. Look at the appalling things it's driven me to! And, to protect myself from discovery, the awful thing I'm driven to next! +++ I hear you asking: *What about the preciousness of life?* It's something we've often talked about. And, in principle, I concur. Really I do! Yes, I wonder how it's been so difficult to live up to such a fundamental axiom — how I could've given way to these twisted personal obsessions and destroyed life so flagrantly! I don't understand it myself. And the inner struggle is tearing me apart. I doubt I can withstand it much longer. +++ During my Sibelius research, I turned up something that struck a resonant chord: a quote from one of his buddies, Adolph Paul, the playwright. He wrote Jean a letter, talking about a play he'd just written. He said: *Do you think people like to be confronted by a crime so psychologically motivated and presented that it loses the very character of a crime? Or are they willing to confront the possibility that madness isn't madness after all?* +++ I expect you're ready to label what I've done as 'Evil' with a neon-flashing capital E. Of course, it's reassuring to think in such terms — easier to resort to the hypothetical existence of some abstract, indefinable quality than confront an unbearable paradox. But, in the end, I'd prefer to go for a concept like 'Accountability'. Doesn't have the same ring to it as 'Evil', I admit, but then we won't need to fall back on any kind of *moral* allusions. We can be pragmatic. +++ A society like ours seems to be based on 'freedom', but obviously there have to be limits. We can't let every individual do exactly what he wants — not when it could infringe on somebody else's freedom and security. So we label these infringements 'criminal' and discourage them with the threat of punishment. Some people see punishment as meting out just deserts for antisocial behaviour. Others see it as a deterrent. Well, maybe it does keep most of the population in check. Look at the mayhem when society breaks down, and the normal restraints are removed: riots, wars, pogroms, ethnic cleansing sprees. Previously law-abiding citizens let out their suppressed aggression and hatred. Yes, maybe the deterrent idea works for most people. But what about the others? A repeat offender's urge to break the rules seems more deep-seated, more like an intrinsic aspect of his personality. Would it be cheating for me to suggest inescapably genetic? Anyway, he doesn't see punishment as a deterrent. It's just an annoying obstacle to be avoided, and the compulsion to 'err' overrides the threat. +++ I've wondered which camp I belong to. Looks like the second, doesn't it? But I feel a bit borderline. In the end, I don't know if locking me away for a while would change anything — not now I've got a taste for my sins. I'd probably still be searching for that ultimate experience and start all over again when they let me out. So it wouldn't be safe to try the experiment. +++ But I'd like to ask you, do you think these cravings I suffer are truly my own fault? Couldn't it just be an illness — like drug addiction, or alcoholism, or compulsive gambling? Was it just bad luck to be born with an infirmity like mine? In essence, is it any different from being born with some *physical* infirmity: cerebral palsy or blindness? I suppose you'll point out how someone with a physical disability strives to make the most of what fate and DNA have dealt them. They can expect support from family, friends and society at large, but they wouldn't wish to subject others to the fruits of their own suffering —

even if they could figure out a way to do it... just like a person with HIV has no right to infect others, whatever inner bitterness they might feel. +++ Truth is I don't know! All this ethical stuff seems so messy to me. Sometimes I've imagined discussing the whole thorny problem with you — of making confession, you could say — especially in the long night hours. Rather like Sibelius conducting his Eighth Symphony, I've even dreamt of doing it — vivid, emancipating dreams of redemption where your readiness to accept and forgive me have held absolute clarity and certainty in my mind. But to do the same thing for real — in front of a live audience, so to speak... Could I ever find the courage? +++ If I've truly managed to love someone, I suppose it must be you. The capacity to feel a sense of loyalty and empathy for at least *one* other human being on the planet has been a thing to treasure in my otherwise narcissistic life. Your joys and sorrows have been mine — even your successes with women... Well, you've always had more luck in that direction. But, amazingly, I've never resented it, never tried to compete with you. No, I'd never allow our friendship to be tainted with jealousy. Significant, don't you think? +++ I know, even if you *could* forgive me, you'd insist I should've tried harder to overcome my driven urges. The trouble is they aren't exactly driven — not in a furious way. It's more of a subtle, relentless undercurrent that carries you from one small step to the next. Each step seems harmless in itself, but cumulatively they bring you to disaster. And, when that happens, I suppose one has to accept the consequences. If an individual's incapable of controlling his destructive behaviour, society's going to want to do it for him. I understand it's inevitable that people feel pity for the victims. That's a right and proper response. But, as you slam the cell door shut and throw away the key, spare an ounce of pity for the other victim — the one who couldn't resist the unhealthy impulses in his dark and misshapen soul.

++

Set about ten yards off the road, with a gravelled track for access, and overarched by luxuriant horse chestnut trees, the single-storey, red-brick building looked insignificant enough. It seemed to have once comprised a pair of adjoining garages, though one of the doors was now bricked in.

On the mad dash here, Miranda had requested backup. Uniformed officers were fanning out on all sides, as she and Tero approached rapidly from the front. The one remaining cantilevered door was locked, but peering through the small dirty window beside it, Miranda could make out a pale-coloured vehicle in the gloomy garage interior.

"It's a VW!" she whispered, in burgeoning hope — although, from this angle there was no way of seeing the registration. "Pray, God, we're not too late!"

She ran to the small window fronting the other half of the building, hoping to confirm her sister's presence inside. The glass had been painted over. And, as a burly officer prepared to attack the garage door with an iron battering ram, Miranda could wait no longer. Scanning the ground at her feet, she reached down with both hands to pick up a large angular rock.

He was perched on the edge of a hard-backed wooden chair — leaning forward, forearms on knees. Rosie slumped before him in the old armchair, fully-dressed and semi-conscious, her head lolling uncertainly against one shoulder. The noose still encircled her neck exactly where he'd placed it an hour earlier — although not tight enough to threaten blood flow or breathing. A hypodermic syringe and several ampoules of anaesthetic — some empty, some full — lay nearby on the workbench.

He'd been talking to her spasmodically. He doubted she could hear him, even if her eyes were marginally open, but he went on regardless: "... so, you see, Rosie, without realizing it, you were privy to some seriously incriminating stuff. What if you'd let any of it slip to Miranda? Then things got even worse. As you were rushing off to your cello lesson yesterday, you grabbed those letters in the hallway. Trying to help out — being your usual sweet-natured self. Unfortunately, along with all the scholarship and job applications was a very different kind of letter, one with an address that might've aroused your curiosity: 'The Ainola Residence'. Perhaps you paid no attention to it, I don't know... but how could I take that chance? The risk of Miranda finding out something dangerous had escalated by several orders of magnitude. Which is why, Rosie, most regrettably, I came to the decision I'd have to do something about it. Yes, something about *you*, I'm afraid. And here we are... all ready to rumble."

He reached for a small flat tin lying on the workbench, drew out a cheroot, placed it between his lips and carefully lit it.

"Surprise you, does it, seeing me smoke? Just an old weakness rebreaking the surface — keeping all the *new* ones company, you might say."

There was silence while he drew long and smoothly on the cheroot; then trickled smoke slowly from the corners of his mouth.

"I've already planned the seventh and final missive to Ainola. It goes: *Looking back, every one of my symphonies appears a torment to me. But they cannot be rewritten. They must remain as they are.* Trouble is I'm not so sure any more... that, at least, this *last* one can't be rewritten. No, I doubt whether I can go through with it this time. Although you can surely see what a dilemma I'm in! If I let you live, they'll incarcerate me — lock me up for good. Then life won't be worth living. On the other hand, if I destroy *yours*, Rosie, how can I live with myself anyway? I'll lose every last vestige of self-respect, and blight whatever life's left to me — make it, in effect, unliveable. At your dinner party a few weeks back, Miranda was talking about her 'victim-anonymity principle'. She said: in the absence of passion, lust or anger, cold-blooded violence can only be inflicted on an *anonymous* victim. That way, the victim remains objectivized and doesn't signify a *real* person to the attacker. I can see what she meant. Getting rid of the Bäckström woman was one thing: it was pure retaliation. She was a scheming, self-serving bitch. Anyway I'd only met her the once. I didn't really know her. And with those other girls... well, all I could think about was their bodies, of possessing them physically. But, with you, it's quite different, Rosie. We've grown close over these last weeks. I've taken so much pleasure in your company — in your spontaneity and your poignant innocence — not to mention the extraordinary way you wield a cello! Yes, you've become dear to me. Like a sister. Theresa's the only other woman I've had such chaste feelings for. So how can I destroy all that and obliterate everything you are and everything you represent? On the other hand, how can I not? Damned if I do or don't, isn't it?"

429

At that moment a repetitious thundering began at the door of the adjoining garage. The whole building was shuddering. Seconds later, the small window at the front of the workshop shattered into fragments, shards of glass skating across the floor at his feet. He jumped up, knocking over the wooden chair, panic flooding his body.

Miranda was at the window, shouting: "Rosie! Rosie, are you all right? For God's sake, Phillip, leave her alone! There's no point any more."

"And if you think this is the *seventh* one," Tero shouted, his face just visible beside Miranda's, "your freako other-half's beaten you to it!"

"Let Rosie go!" Miranda pleaded. "You can't really want to hurt her. It's all over, Phillip! Give yourself up!"

They watched through the broken window as their quarry levered his tall, bony frame onto the workbench, trying to reach the larger window as an escape route. Hopeless, of course. He realized they must have every exit covered. But then something unforeseen occurred, and with horrifying speed. Losing his balance, he clutched for a handhold, upsetting the demijohn of liquid ether, pulling it down as he himself fell to the concrete floor. The glass smashed. The highly flammable liquid scattered, drenching his clothes and hair — was at once ignited by the still burning cheroot he'd thrown down seconds earlier.

And yet, even now, in extremis, and amidst mortal fear and agony, an irrelevant thought flickered across his consciousness. As searing hot fumes penetrated deep into his lungs, Phillip Burton no longer doubted that the legendary manuscript for Sibelius's Eighth Symphony had been consumed by fire.

Tapiola

Symphonic Poem
Largamente—Allegro moderato—Allegro—Allegro moderato—Allegro—Allegro moderato

* *

~ **B**loody single-sex schools! They're an abomination! Anyone espousing them should be stood against the quadrangle wall and shot.

~ *Extreme! But, in essence, a sound argument.*

~ My sodding mother's idea, of course — sending me off to boarding school. Part of her social-climbing agenda. Father never would've thought that one up on his own. Weren't *you* the lucky bastard? Day grammar school, for Chrissake!

~ *Boys only, though. No way of meeting any girls. Most of us didn't even manage out of school hours. No idea how to go about it! They always seemed so unobtainable. I should've joined a youth club, amateur dramatics or something. All I ever got to do was ogle them in the street.*

~ That's what I mean... You lucky bastard! We never even got *that* close. Locked away from the rest of society... Queer's paradise, of course. Got to say that for it. Fine, if you were into that sort of thing. After a couple of miserable gropings in the showers, I realized I wasn't.

~ *Looking back, it's like girls were some kind of alien species.*

~ Scarcely human.

~ *Little more than sex-objects.*

~ Raw material for our mewling adolescent fantasies.

~ *Took me a few years in the real world to shake all that off... the distorted mindset, I mean.*

~ I doubt *I* ever did!

433

Tapiola

~ *So is that your excuse for what you did to those unfortunate women?*

~ No, that was just part of my interminable search for reality.

~ *Don't be facetious!*

~ I assure you, I'm not! It's the emptiness, you see. That's the *real* source of all the trouble. I've sometimes wondered if boredom and depression are built into humanity as evolutionary strategies. They force us to fall back on the old faithfuls — on our basic instinctive survival appetites: the last things to desert us when all else fails.

~ *Sorry, I don't get it!*

~ I'm only saying that when we get bored or depressed we end up eating too much, or indulging ourselves in sexual excess.

~ *And that's some kind of evolutionary strategy?*

~ What the hell other purpose could it serve? I can't see boredom and depression carrying much survival value in themselves, can you? I'm starting to suspect a lot of the things we humans get up to are just responses to this built-in sense of meaninglessness. All those side-issues: art, religion, war, drugs. Some of them work by revving up the adrenaline flow — the body's natural response to fear. And, of course, fear's another survival device we can rely on to give a sense of reality. I mean, why do so many of us look for cheap thrills? Why do people climb mountains? Drive too fast? Gamble their homes away? And then there's the phenomenon of spectator sports? Some bloke pays good money to sit on a hard seat and watch a bunch of other blokes kicking a ball round a field. Why's he there? Obviously because every time the ball gets near one of the nets, a massive dose of adrenaline floods through his system. It's a dependable buzz. Takes his mind off all that emptiness.

~ *Too bloody cynical for my taste!*

~ Oh, it's easy for *you* to talk! You've got your musical creativity, haven't you? You and Sibelius, and the rest of you bloody artists. It all works as therapy for you: a chance to express the very essence of that human void, that chronic sense of meaninglessness, the 'cosmic loneliness' that Nick mentioned in his last lecture.

~ *I suppose you're right — at least, as long as the inspiration lasts...*

~ But what've *I* got? A talent for playing the fool — for clowning it up in public! Believe me, that only goes so far. It doesn't help much to keep one from the edge of the abyss.

* *

The rowlocks creaking rhythmically. The gentle slap of the oars dipping in and out. The trickling of droplets back onto the mirror-like surface with every return stroke...

"You've drifted off again," she commented.

"Sorry!" He shifted position in the stern of the boat; offered a brief smile in further apology. "It's just that, since his death, I've been looking back over those last few weeks. And I find myself holding make-believe dialogues with him... you know, weaving fragments of conversations that actually happened with fragments that might've happened — though now, of course, it's too late. I remember your father describing the same kind of thing back at your dinner party in April. And it's been happening to me a lot recently. I suppose I'm trying to come to terms with it all, to understand how he could've sunk into such depravity."

She glanced over her shoulder to check their position, stopped rowing and shipped the oars. The warm hollow resonance of wood upon wood echoed in reply from the surrounding shoreline before a windless silence crept back in to fill the vacuum. In its turn, the lake's magic mirror echoed a perfect, inverted and indigo-tinted image of the pine and spruce forest that encircled a vast cirrus-flecked sky. Little more than an hour and a half to midnight, but the sun still hovered hypnotically above the horizon. A Midsummer's Eve bonfire glowed on a rocky promontory at the far end of the lake.

Suddenly a bright peal of laughter, followed by a softer baritone chuckle and the metallic clattering of kitchen utensils reached them across the three hundred yards that separated the boat from the cottage. Rosie and Nick were busy preparing the evening meal.

"I was afraid we'd never hear her laugh again. She's proved more resilient than any of us gave her credit for. Still has the occasional nightmare, of course. She didn't want to talk about it at first. It's only the last few days she's opened up — started helping me piece everything together."

435

He nodded. "I can understand her reluctance. It's hard to face the fact that someone you've known as a friend — for so many years, in my case — could be capable of such atrocities."

"I was appalled myself when I saw that picture of him crouched over his hit-and-run victim. That was the moment I realized how deeply he'd been involved. And then he abducted Rosie. I suppose it's crazy, but my first reaction was to try and phone him. Don't know whether I wanted to plead with him or scream abuse. But his mobile was switched off... which also made it impossible to trace his location. Did you know he was renting a lock-up garage in Haaga?"

"Never said a word."

"We were lucky to get there in time. But, if it's any consolation, I don't think he would've hurt Rosie in the end. He'd had her there for well over an hour. Apart from keeping her sedated, he didn't lay a finger on her."

This was painful ground. She wished their first meeting in a month could have been less distressing... although she fully understood his need. He'd left for Britain so soon after that final tragic episode, and with so many unanswered questions. There were things she could learn from *him* as well. On the drive from the airport this morning their conversation had been desultory and strained. They'd both known that, sooner or later, the ghosts would have to be laid to rest.

"Tell me more about this hit-and-run accident," he said.

"It was back in November. He knocked down a jogger in the early hours of the morning. We presume he was driving over the limit."

"He had a history of that."

"It's probably why he passed the old Renault over to you and bought himself a new VW — to be shot of the daily reminder."

"I thought he was doing *me* a favour!"

"There was a woman with him in the Renault when the accident happened — a journalist — and she took a photo of the whole thing... started blackmailing him with it. We tracked through their internet log-ons and their banking records. She'd already extorted quite a large sum from him before he made his move. I suppose you knew he'd inherited half a million from his uncle?"

"The first I heard about it was when his mother told me at the funeral. Anyway, you've explained his reasons for getting rid of the journalist woman. What I don't understand is why he had to kill Liisa."

"He didn't. He couldn't have. An hour or more either side of the critical time he was sitting with *me* in the Ateljé. Fact is I gave him a perfect alibi for that first murder. Eventually you turned up at the restaurant too. Then around midnight you both walked me home and, as I understand it, the two of you went off to Humalistonkatu for a nightcap."

"That's right."

"But, after he left your place, he must've decided — God only knows why! — to walk down to Sibelius Park. He found Liisa's body there at the Monument, and that must've been when he got the idea of using her murder to cover up one of his own. At the time, he had no idea there was any connection between you and Liisa. He'd never seen her before. But he adapted what he found at the murder scene and added some extra details of his own: like giving a sexual slant to the crime. Our DCI later admitted he'd had reservations about anyone attempting a sexual assault outdoors in such freezing conditions. The temperature dropped to minus twelve that night."

"Brass monkeys, etcetera..."

"Exactly! But he then doctored the crime scene even further by propping the violin up against the rock below Sibelius's head as a kind of dramatic touch. And he took Liisa's fourth finger away with him. His plan was to send us a taunting letter via the Ainola Museum with a quotation from Sibelius in Swedish. Swedish was one of the languages he did at university, wasn't it?"

"Yes."

"And he placed an inked print from Liisa's finger at the bottom to authenticate the letter. He then matched the follow-up killings to this same set of characteristic features. All very intricate — over-intricate really — but I'm ashamed to say he had us fooled."

"So, if he didn't kill Liisa, who did?"

"A porter at the Helsinki Conservatory. Jorma Mannila."

"I remember him! Weird as hell. An obvious suspect, I'd've thought. How come you took so long to spot him?"

"It's always a problem with a major case like this — coordinating everything. So many personnel involved. There's a risk of jobs getting done twice unintentionally, or not getting done at all. The Conservatory's computer worksheets seemed to eliminate Mannila. They indicated he was on evening shift when Liisa was murdered. No one took the other porter, Olli Koskinen, seriously as a suspect — much too old and frail — so Koskinen didn't get questioned enough at the beginning. He'd had a terrible toothache on the Thursday night, and he needed to get to a dentist. First thing next morning he phoned Mannila to ask if they could swap shifts. Mannila agreed, but he did something odd when he arrived at work that Friday morning: he punched *Koskinen's* code number into the clocking-in machine instead of his own. Koskinen took over at 3.15 pm, and Mannila explained he'd exchanged the codes to make the record look neater — to keep their shift-swap an unofficial, no-questions-asked affair. Koskinen was obliged to continue the pattern by using *Mannila's* code for the later shift. That's how the computer record got reversed."

"So you think Mannila was manufacturing himself an alibi?"

"No, I'd be surprised if he was that well organized. Most of his actions strike me as irrational and unplanned. Koskinen told us that Mannila had done this same clocking-in trick a few months earlier when they'd swapped shifts for some other reason. It's just another example of the strange way Mannila's mind works. But it really messed up the investigation. By the time Koskinen was questioned more thoroughly, he'd convinced himself his emergency visit to the dentist had been on *Thursday* morning — *not* Friday — which made the shift-swap seem irrelevant to the murder. In fact, he never even bothered to mention it. An important part of succeeding with an investigation is knowing the right questions to ask. If we'd spotted the discrepancy sooner, we might've prevented some of those other young women from dying."

The pain and guilt were evident on her face, but there was no obvious way to comfort her. He tried another question: "You said Liisa's fingerprint was used as a kind of signature on the first letter. Was that his only reason for cutting it off?"

"No, you see, the finger idea was originally the *porter's*. In his subsequent ramblings Mannila admitted how he tried to take Liisa's finger but the secateurs got jammed... so he had to leave without either the finger *or* the secateurs. This whole grisly business originates from more than twenty years ago. Mannila's mother lost her right-hand fourth finger in an industrial accident, and she explained to little Jorma how it was punishment for her sins: she was being punished down here on Earth so that, when she died, they'd let her straight into Heaven. All three of Mannila's victims were sinners in his distorted vision of the world. He believed he had a duty to send them directly off to their Maker before they could slide any deeper into wickedness. By removing their fingers he gave them a chance to atone for their sins and achieve grace! The man's obviously deranged. He was always unstable — bound to his mother in a claustrophobic love-loathe relationship. But, when she died last Christmas and left him on his own, he seems to have slipped right over the edge. I doubt he'll ever get to trial. But we've managed to piece a lot together from his uncontrollable outbursts. He has a sort of feral cunning, but that's combined with a self-righteous certainty that he's God's chosen instrument on Earth. His need to instruct us of the fact overrides his survival instincts. And aside from what he's given us directly, we visited his garden allotment in Käpylä — a place he'd been going to with his mum since childhood. Inside the allotment shed we found a sort of shrine to his mother with a large framed photo of her when she was about twenty. The resemblance to Liisa Louhi is uncanny. He'd also constructed a couple of smaller shrines — one for Liisa and one for his second victim Jaana Saari. He'd had more luck removing Jaana's fourth finger, so that was included, gruesomely cushioned on a bed of cotton wool in a little ornate wooden box!"

"I don't get why he had to kill them at all. What terrible sins had Liisa committed to deserve such awful punishment?"

"No sins as we'd perceive them, but I think Liisa's personality was part of the problem. Her tendency to flirt with every man she came into contact with was probably her undoing. You can imagine her occasionally asking Mannila for help — quite innocent little favours, of course — but smiling a tad too sweetly, standing a little too close. He wasn't equipped to interpret these harmless signals for what they really were. In his own painfully repressed fashion, he must've fallen in love with her. At first he thought she was pure and untouchable — like the idealistic image he'd created of his mother. And you have to remember, Liisa was an extraordinary Mrs Mannila look-alike. The trouble was, when he found out the truth that Liisa was far from untouchable — that someone was doing a lot more than just touch her — he felt betrayed. He transmuted his personal jealousy into something else — into God's wrath which he persuaded himself he was duty-bound to assuage."

"Are you saying my affair with Liisa was what triggered this whole thing off?"

"In a sense, yes."

"But how did he find out? About me and Liisa?"

"No curtains on your bedroom window, are there? And it looks straight onto the park. I went and checked myself last week. There's a balcony runs around the top floor of the library with a fire-escape ladder straight up to it. Standing on that balcony gives a direct view into your bedroom — makes me blush to think of it! — so he could've watched every little move you and Liisa were making that Friday evening. I imagine it was then he decided to weave his first noose from the speaker cable he found in Liisa's handbag."

"He had Liisa's handbag?"

"Yes, he'd followed her from the Conservatory that afternoon... first to her accompanist's flat in Mariankatu, and then to the Forum Shopping Centre. She put the bag down to try on a coat and he snatched it. Plain nosiness, I suspect. He just wanted a look at her private possessions... and to handle them, of course. We found some of Liisa's stuff — lipstick, blusher, things like that — as part of her allotment shrine. He appropriated what he wanted, and chucked the bag with the rest of its contents down the back of the Conservatory concert hall. A careless thing to do, but a lot of his behaviour was irrational."

"You said Mannila had *three* victims. Why did he kill the other two?"

"When Liisa didn't live up to expectations, Mannila transferred his infatuation to Jaana Saari. She was also very beautiful in an innocent, angelic sort of way. But he later caught her and her boyfriend graphically groping each other in a Conservatory corridor. That tipped him over the edge again. He stole an electric cable from a MiniDisc recorder left in one of the classrooms and, the same afternoon, he followed Jaana home — via her piano accompanist's flat

— and strangled the poor girl on the stairs of her apartment block. The reasons for killing the accompanist, Hanna Kettunen, were even more obscure."

"I remember her from one of my counterpoint classes."

"She'd been acting as an accompanist for both Liisa and Jaana, and Mannila got it into his head she was somehow responsible for corrupting them. He'd followed Liisa to Hanna's shortly before he watched you and Liisa carousing in the bedroom. Then Jaana went and visited the pianist almost immediately after he'd caught her heavy-petting with her boyfriend. Apparently that was enough to form the connection in his mind, bringing retribution down on Hanna as well. She doesn't seem to have merited a shrine in the allotment shed, but he did have the mercy to cut off her finger and give her a chance at Heaven like the other two! We'd been a bit puzzled by the sequence of secateurs used for the seven finger amputations. We realize now there were *three* pairs: Mannila's original *Jardine 360s*, which he was forced to abandon at the Sibelius Monument. They passed over, of course, to his copycat, who struggled with two more victims before deciding to replace them with a more effective, heavier-duty pair for victims four and six. Meanwhile, Mannila bought himself another pair of *360s*, which he used on the fifth and seventh victims. Something else that confused us was the fact that Mannila didn't sexually violate any of his victims. Certainly we can assume a sexual motivation behind his killings, but at a very suppressed level. Also, throughout the investigation, we were looking for a connection between the Conservatory and the non-Conservatory victims. But there *was* no connection. Even the violin motif had nothing to do with Mannila. His three Conservatory victims all played different instruments — violin, horn and piano. Apart from the fact that the first two reminded him of his mother, he knew them all through his work. None of the other four victims had anything to do with either Mannila or the Conservatory — or, for that matter, with each other: a photojournalist, a Sibelius Academy student, a part-time prostitute, a school-girl — no connection at all! And there's something I'd like to ask you. That same evening Christa Bäckström was murdered, you went to a late-night movie, didn't you? And you both claimed you'd met at the Kamppi Pizza Hut at 10 pm. That wasn't true, was it?"

"No, ten was the time we'd *planned* to meet, but I was half an hour late. He persuaded me to go along with the ten o'clock lie because it would help get me off the hook. Back then I was still a suspect."

"But he could only have arrived at Pizza Hut moments before *you* did. At ten o'clock he was still in Roihuvuori dealing with Christa Bäckström's body. So lying about the time wasn't to protect *you*. It was to give *himself* an alibi."

"Mm, I see that now. But, at the time, I was grateful for anything that would get you lot off my back. I never told you, by the way, I requested a breakdown of my March calls from the telephone company. I wanted to prove I'd made that nine o'clock call from my flat. But it wasn't there! It was missing from the list."

"Yes, there was some kind of glitch at the exchange that evening. Nothing got recorded for a couple of minutes around 9 pm."

He took a few moments to absorb this, and frowned. "I wish you'd told me! I got a really creepy feeling about it. I started wondering: What if I really *did* kill Liisa and then somehow managed to blank it out of my memory?"

She shrugged. "It's all history now."

"But there's still a lot I'd like to know. He was my friend, for Christ's sake! I can somehow understand why he'd want to kill this Bäckström woman — if she was blackmailing him. But what about the other three?"

"We presume the experience of murdering Christa Bäckström turned him on to the whole idea. From that point onwards he killed for nothing more than his own sexual gratification."

"Oh, my God! Well, it's true there were rumours at university that he'd been stalking and harassing an ex-girlfriend — that he'd even date-raped another girl. I didn't give it any credence at the time. But, after all this, I've started to wonder..."

A further unpleasant thought seemed to strike him: "What about Rosie? How could he even have contemplated hurting Rosie? He seemed genuinely fond of her."

"That was self-defense. Rosie vaguely remembers him telling her — through an anaesthetic haze — about how she knew things that could damn him."

"I don't understand."

"All right, I'll explain. But first I've a couple of questions for *you*. That last evening, when Liisa stormed out of your flat and off to her death — did she threaten to expose your affair to the Conservatory authorities?"

"Yes, but I wasn't going to tell *you*. You'd've taken it as a motive for killing her."

"I suppose you're right. But there's something else. Think back to the evening of Dad's lecture — the one he gave on the Fifth Symphony..."

"The one only Rosie and I made it to?"

"Exactly! That evening I had a meeting with... well, a work-related meeting... and Phillip didn't make it either because of a stomach bug. While you were there in the lecture hall, Mannila murdered Jaana Saari on the stairwell of her apartment block."

"Which finally gave me a proper alibi. You called Rosie in the middle of our Cello Sonata run-through to tell her about it."

"But did you pass that news on to Phillip the same evening — about the murder, I mean?"

"I know I phoned him when I got home. And the murder happened in Kuusitie, didn't it? — just round the corner from his place. I'm bound to have mentioned it, I suppose. Truth is there was a time when I wondered if he'd done that murder himself... to provide me with an alibi."

She stared back in astonishment. "With hindsight, we know he *was* a murderer, of course. But thinking his motive could've been to protect *you!* A bit far-fetched, don't you think? And the irony is Jaana Saari was the first girl since Liisa he *hadn't* killed! What I want to know is, when you spoke to him on the phone, did you say I'd told Rosie the latest murder was part of the same series?"

"Probably."

"Because it seems to me he drew his own conclusions from that. The very next day, Rosie paid him a surprise visit — to find out if he was feeling better — and he made a serious mistake. There were some books left open on his desk, right where she could see them. One was Tawaststjerna's biography of Jean Sibelius in the original Swedish, and beside it was Robert Layton's English translation."

"I remember, he picked up the Tawaststjerna in a second-hand bookshop last autumn. I was with him at the time."

"Well, he'd decided to send a letter to Ainola on his mystery colleague's behalf — to keep up the pretence there was only one murderer. So he must've been looking for a suitable quotation and checking the Swedish against the English version. Rosie didn't know about the letters — I never tell her much about my cases — but if she'd mentioned the Sibelius biographies to me, I'd certainly have made the connection. A little later, when they were having tea in the kitchen, he made a worse mistake. He asked her about the previous evening's murder and whether the girl's finger had been amputated again. He was wondering whether to put a fingerprint on his 'letter by proxy'. But Rosie didn't have the slightest idea what he was talking about, and then he realized how badly he'd slipped up. The business of the finger amputations was restricted information. He shouldn't've known anything about it. So he tried to cover his mistake by implying he'd heard about it from *you* — and that you, in turn, had got it from *me*."

"Not true!"

"Of course it wasn't, but he made Rosie promise to keep it to herself — which she did, at the time. But the sixth Ainola letter was the last straw. You remember Rosie took a bunch of letters from your hallway so she could post them for you?"

"Yes, she took them out of Phillip's jacket."

"But the letter addressed to 'The Ainola Residence' was in his pocket as well and she pulled it out with the others. It puzzled her a bit to find one of them in a separate grip-seal plastic bag — he'd done that to keep it forensically clean — but when she got to the postbox she just slipped it out of the bag and posted it with all the others."

"Did she notice the unusual address?"

"Yes, but again without realizing its significance."

"He must've been terrified she'd mention it to you. I suppose that's why he decided to..."

The sentence remained unfinished.

Neither of them spoke for a while. Eventually she draped one arm over the side of the boat and dipped her hand into the motionless water — gauging its temperature: "Go swimming later, shall we?

From the sauna?"

He nodded absently, formulating his next question: "At the very end — in that garage place of his — he set himself alight, didn't he? I've been wondering... Do you think he died in terrible agony?"

Against her will, she recalled Tero's comment as they were standing over the charred remains: *Must've forgotten to read the warning on the packet... how smoking can damage your health.* She dispelled this grim memory, and said: "All I know is we were lucky to get Rosie out before the whole place went up like a furnace."

"I went to his funeral last week, while I was in England. I'd never had much to do with his mother. She's an awful dragon! But I couldn't help feeling sorry for her. She complained how long it had taken to get his body back from Finland. A calendar month exactly, so she told me, from the day he died to the day they buried him... which should've been his birthday, by the way. And then she said: *It's a terrible thing to outlive one's only child."*

"True, but what about the *victims'* mothers? What about *their* suffering?"

Three days earlier, Beatrice Gröndahl's adoptive mother had tragically taken her own life. Working in a hospital, she'd had access to what was needed, and presumably had felt unable to face a future of vicariously reliving her daughter's final hours. In a sense, there *had* been an eighth victim after all.

"I suppose nobody knew him as well as I did," he went on listlessly, stretching his legs along the barrelled bottom of the rowing boat, "but he could still surprise me. He had this mad, reckless streak in him. On occasion he'd put himself at risk quite unnecessarily. Once I even saw him hang by his fingers over an eleven-storey stairwell. But the last couple of years he seemed to have been on his best behaviour. I thought he'd grown out of all that. How wrong can you get! And now I keep wondering, should I have tried to talk to him more? If I'd known what was going on, I might've been able to help him. He always took an interest in *my* life. I tended to think he was interfering. But those last few weeks, I was so absorbed in the Cello Sonata, I didn't spend much time with him at all. When we *did* meet, he kept giving me this maudlin spiel about the sacred bonds of friendship — how one should be able to confess even the most terrible of sins to a close friend. I thought he was angling for me to own up to Liisa's murder. He seemed to believe I'd done it. But, looking back, perhaps he was just plucking up courage to confess to *me.*"

"Would you have reported him if he had?"

"I keep asking myself the same question. I suppose I'll never know. He seemed to be going to pieces at the end."

"We asked his ex-employers why he'd lost his teaching contracts. They said he'd become unreliable. Sometimes he just didn't turn up. Once he even arrived drunk to the embarrassment of the whole class."

"So do you think he'd somehow gone mad — that he couldn't help himself? Remember the man who started laughing at his wife's funeral? Could it be something like that."

"I'm sorry, but you're too charitable. Rape and murder aren't reflexes. They're controllable urges. He *chose* to give way to them."

"But surely he must've felt guilt about what he'd done?"

"Hardly of much consequence to the victims! Or to their families! Why should *they* care if he suffered the pangs of conscience? Four young women are dead. They're gone for ever. And he made it happen. I've no doubt he looked for ways to justify what he did in his own mind. He had to live with himself, didn't he? But, in the end, it's all bullshit... Hey, perhaps we should try a little thought experiment. It's a sort of fable really — about date rape rather than sexually motivated murder — but the principle's the same."

She omitted mentioning the fable's provenance: that it was Panu Marski who'd picked it up at his forensic psychologists' conference in Boston; and passed it on to her during their 'little assignation' — as present company had once jealously described it! — in the little café opposite the library.

"Strangely enough," she said, "it resonates with a story you told me a few weeks ago — the last time you were here at Tapiola."

"Okay, I'm all ears..."

"I want you to imagine you're sitting alone in a bar somewhere. A girl comes over and sits down on the stool next to you. After a while you get talking, and she tells you some really interesting stuff. She's stinking rich, she says: several million in the bank, a big house on the west side which has a fully equipped and operational recording studio in the basement. It used to be her husband's, but he was killed in a skiing accident a couple of months ago. Her own parents are dead. And she doesn't have any children or brothers and sisters, so she's been wondering who should inherit everything when she's gone. Now she's come to a decision. You seem like a nice guy. She's going to leave it all to you. Drawing a document out of her handbag — her last will and testament — she fills in your name as the sole beneficiary and gets two passing waiters to witness her signature. Then she seals the document in an envelope and asks the barman to put it somewhere for safekeeping. You're astounded by this sudden turn of events. But there's something important she wants from you in return. She takes you by the hand and leads the way up ten flights of stairs to the roof. She tells you she's just been diagnosed with terminal cancer. The doctors give her a couple of months at most, and they've admitted the last weeks will be painful. That's why she's decided to exercise her free will and end her life right now. She's going to jump off the building and avoid all that pointless, long drawn-out suffering. It's all explained in the will, she says — so there won't be any comebacks for you. She just needs to have you there... to help her find the courage. Many things go through your mind: for example, does she have the right to choose her own place and time of death? Well, that's not much of a problem. You've always held the opinion decisions like that should be left to the individual. The truth is your thoughts are focusing more and more on the money and the big house. And, of course, you've always dreamed about owning your own recording studio. Suddenly these things seem amazingly within your reach. Why shouldn't you accept her offer? She clearly wants you to have them all. You set about reassuring her that she's doing the right thing — that jumping is the best option left open to her. Your powers of persuasion appear to be working. She climbs up onto the parapet and steps closer to the brink. The final moment of choice is upon her. Just one last step and all those riches will be yours. It's what she wants, isn't it? She's made it perfectly plain. But then the girl looks down — past those ten storeys to the pavement below — and, at the last moment, she changes her mind. She doesn't want to jump any more. It was all a big mistake. She's not going through with it. So what do you do? Well, it's obvious, isn't it? You push her over!"

447

Tapiola

There was an audible gasp from the stern of the boat.

"In effect, that's what the date rapist does. He gets so fixated on what he wants for himself — what he's going to gain from the woman — that *her* wishes are no longer of consequence. As far as he's concerned, she ceases to exist as an independent, free-thinking spirit. Her claim to autonomy and her humanity are ignored. He blanks them out. She's become nothing more than the object of his selfish personal desires. Meanwhile he finds various ways to excuse himself. It's what she really wants. She's still gagging for it, whatever she says now. She probably likes things rough. She's only playing coy to spice things up a bit."

A startled pheasant broke cover somewhere in the forest with a screech and a clatter of wings. Both turned their heads instinctively towards the sound. Although the disturbance was short-lived, it renewed their awareness of the peace and beauty surrounding them.

She hadn't been talking especially loudly, but now modulated her voice to an even softer level: "A man who's prepared to kill to satisfy his sexual cravings is like the date rapist. A more extreme version, of course! But he still fabricates explanations for himself as to why he does it. They're all spurious because the bottom line is this: he's putting his own sexual gratification above another person's right to live. That's totally unacceptable. It's unpardonable. There can be no exceptions or excuses. Absolutely *no* mitigating circumstances."

"Of course, you're right," he nodded. "But are things ever really that black and white? Aren't we all possessed by our share of angels and demons? Isn't each of us a battleground for good and evil?"

She didn't reply. She was studying him, trying to fathom what her true feelings were for this reclusive, self-absorbed man who'd managed to rekindle her dormant emotions and her sexuality. What did she really want from him? For now, each could offer something the other needed, but what would come of their relationship in the long term? There were aspects of his personality she already found disenchanting. He probably had similar feelings about her. And the ugly focus of their recently shared experience introduced another kind of strain. To be in each other's company was to be constantly reminded of the horror... Although they did still have a few things going for them. Their work lives were demanding, and for both a consuming passion. At least they'd be able to accept that in each other more readily than most couples.

"I've been offered a research post at Warwick University," he said. "I went for an interview last week. A small amount of teaching. Mainly a chance to get on with the composition. Salary's not bad."

She held his gaze for a while... and then turned away, looking across the lake to the distant bonfire. It still flickered in the orange-hued light of the converging suns — one real, one reflected — that continued to slide lazily and imperceptibly along the horizon.

"I think I'll take it," he added.

She gave a vague nod. "Suppose you should," she said, and reached for the oars — busying herself — relocating them on the gunwales of the boat, lowering each one with care into its U-shaped iron rowlock.

"I've been wondering," he said, "about these internal dialogues I keep having with him. Do you think maybe he had the same kind of conversations with *me* — in his own head, I mean? That he might have made some sort of confession to me in *that* way, at least?"

"It's possible," she said, more to provide comfort than because she had any genuine opinion on the subject... although she had noticed how the *Dear A.* that began each of the Ainola letters could carry more than one interpretation. "Before the end," she said, "he may have regretted what he'd done... perhaps been ashamed of what he'd become. We'll never really know. He's no longer here to ask. Though, like you, I'm having trouble understanding that downward spiral — how he could've allowed himself to get drawn into such an obscenely evil mind-set. I suppose it's always the same. There's only so much we can discover after the event. Everything else remains hidden. The whole story, the whole truth... only God and the angels will ever know that."

"And the demons," he reminded her. "You left out the demons."

Her father was now at the cottage door, beckoning in an animated fashion.

"You're right," she said, deftly working the oars to swing the prow of the boat shorewards. "We must never forget the demons."

ACKNOWLEDGEMENTS

Immense gratitude to Carol Norris & Phill Lewis who patiently read the first draft, chapter by chapter, as it was being written; also to those who generously read the intermediate draft manuscript: (in Finland) Joan Nordlund, Flis & Hennu Kjisik, Marjana Johansson, Paul Westlake, my son Roy, Risto Raitio, Nick Burton, and Neil MacLaverty; (in the UK) Vera Pelley, Anne Cartwright, Mary Wright, my sister-in-law Lyn, and my parents Joan & Pete; and to Carol again for her painstaking work editing the final version. I'm indebted to you all. Your feedback was invaluable. Many thanks also to Ritva Forslund, Risto Hartikainen, Angela Hoy, Keijo Kettunen, Matti Lehtonen, Anna-Liisa Naskali, and Eva Uggla, for their much appreciated support.

My very sincere thanks to Prof Veijo Murtomäki for reading through the Sibelius lectures and making numerous valuable suggestions; to Dr Antti Virtanen for discussing several points of forensic pathology; to Dr Risto Evala for the anaesthetic angle; to rikoskomisario Jari Koski for clarifying some questions of Finnish law and giving me a virtual tour of Pasila Police HQ; and to Alžběta Jamborová, Hernán Milla & Juan José Mudarra for the Moravian and Spanish bits. Any errors or discrepancies remaining in the novel are entirely of my own making.

Considerable thanks are due to my colleagues at the Helsinki University Language Centre for their long-suffering friendship; to Harri Niemilä, Kari Kääriäinen & Ian Gamble for their technical support; and to staff & colleagues at the Academy & Conservatory, who have always been so helpful and in no way resemble anyone in my fictitious narrative.

I also wish to express a deeply felt appreciation of my friends, family (& extended family) in the UK and in Finland, for their continuing love and support.

And an enormous thank you to all of my students at the Sibelius Academy, the Helsinki Conservatory (Stadia), and elsewhere. You have taught me so much.

Some of the sources I drew upon in the writing of this novel were:

Sibelius *Erik Tawaststjerna (translated by Robert Layton)*
Sibelius *Robert Layton*
Sibelius: a personal portrait *Santeri Levas*
The Symphony: A Listener's Guide *Michael Steinberg*
How the Mind Works *Stephen Pinker*
Phantoms in the Brain *V.S.Ramachandran & Sandra Blakeslee*
The Jigsaw Man *Paul Britton*

THE AUTHOR

Simon Boswell was born in south London, grew up in Bristol, and did a Bachelor's degree in Civil Engineering at Birmingham University. He followed this with a University of Aston postgraduate diploma in the Teaching of English as a Second or Foreign Language, and has since lived in Finland working as an English teacher. He also studied composition with Einojuhani Rautavaara at the Sibelius Academy, where he now holds a full-time lectureship in English. For many years, his working life has been focused on developing and teaching music-related English courses for students at the Sibelius Academy, the Helsinki Conservatory, and Stadia (polytechnic college). *The Seven Symphonies* is his first novel.

FINAL COMMENTS

The drug *Comatin* does not exist. It is a literary device.

Although otherwise implied in the novel, there is neither a forensic laboratory nor a morgue in the Pasila police station building. They are situated in Espoo and Ruskeasuo, respectively.

For simplicity's sake (and to avoid unnecessary confusion for non-Finnish readers) no distinction has been made between the Helsinki Conservatory and the Stadia Polytechnic College.

The Wegelius Hall appears rather larger in this novel than in real life. There were other possible venues for staging the Sibelius lectures. I used 'Wegelius' for no better reason than I like the name!

Finnish readers may discover further deviations from reality in the Helsinki setting of this novel. Some I am aware of myself, others may have escaped my notice. I ask you to be indulgent, and remember: it's only fiction.

If you've enjoyed this book, please email your friends about it, point your workmates to the website (even link to it from your own), mention it in chat rooms and post messages on newsgroup billboards; please shout it from the internet rooftops! For a self-publishing author without large-scale corporate backing, word of mouth is a powerful ally.

Greetings Evolution Gamers worldwide! Information about The Evolution Game can be found via:
http://www.sevensymphonies.com/evolutiongame.html

For further information or to contact the author, please visit:
http://www.sevensymphonies.com

Lightning Source UK Ltd.
Milton Keynes UK
14 October 2009

144969UK00001B/224/A